THE DRAGON MARKED CHRONICLES:

CHRONICLES:

PRINCE OF DRAGONS

Books By Jay Lynn

The Dragon Marked Chronicles

The Dragon Sage

Prince of Dragons

Mission Stone: Quest of the Five Flames

THE DRAGON MARKED CHRONICLES:

PRINCE OF DRAGONS

JAY LYNN

First print edition 2020
ISBN-13: 978-0-9993273-5-7

Book cover design by: brosedesignz
Editing by: H.B.

For Holly and my Readers

MAP

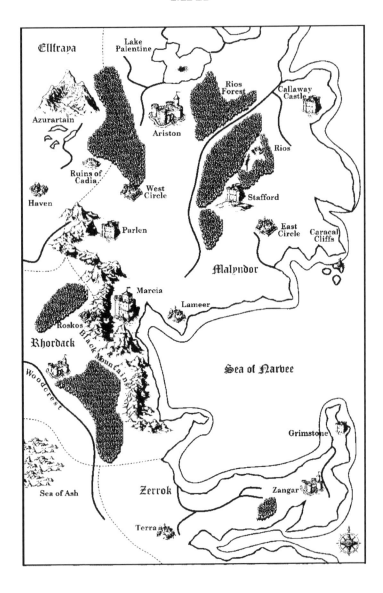

CHAPTER 1

Cantering across an open meadow the wind brushed Alec's face and hair. Briefly closing his eyes, he never felt freer. He regretted the action immediately. Flashes of smoldering corpses greeted his shut lids. Alec's eyes shot open. Glancing to the side he looked over at his partner, Isabelle.

Beaming, she rode the dark brown bay easily and seemingly without care.

Alec sighed. She hadn't noticed his momentary lapse. The sorcerer mentally shook himself. He shouldn't have forgotten, even temporarily, the urgency of their mission.

Newly appointed to the Emerald Sages, this was their first official assignment. Alec released a short humorless laugh. If someone told him a year ago he would be living in Malyndor and working as a sorcerer for the king, he would never have believed them. To think so much had changed. In almost a year to the day, Alec had earned his freedom from his Zerrokian master, became a Stafford soldier, learned he possessed magical abilities, befriended a dragon, dueled with another dragon, and then became an Emerald Sage.

Giving his head a light shake, Alec peered at Isabelle once more. Lately, they seemed to be teamed up a lot. The warrior felt the one corner of his mouth twinge with a faint smirk. By some miracle she wasn't talking a mile a minute.

It could be worse, I guess. He could have been made to go with Jerric.

Having gotten past her initial fears of battle, Isabelle was growing into an asset. What's more, she was also a trustworthy friend. In a time with traitors lurking in the shadows, Alec wouldn't have chosen another for such a dangerous mission. The only ones they would be able to rely on, were each other.

'Remember, creation spell first.' Alec recalled Malcolm reminding him as he got ready to depart.

The great sage wanted to speak to him about something important, but after growing quiet for a minute or two, he told Alec it could wait until his return.

I wonder what it could be, he thought, not for the first time.

The surrounding fields were slowly consumed by the dense forest encasing the Black Mountains. A more northern route into Rhordack allotted them some much needed time within the ally kingdom. Otherwise, how else would they be able to judge if an evil force was lingering about? The pile of corpses invaded Alec's mind. Something tainted was most certainly there.

Though King Soren hadn't reported anything unusual, Layfon strongly believed The Pure were using the mountainous terrain along the coast as cover. With various assaults on Malyndor's most guarded strongholds, Rhordack was the most logical point of entry. Security was tight along the Sea of Narvee, and the kingdom's spies gave no mention of The Pure's army coming by vessel.

2

Wherever their enemies may be hiding, they had to find them. At this rate, the Zerrokian Crown would fall. Then, Rhordack would crumble, leaving only Malyndor to fight off the coming storm.

A few miles after descending into the middle realm, Alec dismounted.

Bringing her steed to a halt, Isabelle frowned. *What is he doing?* She watched as Alec pressed a finger to his lips. Isabelle nodded. Getting down, she followed behind as he weaved his way through the brush. A good twenty yards from the path, Alec reached up and secured his reins to a branch, then aided Isabelle in doing the same. The prickly underbrush caught her clothing and scraped her skin as she trailed behind him.

"Is this really necessary?" she mumbled with a hiss.

"Quiet!" he ordered softly.

Scowling, she did what he said. Alec was much better suited in judging the situation. None of her training thus far required such stealth. Fighting the urge to ask the numerous questions plaguing her mind, the sorceress kept her head down and her gaze forward as she stayed within the camouflage of the forest.

Eyes continuously scanning the area, Alec tried to pick the best route through the foliage. *Isabelle should have stayed with the horses.* Traveling with her was no better than a herd of steeds.

They were getting close. The sound of snapping twigs caused him to flinch. Holding up a hand, Alec motioned for the sorceress to remain behind while he crossed the road. Melting into the shadows, he traveled further up the path and disappeared from Isabelle's view.

Another two hundred yards and the road split, rounding a bend. It was there that Alec heard the first whispers of voices. Settling against the thick trunk of a tree, he watched and waited. The stillness of the forest primarily alerted him to the coming patrol. Dark eyes tracking the two men's movements, Alec's hand tightened upon his blade. The uniforms they wore were not of Rhordack's grey wolf, but the white mark of The Pure. Three vertical lines adorned the front of the soldier's tunics, as well as the pauldrons covering their shoulders.

Alec lingered there until they vanished into the forest. His grip loosened slightly. It would be so easy to dispose of them. However, slaying the soldiers would defeat the purpose of his mission. The enemy was not to know they were there.

The soft sounds of voices still had not dissipated.

Making his way up the road, Alec followed the noise. Deeper into the woods he came upon their makeshift camp.

Four soldiers sat around the fire ring cooking their meal and smoking. Tents were hoisted at the rear of the camp beside a crude fence post where several horses were tethered.

Opposite his position, another patrol appeared through the trees.

Backing away, Alec crept through the underbrush and retraced his steps. Passing by the fork he searched for any sign of the first patrol. Seeing none, he continued on towards the main path. Visually scanning the trees, Alec didn't stop until he spotted a glimpse of Isabelle's blonde hair and dark green uniform. She blended in fairly well with the forest. Eyes passing up and down the road, he quickly slipped over to rejoin her.

A smile spread across the sorceress's face. Opening her mouth with a deep breath, any forth coming words were cut off as Alec urgently shook his head. Blinking several times, it took her a moment to register he was pointing in the direction from which they came. Isabelle managed a nod.

Once again the sorceress was following behind as Alec navigated through the trees. A few minutes passed prior to Alec stopping and clicking his tongue.

A soft answering neigh sounded through the woods.

Adjusting their direction, Alec headed straight for the clever steed.

Beaming, Isabelle nuzzled the grey horse's nose. "Good boy, Cloud."

"Not yet."

Scrunching up her nose, his partner made a face, but said nothing. Returning to the road the two companions mounted up then headed north.

Hands gripping the reins tightly, Isabelle twisted in her saddle to peer behind. Frowning, she gazed at Alec.

Looking straight ahead, he didn't meet her eye. Cutting through the woods he remained silent even after several minutes passed.

Isabelle raised her brows and stared at the warrior. "Well?" she questioned at last. "Why are we going this way? We can't possibly be done yet. Was there something wrong with the road? Did you see someone? Why aren't you saying anything?"

Alec gave her a sideways look. "Perhaps, because you're not giving me a chance."

Isabelle rolled her eyes. "My horse's foot. You had no intention of saying anything till I questioned you. I swear you do this on purpose." For a brief instant, Isabelle knew she saw the hint of a smirk. Drawing back, her mouth hung open. "You do, don't you? One of these days Alec—"

"Yeah?"

Fighting a laugh, the sorceress shook her head. "Keep it up and you shall find out."

Alec chuckled, urging Cloud ahead as he jumped over a shallow creek.

Isabelle tapped the bay's sides and caught up with Alec easily.

"So?"

This time the warrior met her gaze. "Troops of The Pure were stationed by the road."

"The Pure? Already?" Isabelle whispered, instantly lowering her voice.

This was not good. They hardly passed into Rhordack and they were running into advanced enemy forces. How many more might be hiding in the lush forest waiting to strike?

Alec dipped his head in a quick bob. "Appeared to be a scouting patrol."

Isabelle frowned, her brows lowering. "Then why are we riding in the other direction? Shouldn't we…you know…take care of them?"

"Armies notice when their scouts go missing. A pile of corpses would alert too many to our presence."

"I suppose you're right. So, where *are* we going?"

A small half grin made an appearance. "Around them," Alec answered nonchalantly.

Shooting him a glare, Isabelle snapped the reins, urging the bay to canter ahead. The quiet sound of Alec's laughter followed behind her, causing the sorceress to shake her head. A smile of her own spread across her lips. *The man has a better sense of humor than people know.*

She led for another few hundred yards prior to dropping back to rejoin her companion. *He's lucky he's so cute,* Isabelle thought mildly. Little was said as they traveled through the forest.

Alec carefully steered them onto a slightly higher mountain path which ran parallel to the main road. More of a hunting trail than anything else, it weaved its way among the surrounding hills and along a nearby river. Eventually, they were forced to descend back down to their original path. Alec went on ahead, leaving Isabelle in the strangely quiet woods. His return brought news of another scouting party hidden within the dense terrain.

Carefully skirting around them Alec turned east, taking Isabelle higher into the mountains.

"Alec," she called out quietly. "We're going the wrong way. Isn't the village we seek to the west?"

He dipped his proud head. "This is a necessary detour."

Gripping her reins, Isabelle pursed her lips. Why couldn't he trust her enough to share his plan? The sorceress knew he had one. Scowling at his back, the rest of the journey was made in an uncomfortable silence.

As they trotted up towards the main gate of Roskos, Alec hoped the villagers would be willing to offer him aid. He had a bad feeling about this mission. Years of battle taught him to trust his instincts. Isabelle might disagree, but preparing for the worst would only increase their chances of survival should they unexpectedly run into a greater number of Zerrokian troops.

It was cooler up in the mountain village and Alec reveled in the refreshing change of humidity. The valley floor was blistering shortly after the sun rose with the break of dawn.

While Alec slowly road up the path, a few people smiled and waved. Considering he only came with the Marcian patrol once, Alec was surprised they remembered him. Reaching the town square, he gazed at the familiar sight. The warrior could feel his partner's eyes on him as he remained seated upon Cloud. When she went to dismount, he stayed her movements. Tall and proud, the sorcerer waited quietly as if made of stone.

Crossing her arms, Isabelle slumped in the saddle. *What are we waiting for?*

After a few minutes, an older man ambled towards them, cane in hand. Once he was ready to receive them, Alec descended from his steed.

"Greetings, elder Jorrin," Alec said as he and Isabelle approached. "How has the growing season faired?"

A smile materialized on his wrinkled face. "Alec? I almost didn't recognize you without the Marcian crest. Who might your new companion be?"

"This is Isabelle." He turned to his partner. "Isabelle, this is Jorrin, the village elder."

"It's nice to meet you."

7

"A pleasure young lady."

"Jorrin, is there somewhere we can talk in private?"

The man's bushy brows rose. "Come with me," he replied after a moment.

Walking back in the direction he came from, Jorrin led them down the street and into a small hut. As they strolled towards the building two men joined them. Once inside, Jorrin motioned for them to shut the door.

"Pray, make yourself comfortable."

Alec nodded and lowered himself onto a cushion beside the elder.

Sitting on the warrior's other side, Isabelle inched closer.

Peering at her, Jorrin lifted a hand. "This is my son, Rin. The other man is Sean, a friend and council member. Both can be trusted with whatever you have to say."

"Thanks for hearing us out," Alec began, his gaze encompassing them. "Jorrin, do you recall the attacked village Sir Blake and I spoke of during our scouting mission?"

The man stiffened. "I do."

"Isabelle and I have been sent by King Titus to investigate the village. It's believed members of The Pure may be using the area as a secret base."

The men's eyes widened.

"The Pure? Here?" Rin growled.

"That doesn't bode well for us. We aren't able to defend ourselves against an army."

The sorcerer lifted his hands. "We still don't know if they're there for certain. It's our mission to find out, and if possible, discover their plans."

"How can we help? We aren't fighters."

Alec shook his head. "I'm not asking you to fight, but we could use a ride."

Isabelle jerked back while Jorrin flashed him a puzzled frown.

An hour later, the five of them emerged from the hut. Jorrin willingly agreed to aid them, but Isabelle still wasn't so sure. Now dressed in plain peasant's clothing, she pulled her long hair back into a simple braid. Nothing about their appearance or possessions was to resemble Malyndor. Instead, Alec and Isabelle were to pose as Rhordackian commoners traveling to Woodcrest. Since they would be walking once they reached the outskirts of the village, the sorceress chose to wear breeches in place of a dress, as many poorer farmers did. Tying a simple sword on his belt, Alec materialized by her side.

"Here," he said handing her a knife. "Keep this on you."

Isabelle tentatively took the weapon from him. *Here we go.* Taking a deep breath, she started to turn away.

"Isabelle."

She stopped and spun towards him. Looking at the warrior's outstretched hand, she frowned.

"Your ring," Alec clarified softly.

"What?"

"It's a sign of the Emerald Sages. It would give us away."

Only then did Isabelle notice he wasn't wearing his. "But what if we need to escape and prove who we are? Our horses are staying here, and Jorrin's men won't be coming for us for two days. Have you thought this through?"

"We need stealth and a horse makes too much noise. This is what you volunteered for, Isabelle. I told you it was going to be dangerous." Alec lowered his hand. "I won't make you come."

As he was about to move away, Isabelle's hand shot out to grab his sleeve. "No! No, I'm your partner. I swore I'd watch your back."

At the time when Isabelle volunteered, she hadn't thought about the risks. She wanted to be with Alec. They were partners and for some reason, she felt protective of him. She recalled the conversation she overheard between Malcolm and Kalvin.

'He is destined for greater things than we can imagine,' the headmaster had said.

Isabelle might not be as powerful as him, but she could still help. The golden blonde dropped her gaze to the metal adorning her hand. Isabelle just earned the precious item. However, Alec was right. She couldn't risk their lives over a ring. Moving in slow motion, Isabelle slid the jewelry from her finger. Twirling it gently, she reached out to place it in his palm.

"You will get this back," Alec promised, holding Isabelle's gaze for a second prior to meeting up with Jorrin.

Leading the man off to the side, he discreetly gave him their rings along with a purse of coins.

"For the horses, with my thanks."

The elder man's eyes shimmered gratefully.

"If you don't return, I'll send men to Marcia immediately and inform Lord Kegan of your situation."

Alec nodded. "If the worst comes to pass, give him these rings. He will know you speak the truth."

"It shall be done. Safe journey to you both."

"Thanks."

The men shook hands before Alec walked back towards Isabelle. She quickly shifted her attention to their horse, making a show of straightening the bridle.

"Ready?" the sorcerer questioned.

Isabelle put on a brave smile. "As I'll ever be."

Alec swung up into the saddle of the restless stallion then held out his hand. Isabelle stared at him blankly.

"Sorry, we don't have many horses to spare and yours need to rest," Rin apologized as he watched her hesitate.

Isabelle pulled herself together. "It's fine," she muttered wrapping her fingers around the warrior's strong calloused hand.

It never occurred to her they would be sharing the same horse. Arms snaking around his narrow waist, she could feel her cheeks warming. *Why is my heart racing?* Isabelle shook herself. It would be unwise to allow herself to grow feelings beyond friendship for the warrior. Alec's heart already belonged to another. Even so, Isabelle found herself enjoying the experience of having him close just the same.

Rin and Sean rode with them as they descended the mountain and made their way towards the village. The journey was mostly silent until Isabelle loosened her iron grip and began chatting to her more receptive company. As darkness swallowed up the sun's brilliant luster, the riders slowed their pace. Tugging on the reins, Alec crawled to a halt. Eyes scanning the shadowed tree line, he nodded to the others.

"This will do."

To the right, the river bent in a sharp curve then disappeared back into the woods. Alec gestured towards the landmark.

"We'll meet you here two mornings hence. Thanks for your help."

Rin dipped his head. "Anything for friends of Lord Kegan. He looks out for us more than our own kingdom does."

Taking hold of Alec's arm, Isabelle slid down off the horse. Stepping back, she gave him room to dismount, then watched as he handed the reins to Rin.

"Stay safe," he told them spinning the horses in the other direction.

Riding off, Rin and Sean were all too soon nothing but specks in the distance. Adjusting his sword, Alec started walking with Isabelle following close to his side. He strode down the side of the road for a good twenty minutes prior to shifting into the brush.

Isabelle did her best to copy every step the warrior took. One arm clamped over her bag, she ducked beneath a branch Alec held to the side. It was slow moving through the underbrush. Every snap of a twig or scuff of her boot seemed to echo in the sorceress's own ears. As the light faded more aggressively around them, it became increasingly difficult to see.

Alec gripped his own satchel to keep it from swinging as he searched for the easiest route to take through the trees. A faint glow across the road instantly stilled his movements. Gently tapping Isabelle's shoulder, he pointed to the outline of the fire.

She nodded, then waited for his next instructions.

She's learning quickly, he thought pleasantly. It was almost strange for Isabelle not to be asking a thousand questions.

Crouching down across from the sentry post, Alec's dark eyes intently scanned the area. The shadowed figures of four men could be seen in the low fire light. A screen of leaves and moss blocked their left side, which faced out towards the road. If they had stayed on the path, it would have been nearly impossible to spot their enemy. Most likely, the soldiers would have found them first. The glint of chainmail and light armor rid any thoughts of their company being hunters camping in the forest.

After studying them for some time, Alec drew back. Traveling deeper into the woods he looked for a place for them to camp. It was completely dark now, and neither Isabelle nor Alec possessed the right training to stumble around in the starlight. Dawn and dusk would be their greatest allies.

Satisfied they were far enough away from both the sentry and the village, Alec signaled for Isabelle to help him set up camp. They found a rock enclosure which would offer them some protection from the elements. A fire was out of the question, but luckily the night air was still warm. First casting an energy spell to repel unwanted company, Isabelle then added the shielding enchantment she heard Malcolm use at the East Circle.

"Ahhh," she drawled elatedly. "It feels so good to be able to talk, and the best part is—no one can hear us."

He flashed her a half smile. "Neat trick. Where'd you learn it?"

Isabelle hesitated. *Spying on your teacher.* "At the academy."

He nodded, tossing her an apple before cutting them both off a piece of salted pork.

"So...do you think we're going to find The Pure here?"

Alec didn't answer right away. "Hard to say. Someone is here."

Isabelle's eyes dropped, her grip tightening on her food. Nodding to herself, she forced a grin. "Well, then we best find out what they're up to."

"Agreed."

Early the next morning, as the first rays were breaking through, Alec stood in the upper branches of a thick tree while Isabelle dozed below. She only drifted off a few hours prior. Even with using her bag as a pillow, the sorceress had difficulty falling asleep on the hard ground wrapped up in only a thin cloak.

Scanning their surroundings, Alec better studied the village's location. To the west, the rocky, slanted sides of the valley walls made it difficult to sneak around from the rear. The river cut off access from the north, leaving the southeast the most logical route. However, it would mean sneaking past the sentry. Heading east to go around them would take far too much of their precious time.

Climbing down the ancient tree, Alec approached his sleeping companion. Leaning in, he gently shook her.

"Isabelle, time to rise."

The warrior was rewarded with a sudden punch to the jaw.

"Get off me!" came a snapped, sleepy reply.

Sitting up, Isabelle rubbed her face. A confused frown marred her features as she looked at Alec through partially open slits. Staring at him, Isabelle blinked several times. Then, her gaze widened considerably.

"Oh my stars—Alec are you okay? I'm so sorry. I didn't mean to—"

"It's alright," he assured her, holding up his hands to stem her apology. The punch hadn't really hurt. It was her reaction which took him by surprise. "I'm fine, just remind me not to wake you again. Did something happen when you were training with Jerric?"

Isabelle looked away. "Only too many students with too little control," she said coldly. "I don't want to talk about it."

That's a first. "We better get moving," Alec told her putting the strap of his satchel over his head.

Isabelle tilted her head to the side.

"We need to sneak past the sentry to the other side of the village. Once daylight hits, we won't stand a chance."

"So darkness is our only friend?"

Alec nodded.

Isabelle stood and straightened her clothing. "Lead the way."

Only a faint light painted the sky as the sorceress dispelled their barriers. Alec took the front, smoothly guiding them through the brush as they rounded the village with a wide birth. It was a difficult balance keeping distance from both their future destination and the sentry they already identified.

Isabelle's breath caught in her throat as she nearly ran into Alec's stiff form. Peering around him, she froze as she saw a man returning to his tent. It seemed they had come upon another sentry. He appeared to be hiding behind camouflage similar to what the soldiers were using the night before. Backtracking somewhat, they inched their way around the camp. The higher the sun rose, the more every sound seemed to make Isabelle flinch.

Having successfully made it to the southern side of the village, part of Alec wanted to continue on with his mission. Alec glanced back at Isabelle. He might be able to get closer in the coming daylight, but she certainly couldn't. It would be too great of a risk.

14

Instead, the warrior searched for a place for them to wait out the day. Down near a creek Alec came upon some fallen trees. Quietly summoning an earth spell, he dug out a den beneath the trunks and covered it up behind them. From the outside, the area appeared unchanged, hiding their presence.

"So what, pray tell, is the plan?" Isabelle whispered, leaning against the solid earthen wall.

Alec stretched out his legs. "We wait. When the sun starts to set, we'll sneak into the village."

"Arrgh," Isabelle softly moaned. "I hate waiting. Can't we look around a little?"

Alec tilted his head, raising a brow.

"Fine. I'll stay here and try to be patient."

Laughing with a short huff, the warrior closed his eyes. He spent most of the night on watch. It was time for him to get some rest.

"Wake me if you see any scouts," he mumbled.

CHAPTER 2

As streaks of red, orange and pink painted the skyline, Alec and Isabelle crept from their makeshift den. They journeyed back towards the village, taking extra care should the sentries have moved during the day.

One hand holding his bag in place, Alec slowed his pace as they neared the village outskirts. No wall surrounded the perimeter. The farthest huts were empty, left abandoned as a couple of animals claimed them for their own. A few guards were spread out along the edge. Fires came to life as the light faded from the sky.

Pausing, Alec's eyes tracked them quietly. Three soldiers were stationed to the left around the blaze with another three farther along on the right. The men lingered by the embers, never seeming to venture more than a few feet. The spots were spread out enough to leave a dark shaded gap in their line.

Smoothly blending in with the growing shadows, Alec inched closer. He stopped beside the next row of huts. A short stone wall jutted out from the one side, giving the two wizards the perfect cover. Peering into the village, Alec's eyes narrowed dangerously. Throngs of people milled about the

16

streets. Soldiers lined the roads, were gathered outside huts and lounged beside the central well. Everywhere he looked, Alec spied the mark of The Pure. And that wasn't all.

Men clad in chains were working in the forge or carrying crates up and down the streets. Women dressed in tattered rags chopped wood or stood hunched over kettles as they cooked the soldiers' evening meal.

From somewhere within, a woman screamed in terror.

Palm smacking the wall, Isabelle tried to rise.

Alec clamped a hand on her shoulder to still her movements. Jaw clenched, he slowly shook his head.

Damn it.

There was nothing they could do for them now. Whether Zerrokian slaves, or captured peasants, the two sorcerers couldn't defeat an entire army in order to liberate them. Completing their mission would offer the most aid. Alec knew King Titus wouldn't ignore their distress. Forcing his attention elsewhere, Alec's gaze traveled over the soldiers. He estimated about five hundred were currently in the village. The sage then shifted his focus to the forge.

The clang of metal rang out in a constant melody. Near the closest fire, a man lifted a piece of steel for a soldier's inspection.

Alec's brows furrowed. It was a sword.

With a jerk of his head, the soldier ordered the man to toss the scalding blade into a wide trough of water.

Keeping his head down, Alec rounded the back of the hut and moved closer. Isabelle remained back in the shadows while he better studied the armory.

Four pools of water were brimming with weapons. Men stood on the other side, removing the cooling metal to add the finishing components. Afterwards, the completed swords were stored in crates.

The warrior's eyes traveled over the numerous boxes. There were dozens of them, enough to strike Malyndor without anyone being the wiser.

We have to inform the king.

Sliding back, Alec rejoined his partner. They retreated into the woods, leaving the outskirt of the village. The light was quickly waning, but Alec was still able to see fairly well. In another hour, it would be completely dark.

As they headed towards their makeshift den, the sound of soft mumbled voices reached their ears. A narrow road ran alongside the settlement. The sorcerers needed to pass the trail to travel deeper into the forest. With the voices quickly approaching, Alec stepped back to hide in the trees until the coast was clear.

Head down and shoulders hunched, Isabelle flew by.

Alec reached out, trying to catch her, but missed. "Isabelle, wait," he called out in a hushed tone.

Spinning around, she peered back at him with a startled frown. The quick, jerked movement caused her to catch her foot on an imbedded rock. The next thing she knew, a shriek passed her lips as Isabelle crashed onto the ground.

Alec raced to her side as the soldiers hastened towards them from down the road. There was no chance of sneaking by them now. *Damn it.*

"Don't panic," he whispered to Isabelle as he helped her to her feet. "Evening good sirs," Alec began calmly as the soldiers crawled to a halt. "Sorry for the disturbance, my sister's a little clumsy."

Placing a hand on her upper back, he gently pushed her into a bow as he bobbed his head.

Eyeing them carefully, the men gradually released their grips on their swords.

"What are you doing here?" a stout man with a thick dark beard questioned.

"We have a campsite about a mile up the path."

The man's brows lowered. "Our scouts didn't report seeing anyone in the area."

"Not surprised. We only use it when traveling to Woodcrest to see family," Alec told them with a little shrug.

A hand on Isabelle's back, he slowly walked forward to go around them.

The squad leader's eyes looked over the length of the travelers. "Where are you from?"

"Roskos," Alec replied evenly, offering nothing more. These men were taking too keen of an interest in them.

"Where is that?"

"Up in the mountains."

The two sorcerers were almost even with the soldiers.

"Why don't you stay in the village? The woods are no place for a pretty girl."

Crap. "Thanks, but we don't have the money for an inn. Besides, we'll be gone by first light. Family's expecting us tomorrow."

The man held out his sheathed blade, blocking their path. "I insist."

"We're not looking for trouble, sir," Alec informed him in a dark tone.

Eyes locked upon each other, the two men stood frozen.

Chin lowered, Isabelle's gaze darted between them. *This isn't good. These soldiers aren't going to let us go. Why am I so bad at being undercover?*

In a flash, the man drew his sword.

Alec pushed Isabelle behind him, unsheathing his own weapon as the other men did the same.

"Run!" he commanded.

Twisting on her heel, Isabelle took off in the opposite direction as Alec engaged their enemies. His blade sliced through the first man like melting butter. Five men were left standing before his red stained blade.

19

One sounded a horn while the others attacked. Two soldiers in the front simultaneously struck with long sweeping cuts.

Springing off the ground, Alec spun in the air, passing directly between the blades. The moment he landed, he kicked the next soldier in the chest, then parried a blow from the fourth man. Twisting in a circle, the sorcerer knocked their blades away.

The fifth man charged forward, locking his sword with Alec's. Eyes narrowing to slits, he released a deep growl.

Bringing his knee up, Alec struck him in the side. Pulling back, he freed his blade just in time to face the next round of attacks.

Behind him, Isabelle hadn't gotten very far. Moving in from the other side, another squad of soldiers appeared. The sorceress skidded to a stop as she eyed them wearily. A hand went to her belt. The thin blade she wore was more or less useless for her to use against these foes.

I guess I have no choice.

Keeping the knife in its sheath, Isabelle held her hands out in front of her.

"Surgeon, blast," she calmly stated, summoning an energy spell.

The pulse knocked her enemies off their feet. Several arrows flew from the canopy.

Isabelle dodged the strikes, watching with wide eyes as they landed where she had been. Heart racing, she scanned the tree line. Calling up an air spell, the sorceress blasted the area with a powerful gust.

Further down the road, Alec spotted the men lying on the ground near his partner rise menacingly. Distracted by the archers, she didn't see the threat.

The soldiers however, were not the biggest danger to the sorceress. The section of forest they were currently in was close to a steep rocky hillside. The vibrations of her energy blast loosened some of the rock, causing a small land slide which was heading straight for her.

Throwing the man he was fighting off, Alec tightened his grip upon his blade and brought it down with such force that it broke both of their swords. Summoning his own energy spell, the sorcerer swiped his hand in an arch, stunning the remaining soldiers around him. Using the residual energy, he quickly closed the distance between Isabelle and himself.

As the rocks crashed towards her, Isabelle raised her arms to shield her face.

Appearing by her side, Alec wrapped his arms around her, pulling Isabelle out of harm's way as his momentum launched them forward. They rolled onto the ground, sliding into the trunk of a tree. Turning her away from the rubble, Alec shielded his partner as the mounds of rock tumbled onto the forest road and sprayed the area with a blanket of dust.

When it stopped, Alec released her. Tugging Isabelle quickly to her feet he urged, "Let's go."

Once again Alec saved her life, but not without price.

Catching sight of a soldier coming from his blind side, Alec started to turn around and engage him. Two more pounced on him first, taking him to the ground.

Isabelle started to call up a spell when a third man cracked the metal butt of his weapon on the back of Alec's skull, knocking him out cold.

"Say a word sorceress and I'll slit his throat," sneered a cold, grey eyed soldier as he pressed the tip of his sword against Alec's neck.

Clamping her mouth shut, Isabelle let the magic seal in her palm dissipate. There was no way she could defeat these men and protect Alec from this monster. Considering how much The Pure hated sorcerers, Isabelle was sure the soldier would do exactly as he threatened. Raising her hands she could think of nothing else but to surrender.

Another soldier came up behind her. Removing the knife from her belt, her hands were roughly bound as she was gagged with a dirty rag.

"Take them to the compound," the new squad leader commanded.

Helpless, Isabelle was pushed forward towards the village. Behind her, two men unceremoniously hoisted Alec up and proceeded to drag him along. Briefly squeezing her eyes shut, she fought off tears. It should have been her the soldiers captured. Alec would have been able to defeat them. He'd know what to do.

Isabelle couldn't stop a tear from escaping. *This is all my fault.* The bitter truth struck her like a blow. Her combat skills might be improving quickly, but she was nowhere near ready for this type of high risk mission. Isabelle shouldn't have insisted on coming. Her foolishness most likely just cost both of them their lives.

A pain throbbed in perfect rhythm inside Alec's skull. His body felt heavy, strangely so, and ached all over. Floating on the edge of consciousness, he was swayed to let his mind drift in the shadowed clouds of sleep. Here, there were no insidious plots. No stuck up nobles. No endless battles he needed to face. It was all too tempting to remain.

Wake up, a strange woman's voice gently commanded.

Alec heard her once before, on the day of his initiation as an Emerald Sage. At the time, he hoped he was hearing things.

Alakaid, wake up.

A warm tingle traced the dragon shaped birth mark between Alec's shoulder blades. Sleep was instantly the furthest thing from his mind. The pain in his head seemed to worsen. Alec shifted, going to rub his temples, yet was hindered. The rough feel of rope dug into the skin at his wrists along with the odd feel of cold metal encasing his right one.

The sorcerer slowly pried his eyes open. Darkness completely surrounded him save for a large bright bonfire. The first thing he noticed was a crowd of soldiers chatting as they sat scattered around what appeared to be the town center. To his left was Isabelle, tied to a pole on the brim of the fire's light just as he was.

Sitting with her knees pulled to her chest, she gazed at the ground miserably.

A few soldiers sat close by, mocking her as they blew kisses and drank from oversized mugs of ale.

Alec pulled against the ropes, testing their strength.

"Good, you're finally awake," observed a man with long greasy hair hanging to his shoulders.

Downing the rest of his drink, he wiped his mouth on his sleeve as he stared at Isabelle with an evil glint lurking in his eyes. The man rose purposefully and sauntered over towards the sorceress.

Alec stiffened. His narrowed gaze tracked the soldier's every step.

"The boys and I have been ordered to keep an eye on ya," the man said, gesturing towards several of the others lingering by the prisoners. "And it's been mighty boring. I could use a good intrigue. How about we have some fun. What do ya think?" he asked the others, staggering a little as he moved in front of Isabelle. "Your sister's very beautiful."

"Don't touch her," Alec warned in a quiet, icy voice.

Smirking, the soldier knelt down and twisted a lock of her golden hair around his finger.

"What are ya going to do? Nothing, cause that bangle around your wrist ain't for decoration. The carvings negate all magic. Ya can't cast a single spell while it's on." He released her hair and pulled out a knife. "Just sit back and watch the show."

Alec wasn't concerned with the cold metal touching his heated skin. The rules for magic were different for him. With Isabelle's life on the line, he wasn't dwelling on the promise he made to Malcolm either. Alec knew he shouldn't cast without a spell. He knew it would mark him, like the dragon on his back and awaken some unknown danger as if revealing himself to an evil force. At the moment, it didn't matter as his power seemed to take on a will of its own.

Eyes glowing faintly, the flames of the bonfire rose, lighting up the area with greater intensity.

"I warned you," Alec growled frostily.

The square filled with a heavy, charged energy. Objects all around the space shook as they rose to hover in the air. Face a hard mask of stone, even the ends of Alec's hair lifted up.

No one moved as they waited on the brink to see what the sorcerer would do.

"What do you empty headed morons think you're doing?" demanded a stern voice as the camp's commanding officer strode into the square.

Regarding Alec carefully, the man's brows rose slightly as they took in the sorcerer's blazing eyes. He could feel the surrounding atmosphere charged with a dangerous aura the second he strode into the square. Gaze narrowing on the soldier eagerly staggering away from Isabelle, their commander stormed across the stone courtyard. A loud crack sounded as he backhanded the soldier so hard he was knocked off his feet.

"I won't ask again. What the hell do you think you're doing?" Not bothering to give the man a chance to answer, he peered up at the other men stationed in the space. "We are soldiers of the noble Pure. In case you have forgotten, this woman is a sorceress. You touch her and you'll be tainted for life. Any man under my command that's stupid enough to be tainted by a wizard, I'll kill myself. Now back to your posts!"

Nursing his bloody nose, the soldier took off down a side street. His loudest conspirators quickly scattered as well. They were replaced by grim faced guards who eyed the sorcerers without so much as a word.

The objects floating around the square plopped to the ground shortly after the commander slapped his subordinate. Arms crossed, he stood with his weight to one side as he studied Alec.

Sorcerers could be tricky. One never knew what they were capable of, or what types of vile evil magic they might unleash. He would have thought his men would know better than to antagonize a wizard.

Reaching up to scratch his chin, the soldier wondered if it might have been wiser to kill them after they were dragged into his camp. Then again, the money he could make was too good to pass up. Instead, he would sell them off to a nearby lieutenant commander who ran a slave trade operation on the side. This way, the sorcerers would be on their way to Zerrok by first light. Death would find them soon enough.

His spirit calmed, Alec focused on the camp's leader as the man strolled over to a chair by the flames. Considering The Pure's hatred of wizards, he found it interesting they were allowed to live this long, even if it meant the loss of a sale. Once again, Alec was reminded man's greed knows no bounds.

At least we're alive, he told himself, still watching the commander.

Each day alive meant another chance to escape. Somehow, he would find a way to get Isabelle out of here. He should never have allowed himself to get caught in the first place.

Leaning back in the chair, a servant rushed forward to place a mug in the commander's outstretched hand. As his eyes settled on Alec, their gazes locked together in a silent battle of wills.

Unflinching, the sorcerer didn't back down, nor look away.

A smile spread across the soldier's lips. "You have spirit," he said taking a long drink. "If you weren't a filthy wizard, I might have enlisted you. It's a shame to waste a man skilled with a blade."

"What do you plan on doing with us?"

"Sell you of course. There is no greater motive than that. In the meantime, I can't have any of my men damaging the merchandise. So you and your sister will be safe until you reach the next camp, as long as you behave. After that, I don't really care."

He's worried about my power. "Fair enough."

Considering the direction things were heading, it was more than Alec could ask for. Once they were sold, he would have to go from there. Alec suppressed a shudder. To think he was on his way back to the barbaric land of his birth as a slave once more.

CHAPTER 3

Malcolm rushed through the corridors of Ariston Castle as if a demon were on his heels. Heading towards King Titus's study, he stayed not one step as he strode around servants, nobility and soldiers alike. Most of the Royal Guard moved out of the great sage's way as he bolted down the hallway. Those who didn't were nearly run over as Malcolm passed like a dark storm. Having received word of an urgent message from Marcia, he would allow no one to interfere with his journey.

Please don't let it be about Alec, the wizard silently pleaded.

The moment Malcolm read the important summons from King Titus, a knot formed in the pit of his stomach. Alec's mission to Rhordack was near Marcia, and something intangible told him the two were linked.

Bursting through the highly decorated door, Malcolm quickly gazed around the room. Two soldiers sealed the space behind him as his hazel eyes skimmed over the others who were summoned.

Prince Zachary was present along with Layfon Eldridge, Grandmaster of the Emerald Sages, and General Phillip Rickman, commander of the Royal Guard.

"Good afternoon, Your Majesty," Malcolm greeted with a bow.

"Thank you for coming so quickly."

"Not at all, Your Majesty. What news from Marcia?"

Titus took a seat behind his desk and motioned for the others to do the same.

Joining Layfon, Malcolm leaned forward as he waited for the royal to speak.

"I have gathered you here to discuss news of a most disturbing nature. Recently, two of our sages were sent to investigate an executed village near the Black Mountains in Rhordack. There was a possibility of Zerrok involvement in the deaths of the villagers. Both sages are now missing."

Malcolm briefly closed his eyes. Clenching his jaw, he waited for Titus to continue.

"The Dragon Sage left word with the leader of a small mountain village by the border. I am told he had prior dealings with the gentleman while staying in Marcia, and left instructions to seek out Lord Kegan should they not return. Men from the village arrived in Marcia yesterday with the sage's horses, equipment and rings. Since the village is part of Malyndor's protection under our agreement with King Soren, Lord Kegan dispatched soldiers to investigate further."

Titus interlaced his fingers while a frown pulled at his lips. "A messenger hawk arrived only a short time ago. It seems members of The Pure have been occupying the village. However, there was no sign of the sages."

A tense silence fell as his words sank in. It was grave news indeed.

Layfon was the first to voice his thoughts. "What are the chances they're still alive?"

"Alec's smart," Malcolm immediately declared with certainty. "He purposely left behind anything that would tie them to the Emerald Sages, or Malyndor for that matter. The soldiers most likely believed they were ordinary Rhordackian peasants."

"That would be to their benefit," Phillip stated, standing up to hover over a map of the kingdoms.

"They *are* alive," Malcolm firmly insisted. The sage refused to believe otherwise. Rising, he joined Phillip by the map. "Alec spent his whole life around these types of people. He knows how they think. I doubt the soldiers would waste an opportunity to make money. Odds are they're on their way back to Zerrok to be sold."

"Sold as slaves," Titus mumbled unhappily, shaking his head. "I have already petitioned King Soren to send a search party after our comrades. Until I receive an approval, I cannot send a military force through Rhordackian lands outside of the specified region. Hopefully, Soren's soldiers will intercept them. If not, they're on their own for the moment. There was a reason Alec survived all those years in Zerrok. I have confidence he will be able to protect them until we are able to complete a rescue."

Leaning forward, Titus hit a hand on the polished surface of the desk. "That being said, Lord Kegan has already been given my permission to launch a full attack. We cannot ignore The Pure's actions near our border. Rhordack has been severely compromised. Once this threat has been neutralized, we can turn more of our resources to rescuing our comrades. I will not leave our people behind to suffer."

Malcolm knew Titus was right. Still, that did not ease the sour taste in his mouth. Alec's power was great, yet there was only so much one could do when imprisoned behind enemy lines. Part of him regretted urging Alec to promise not to use his magic without spells. If forced to, the wizard would not blame him for breaking that oath. Survival was key. Help would be coming. Malcolm would see to it personally.

Dragon mark or no, he cared too much for his former apprentice to leave him to relive such a twisted fate.

Leaving the study a while later, Malcolm frowned to himself. He slowly headed towards the library with a shadowing pair of footsteps.

The king's younger brother joined his side with an equally displeased expression. "You should not have let him go, Malcolm."

Glancing at Zachary, the sage's brows furrowed. "He's an Emerald Sage, Your Highness. It's his job to undertake the missions he is assigned."

Malcolm continued on his way, but Zachary kept pace with him easily.

"Alec's different, as you well know. I am certain my brother would have agreed. If he knew the truth, I doubt Titus would have put Alec in such a dangerous position."

"My former apprentice was a warrior long before he was a sorcerer. He is not afraid to do what he must."

"It is not his courage which concerns me, it is his life."

Eyeing the soldiers stationed at the end of the hall, Malcolm said nothing.

Zachary slowed his pace, allowing the other man to move on ahead. His voice sounded soft, yet clear, in the corridor as he recited these words:

"Ancient dragons, their magic combine,
the blood of one throughout his line.
Till born a child mightier than any blade,
on whom the mark of power shall not fade.
Once to its owner, the magic returns,
a new light awakens, strongly it burns.
Evil will rise; beast and man must unite,
or darkness reign, and hope takes flight."

Malcolm drew to a stop. Glancing back, a humorless grin touched his lips. "And to think they call *me* cunning."

Zachary closed the distance between them. Lowering his voice, his gaze locked on the wizard.

"So, it is true. To think he's still alive after all this time. Does he know about the prophecy? Who he is? Anything?"

"No."

Zachary's eyes widened as his mouth gaped.

The great sage held up his hands. "I suppose it makes no difference now, but I was going to tell him about the prophecy the night of his initiation. Then, Layfon gave him that mission and…"

The royal couldn't recall seeing Malcolm ever look so torn.

"He wasn't ready when I first met him," Malcolm told Zachary starting again. "I believe he is now, for at least part of the truth. Yet, I couldn't allow him to go on such a dangerous assignment with another burden hanging on his shoulders."

Zachary sighed. "I hate to admit it, but I must agree. Telling him about the dragon prophecy prior to traveling to Rhordack would not have been wise. Hopefully, we can rescue him and the girl quickly."

"I haven't kept this secret to be cruel, Zachary. I did it for Alec, to prepare him for what is to come."

"If the slave traders make it to Zerrok, I worry he might not have a future for which to be prepared."

With the force of a thousand men, Leos crossed the Black Mountains and charged into the Rhordack Valley.

Somehow, The Pure was alerted of the incoming threat, though it offered them little advantage. They believed the lush forest, swift river and steep surrounding hills would provide them ample cover. It might have, if not for the fierce rage of Leos's men.

Jay Lynn

Marcia's soldiers knew of Alec and Isabelle's situation. Having trained with and battled beside the sorcerer, many of them attacked with the overwhelming need for vengeance. The earl personally led his men into the ally kingdom.

The two forces clashed with a thirst for blood. Like an unstoppable flood, Malyndor's troops washed over the village, desecrating The Pure's outnumbered soldiers. The terrain which they believed would save them only served to box them in. In the end, those who surrendered were the sole survivors from the enemy's force.

Freed from their captors, the village slaves gladly shared what they knew about the missing sorcerers.

Leos's heart sank at the news. Apparently, they were moved to another location the day after their imprisonment. To make matters worse, The Pure knew Alec and Isabelle were spellcasters. Each was bound with an anti-magic cuff, though one woman did speak of Alec's power frightening several of the soldiers even with the device.

Knowing their comrades were still alive when they departed offered some hope. Now, the task of tracking down the caravan remained.

Leos pounded a fist against the side of a hut. "Damn it! I will not lose him again."

Sliding further back into the trees, a pair of sharp yellow eyes watched the scene in silence. Suppressing a growl, Cassidy moved through the forest with great speed. She was supposed to protect the marked one. It was her sacred duty. Dragon kind was linked to his fate. After her initial discovery, it had taken some convincing to gain the support of Emperor Draco and Empress Shiori to be assigned his protector. Even so, his safety was not merely a duty. Alec was her friend and she was failing him.

Smoke seeped from the dragon's nostrils. How could the humans allow him to be captured? Cassidy could no longer locate Alec by sensing his power. When she left for Ellfraya, he was still in Ariston. Since he couldn't leave her a message in the city, tracking him thus far hadn't been easy. Perhaps she could find him another way. The dragon knew of a local slave trafficking route. There was much to learn when one spent a great deal of time hiding in the woods. Following it could lead her to the sorcerers.

Reaching a break in the trees, Cassidy flew south. The neighboring town she sought was only twenty miles away on the other side of a mountain. Skimming the clouds, she pursued a lower jet stream in order to shadow the road from the sky. The terrain made traveling with heavy carts a long and slow process. It took three days to reach the border crossing over into Zerrok. By air, it was merely hours.

Every time the dragon spotted a group of carts, she swooped lower, studying the contents to the surprise of the driver and passengers alike. As the main road neared the border it split off. Cassidy hovered in the air. Which way would they go: south to the closest trading posts or east to Zerrok's wealthiest cities?

She chose the eastern route. Larger cities meant greater profit for the slave traders. Surely human greed would have them sell their prisoners in the deeper parts of Zerrok or even the capital itself.

Several miles down the road, the smell of sweat and horses penetrated the air. Four barred carts clattered along surrounded by a dozen men on horseback. Cassidy could hear chains rattling and people moaning within. This had to be it.

Releasing a blaze, the dragon shot a fireball by the front riders. They reared up—displacing the men, while close by, a wagon took off in a frenzy towards the woods. The soldiers driving the carts screamed commands and snapped their whips as they fought to regain control.

Cassidy made another pass, shooting flames along the outside of the caravan. Two riders were killed as the green dragon looped back. Sweeping in low, she knocked the second wagon onto its side.

The front soldiers regrouped, swinging at the fearsome creature as the men she displaced shot at her with their comrade's bows.

Inhaling, Cassidy launched a stream of boiling fire.

Screaming, the men were incinerated as the rear half of the caravan sought to escape. Using her tail as a whip, Cassidy smashed the back wheels of the closest cart. Leaping into the air she clutched the final cage with her talons and tore the roof clean off.

Surrendering to the inevitable, the last soldiers fled.

Peering inside, Cassidy searched for Alec. She recognized none of the frightened people cowering beneath her gleaming scales. Snorting, the dragon moved from one wagon to another. Fairing no better, she clawed at the ground. Head jerking back—she remembered the first cart which had driven off into the forest. Taking to the skies the mighty creature flew off. Sharp yellow eyes scanning the ground through the canopy, she was upon the speeding vehicle in no time.

Eyes bulging from his head, the soldier hollered for the steeds to go faster. Turning around he looked for the dragon, but the air above him was empty. Twisting back, his hands flew up to shield his face as a clawed hand swatted him from the cart. Slashed to ribbons, the corpse sailed into the foliage without so much as a glance from Cassidy.

Gripping the cage, she gently pried open the roof with her teeth.

"Alec, I'm glad you're—"

Her words were cut short as she gazed at the slaves curled up in terror just like the others. Alec wasn't among them. Staring at them for a long moment, Cassidy inched back. Shaking her mighty head she released a pained roar. Stretching out long wings, she rose up into the clouds and headed towards the border with a heavy heart.

It was too dangerous for her to roam aimlessly. Not only did humans hunt dragons here, but there was the Iron Scales

Clan to consider. Banished to the Sea of Ash, the rebel dragons used the southern kingdom as their hunting ground. If they were to discover who it was Cassidy sought, then Alec would be in even greater danger than he already was. Whether she liked it or not, it seemed Alec's rescue would be up the humans.

The wooden cart rocked back and forth as it rolled over the marred surface of the ancient road. Alec watched the passing scenery cautiously from within the confines of their cramped cage. Ten of them were seated shoulder-to-shoulder. Positioned on the center right, Alec was always kept from both the cage's door and the space closest to the horses. Their escorts must have been forewarned about the sorcerer.

The light pressure of Isabelle's head rested against his arm. Glancing at the golden strands he grimaced. Her tense form told him she wasn't asleep. None of them seemed able to do more than doze during the long irksome journey. Sighing, she shifted slightly, confirming his suspicions.

Returning his gaze to the countryside, Alec leaned the back of his head on the bars. With each passing day, their situation appeared bleaker. The traders who purchased them were well organized. They left early each morning from designated Zerrokian occupied outposts. Once locked within the cart, the door wasn't opened again until reaching the following campsite.

Try as he might, Alec couldn't find a way to escape without exposing his true abilities. The outposts were heavily guarded, as were the caravan of wagons traveling south. None of the other prisoners had anything to pick the lock with, even should he find the opportunity to use it.

Why did I make that promise to Malcolm?

Even if he hadn't, Alec knew he would still be using the same caution. Having magic didn't make one invincible. His eyes darted towards his partner. Alec also wasn't the only one an entire army would be focused upon. He exhaled with a huff.

Since entering Zerrok, they'd passed a few large towns and a small city. The other wagons split off here and there. Yet, they stayed on course, heading south without hesitation. As the outline of a large bleak city appeared, Alec's heart sank.

So this was our destination all along.

No sign as of yet marked their location, but Alec didn't need one. Having traveled here three years prior with his master, he knew precisely where they were. It was Terra, a southern city with one of the largest gladiator stadiums in the Kingdom.

Alec's eyes narrowed darkly. Clenching his hands he bit back a curse. Unless fate decided to change its mind and show him favor, there was no escaping this fortress of a city. Alec had tried.

As the horses pulling the carts trotted through the bustling streets, Alec glumly noted the area appeared no different than he remembered. Drab stands lined the busy walkways. When soldiers rode by, the citizens flinched and shrank back into the shadows. Entering the main square, Alec spotted a large wooden stage. A crowd was gathered around as tools, livestock and slaves were paraded one after another across the scarred boards. Around the perimeter, individual sales were taking place in front of wagons and makeshift stalls. Larger crowds and fewer soldiers might offer him the opportunity he was looking for. Stretching his shoulders, Alec tried to work some of the stiffness out of his muscles.

I just need a diversion.

The soldier driving their wagon maneuvered it into one of the few open spaces in the back row. Their journey finally completed, the prisoners were ushered out of the cage. Forced onto their knees, they were each chained to a short pole behind their backs which was permanently cemented into the ground.

Discretely glancing to each side, Alec searched for Isabelle. She was two people to his left. Sitting on her heels the sorceress hung her head as so many of the others did. Body slumped, she didn't bother to peer at those milling about.

Don't give up, the warrior mentally willed her.

Keeping his chin lowered, Alec constantly scanned the steady stream of people. Talking amongst themselves or lounging by the wagon, the soldiers were paying little attention to their slaves. If he set fire to a few of the empty carts it should be enough for Isabelle and him to disappear into the crowd. Clutching the chain binding him to the pole, Alec was just about to melt it when a foreboding chill ran down his spine. He stiffened. Tilting his head slightly, he gazed farther down the row. Eyes widening, he muttered a curse. His luck was taking a dramatic turn for the worse.

Meandering past the stalls was none other than Markus Duncan, Alec's former master.

Alec didn't bother hoping the vile man wouldn't see him. He knew the instant Markus's cold eyes were upon him.

The man suddenly stopped. His gaze narrowed briefly with a frown before his brows shot up to his hairline. Just as quickly he scowled, clenching his hands into fists. Pushing his way through the crowd, Markus headed straight for Alec.

A shadow passed over the warrior as Markus leered at him. Lifting his chin, Alec defiantly met the man's blazing irises.

Lip curling back in a snarl, Markus grabbed hold of the open collar of Alec's dirty shirt and jerked it over to reveal the distinct crescent-shaped scar which wrapped over his left collarbone. A satisfied gleam lit his face.

"How the tables have turned," Markus drawled. "I've been looking forward to when our paths crossed again."

Alec didn't so much as blink. "Is that so? The way I've heard it Markus, you're telling everyone I died from my injuries. What's the matter, too embarrassed to let people know I won my freedom because you lost a bet?"

The slave owner's hand connected with Alec's cheek with such force that even Isabelle flinched.

Two of the soldiers broke off from their conversation to glare at Markus.

"Hey! Keep your hands off the merchandize. No roughing them up unless you're buying."

Isabelle paled as she watched the events unfold. *This horrible man was Alec's master? No wonder the poor guy had issues.* She pulled against her chains. How dare he lay a filthy hand on her friend?

Eyes locked on Alec, Markus didn't bother glancing at the soldier speaking to him. "I'll take him."

Their captain's head snapped up. Markus hadn't tried to haggle, ask about the slave's history or even bother finding out the price! A smile found its way to the greedy man's face. Lifting a hand, he casually pointed towards Isabelle.

"How about his sister? Want her too? I'll give you a deal on the pair."

"Sister?" the slave owner echoed oddly.

Slowly, his gaze shifted to peer at Isabelle for the first time. His focus had been so intent upon Alec, Markus hadn't noticed any of the other slaves for sale. Gradually, his eyes traveled the length of her.

The woman was smudged with dirt from her head to her toes. Her blonde hair was a knotted mess and her clothing bore a few tears. Even so, the filth could not hide her attractive features or becoming curves. Cleaned up, she would be a beauty.

Markus snorted. Siblings? This woman and Alec didn't look a thing alike. The warrior's dark hair and eyes were polar opposites of Isabelle's light green eyes and honey-colored hair. They might not be aware of it, but Alec had no way of knowing who his family was. This girl was *not* his sister.

Markus noted her glaring at him and almost laughed. She did have spirit though.

"Yeah, they were traveling from some tiny village when captured," one of the men was saying, interrupting Markus's inner thoughts. "Weren't easy to get. The soldiers who sold them said they took out at least six skilled men."

"You don't say," he mumbled sardonically.

Considering Alec's skills as a gladiator, that wasn't surprising information. Markus wouldn't admit it, but Alec was the best fighter he had ever owned. It appeared he hadn't stayed in Malyndor with the dim-witted noble. Got himself a little girlfriend along the way, too.

"Got some nasty powers," the captain added.

Markus blinked, his brows lowering to a point. "Powers?" he questioned with disgust. "She's a spellcaster?"

"They both are. The anti-magic cuffs are included in the price."

"Two sorcerers huh?"

Markus's nails dug into his palms. It all made so much sense. No wonder Alec was capable of such incredible feats, like defeating Titan. He was using his filthy powers. Not this time. Markus was going to get back every cent he lost from Alec's ill-fated win.

"So what do you think? Do you want them both?" the soldier asked.

With Markus's eyes boring into him, Alec knew what the answer would be.

"You have yourself a deal."

Money was quickly exchanged prior to the pair being unchained. Snapping his fingers, Markus summoned a few of his men who appeared like wraiths. A guard grabbed each arm as both Alec and Isabelle were hauled through the market.

The sorceress's heart was drumming so loudly she could hear it thumping in her ears. *What should I do? What should I do?*

Isabelle asked herself over and over. What *could* she do? If there was a way to escape she knew Alec would have done it by now.

Thinking of Alec, Isabelle glanced at his stiff back. He hadn't said a word since his unpleasant exchange with Markus. She would *not* call the monster her master. Was he so quiet because he knew what fate awaited them? Isabelle fought a shiver. Nearly tripping, she was roughly hauled to her feet.

"Hey, you don't have to drag me about," Isabelle snapped at the men pulling her along. "You're hurting me. Where are you taking us? What is this place?"

"Quiet!" the one man commanded, giving her a quick jerk as they walked into the ever gloomy shade of a huge arena.

Smirking, Markus peered back at her. "Got quite the mouth on you. Alec was the one I wanted, but I just may find a use for you after all."

Laughing cruelly, he continued to lead them inside the stadium.

Alec clenched his jaw as he was once more taken through the twists and turns of a colosseum's underground corridors. Flashes of old memories he believed to be locked away resurfaced.

Halfway up a hall, Isabelle and Alec were dragged into a room with four cells. The one on the far left stood empty. However, the rest were filled with the bloodthirsty eyes of Markus's slaves.

Scanning the space, Markus pointed to the empty cell. "Lock them in there for now. I don't care what you do with them; just make sure you keep them alive. I have plans for this creature now that he's returned to his master."

With a booming chuckle, Markus disappeared back up the corridor.

The four guards smiled at each other gleefully. A man continued to hold Isabelle while her other escort joined Alec's captors.

The warrior felt a sharp kick to the back of his leg.

"Get on your knees worm," growled one of the guards.

Forced to the ground, two men held Alec's arms as a third stood in front of him. Cracking his knuckles, he smiled as he pulled back his arm to land a solid punch in the warrior's gut. The next one connected with Alec's cheek as the guard merrily continued the beating.

"Leave him alone," Isabelle commanded, squirming relentlessly.

"Shut up."

"Ouch!" she cried as her captor pulled at the chains binding her wrists.

He laughed cruelly, eyeing her flushed cheeks and flashing eyes as he turned back to watch Alec's guards switch places. The next instant the solid toe of a boot connected with the back of his calf.

"I said leave Alec alone!" Isabelle repeated, kicking him again.

"Why you little—" Snarling, he backhanded her, knocking the sorceress off her feet.

Hearing Isabelle's cry of distress, Alec's demeanor instantly changed. Stiffening, his aura started surrounding him with a dark tint.

"Don't touch her," Alec ordered icily.

The guard attacking him ceased his blows for a moment. He snickered loudly, his arm still raised until Alec lifted his eyes.

The warrior's murderous gaze was as effective as a spell. No further sounds came from his oppressor. Rooted to the spot, he hardly dared to breathe.

Tugging his hands apart Alec broke the links of the cuffs, throwing the two men holding him onto the dirty stone floor. Alec then purposely rose to his feet. Ignoring the other guards, he sped across the room in a flash. Grasping the man standing over Isabelle by the throat, the warrior proceeded to

Jay Lynn

slam his back into the wall. Face inches away, Alec glared at him with the intensity of a coming storm.

"Listen closely, you filthy piece of slime," the sorcerer began. "I don't care what you do to me, but if you ever touch her again, I will tear you apart. Is that clear?"

The man wheezed, unable to speak. Clawing at Alec's steel-like grip he managed to nod his head. When he was finally released, he gasped for air as he leaned heavily against the wall.

Taking the keys off the man's belt, Alec unlocked Isabelle's chains and jerked his head towards the open cell.

Isabelle didn't need to be told twice. She bolted across the room and slipped inside without a word. Turning back to peer through the bars, Isabelle gaped at her friend. *I've never seen him like this before.* The blood smeared over his face, along with his blazing eyes, made the sorcerer look like a demon. She shuttered and crossed her arms.

Dropping the keys, Alec slowly walked towards the spot where he had been. His steps came to a halt by the fresh drops of blood spilt from his beating. Remaining silent, the warrior lowered himself back onto his knees and placed his arms behind his back.

The guards watched him with wide eyes. Gazing among themselves, they made no move to attack the new slave. Prompted by the others, the youngest man cautiously inched forward. Gripping the broken cuff around Alec's wrist with trembling fingers, he removed one, then the next, before quickly dashing away.

"In your cell," their leader barked, pointing to the still open door.

Alec took his time rising to join Isabelle inside of the cage. His wrathful behavior wasn't merely for the benefit of the guards; it was for the other slaves as well. Isabelle would be a constant target here. Female slaves were not usually kept among the men inside the arena. Alec was partially thankful. This way, he would be by her side to protect her.

The moment the lock turned in the aged steel door, all of the guards hastened from the space.

Several of the gladiators hooted and hollered after them with glee. Although some still leered at Isabelle, none of them directed any remarks her way. They knew they wouldn't be able to touch the woman as long as her protector was still alive.

CHAPTER 4

Lingering in the shadows of a narrow alley, Jerric crossed his arms with a huff. It was well past midnight, and the air was brisk as a chilling wind blew through the streets of Ariston. Pressing his lips together in a thin line, he leaned forward to peer up and down the dark side street. Save for a stray cat or two, it was empty.

"He's late," the master sage growled under his breath.

Shifting his weight from side to side, he pulled his cloak more snuggly around him. If his contact didn't show soon, he would leave. Edging towards the corner of the building, Jerric scanned the main street. Occasionally, a carriage rattled by in the dim lamps' glow or a small group would stroll noisily down the cobblestones, but that was all. With the pubs still open, not many people loitered in the street.

"Looking for someone?" questioned a quiet voice from behind him.

Spinning around, Jerric glared at the figure standing several feet away.

"Good of you to finally make an appearance. How long were you planning on making me wait?"

The short man's face was hidden by the hood of his cloak. Still, his proud stance seemed to radiate a shroud of indifference.

"I had other priorities," he answered vaguely.

"Indeed? You should remember that without my help for all these years The Pure wouldn't have gained the power it has. Nor would your forces have been able to infiltrate either of the magical academies, not to mention the Royal Palace."

"You dare to brag about such failures? I care not how long you've been skulking around for your own gain. Your job was to help us weaken the Malyndorian Crown and eliminate the Master Sages, neither of which you accomplished. Do not fool yourself into thinking your value was not affected. The Pure do not take kindly to mistakes."

Jerric jerked back. Scowling, he peered down his beak-like nose at his guest. "That wasn't my fault. Malcolm's filthy apprentice interfered. The boy has great power, but I managed to take care of him."

The cloaked man was quiet for a few seconds. "So you were the one to send him and the girl to Rhordack."

The sage shrugged. "I simply convinced certain sorcerers that he was the best choice."

"There might be some use for you yet, Master Jerric. My sources informed me they were both sold in Terra."

Jerric smiled. It seemed the arrogant slave was back where he belonged.

"He won't be leaving Zerrok alive this time. I just wish I could be there to watch them both die."

Isabelle stood as still as a statue while gripping the handle of her hatchet so tightly her knuckles bleached white. The pressure kept her hands from shaking. Unfortunately, it did nothing for her knees, which were threatening to buckle. Above her, the noise from the crowd was almost deafening.

On the arena floor, numerous battles were taking place all around.

How did Alec do this? she thought frantically.

The large space was oval in shape. The far end had a massive gate flanked by two smaller ones. Three doors were spread along both side walls ending with two more gates at the rear.

Isabelle didn't know what could possibly be unleashed from the large steel doorway and she didn't want to know. She had her hands full staying alive as it was.

Two dozen gladiators fought throughout the arena. For some reason, everyone seemed to have swords save for Isabelle and Alec. The sorceress glanced over to where he stood engaged in combat against another slave. The competition had just begun, yet the others appeared to be mostly zeroing in on her partner.

A badly scarred man came at her. Instinctively raising her hand, she summoned a spell.

"Surgeon, blast."

The cuff on her wrist glowed faintly then stopped. Eyes darting between her hand and her attacker, Isabelle gulped. *Crap! I forgot about this stupid thing.* She lifted the hatchet and planted her feet. The man would be upon her in a heartbeat.

A blade shot in front of Isabelle's face, blocking her foe's sword. Pushed back, the man emitted a primal like growl before launching forward to strike at her savior instead.

Both hands gripping his weapon, Alec followed with a series of powerful attacks.

The other man blocked the first few, but couldn't keep up with Alec's speed.

There was no way Alec was going to lose to any of these fighters. The warrior couldn't afford to. Markus's words prior to the battle replayed themselves in his mind.

'You can't refuse my orders this time, Alec,' he sneered coldly. 'If you don't want that girl to keep my men company for the rest of her days, then *every* match you fight…kill them all.'

Face a mask of stone, Alec drove his blade into his opponent. Pulling his sword free, he turned to meet another gladiator.

"Eeek!" Isabelle squeaked, jumping back. She hadn't seen the second man closing in upon her.

Twisting his wrist, Alec slashed him from shoulder to hip.

"Thanks Alec. Where did you find the sword?"

"I borrowed it," he answered gesturing in the direction he originally came from.

While Alec joined her side, Isabelle glanced to the left. Sure enough, a man was lying on the ground with a hatchet planted in his skull. Face paling, the sorceress fought to keep from vomiting.

"Do you have to slay them? Can't you just knock them out?"

Alec paused, watching two more gladiators approaching them. Jaw clenching, he refused to meet her eye.

"I can't, Isabelle."

She jerked back slightly. *Can't?* Had the blood and gore of the colosseum gotten to him already? Was Alec morphing into one of those mindless, murdering weapons? No. She wouldn't believe that. There was something almost desperate in his gaze. Isabelle lifted her eyes to peer up at the stands. Markus was there, not even bothering to hide the wide grin covering his lips.

This has to be his doing.

Alec wasn't a merciless killer. Before the match, their owner pulled him aside. Isabelle hadn't heard his words, but she would bet he was the reason for Alec's odd behavior.

Blocking out the sound of his opponent's cries of pain, Alec battled one after another until only he and Isabelle remained. The crowd yelled with glee as the blade slipped from his loose fingers. Refusing to even glance at the faces above them, Alec placed a hand on the small of his partner's back and led her from the bloody stage.

Wrists bound in chains, they were taken back through the twisting bowels of the colosseum. The men trapped inside the steel cages hollered and screamed as the two newest slaves were dragged past. Reaching through the bars, several of them tried to grab Isabelle.

One man managed to catch her arm. His grimy fingers dug into her skin as he gripped the bars with his other hand.

Alec pulled the two guards holding him over to the side as he lifted his leg to slam his foot against the slave's exposed hand.

The man screamed as his fingers were crushed against the bars. He immediately released his hold of the sage.

By the time they were able to tug Alec off, the damage was already done.

"Never touch her," the warrior warned.

Forced back down the corridor, Alec's eyes continued to scan the cells. He would find no allies this time. There were only the deadliest of foes. Once the door to their cage was secured behind them, Alec's shoulders finally sagged. Exhaling, he lowered himself to the ground.

Placing her hands on her hips, Isabelle stood over him with a frown.

"What in the world has gotten into you? I've never seen you go on a rampage like that. Seriously Alec, I know we're being forced to fight, but that doesn't mean you have to slaughter people."

Alec snorted. Sometimes she could be so naive. They couldn't afford to appear weak, even if Markus hadn't commanded him to behave like a savage.

"This isn't the academy, Isabelle. Being soft gets you killed."

Eyes widening, her head jerked back as if he had slapped her. "What did he say to you?"

Alec tilted his head.

"Don't pretend you don't know of what I speak," Isabelle told him testily. "Markus. What did he say?"

Not as naive as I thought, Alec mentally corrected. Sighing, he gave her a helpless shrug.

"Kill them all, or you pay the price."

Blinking several times, Isabelle's mouth tightened at the corners. "That bastard."

Alec's brows rose to his hairline. He couldn't have heard her right. Isabelle rarely swore.

Hands dropping to her sides, she placed a palm against her cheek and peered at the dirt floor. Isabelle's entire body seemed to droop. Her lips started to move, yet no words came out. Finally shaking her head, Isabelle slid down the wall to sit beside him.

"Sorry," she whispered.

Alec flashed a humorless smile. "I'm not going to let anything happen to you."

The sorcerer would not break his promise. Closing his eyes, Jade's face came to mind as he gripped the chain still around his neck. *Wait for me, Jade. Somehow, I will return.*

A wisp of hair brushed the side of Jade's cheek. Tucking it behind her ear, she continued to stroll along the edge of the bustling street. Various carts wheeled by as vendors finished setting up for the annual harvest festival. Decorations hung above the walkways, covered the fronts of shops, and even adorned every flag pole displaying Stafford's dual sword crest. Like clockwork, almost all of the preparations were ready for the start of the celebration this Saturday.

Jade smiled softly. Peering around at the beaming faces, and listening to people's laughter, she sighed wistfully. *There is such a wondrous sense of excitement in the air this year.*

Suddenly, her footsteps drew to a halt, as did the two soldiers discretely escorting her.

Across the road, a man dwelt in the shadows of an alley. Nearby was the side door to one of the shops. An arm hidden behind his back, he glanced at the entry, then peered about cautiously.

Unconsciously, Jade's fingers snaked around the steel grip of her sword. Eyes narrowing, she inched forward with her bodyguards.

The side door flew open. A woman stepped into the alley, nearly running into the man hiding in the partial darkness. She shrieked, pressing a hand to her heart as the man revealed a bouquet of flowers.

Exhaling, Jade watched as a large grin stretched across the woman's face. Releasing her grip, the noblewoman leaned a hand against the sheath. *Thank heavens. It was nothing after all.* Only recently did Garth give her permission to wear a blade outside of the practice field.

A sword was a weapon, he told her. While to some it was a deterrent, to others it would be an invitation to test their blades. A swordsman should never carry a weapon unless they have the skill and resolve to use it.

Jade knew she was ready, even if the duke was less than pleased with her decision. Still, part of her was thankful she had yet to draw her sword against a foe. As Jade began to walk down the street once more, she passed the couple who sold her the hair ribbons she purchased last year. Smiling brightly, they engaged in small talk for a few minutes before Jade continued on with a wave. Reaching behind her, she twirled the ends of her long dark hair. She didn't have her green ribbon any longer.

A sharp pang squeezed Jade's heart. She didn't regret giving Alec the token on the day he departed Stafford. Sadly, it was the last time she saw him.

The spark faded from Jade's emerald green irises. If she shut her eyes, she could picture her beloved warrior with ease. Thinking about his intelligent, chocolate-colored gaze and his playful half smirk caused the pressure in her chest to increase. There was no word from Alec for several weeks now.

Garth, his closest friend, received letters here and there. By what Garth told her, Alec traveled to Marcia after departing. While training soldiers, he met up with a fellow sage named Isabelle. Alec then made his way to Ariston with Malcolm where he recently was initiated as an Emerald Sage.

Glancing up at the sky, a grin spread across Jade's lips.

He did it.

Alec became an Emerald Sage, just as he planned. The smile slipped. *Why has he not returned?* The warrior promised to come back when he was someone worthy. The man she loved was one of his word. So where was he? He gained the honorable title of a King's Sorcerer. What more did he need?

Frowning, Jade's steps slowed. Had something happened to him? Jade heard rumors about two sages who went missing during a mission. The latest news suggested they might be in Zerrok.

Jade shook her head, ridding herself of those thoughts. Alec would never go anywhere near the southern kingdom again. She saw for herself some of the suffering he endured there. Then what could it be? Biting her lip, Jade peered around. Children laughed and played while couples walked by hand in hand.

"Isabelle," Jade whispered darkly.

The sorceress's name seemed to magically appear on her lips.

Garth briefly mentioned her after receiving one of Alec's letters. If she wasn't of some importance, Alec wouldn't have written about her. He wasn't one to waste words. The warrior's correspondence was always short.

Who is she?

Jade's fingers curled around the hem of her tunic. Pressing her lips into a flat line, her body tensed. Nodding to herself, Jade exhaled with a sharp huff then suddenly spun on her heel. The noble passed between her two startled guards as she quickly retraced her steps towards the castle. The need for answers drove her forward to the point that Jade was nearly sprinting as she reached the front door. Handing her sword to one of the soldiers, she grasped the door handle. Taking a deep breath, her shoulders pulled back and chin lifted. Jade forced herself to slow her pace as she strode gracefully into the gleaming foyer.

Garth no longer lived in the soldiers' barracks. A few weeks ago, he finally agreed to move into the castle where the higher ranking members of the Stafford's Guard resided. At first, he had been adamant to change. Jade wondered if part of him was against leaving the room he shared with Alec so soon after the warrior's departure.

Traveling down the corridor, Jade passed the hall leading to the healer's quarters. Jade smiled as she ascended the stairs to the next floor. Perhaps Kayla had some influence on the drill instructor's decision.

Nearing his door, Jade hoped the former gladiator was in. The new recruits were given the week off to visit family and assist with the festivities. He might not be teaching any classes, yet, that didn't mean he wasn't training himself.

Knocking on the solid wooden door, Jade tapped her fingers against her leg as she waited for the sound of Garth's voice. Leaning forward, she tilted her head to the side. Previously with Alec, Jade learned the hard way not to burst into a man's room without permission. Just thinking of him shirtless caused her cheeks to flush.

Why am I thinking of that now? Stay focused Jade.

She was here to find out more about this unknown woman, not to be reminded of this relentless longing.

The thump of footsteps on the other side of the entry pulled Jade back to current events. She straightened just as the door opened.

Eyes widening slightly, a grin spread across Garth's face. "Lady Jade, what brings you here?"

"Greetings Garth. May I have a few moments of your time?"

"Of course." He opened the door wider and stepped to the side. "Come on in."

Jade had yet to visit his new chambers, and normally wouldn't do so without Ariel, but this could not wait. She trusted him. If people wanted to talk, then they may do so.

Garth offered her a distinctively feminine chair with a floral pattern. Peering around, Jade noted a few other pieces Kayla must have picked out in the sparsely decorated space. *I am pleased for them.*

"How are you settling in to your new room?"

"Quite well, thank you."

"I am glad. It must have been cramped in the barracks. I hope you are enjoying some time without your students. It is a lovely day out. I regret I shall not be able to resume our lessons until after the festival. It should be splendid this year. I do hope you are planning to attend."

Cease rambling.

Raising his brows, Garth watched her for a few moments without a word. Interlacing his fingers, he leaned his elbows on his thighs.

"Jade, what's the true nature of this visit?"

Opening her mouth to speak, Jade closed it again while giving her shoulders a small shrug. "Have you heard anything from Alec?"

The warrior released a sigh. "No, not lately." He forced a smile. "I'm sure everything is fine. Alec's certainly capable of taking care of himself. Tensions with Zerrok are keeping everyone busy in the military. I'm sure he's just working around the clock somewhere for King Titus."

"Rumors speak of two missing sages. Do you...do you think Alec is one of them?"

"No," Garth immediately refuted, shaking his head. "No, I doubt it. I've heard this rumor as well. Sir Roderick said the word from Ariston is the sages are in Zerrok, and a rescue party was already dispatched. Alec would never go near Zerrok. It has to be something else occupying him."

"Then why has he not returned? Or written as of late?" Jade questioned forcefully through clenched teeth.

Garth shook his head, gesturing with a hand. "Like I said Jade, he's probably delayed because of his duties. As much as we might want our warrior back, orders from the King come first."

Pursing her lips, Jade's gaze dropped to the chair's arm. Picking at a piece of fuzz she didn't meet his eye.

"What about Isabelle? Might she be the reason?"

The soldier was forced to hide a smile as he leaned back. Garth knew there was nothing for the noble to fear. Alec wasn't fickle. Though the sage tried to hide it, Garth saw how much Alec cared for Jade. She needn't worry that he would betray their secret either.

"Jade, from the moment I met Alec, he has been a man of his word. He promised to return, and I *know* he will, because what he loves most is right here."

Jade's head jerked up as she stared at the warrior.

Garth steadily held eye contact.

Lip quivering, Jade blinked rapidly and turned away. *So, he does know. I wondered if he might have discovered it.* More people guessed her and Alec's feelings than she liked, but Garth's words warmed her too much to fret about it now.

"You really think so?" she whispered.

"Look here."

Garth rose and removed a plain wooden box from his desk. Returning to Jade's side, he pulled off the top and held it out to her.

"He doesn't come right out and say it, but every one of these letters have thoughts of you."

"Indeed?"

Taking the box, Jade gently set it on her lap. Picking up the pages she read through them one after another as Garth lowered himself into his seat. Her movements were slow, hesitant at first. Jade had no problem reading Alec's messy script. The more she absorbed his words the faster her heart began to race.

Hope your sword lessons aren't becoming too dangerous. Wood ones might be better.

You should see the ocean out here. The green color reminds me of Stafford.

Cloud and I miss our daily rides.

Jade stared at the words unable to look away. On the surface, his comments might not appear special, but Jade could see what Garth meant. Alec was talking about her! She was the only one Alec used wooden swords with regularly. Alec once compared the shade of her eyes to the ocean and Alec always escorted her on her daily rides.

"I miss you, too," Jade whispered to the pages, gripping them tighter. Holding something he touched as well warmed her as if it connected them together. "Then who is this Isabelle?" she questioned, peering over at Garth.

He smiled indulgently. "She's a fellow sorcerer that Alec met at the East Circle. At first, he seemed to find her annoying. They've been training together here and there since he left. She was recently made his partner after joining the Emerald Sages. Isabelle is a friend and someone he appears to trust. It's good for him to find some allies. Alec's going to need them in his line of work. You have nothing to worry about Jade."

So he says, Jade thought bitterly, thinking about how this other woman was traveling all over Malyndor with her Alec. Jade sighed. Realistically, she couldn't be jealous of every faceless woman he worked with. Sometimes love could feel like a curse instead of a blessing. Garth was right. Alec needed allies. In the end, all that mattered was that he returned safely.

In the blink of an eye, Saturday descended upon Jade with a whirlwind of activities. Trying to enjoy the celebration, she allowed herself to get carried away with the festive diversion all week.

By the night of the closing dance and feast, she almost forgot the lingering ache in her chest. Almost. Sitting at the high table, Jade gazed at those twirling around the room with a well-practiced smile. It was here, only a year ago, she danced with Alec.

A warm breeze caressed her skin, reminding her of his gentle touch. Jade's eyes lowered to the table while she clutched her hands together.

Appearing through the crowd, the Thornbrook children suddenly rushed to the noble's side. Hearing their voices, a real grin found its way to Jade's lips. There was not a day in which she wasn't pleased to see them. Within moments, the noble found herself spinning the three younger ones across the polished stone floor.

Linus stood to the side, arms crossed, as he watched the others quietly. The children knew Alec was working as a King's Sorcerer, but his inability to join them at the festival dampened their spirits.

Lia and Simuel didn't understand the importance of the warrior's new position.

While Linus did, his dreary mood had yet to lighten.

Jade sympathized. Ever since Alec saved Lia from that fire he'd become a hero to the boy. Being a wizard hadn't lessened Linus's admiration. It seemed in his mind, there wasn't anyone who could compare to the warrior from his homeland.

Grasping the boy's hands, Jade pulled Linus out into the throng with the other dancers. As he tried to pull away, she spun them in a continuous circle. A few seconds later, he was laughing along with Jade.

Later in the evening, Jade strolled back to her table after bidding her favorite children farewell. Her father was awaiting her there and he was not alone. Jade's smile faded.

Not another suitor, she inwardly groaned.

Instead of the parading of possible husbands lessening after the incident with Lord Percy, it had gotten worse. For Jade, it seemed as if every week one man or another was brought before her. Shouldn't Malyndor have run out of eligible nobles by now? As the introductions were made, Jade pasted on a hollow smile. Her mind drifting, she paid zero attention to what was actually being said. Jade couldn't remember the lord's name even if her life depended on it.

When the man asked her to dance, she was obligated to consent. He slowly twirled her around the floor, watching the expressions of the other nobles present.

Jade distinctly felt like a doll on display. Her body fought the urge to recoil from his touch. *I cannot take much more of this.*

When he spoke to her, the man only carried on about himself. He didn't even seem to notice Jade's lack of interest. Each second she was forced to spend in the lord's company condemned him in Jade's mind. He didn't have a hope of making a match with her.

Somehow, she made it through the remainder of the evening. The joy Jade felt at the start of the celebration long since dissipated. When she was finally able to escape, Jade laid in bed for hours, unable to drift off to sleep. In the times she did doze, her mind tormented her with vivid dreams of Alec. Why did spending time with these men cause her to feel as if she was betraying him? The infuriating man never said he loved her!

But he refused to say he did not, her mind countered reasonably.

Jade let out a ragged sigh. The words hadn't been needed. Jade knew how he felt and more importantly, the feelings in her own heart. Her father's poorly disguised match-making could not continue. It appeared to be time for Jade to speak with him about this matter.

Walking the corridors the next morning, without meaning to, Jade found herself in front of Edmund's study. She was trying to decide how best to make her case. Taking a deep breath, Jade knocked on the door before she lost her nerve.

Calling for his visitor to enter, Edmund glanced up, then grinned. It had been awhile since Jade stopped by his office.

Last night must have gone better than I thought, Edmund happily mused.

So far, Jade had yet to show any interest in the lords who visited the castle. At times, she seemed to be willfully trying to scare them off. He recalled Lord Percy's reaction after Jade's training session with Garth.

Young women are such a mystery.

Wasn't getting married and having a grand wedding one of their greatest desires? It would appear he thought wrong.

Focusing on the slight woman standing in front of his desk, Edmund noted the determined gleam in her eyes. Edmund held back a sigh. It would seem she hadn't come to announce her infatuation for anyone.

His eyes quickly traveled the length of his daughter. Jade had grown and changed much since her journey to Zerrok, but it appeared the transformation had not ceased. An air of confidence shrouded her. For the first time as he gazed upon his daughter, Edmund saw not his little girl, but a woman capable of leading their people. *When did this happen?* Despite her stubbornness, he was proud.

Rising, the noble gave her a hug all the same. He could feel Jade squeeze tightly, desperately, in return. Pulling back, he gently led her to their favorite spot by the windows.

"Tell me my jewel, to what do I owe the pleasure of your company this morning? I trust you found the festival diverting."

"I found it fairly adequate." She flashed him a small smile prior to taking a deep breath. "In fact, it is in regards to last evening which brings me here."

Edmund instantly perked up. He must have misjudged the light shining in her eyes. *Which lucky lord could it be?*

"Pray, continue. You know you can tell me anything."

I hope that is true, Jade thought, gripping the skirt of her dress. Smoothing out the fabric, she let the words trapped within her flow out.

"Father, I love you very much. I know you are merely seeking what you believe to be in my best interest, but pray, I ask for you to discontinue with your matchmaking hence forth."

Edmund's expression morphed into a scowl. "If you are aware it is for your best interest, then why request me to cease with the introductions? Do you not desire to make a proper match?"

"Of course I do, Father." Jade clutched her hands together and peered out at the rain splattered glass. "More than anything, I seek a man who will be the best match for not only myself, but Stafford as well." She turned back to gaze at her father. "These lords as of late are not the right fit for me or our people."

Crossing his arms, Edmund's eyes narrowed. "Is that so? And what was so exceedingly wrong with my choices?"

Jade shook her head. "I mean no offense. It is not easy to find someone with the proper character to follow in your footsteps. Should I not, at the very least, like the man I am prevailed upon to marry?"

Holding Jade's unwavering gaze, the duke exhaled deeply through his nose. "What type of man might that be?" he questioned a little too sharply.

"One that is not completely self-centered would be a welcome start," Jade nearly snapped in return.

Their tempers were much more alike than either one was willing to admit.

Jade refused to advert her eyes. She wanted— no needed, her father to understand.

"My entire life, you and mother have spoken of what is proper for those of privilege. I do not think it is unreasonable to seek a husband who bears those qualities. I seek someone who is smart, strong and courageous, yet still kindhearted enough to see people *as* people, not merely a means to get what he wants. Someone who sees *me* as more than an asset to trade for greater wealth and power. I deserve that and so does Stafford."

The duke could feel his jaw tense. Jade's speech wasn't fooling him. As heartfelt as her words might have been, he could still see the hidden meaning behind them. Her list of qualities wasn't designed for any lord to live up to. They were derived from an already chosen suitor.

It didn't matter if he paraded a hundred, or even a thousand men before her. Jade's mind was already made up. After all these months, she hadn't forgotten about Alec. He knew Garth was the only one to receive any type of correspondence. Therefore, Edmund couldn't fathom how the warrior was influencing her despite the distance between them. There was no denying it. It was lingering still, from Jade's lessons with a blade, to the defiance dancing in her eyes like a flame. *I should have done something sooner.* Had he been aware of this unhealthy infatuation with a man of lower birth, Edmund would have.

Hands curling around the arms of the chair, Edmund slowly rose to his feet. Face twitching, he stared at his daughter like a looming thunderstorm.

"As your father and patriarch, you shall heed my words, Jade. You are the daughter of a Duke, and as such, you *will* marry a man of noble blood and *only* a nobleman. I shall not give my blessing for another. So forget him."

Him. Jade knew at once to whom her father was referring, even though his name was yet to be said. Leaping to her feet, she glared up at him.

"Why do you disapprove of him? I thought you liked Alec? Did he not save your life?"

"He might be a great warrior, but he is not worthy of you!"

Tears welled up in her eyes as Jade raised her chin. Finally, she understood why Alec left to make a name for himself. He was right. Edmund would never approve of him even after all he had done.

"He is the only one worthy," Jade managed.

With a choked sob she fled the chamber, nearly crashing into her mother who was standing on the other side of the door. Sailing past her, Jade didn't trust herself to speak as she raced back towards her room.

Closing the solid wooden door with a soft click, Leona glided over towards the desk and took a seat.

Edmund plopped down in his chair behind the massive piece of furniture. Eyes closed, his fingers rubbed his right temple while the noble released a frustrated groan.

"Are you proud of yourself dear?" Leona questioned smoothly in a calm voice.

Edmund's hand froze. Blinking, he peered over the desk's polished surface to look at his wife. His arm dropped.

"Not you as well, Leona. You cannot possibly approve of her choice. You more than anyone have taught her the importance of marrying someone suitable."

She nodded gracefully. "Indeed, I have. I admit, my love, I was a trifle surprised to see them growing so close."

"You knew about this?" he growled in return.

"Anyone with eyes could see it."

"And you allowed it to continue?" Pounding a hand on the desk Edmund turned the chair so he could face his wife. "Leona what were you thinking? Our daughter refuses to even consider another suitor because of him."

Ankles crossed and hands resting lightly on her lap, the duchess waited a few moments prior to asking, "Why do you disapprove of Alec so greatly? I distinctly recall you being quite fond of him."

"I have nothing against him as a swordsman or even as a sorcerer," Edmund began, leaning over the desk. "But for our daughter! Come now, he was a slave fighting as a gladiator. He cannot possibly compare to the lords I have selected."

Edmund's head jerked back as he distinctly heard Leona emit a noise which sounded very much like a snort.

"My love, you are misguided. I do not include you when I say this, but having noble blood does not automatically make you above reproach. Too many are driven more by their ambitions than a desire for a respectable companion. Having lived through a similar experience myself, I understand her distaste in being treated like a mindless doll. Far too many are vain, selfish and see women as beneath them. It is no wonder Alec earned her affections; her other suitors pale in comparison."

Edmund blinked rapidly. Did she just say Alec was better than these noblemen? That he was better than the men Edmund was choosing for their daughter? The duke raked his fingers through his hair.

"Do not be so foolish, Leona. You have been blinded by that man's charm."

"Lord Vincent was charming, Alec is anything but."

Edmund scowled at her.

The duchess fought a smirk. "Tell me Edmund, what qualities do you seek in our daughter's suitor?"

Slumping in his chair the duke's eyes momentarily dropped to the desk. He took several slow, deep breaths.

When he began talking again he started out quietly, as if speaking to himself.

"The man must be intelligent to begin with and treat Jade well. Strong...a good leader...a fine warrior would not hurt. More than anything he should be someone our people can rely on, look up to, no matter if it be times of privilege or strife. I want the next duke to rule as we have, with a just fist and a compassionate heart."

Leona smiled fondly. "You are a fair and just man, Edmund. I am proud to be your wife." She stood and rounded the desk, lingering by his side. "Name one of those qualities Alec does not possess. I could understand your disapproval if the man in question was a simple farmer, or one of the footman, but he is not. Look at what Alec accomplished. The impression he left behind, from Leos to Malcolm. Grandmaster Malcolm, the greatest sage of our time, took Alec as only one of three apprentices. Perhaps, you should think of that instead of the slave from Zerrok."

Bending down, Leona placed a gentle kiss on his forehead prior to leaving the study.

Edmund leaned his head against the back of the chair. "Women!" he muttered to the empty space.

When had his wife shifted her alliances? He never would have imagined her approving of Alec over any of Jade's other suitors. Was the kingdom going mad?

Running a hand over his face, Edmund stared blankly at the wall. Was it possible Alec had more worth than he gave him credit for? The man could not help the situation to which he was born. Yet, during his time here Alec certainly left an impression as Leona said.

At first, Edmund considered him a possible threat. After Alec saved him and his men in the Rios Forest, he came to see him as a great warrior. Quiet and slightly withdrawn, the man gradually came out of his protective shell to become a major part of the running of Stafford. His impressive skills in combat with both sword and sorcery were matched by his strength as a leader.

Tapping his fingers on the arm of the chair, Edmund was forced to admit Leona was at least partially right. Malcolm did take a special interest in Alec. He could have easily let another train the new sorcerer and even left with Alec when he departed for Marcia. There wasn't a single time Alec showed off his powers or abused them.

In his mind's eye, Alec's history with the Stafford's Guard seemed to flash before him. Edmund was reminded of when Alec nearly drowned in the creek, his restraint against Vincent, and the way he helped Jade overcome her fear after she was attacked. Perhaps, it was time to stop thinking of him as a former slave, and see him in a different light. In that regard, part of him was as equally guilty as some of his men.

CHAPTER 5

Carefully shifting his feet on the roughly tied logs, Alec gripped his knife as he studied his new battlefield. Begrudgingly, the warrior had to admit Markus outdid himself for Alec's first ever water match.

The entire arena was flooded to create a man-made lake. The only area within the stone pit which could be considered land was a sand mound pressed against the upper right corner. A tall thick pole jutted out of the sand against the wall to hoist what was considered the "prize" of this particular competition.

Upper body bound by ropes, Isabelle kicked her legs as she swung unhappily from near the top. Whoever was deemed the winner would get to keep her in their cell. Alec would be damned before he allowed that to happen.

The warrior shifted his focus back to the more pressing problem at hand: his battleground. A total of four gladiators armed with knives were positioned at the corners of a large, thirty-foot platform. The structure was nothing fancy, just heavy timber lashed together. Water seeped through the cracks around his feet. Worse, every time one of the fighters moved, the whole platform bobbed. Keeping it from flipping over entirely would be a feat in and of itself.

The man across from Alec glared at him thoughtfully. "I know you. You're the wench's brother."

Alec didn't bother to answer.

"He is? Good," another gladiator interjected. "Let's kill him first. Then, we can fight each other for the girl."

"I'm game," the last man agreed.

All three started towards the fighter. The platform swayed, tipping in Alec's direction as everyone's weight shifted at once.

"Hope you guys can swim," Alec quipped. *Nathan, I owe you one.* He was glad the soldier had taught him.

Their movements ceased immediately. Glancing at each other, the gladiators nodded. The man opposite Alec once more strode forward while the others remained in place.

Alec willingly met him at the center of the platform.

Slashing with his knife, the slave charged full force at Alec.

Ducking under the attack, Alec followed with a strong kick to the man's side. His opponent dropped his left arm to cushion the blow while Alec twisted back with a long horizontal cut.

Jerking away, the man barely escaped. Striking low, the fighter aimed for Alec's knee.

Jumping up, Alec easily dodged it as he somersaulted over his foe's arm. As he was about to land a killing blow, the two men waiting in the wings rushed forward. Alec was forced to draw back to get out of the line of fire.

"Alec!" Isabelle shouted, kicking her legs ferociously as she sought his attention. "Alec!"

Catching a man's arm, Alec leaned back as a knife slashed by his face. "I'm a little busy."

"No Alec, there's something in the water!" she frantically replied.

A large, long silhouette glided through the somewhat murky lake below. Isabelle's eyes tracked its movement as the creature slipped past her and headed straight for the structure rocking on the water's surface.

Right after Isabelle's warning, something nudged the platform as if testing it. The next thing Alec knew, they were all thrown off their feet as the over-sized raft was hit below the left edge.

"What the hell was that?" a slave questioned.

A scaly, serpent-like back broke through the surface of the water a few feet off as their new nemesis made another pass.

Instead of attacking again, the creature headed away from the platform. Still flailing about, Isabelle hung from the pole like a worm on a hook. Her constant movements attracted unwanted attention.

Charging up from the depths, the large serpent snapped its jaws at the sorceress.

Lifting her legs, Isabelle shrieked as a wide mouth, filled with large foot-long fangs, snapped to a close only a few feet beneath her.

The other gladiators were no longer looking at Alec.

"Was that a snake?" one asked incredulously.

"There's no way in hell that was a snake. The thing was huge," a second answered, gripping his knife as his eyes scanned the water.

"Isabelle, are you alright?" Alec hollered to her.

"Surely you jest. No, I'm not alright. That thing tried to eat me!" she shrieked.

The warrior's gaze tried to track the serpent, but he was having difficulty seeing it from so close to the surface.

"Isabelle, I know you're scared, but I need you to be my eyes. Do you know what it is?"

Inhaling with a shaky breath, the sorceress tried to focus as she nodded.

"Y-yes and it's coming your way." She peered at the water, following the figure slithering back towards her friend. "I've seen pictures of it at the academy. It's a drakon, also called a Water Dragon. They average about twenty-five feet long and are very rare. Normally, they live in deeper parts of the ocean, and are known to be extremely territorial."

"Water Dragon? Does it breathe fire?"

"No," she began to answer as the drakon charged the raft. "It's coming towards your right! Watch out for its poisonous—"

Isabelle's words were cut off as the drakon shot out of the water and spewed a thick grey mist over the surface of the platform.

Alec covered his mouth, trying not to breathe in the toxins as his eyes burned. Nearby, the other men where unleashing various cries of alarm. The logs jerked to the side as the drakon snapped his jaws around one of the gladiators and pulled him under. He could hear Isabelle's voice calling out to him, but her words were difficult to decipher amidst the general commotion of both the arena and the stands above.

Closing his watery eyes, Alec tried to clear his vision. It didn't change the darkness which greeted him. The platform rocked violently. Still clutching his blade with an iron grip, Alec held his hands out by his sides as he fought to keep his balance. Another scream erupted close by. The warrior was tossed from the logs as the drakon dove onto the raft, killing one of the gladiators and breaking the structure apart.

Alec was suddenly stripped of his breath as he plunged into the icy lake. Clawing his way back to the surface, he jerked his head from side to side, yet couldn't make out anything other than black shadows.

Wading in the water, Alec listened for Isabelle's voice so she might guide him towards the sand. The garbled pleas of the last remaining fighter as he struggled to stay above the surface cut through everything else. Then it was gone, leaving nothing behind but the joyful screams of the crowd.

Alec knew who the drakon would seek out now. Blinded by its poisons, he was a sitting duck. No one, not even Isabelle, who was still swaying from the rope, could aid him.

The scrape of hard scales suddenly brushed by Alec's side. He could feel the swift change of the water's flow as a powerful form swam past. Coiling around his ankle, the drakon's tail pulled Alec down into the depths of the lake. Running his hand over his leg, Alec plunged his knife into the creature.

A hissing shriek vibrated through the water as Alec was instantly released. It would be coming for him, though from where?

Behind you! the strange woman's voice warned him as Alec felt his dragon mark warm.

Twisting around, Alec held his hands out in front of him. *Sorry Malcolm,* he thought sadly. If he wanted to live, if he wanted Isabelle to survive, then he would have to break his promise.

A soft flash of light passed from his hands through the drakon as Alec silently cast a paralyzing spell. The murky water absorbed every beam, locking the secret of Alec's creation-less magic below the surface.

Reaching out with the blade, Alec tapped the drakon. It didn't budge a single muscle. Swimming closer, he searched for the creature's throat. It would be better to slit it open than to use his powers to obliterate the serpent. This way, no one would know what he had done.

Surprisingly still, Isabelle stared at the lake. She didn't dare move or speak. It felt like an eternity since Alec was dragged down into the darkness.

Come on, she silently pleaded. *Alec, where are you?* He couldn't be dead. The sorceress refused to believe it.

The surface rippled.

Leaning forward, Isabelle watched as the long serpent's body bobbed to the top of the water. Black, inky blood swirled around it in a growing puddle. Popping up by its head was the sorcerer himself.

Gasping for breath, Alec coughed as he sucked in some much needed air.

Isabelle called out to him.

Twisting his neck, Alec tilted his head to the side as he sought the direction from which she was summoning him. Cutting through the water with powerful strokes, Alec swam to the sand mound and trudged onto its dry land. His vision was improving quickly, yet he still couldn't make out anything useful.

Relying on Isabelle's guidance, he managed to find the rope holding her aloft and lowered her to the ground. The instant the warrior sliced her bonds, he was knocked back as his friend's arms curled around his neck.

"Don't ever scare me like that," she commanded with a sob.

Alec managed a short huff of a laugh. "I'll try not to."

"Alright then," she whispered back.

In that moment, as Isabelle briefly tightened her embrace, she thought nothing could stop this man. Who else could accomplish the feats he did? To her, Alec was invincible. Isabelle had no idea how wrong she was.

The following day, Alec was taken away from their shared cell as Isabelle was left to pace the floor impatiently. She didn't know how long she was forced to anxiously wait. When the door to their chamber creaked open, she stopped and raced to the bars.

Alec, surrounded by guards, slowly shuffled towards her. Isabelle's face lit up with a grin. When she fully saw him in the dim torches of the chamber, her expression instantly fell.

His skin was a pale sheet beneath the layer of blood covering the side of his face. The red stain soaked his hair and was still slowly running down his throat. Splashes of blood colored his entire body. Thankfully, it didn't appear to be his own. As Alec drew near, there was a distinct tremble to his hands as well as an unusual slump to his proud shoulders. The warrior's eyes however, were the most troublesome. The normally sharp, watchful chocolate irises had a dull, somewhat glazed look about them.

Sluggishly walking into the cell, Alec dropped down on the floor by the back wall. Curling his legs up to his chest, his body continued to shake as he slightly rocked back and forth.

Locking the cell door, their guards smirked. They glanced at each other prior to departing with loud chuckles.

On the other side of the room, a few slaves jeered and called out some taunts.

Isabelle ignored them. Her attention was solely on the warrior. After more fights than she cared to think of, Isabelle knew some of the terror that a gladiator faced in the ring. A shudder raced through her body that she couldn't suppress. The few times she battled pushed her beyond limits she never knew she had. As a result, the sorceress's hands were no longer clean of blood. To think, at one point she wanted real experience.

Alec on the other hand was always a source of calm and complete control. Looking at him now, the warrior was merely a hollow shell. There was no spark left. Whatever took place levels above them in the arena did what Markus sought all along. He'd finally broken Alec's spirit.

This is all my fault, she thought, for not the first time.

Isabelle tried to swallow the lump stuck in her throat. There had to be something she could do to help. Eyeing the blood covering him, the sorceress grabbed a few rags and a little bowl of water used to catch droplets from the ceiling. First things first, she could at least get him cleaned up.

Setting the items on the floor, Isabelle knelt in front of him. Dipping the cloth in the water, she started wiping the stain from the side of Alec's face.

He didn't so much as even acknowledge her presence. Rocking quietly, he stared at some invisible point on the ground.

Pausing, Isabelle leaned closer.

"Alec?" she softly called.

He said nothing.

"Alec, I'm going to clean you up, alright?" She waited a moment. Receiving no hint that he even heard her, Isabelle continued speaking. "I don't know what happened, but whenever you want to talk, I'm here."

Another seemingly long minute passed prior to his voice breaking the silence.

"I killed them," Alec whispered, his words painfully raw.

Isabelle's hand stilled for a second. Blinking, it took her a brief span of time before she was able to speak. "You did what you had to."

"I killed them," he repeated without the slightest change in his behavior. "I killed them all."

Isabelle couldn't bear to ask who. In a sense, it didn't matter. Each life Alec took within the arena was like another weight around his heart. She knew they would stay with him always. Yet, something about today's battle seemed to be affecting him differently than the others. It was torturing him, pushing him past broken and to the point where he might shatter all together.

There must be something I can do. I can't let Markus destroy him.

"It's not your fault, Alec. Markus is forcing you to do this. He's the one to blame for these misfortunes."

Alec's hands gripped his knees, squeezing tightly as the rocking still didn't cease.

"Kill them all," he muttered. "I have to kill them all."

A deep frown creased Isabelle's brow. Having finished cleaning the skin on his face and neck, she studied him again. There was no improvement to the haunted look in his frighteningly dull eyes.

He's losing it.

A pressure tightened around her heart with the intensity of a vise. Isabelle instinctively knew she had to do something, anything, to snap him out of this traumatic state immediately or risk Alec slipping away permanently.

Gently placing her palm over his cheek, the sorceress turned Alec's face towards her.

He's eyes didn't meet her gaze. They remained unfocused, empty.

Isabelle couldn't say what made her do it. At the time, it seemed like the only way to reach him since words held no sway. Cupping his face with both hands, Isabelle leaned forward and covered his lips with her own before she lost the nerve. It was not a soft and gentle kiss, but a firm meeting of mixed pain and passion. Isabelle placed everything she could into it. Things that even words could not express. She kissed the broken man before her with the compassion of a dear friend, with the love of a woman who knew he would never love her back, and with all her heart.

Pulling back slowly, she peered into Alec's eyes. The dark pools were brimming with sorrow as he finally gazed at her. He didn't say anything. There was no need. Closing his eyes, Alec dropped his chin to his chest and buried his fingers in his hair.

"They were so young. Barely older than Linus."

Isabelle blinked, unsure if she heard him right.

The warrior's low voice sounded again in the same gruff mumble. "They were so frightened. I—I can still hear them begging me to stop. And I slaughtered them all as he stood there…smiling."

Alec didn't need to say who. Isabelle knew it was Markus. Her jaw tensed. If it was the last thing she did, she would get him for doing this to her friend.

"I'm so sorry, Alec."

Her arms wrapping around him, Alec willingly allowed Isabelle to pull him to her shoulder. He said nothing more as they sat together in the dismal space. A few quiet sobs shook his body as Alec finally allowed himself to morn the lives cut painfully short at the command of his sick and twisted master.

Edmund strode away from the stables as he crossed the courtyard towards the castle. He spent most of the morning checking in on a few of his stewards. From time to time it served him well to make an unannounced visit. This way, he could best witness the true character of those charged with watching over his fief.

Across the courtyard, Roderick made a beeline for the duke.

The noble frowned as he gazed at the other man's set expression.

The knight bowed quickly prior to joining Edmund's side. "Your Grace, I just received the latest report concerning the two lost assets in Zerrok," he told him quietly, glancing around at the people milling about.

Edmund's steps paused. "Are they alive?"

Roderick sighed, shaking his head. "I don't know. His Majesty is officially postponing the search. They've found no leads on either their location or the soldiers who were selling them. Apparently, it's as if they've disappeared without a trace."

"A difficult choice to make. I doubt Malcolm is taking it well."

"To be sure. He won't give up—not that we should."

Edmund tilted his head to the side. "It's been several weeks. Do you believe they are still alive?"

Roderick lifted his gaze to peer over at a few soldiers making their way to the indoor training hall. He saw firsthand some of what Alec endured. If anyone had the will to survive slavery a second time, it would be him.

"I've learned not to underestimate a stubborn warrior," the knight finally declared, turning back to his lordship. "Malcolm's right to believe in them."

Edmund nodded thoughtfully, "Then we shall offer whatever aid we can. Contact Theron Kinsley and everyone you can who is connected to our trade network in Zerrok. Find him, Roderick."

Edmund knew he couldn't leave Alec to rot if there was a chance he did indeed survive. He still owed the warrior for saving his life.

Just then, Jade strolled around the back of the castle and headed towards the portcullis along with Ariel and three guards.

Eyes following her movements, the duke glanced back at his right hand man. "Jade is not to know of this."

"You have my word."

Days gradually passed as Isabelle unhappily waited in the confines of their prison cell, or at least what she thought was days. It was difficult to decipher any true sense of time. However, the dwindling number of slaves sharing their chamber allotted her some idea. Markus would be coming for them soon. They had been in the arena long enough to have a general layout of the facility. There must be some way to escape. The sorceress was having trouble coming up with anything and Alec was of no aid. She glanced in his direction.

Alec had seldom moved since his return from the colosseum. His shaking ceased and some color once more shaded his skin, but still, he was far from himself. Slumped against the jagged stone in a dark corner, he gazed blankly at one of the other walls.

Isabelle sighed. She might have helped pull the warrior back from the brink of madness, yet he was nowhere near healed. Isabelle was at a loss. He barely ate and spoke even less. There were times she actually missed the taunting calls from the other gladiators. Otherwise, they were all just sitting there in a strained silence.

Getting up to stretch, Isabelle strode over towards the iron bars. Leaning her head against the cool metal she exhaled with a long dramatic hiss. Fingers tapping one of the bars, she fought the urge to start pacing.

Alright, I've had about enough of this!

Pushing away from the metal wall Isabelle tromped over to her friend.

"How long are you going to sit there all depressingly?" she demanded, placing her hands on her hips.

Alec glanced up at her, but didn't bother to respond.

"Come on Alec, this isn't like you. You're not training. You're not talking. You're just sitting there like a lump. Enough already, we can figure this out."

"There is no way out, Isabelle," he said emotionlessly.

Her head snapped back. Alec was a master at hiding what he was thinking. This emptiness however was frightening. Somehow, Isabelle needed to reignite his spark. Nothing she did seemed to work. *How can I reach him?*

Sighing, the sorceress crossed her arms and began to pace in front of him. As she strode back to his side of the cell, Alec turned his head, leaning it against the stone wall. The fire's light caught the glimmer of something peeking out of his torn shirt. Isabelle frowned, drawing to a halt. Suddenly, her eyes widened. Quickly closing the distance between them, Isabelle knelt down by the warrior's side. Just as she thought, Alec was still wearing the chain necklace with the dark green hair ribbon. This had to be the one thing guaranteed to bring him back. Reaching forward, Isabelle gently pulled the jewelry free from his tunic.

"Alec."

He didn't shift his gaze.

"Alec," Isabelle repeated, moving her face in front of his line of sight.

Blinking, he looked at her solemnly.

"I know this hasn't been easy on you, and you've been forced to do terrible things, but you must hold fast. You need to survive. Because I need you, and I'm not the only one." Grasping his hand Isabelle wrapped his fingers around the necklace. "Someone else is awaiting your return. If she cares for you even half as much as I do, then she *is* waiting, Alec. Are you really going to make her wait forever?"

Alec's brows crinkled with a frown. Fingers tightening around the chain he lifted his head off the wall. Straightening, the warrior's eyes scanned the ground thoughtfully.

Jade.

Her name seemed to ring out in his mind from afar. Pulling the necklace away from his body, Alec studied it as if for the first time. The entire piece was smudged with dirt as well as specks of dried blood and the silken ribbon bore some fraying along the edges. The sight was like a shock to his brain.

"Jade," he whispered.

How could he have possibly forgotten her? Forgotten that the woman he loved was in Stafford at this very moment wondering when he was going to come back. Trapped in this dungeon, the outside world had all but faded from his mind. Nothing seemed to penetrate the cloud of despair and misery consuming him since the last slaughter Markus forced upon him. At some point, Alec came to believe he warranted such a death. Hence, here he sat, numbly waiting to draw his last breath.

The warrior was reminded who the real enemy was: Markus. Someone needed to ensure the vile man paid for all the countless lives he cut short. Such a monster could not be allowed to run loose for all time.

I can't die here.

No. Not in this place. Isabelle deserved better than this fate. Wasn't that the reason he had been following Markus's commands like a dog?

Alec's eyes dropped to the engraved cuff around his wrist. To survive against the drakon he had already broke his promise to Malcolm. To escape, he would have to do it once more. Hopefully, he could do so without revealing his true capabilities. It was a risk Alec was willing to take. Otherwise, they stood no chance of leaving the arena alive.

Alec made Jade a promise; he wouldn't go back on his word to her no matter the cost. *I'm coming.* Dark eyes filled with a new vigor, the sorcerer rose to his feet and clenched his fists. His gaze connected with his partner's.

"Thanks Isabelle."

Her whole body seemed to sag as she exhaled. Flashing him a weak smile, Isabelle tried to hide her relief.

"Yeah, well…I was tired of you moping about, that's all."

The sorceress gasped as she was suddenly pulled into the warrior's embrace. Unable to process his strange behavior quick enough, she stood frozen as he gave her a gentle squeeze before stepping back. A few tears rolled down her cheeks.

"You jerk," she sniffled.

"I know," Alec countered with a classic half smirk.

Seeing the old Alec once more, Isabelle's lower lip quivered. Launching herself forward she wrapped her arms around his chest and clung to him.

"I was so frightened that I'd lost you. You've been like a zombie for days or weeks or whatever it's been. It's impossible to tell anything in this infernal dungeon. I didn't know what to do. You have no idea how glad I am to have you back."

Alec couldn't suppress a light chuckle.

"Forgive me. I didn't mean to worry you."

"I know," Isabelle told him moving back to wipe away the moisture by her eyes. "And of course I forgive you. How could I not?"

"Good, for we have work to do."

Isabelle tilted her head. "We do?"

Leaning closer, Alec lowered his voice, "We're going to escape."

CHAPTER 6

As painful as the wait might be for his impatient partner, Alec knew the only way to break out of the Terra Colosseum would be from the arena itself. The depths of the slaves' cells were too heavily guarded. Grimstone was a completely different situation. Alec was housed alone in an end chamber with the exit to the dungeon relatively close by. Here, several rooms separated them from any known stairs to the next level. At least two dozen men blocked the way out, and that would be before the other slaves raised the alarm of their escape.

No, the arena was their best shot in making it out of the colosseum. After that, Alec would worry about finding a way out of the city. With their powers restored, the sorcerers should be able to make it out of Zerrokian territory.

The tricky part was making sure Isabelle joined him in his next battle. Alec didn't care if she had to scream and throw a tantrum in order to accomplish it. It wouldn't be the first time she yelled at their guards.

As fate would have it, a troop of soldiers appeared in the chamber without warning. Walking towards the bars, Alec crossed his arms as he studied the dozen men.

"Clear the cells," a man commanded pointing to the few slaves remaining. "Markus wants them all."

Alec glanced at Isabelle.

She nodded silently in return.

The time had come.

The high pitched squeak of aged metal sounded throughout the room as the cages were opened. Quickly cuffed, the slaves were pushed forward, then marched through the underbelly of the arena and up into the tunnels outside the ring.

At the entrance, each slave was handed a random weapon. One of the men shoved a battered axe in Isabelle's hands while Alec was given a sword. They were then hustled towards the opening with a strange urgency. After all the gladiators in the tunnel entered the space, the gate firmly slammed onto the dirt floor.

Jerking around, Alec peered at the various entries throughout the arena. All of them were either shut, or closing, as the last of the slaves were being ushered inside. Alec knew what closed gates meant. As an investor, Markus had sway over the matches. Surely this time he was sending a creature to finish Alec off. His old master must finally be tired of playing his game.

I wonder what it will be.

Beside him, Isabelle shivered as a breeze brushed their skin. Having spent the last year in Malyndor, Alec guessed there was at least a fifteen degree difference between his new home and the more southern kingdom. It had gradually become cooler here, leading him to believe it was probably in the early months of winter. Were they really trapped here for that long?

There wasn't time to contemplate the length of their imprisonment. A gladiator came flying out of nowhere with his sword aimed ready to strike. Pushing Isabelle out of the way, Alec blocked the blade with his own weapon. Twisting the hilt, he slashed the man across the gut. Without even glancing back, the warrior kicked a fighter zeroing in from behind.

To his left, another man raced forward. Their blades connected in a clash.

Arms trembling from the force of the attack, Alec's foe growled as he pressed the weapons away.

Alec didn't allow him a reprieve. Striking at the man's knee with his foot, the warrior then pulled his enemy off balance. The next instant, he lodged his battered sword into the man's chest.

Behind Alec, his previous attacker was coming at him again. Leaping into the air, Alec spun around, ripping the weapon out of one victim only to plant it into the body of his next.

"Look out!" Isabelle called from his blind side.

Racing forward, she positioned herself in the gladiator's path. Isabelle blocked the mace with the long handle of her axe. The wooden shaft cracked.

Appearing by her side, Alec drove his blade beneath the locked weapons and into Isabelle's attacker.

"Are you alright?" he questioned, scanning her for injuries prior to moving away to meet an advancing foe.

"Yeah, I'm fine. Why are the gates shut?"

Alec was too preoccupied to answer. Mentally, he called the gladiators around him all kinds of fools. Couldn't they see the biggest threat was yet to be unleashed? Destroying each other was only serving to immensely lower the odds of their survival.

Four men charged on all sides. Standing back to back, Alec and Isabelle braced themselves.

A thin man holding an axe was the quickest to reach them.

Catching the assault with his sword, Alec reached out, grabbing the man's wrist. Keeping the weapons pinned together he stepped back and pulled his opponent off balance as he twisted the axe out of the gladiator's grip.

Isabelle spun around, implanting her weapon in the man's back.

Farther away, a spear came flying at them. Alec dove to the side, knocking his partner out of its path. Before they could rise, another gladiator pounced. Alec held his sword long ways as he blocked the attack. Hand pressed against the flat side of his blade, he kept the weapons away from landing a killing blow. Blood seeped onto his palms as the sharp edge of his sword was forced down into his skin.

At an advantage, their enemy leered down at Alec as he used his weight to inch closer to the warrior's neck.

Straining, Alec fought to keep the sword at bay as the two remaining fighters neared them.

Rolling to the side, Isabelle slashed at the back of the man's leg.

Howling in pain his right one crumpled.

Driving his foot into the man's chin, Alec slid out from beneath the fighter's blade. Cutting the man's throat, he turned to engage his next opponent.

The man who threw the spear charged straight at Alec, tackling him to the ground.

Alec lifted his blade to strike, but was hindered as the other fighter twisted his sword from his grip. Rapidly striking his opponent with his fist, Alec flipped them over so he was on top before the gladiator could pin him down.

"Isabelle, axe!" Alec shouted over his shoulder as the first man moved in with a lethal grace.

Blinking, the sorceress shook her head as the words sank in. She then quickly threw her weapon.

Reaching back, Alec grasped the hilt of the axe. Swinging it at an angle he rotated his wrist to slash the man standing over him along the waistline. Twisting the blade, Alec swept his arm in the other direction.

Isabelle glanced away as the sorcerer finished off the last of their current attackers.

Just as Alec was rising to his feet, the ground rumbled throughout the arena. The massive gate on the other side began to open. Across the space, many gladiators ceased their fight as they realized what Alec already knew. The worst was yet to come.

Now's our chance, Alec thought, glancing around at the distracted stands.

Grasping hold of Isabelle, Alec directed her to a more shadowed section along the wall. Positioning her in front of him, the sorceress kept watch as planned while Alec concentrated on their engraved cuffs. Within moments, two pools of melted metal lay on the dirt floor.

Isabelle gazed at the remnants with a slack jaw. Closing her mouth, she was about to speak, but suddenly stopped.

The sounds of heavy chains dragging over the ground rang out with increasing clarity. Eyes narrowed, Alec watched a form appear in the darkness of the tunnel.

Isabelle shrank back as it breached the shadows to step into the light.

Alec on the other hand, emitted a bark of laughter.

"You've got to be kidding me! *That's* what Markus has sent to destroy me?"

The cruel slave owner very well may have signed his own death certificate, for he sent a dragon to kill the Dragon Sage.

Much like the griffin, this dragon was a pitiful sight. His wings were bound tightly to his body and thick irons weighed down each of his limbs. Various chains also hung around his neck like broken leashes. The red scales covering his body were dull from abuse, caked with dirt and missing completely in a few places. Even worse, one of the great horns on his proud head had been broken off.

Alec's hands curled into fists. This dragon might be larger and a different color than his friend Cassidy, but the reminder of her served to strengthen his resolve. How dare Markus treat the noble creature this way?

The initial shock having worn off, gladiators throughout the ring charged forward in rippling waves.

Swinging his massive tail, the red dragon swatted the pests away like flies. Whether out of fear or blood lust, the slaves did not cease their assault. Overrun by sheer numbers, the dragon roared as he was struck with dozens of blades. Baring his teeth, a burst of boiling flames cut through the gladiators and shot across the arena.

Still standing by the wall, the sorcerer watched the fire speed by. Good, the dragon hadn't lost its spirit. Part of him worried the creature might have succumbed to his imprisonment as Alec almost did.

"Isabelle," he began glancing over his shoulder at her. "Do you trust me?"

Blinking, she frowned. "Absolutely."

"Good, for we have a dragon to set free."

"We—what?" she croaked, her eyes growing wide as her head jerked back.

Isabelle didn't even bother to pretend she understood what Alec was thinking. She did trust him. So, she trailed behind and prepared herself to meet her first fire-breather.

Charging towards the line of gladiators battling the dragon, Alec summoned a wind spell and swept his hand to the side. The gust threw the men backwards away from their target. Arching his arm in the other direction, the sorcerer then cleared the other side. Picking up a discarded mace, he raced forward.

"Tsumorri, ice," Alec said, calling up another enchantment.

Pointing his hand at the closest chain, Alec froze the metal surrounding the dragon's right front leg. Gripping the mace with both hands, he encased it in a shielding spell as the sorcerer brought the weapon down onto the frozen steel with all his might. The chain shattered, freeing the dragon's leg.

A gladiator attacked Alec from behind with a roar.

Raising her blade, Isabelle blocked the strike.

Alec slid in beside her to smash their foe in the face. Spinning back, he met the dragon's puzzled green gaze.

"If we free you, will you help us escape?" Alec questioned, no longer caring who might hear him.

The fire beast jerked back.

Beside the sorcerer, his partner's jaw dropped.

Recovering quickly, the dragon immediately replied, "Free me and I will take you wherever you wish to go."

Alec bobbed his head. He turned his attention to Isabelle as he gestured towards the dragon. "We need to remove all these chains."

"Alright," she agreed a little shakily. "I'll summon a barrier while you start." Keeping a careful distance from the dragon, Isabelle called up a giant energy shield. It took more power than she imagined to hold it in place. "Alec, if I move, the spell will dissipate."

Creating a flaming sword, Alec glanced over his shoulder. "It's alright. Just focus on holding them off."

The magical blade burned brightly as he sliced through the metal binding the dragon's wings and continued down the length of him. Leaping over his tail, Alec removed the chains on the other side in a matter of moments.

High up in the stands, Markus gripped the edge of the owner's box so tightly there was no color left in his appendages. Alec was doing it again. The filthy slave was using trickery and magic to steal the victory which should have been his. Markus had no idea how he or the wench had managed to free themselves, but he would be damned if he stood by and let them disgrace him a second time. Prying his fingers from the rail, Markus jerked away as he began to push himself through the startled crowd.

His blazing sword dispelling, Alec gazed in Isabelle's direction. He had removed the last of the chains from the dragon, yet there was no telling if the fearsome creature would actually wait for them before taking off. They needed to get on his back and quickly.

"Isabelle, let's go!"

Twisting around, the sorceress watched as the great dragon spread his mighty wings. Beside him, Alec stood on the back of the creature's arm with his hand held out towards her. Isabelle was only able to gape as her feet refused to obey her.

"Come on," Alec urged. "Trust me."

Gulping, Isabelle raced to the sage before she came to her senses. She allowed Alec to pull her up beside him, then onto the dragon's back. Alec's arm protectively curled around her as they started to lift off the ground.

Screams erupted from the stands as people tried to flee in all directions.

Wings spread wide, the red dragon hovered above the arena with two humans nestled at the base of his neck, and a mouth full of fire.

It was anyone's guess as to what was to come. Boiling flames struck the crowd near the owner's box. Gliding closer, the dragon landed amidst his destruction however his target didn't seem to be present. Scanning the area the dragon searched the frighten crowd. Both Alec's and his eyes seemed to lock on the same person at once: Markus Duncan.

Pushing his way through the terrified masses, Markus suddenly felt a hot, steam-like breath blow down upon him. Twisting slowly, the man glared at his foes without an ounce of remorse.

A glint of metal flew through the air straight at Alec's head.

Eyes never leaving his master's face, Alec didn't even bother to raise a hand to block the attack. The knife slammed into a glowing shield as the sorcerer's aura created a protective barrier around him.

"Your evil ends here, Markus," Alec declared.

Entrapped in the swirling cloud, the knife froze for a moment prior to reflecting right back at its owner.

Markus was forced to dive out of the way. Flipping onto his back, he peered wide-eyed up at the dragon just as the creature darted forward to bite him in half.

Chomping down on his victim, the dragon released a deep roar, then took off into the heavens. At first, he strained against the force of gravity. Yet, the pleasure of the open skies after being imprisoned for so long outweighed any hardship.

His upper body lifting, Alec's eyes drifted closed as a wide smile spread across his lips. With the wind whipping through his hair, he would have stretched out his arms if not for Isabelle gripping them so firmly.

Shoulder's hunched, she sat with her eyelids squeezed tight.

The dragon flew north until the outline of the grim city was no longer in view. When the skies appeared clear, he glanced back to address his passengers.

"Where would you like to go?"

Alec leaned forward, raising his voice to be heard over the strong breeze. "Can you take us to Malyndor?"

"Of course, any certain location?"

"Do you know a city called Marcia? It's on the southwestern border."

The dragon nodded his head. "I know it. Tell me, what is the name of my rescuer?"

"The name's Alec, and I think we rescued each other. This is my friend Isabelle. We're both Emerald Sages working for King Titus. What is your name?"

The dragon smiled. "I am called Ardys."

Alec shifted his attention to the blonde curled up in front of him. "Isabelle, this is Ardys. He's agreed to take us to Marcia."

Without opening her eyes, Isabelle patted the great red dragon's neck. "Thank you, Ardys," she squeaked.

"Anything for the marked one."

The dragon's words were like an invisible blow. The grin vanished from Alec's face. Marked One. The black dragon who challenged him used the same words. *What does it mean?*

"Another dragon called me that. Why?"

"You bear the mark of the dragon. I can tell because only a human with magic in his blood would be able to understand us."

Magic in my blood, Alec mentally repeated. So he was right. Malcolm had said that as well. Was this what the great sage wanted to speak to him about prior to his departure?

"I would have recognized you at once, but something is shielding your magic," Ardys told him, breaking into Alec's thoughts.

The sorcerer frowned. Was such a thing possible? Sorcerer's created barriers around objects all the time, but one's aura, their magic, wasn't a physical item. His gaze passed over Isabelle. Perhaps she would know. Isabelle did have a thorough knowledge of spells.

The sorceress shivered, going so far as to release one hand from his arm to wrap it around herself.

Alec felt a chill race through his own body. While lost in thought, Ardys rose higher into the clouds, blocking them from view. The air surrounding them was much cooler. Exhaling, he could see his breath linger in a cloud of mist. Never having flown, Alec didn't know how long it would take for them to reach Marcia. Whatever length of time that might be, if he didn't warm them up, then they could freeze to death before even nearing the border.

If she knows I'm using magic the whole way she'll only nag me.

Instead of summoning an air spell, Alec concentrated on the currents flowing around them. Warming the air, he circled it around in a continuous ring. After a few minutes, Isabelle's shaking lessened. It was the least he could do to thank her for not freaking out when she saw a taste of what his strange magic was capable of.

Soldiers marched along the battlements of Marcia Castle, wrapped up in their cloaks as they braved the chilly winter air. It was a relatively quiet day. Thick clouds swirled above as they released flecks of snow. A form appeared in the distance, moving through the specks of white towards the castle. Pointing towards the growing mass, soldiers started to race to their posts. The red dragon flew closer, raising an instant alarm throughout the city. No one could recall the last time there was a dragon attack.

Within a few short minutes, Ardys was upon them. Arrows flew through the sky as soldiers loaded heavier weapons to repel the assault. The arrows struck a glowing force field then dropped from the heavens. Jerking back, the men stationed on the wall released various exclamations.

Flying over the battlements, the great dragon landed in the middle of the training grounds behind the castle. A voice called out to them above the chaos.

"Soldiers of Marcia, stay your weapons. We mean you no harm. We're Emerald Sages in service to King Titus. This dragon was aiding us in our escape from Zerrok. He will not harm you."

"Who dares to bring a dragon into Marcia?" Captain Cedrick demanded harshly.

"I'm the Dragon Sage," Alec told him, since he had no other proof from this distance to confirm his claim. "This here is the Just Sage."

Cedrick scoffed, not even considering his words. "A likely story, but you'll find no fools here to believe you." The soldier signaled for his men to commence with another attack.

"Alec?" Sir Darin questioned racing into the space. "Hold your fire!" he commanded gazing at the sorcerer standing on the back of the great red dragon. "Alec, what are you doing on a dragon? Never mind," the knight added shaking his head.

It didn't matter how he got here, all that mattered was Alec was still alive. A dark cloud had descended upon his lordship ever since men arrived from Roskos to inform them the sorcerer was missing.

"Stand down at once!" Darin snapped upon seeing several soldiers still ready to strike. Cautiously approaching the dragon, the knight lifted a hand to help Isabelle down, then drew her away from the creature.

Alec slid to the ground, but made no move to join the others. The sorcerer took a few steps back as Ardys turned to face him. Not a word passed between the two as they stood watching one another.

Suddenly, Ardys lowered his head, dropping his face so the large jewel on his forehead was within Alec's reach.

Holding his hands out to the side, a brisk wind swirled around the sorcerer. Eyes faintly aglow, he called up a spell.

"Surgeon," Alec said, forming white circles before his palms. He added the words of power just as he was about to touch the dragon's gleaming red jewel. "Restore."

Like a tidal wave, Alec's magic erupted from the point of impact. It flowed over Ardys as the energy revitalized his entire body. The missing scales reappeared, injuries healed and his broken horn rebuilt itself. No longer was a battered and worn creature slumped in the yard. Instead, a proud, gleaming bright red dragon stood before them as if reborn.

Ardys nudged the sorcerer with his head. "Thank you. We shall meet again."

Stretching his wings, he took to the skies with a roar and disappeared from sight.

Isabelle stood watching the event with wide eyes. How did Alec's power keep amazing her? Was there even a limit to his abilities?

"Alec, that was incredible!" she shouted walking towards him.

As he began to turn, her steps drew to a halt. Beneath the layers of dirt and blood on his flesh and clothing, Alec's skin was deathly pale. She knew just by looking at him that his aura was dangerously low. It had to be more than the spell he cast to drain the sorcerer like this. It struck Isabelle that the air around them instantly grew warm while they were flying. Half frozen, she didn't realize what it meant at the time. Alec was using his powers during their entire flight! *What was he thinking?*

Isabelle got to neither yell at him nor thank him.

Flashing her a worn half smile, Alec collapsed onto the ground. The final thing he heard, as everything faded to black, was Isabelle screaming his name as it melted into Jade's voice.

CHAPTER 7

The conscious world came back to Alec gradually. Broken bits and pieces was all he could remember of what took place after healing Ardys. It was a jumbled mess of voices and faces which faded in and out like the morning tide. Trying to make sense of it only served to increase the pain drumming inside of his skull. Still, Alec didn't regret his actions. Ardys deserved to be healed.

Opening his eyelids a slit, his familiar surroundings slowly came into focus. Heavy maroon drapes hung from the large windows blissfully blocking out most of the daylight. On the far side of the room, one curtain was left partially to the side, keeping the chamber from being cast in complete shadow. A large oil painting of a ship hung on the nearby wall above a set of beautifully handcrafted chairs. Alec closed his eyes and reopened them. Sure enough, he was back in his room in Marcia Castle.

Rolling onto his back, Alec stiffened. He wasn't alone.

Curled up beside him on top of the covers was Isabelle. A thick blanket was spread across her lower half and her long blond locks were messily sprawled in every direction.

Alec tried not to groan as he pulled himself up against the pillows. His muscles burned unhappily in protest. Sighing, Alec welcomed the irritation. *So, I'm alive after all.* Despite the odds, he made it. Peering down at his sleeping intruder, the warrior gently smiled. *They* survived, he amended.

Unable to drift back to sleep, Alec tried to ease himself out of bed without waking Isabelle. Once his feet hit the floor the room began to spin. He grabbed the side table to steady himself and closed his eyes, willing the unpleasant side effect to cease. As soon as he regained his balance, Alec crossed the chamber towards a pile of neatly folded clothes on his dresser. A full-length mirror stood beside it. Gazing at his reflection, Alec winced.

His face was covered with bruises in various stages of healing. The pattern continued sporadically over the exposed parts of his chest and arms. It would take some time for the marks from his guards to vanish. The cuts on his hands and limbs from the arena were cleaned and bandaged. Alec looked at the wrapping sourly. It seemed Zerrok gave him more scars to add to his collection.

Glancing at his reflection, something else caught his eye. The chain around his neck had been polished to a shine and the green ribbon cleaned.

Isabelle must have taken care of it. She knew what it meant to him. Still, she could not remove the specks of blood staining the rich material.

Alec was hit with a flood of unwanted images. Dropping his gaze, he clenched his fists as he turned from the mirror. He could see the faces of each person who met his blade. Could hear their final cries of pain and feel the warmth of their blood covering his hands.

What kind of monster am I?

"No," Alec told himself firmly.

He would not let his thoughts go down that path again. Markus was to blame for each slaughter, not him. The vile man was no more. He could harm no one else. Alec took a deep breath and let it out slowly. Somehow, in time, Alec would have to try and let the pain and anger go.

What about Isabelle? his mind questioned.

The sorceress might not have gone through such horrors if not for him. Markus actually dangled her as bait for a drakon.

Alec kept his word, and protected her from any physical harm, but he couldn't save her from getting mixed up in the ugliness of his past.

Would she be willing to forgive him? Or still even want to be his partner now that she knew his secret connection to dragons?

With a sigh, Alec tore his gaze away to peer at something else. His dark eyes focused on the items laid out on the dresser. Next to his clothes were the weapons he entrusted to Jorrin as well as his ring. Sliding the metal back on, the warrior's fingers lightly glided over the surface of his sheathed blades. Just touching the weapons seemed to calm his spirit. As Roderick once said: 'Alec might be a sorcerer, but he was a swordsman first and foremost.'

Grasping his sword, his hand clutched the hilt and pulled the blade free just enough to look at the mark engraved upon the steel. Light from the window reflected off the metal. The etched dragon stared back at Alec with knowing eyes. This mark meant something, Alec was sure of it, but what?

"It suits you," Isabelle said softly.

Alec's head jerked up. He'd been so lost in thought he didn't hear her.

Grasping the blanket wrapped around her body, Isabelle flashed him a watery smile.

Re-sheathing the blade, Alec set it down and turned towards the sorceress. He wasn't able to utter a word before she launched herself at him.

The blanket slid to the ground as she snaked her arms tightly around his waist.

"I'm so sorry, Alec," she sobbed, pressing a wet cheek against his chest. "I never should have gone with you to Rhordack. I wasn't ready for that type of mission. All I did was cause trouble. There were so many times I thought you were going to die. We could have been killed. We should have been killed. I'm so sorry. I'm so sorry."

Isabelle's body shook as she clutched the startled warrior. It seemed the two of them were blaming themselves for the afflictions they both endured when neither was at fault.

To think I was worried about her forgiving me.

Cupping Isabelle's shoulders, Alec pushed her away slightly so he could gaze upon her.

The sorceress hung her head and refused to meet his eye.

"Isabelle, look at me," he encouraged, bending down and twisting to try to see her face.

She shook her head, continuing to sob quietly.

"Isabelle, look at me," Alec ordered in a firmer tone.

Slowly, she lifted her gaze.

"That's better," he began, softening his voice. "Now you listen well, my friend. None of it was your fault. Things happen," Alec told her with a shrug as Isabelle started to wipe her eyes. "Sometimes it's just out of our control. If nothing else, I'm glad I had such a stubborn, outgoing partner to back me up. I couldn't have gotten through it without you. Truthfully, I blame myself. If not for my past with Markus, you would never have been sold to the arena. I hope you can forgive me."

Isabelle offered the warrior a sweet smile. "Of course I do. I guess Markus is the real villain. What a despicable man. He got off too easily if you ask me."

"Is that so?" Alec laughed lightly.

"Yes. Getting eaten was too quick of a death. Hopefully, he doesn't give Ardys a stomach ache," she giggled. Exhaling with a sigh, Isabelle watched Alec with a thoughtful frown. "You know Alec, your past was not the cause of that monster's actions. If you think about it, your skills saved us. You should be proud."

"Proud?" he echoed shaking his head. "I don't know if I could ever be proud of being a gladiator, but it did come in handy."

"That's for sure," she agreed with a smile. "Your lessons were a help as well. No wonder you're so apt with instructing troops."

"Thanks."

Alec wasn't the only skilled one. Isabelle had a vast knowledge of various types of magic. In some ways, she reminded him of Malcolm. During their imprisonment, she'd taught him a few new spells and told him about some advanced training she'd begun with Master Breanna. Perhaps she could shed some light on the questions plaguing his mind.

"Isabelle," the warrior said shifting his weight from side to side.

"Yes?"

"Is it possible to shield someone's magic?"

She instantly stilled. Looking at Alec's suddenly serious expression, Isabelle frowned. She knew he wasn't asking this question on a whim.

"How do you mean?"

Alec raked a hand over his long, somewhat tangled, hair. "I was wondering if there was a way to disguise a person's magic from being detected by others."

"Do you think someone is trying to block your magic?"

He shook his head. "No, not block it. More like hide it."

"Why would you think that?"

Alec should have known Isabelle wouldn't simply answer his question. *Ah, what the heck,* he thought, giving in to the inevitable. She already knew he could talk to dragons, so what harm could there be in telling her?

"Ardys made a comment to me. He said something was shielding my magic. And that wasn't the only time I was told something to that effect."

"By another dragon?" Isabelle ventured.

Alec didn't answer her, telling the sorceress she guessed correctly.

"Wow, you really are the Dragon Sage." Glancing at the floor, she tapped a long finger against her lips. "I've read about shielding magic, so it can be done. However, not just *any* sage can do it. It's an advanced technique, requiring knowledge of Elan to complete the incantation. If I had to guess, only a Master Sage would be capable of completing such a complex spell."

"A master, huh?"

"Yes, and there's one more thing. It's not possible to enchant a person like that. Whoever it was would have to use the spell on an object...an object *always* in your possession," she stressed.

Alec's hand drifted towards his necklace of its own accord. The chain was a gift from Malcolm. His teacher would, without a doubt, have the knowledge and power to cast such a spell, but why? It seemed his delayed conversation with the sage was growing even more important.

"Thanks Isabelle. I appreciate your aid."

Her eyes twinkled happily. "That's what partners are for."

They spoke for a little longer, then Isabelle excused herself to change and detangle her hair. Having refused to leave the warrior's side until he recovered, she was in as desperate of a need for a bath as he was.

After the door clicked shut behind the sorceress, Alec rang for a servant. Picking up a knife he headed towards the washroom. While he waited for a bath to be prepared, the scuff on his face was going to be the first thing to go.

More than an hour later, Alec emerged from his bathroom freshly scrubbed and shaven. It was the most human he'd felt in a long time. Tying his belt over his new tunic as he strolled back into his bedchamber, his steps suddenly came to a halt. Half a smile appeared on the side of Alec's face. While he was gone, Isabelle's presence was replaced by Leos.

The gruff earl stood by a window with a hand resting on the frame. A thoughtful frown pleated his brows as he gazed out at the mountainous terrain. The moment Alec came into view, he spun around and strode across the space.

Alec tried not to wince as he was tightly embraced. With a chuckle, he willingly returned the gesture. He missed the warrior as well, and was starting to get used to such signs of affection.

"I knew you were alive," Leos declared stepping back with a bright grin. "I was not going to misjudge your survival skills yet again. I knew those pompous windbags in the capital were mistaken."

Alec's smile faded. "Guess I shouldn't be surprised that we were abandoned."

Leos shook his head. "Not everyone gave up. Malcolm never stopped seeking your location. King Titus has been continuously working with Rhordack to find new leads, and even Duke Stafford contacted everyone he knows in Zerrok. There just weren't any clues. It was as if you both vanished. I spent weeks looking for you myself."

The warrior blinked. "How long were we gone?"

"Over three months. Since the soldiers you were sold to never returned to their base, your trail was almost impossible to track."

"I wonder why they didn't go back."

The noble shrugged. "Perhaps they discovered it was no longer under their control. My troops wiped out both settlements under The Pure's command."

"Perhaps," Alec agreed.

There was no way for them to know for sure. The Pure did seem to be filled with some slippery individuals. There was also the leak within the sages to consider. Had they found the traitor while he was imprisoned?

"Feel up to joining me for a walk?" Leos questioned, breaking into Alec's private thoughts.

The offer of fresh air and open spaces was too tempting to pass up. Pulling his cloak around his shoulders, Alec strolled beside the earl as they traveled through the castle and out into the courtyard.

During their journey down the corridors, Alec noticed he was receiving some unusual looks. Once outside it intensified. Soldiers, servants and nobles alike were watching Alec with a variety of poorly disguised stares. As the sorcerer kept pace with Leos, his eyes scanned the courtyard. There were some who smiled and bowed, others who gawked, and a few who either tracked his movements suspiciously or backed away as they whispered behind their hands.

Alec bristled. Riding a dragon into the castle grounds had not been to his benefit. Every time he was free of people's fearful glares, something would cause them to arise anew. Would he never escape their constant judgments?

Trying to focus on anything else, Alec followed Leos up onto the battlements. They slowly moved among the soldiers until they came to a quiet spot overlooking the city. Those in the courtyard could not see them from here. Exhaling, Alec's shoulders sagged as he leaned on the stone wall.

Below, people flowed through the maze of streets which descended the mountain. Snow had fallen recently, covering the rooftops with a blanket of white and leaving melting mounds beside dwellings and on street corners. Well acquainted with heavy snowfalls, the weather did not hinder the bustling city's activity.

Gazing over towards the valley where he met up with Cassidy, Alec wondered how the green dragon was fairing. He hadn't seen her since before his initiation into the Emerald Sages. Had she found a more 'interesting' human to watch over? Alec doubted it. Cassidy knew more about his strange connection to dragons than she claimed. He was tired of being kept in the dark.

Alec lightly pounded a fist on the stone wall. At least Leos was always straight forward with him. He glanced to the side. The noble was looking out at the city with a slight smile.

Following his gaze, Alec too, peered into the distance. While the state of the kingdom might be unknown, at this moment, it didn't seem to matter. On top of the battlements everything was quiet and peaceful.

Too bad I can't stay here forever.

"Amazing, is it not?" Leos asked breaking the surrounding silence. "I come up here to remind myself what it is I am protecting. Did you know our lands stretch from the sea all the way to the top of the Black Mountains?"

Alec shook his head.

"For two hundred years our family has been guarding Malyndor from this spot. It is a noble task which cannot be left to just anyone."

Brows lowering somewhat, Alec watched the earl carefully. They had spoken at length many times, yet the warrior could not recall him behaving so strangely. Did he really say 'our' instead of 'my'? Alec pushed the thought aside. He must be reading too much into it. Turning, he propped a hip against the wall as the earl continued to speak.

"A lot has happened since our paths first crossed. I must confess, Alec, my reasons for bringing you to Marcia were quite selfish." Leos watched as Alec smiled. "Do you remember our last meeting when you were a boy?"

"Of course."

"I never told you, but I went back a few weeks later...for you."

Alec froze. Eyes locked on Leos, he didn't dare move a muscle.

"Not just to see you, but to buy your freedom, Alec. You were the son I was never blessed with. I wanted to bring you here, to Marcia, and make you a part of my family. Those wishes have not changed."

The warrior opened his mouth, then closed it. He must be misunderstanding the noble's words.

"Leos, what are you saying?"

The other man released a short laugh and shook his head. Placing a hand on Alec's shoulder, he clarified, "Alec, I want you to become an official member of the House of Kegan, as my son and heir."

Alec simply stared at him. Then, blinking rapidly, his brain tried to process a reply. Leos wanted *him* as his son? He was no one, just an expendable peasant with no last name and a knack for finding danger. He couldn't possibly become a noble. It didn't work that way.

"I was a slave," Alec finally managed. "There's no way I could become a lord or be responsible for protecting this city and all these people. I'm no one, Leos," he said bitterly looking out beyond the battlements.

The noble didn't back down. His hand still resting on the warrior's shoulder, he gave it an encouraging squeeze.

"One's birth does not define the type of man he is or his worth in my eyes. It is a man's actions which define him. Just look at Lord Vincent. He was born with all the wealth, privilege, and power a man could desire. Yet, he lacks half the strength of character I have seen in you time and again. You are far more worthy than you realize, Alec. You must stop thinking of yourself as a slave. It is not who you are."

Gaze lowering, Alec gripped the unyielding stone beside him. Leos's words impacted him with the effectiveness of a blow. The sorcerer joined the Emerald Sages to become more and gain the merit he needed to ask for Jade's hand. Somewhere along the way, he forgot all that he had accomplished. His return to Zerrok only served to deepen the doubts still plaguing him. Malcolm never thought him insignificant. Neither did Leos. Even Roderick now treated him with the utmost confidence. In the eyes of those who mattered, Alec earned his place because he proved himself. What could make a person more worthy than that?

"I would be honored to be a part of your family," Alec answered at last, meaning every word.

Lunging forward, Leos grabbed Alec in a bear hug. "Well kiddo, you better get used to calling me father."

Sitting in his chambers, Alec stretched out in a deep armchair with a book propped open on his lap. The sorcerer hadn't found much tranquility since arriving in Marcia and he was enjoying some time to himself without either Leos or Isabelle hovering close by.

Suddenly, the door to his room flew open.

A knife practically materialized in his hand as Alec bolted upright.

Chest heaving, Malcolm stood in the entry encased in a damp, dirt stained cloak. Striding forward, he approached Alec just as the sorcerer sheathed his blade. A hand grasped each shoulder as the wizard bent down to study his former apprentice.

"Alec? That is you isn't it?" Malcolm questioned, looking him over. Sighing, the sage's shoulders sagged as he dropped into a neighboring chair. "I told those fools you were alive. Still," his gaze lowered to the ground, "I failed to protect you, yet again."

Again? "My capture wasn't your fault Malcolm," Alec dismissed with a wave of his hand.

The wizard shook his head, causing the younger sorcerer to frown. "I never should have allowed you to go. You have a gift, Alec, and I've done my best to look out for you, to protect you. Though, I suppose I've ended up sheltering you too much. In some ways, *I'm* the old fool."

Brow lifting, Alec pulled back. His heart started to pound in his chest. Instinctively, he knew this was the talk Malcolm wanted to have with him prior to his departure.

"Does this protecting include enchanting my necklace to shield my magic?" he ventured.

Malcolm looked at him incredulously for a moment, then his shoulders sagged with a sigh. "That is part of it," he admitted. "How did you know?"

Alec didn't answer.

The sage held his gaze for a second before the warrior broke eye contact. Continuing to watch his former apprentice, Malcolm nodded to himself.

"I see. What precisely did the dragon tell you?"

The warrior's eyes snapped back to Malcolm's face. At first, he couldn't answer. *He's not fishing. He knows. How does he know?*

The corners of his mouth dropping in a frown, Alec bristled. "Dragon's don't talk."

"To normal sorcerers, no. But to you they should," Malcolm leaned forward, resting his elbows on his knees. "I meant it when I said you were special, Alec. Do you remember the night I came to the barracks to assess your power after you were injured?"

"Not much of it."

Malcolm bobbed his head. "I saw your mark."

Alec straightened. "Wait, you've been aware of it this entire time?"

"Yes, and it is a sign of greater power then you could possibly imagine. Would you have believed me if I told you when we first met that you would be able to speak with dragons?"

Exhaling with a long hiss, the sorcerer raked a hand through his hair as he leaned back in his chair.

Malcolm tilted his head to the side. "The red dragon wasn't the first, was it?"

Slowly, Alec shook his head.

"You surprise me, my boy. It seems I'm not the only one keeping secrets."

Alec shot him a quick glare. "Alright, so I can talk to them. What does it mean?"

"You're not cursed, if that's what you're thinking."

A deep frown touched Alec's lips. What, was the sage reading his mind now? Unsure if he should be cross or elated that Malcolm knew about his mark, Alec told himself to be calm. The wizard was kinder to him than anyone but Leos. He wouldn't seek to bring him harm. Of that, Alec was certain. All he wanted now was answers.

"Then why am I marked?"

"About five hundred years ago, when Malyndor was first forged out of the ashes of the Great Dragon War, a prophecy was foretold by a trusted seer. According to ancient records, he said this:

'Ancient dragons, their magic combine,
the blood of one throughout his line.
Till born a child mightier than any blade,
on whom the mark of power shall not fade.
Once to its owner, the magic returns,
a new light awakens, strongly it burns.
Evil will rise; beast and man must unite,
or darkness reign, and hope takes flight.'"

"Only a select few know those words and their significance to the dragon mark you bear," Malcolm finished, his gaze never leaving Alec's face.

Rising to his feet, Alec pressed his fingers against his temples. "Wait, so there was a prophecy that someone would be born with this mark? And you said something about dragons combining their magic. Combine it with what?"

Malcolm gave him a look that told Alec he already knew the answer.

"Surely you jest," the sage scoffed. "I have dragon's magic?"

"Is it that difficult to believe? Come now, Alec. Name another sorcerer who can cast spells without a creation spell. Speaking with dragons is only a taste of your true power. There is magic in your very blood. You are a link between our kinds. And as such, your destiny will change the fate of this entire kingdom. You are very important to the King."

Alec blinked, then shook his head violently. "I don't want to be the...the kingdom's savior," he declared slashing the air with his hand.

Helping people was one thing, but this kind of power would bring all the wrong types of attention. Every noble in the land, and possibly neighboring lands, would be seeking for him to join them. Leos and Jade were different. Alec knew there were some good nobles out there. However, many only cared for themselves and the warrior refused to be a pawn. No one was going to use him again.

"I won't be a tool for a bunch of pompous, egotistical nobles," the younger sage ground out in a low voice.

Interlacing his fingers, Malcolm waited a moment to speak.

"Alec, that is not what I meant, but as an Emerald Sage, you do already work for the Royal Family. Who, in case you have forgotten, are nobles as well as good people."

Alec glared at him. Crossing his arms, he turned away.

"With everything you've gone through, I know this isn't easy for you to hear. After you're done plotting my demise, perhaps you will see why I did not inform you of this sooner." *And won't be telling you the entire truth today.*

Unable to remain where he was, Alec's long legs carried him from one side of the chamber to the other.

Malcolm said nothing further.

Privately, Alec agreed with his teacher. Had he been informed of this ancient prophecy while still under the sage's tutelage, he might have boarded the closest ship and sailed as far from the western kingdoms as he could get. Returning to the other sorcerer, Alec stopped beside his chair.

"What happens now?"

"Nothing," Malcolm replied simply.

Alec's one brow rose.

The great sage laughed. "You don't need to look at me like that. As I'm sure you are aware, your powers are still growing. Focusing on controlling them is a must. Take some time to process what it is you are destined for."

"There's more to this prophecy, isn't there?" Alec observed.

"Yes," Malcolm answered dipping his head. "And I promise, I'm not doing this to be cruel. I want what's best for you. We shall discuss it soon; but for now, I do believe I've given you enough surprises for one day." *Anymore and his powers might lash out.*

The sage doubted Alec was aware that his aura started to glow faintly while he was pacing. His magical abilities were rapidly increasing. Another upset at this time could shatter his control. The Cunning Sage knew he couldn't risk bringing any other secrets to light. The darkest ones would have to wait.

A hand flew through the air as it connected with Vincent's cheek. Biting back a curse, he could taste a few drops of blood from the new cut on his lip. Eyes blazing, the Earl of Parlen glared at his son with a sneer.

"I do not want to hear another word about Lady Stafford. As far as I am concerned, you have done quite enough damage to our family's honor over that girl."

"I thought you would be pleased with my choice. She's the daughter of a duke." Vincent didn't dare say her name this time.

"It would not matter if she was the daughter of a king at this point," the earl scoffed. "You have no chance of making a match after your last stunt. Do you know the type of mockery you have brought upon us? My own son, banished from another lord's holdings over a battle with a lowly soldier, of all things!"

Spinning away, his father strode over towards his desk.

"It was only temporary," Vincent whined.

His six months leave from Stafford was over, yet his father had not agreed to him returning. Vincent curled his fists as his gaze dropped to the floor. He had been so close to securing Jade as his bride. Even now, Alec still seemed to be causing him issues. To think a filthy peasant could be such a thorn in his side.

"Yes," his father was saying picking up a letter. "The fact that Duke Stafford chose not to take the matter of your behavior up with the King was your only saving grace. Fortunately, this embarrassment can be put behind us as long as you do exactly as I say."

"Of course, Father."

He wasn't going to argue with him if it meant winning back some freedom to pursue his own goals.

"Lord Kegan of Marcia is finally naming an heir. There is to be a ball in his honor." The earl flipped the letter over and then back with a frown. "No name has been given. I never took Leos as one for a flair for the dramatics."

He cleared his throat, setting the paper down. "I want you to attend. You are to make friends with the future earl and win back some good will with the other nobles. By no means are you to bother the Staffords. I mean it, Vincent," his father told him pointing his finger. "Any embarrassment and I shall deal with you accordingly."

"You have my word, Father. Lord Kegan's new heir will well remember me."

"Good. Now be off with you," the earl said, making a shooing motion with his hand. "I have work to attend to."

CHAPTER 8

The city of Marcia was abuzz with excitement. The winter season was entering its final months, yet the much desired spring was not the cause of the invigorating energy. After years of waiting, their beloved Earl had finally chosen an heir. Only those within the castle knew his identity and by strict orders they were guarding the secret jealously. Tonight, Lord Kegan would be introducing his new son at the magnificent celebration in his honor. Till then, everyone from lords to peasants could only guess and wonder.

Riding through the snow dusted streets with her family, Leos's heir wasn't the only gossip Jade could hear outside the carriage. Curtains pulled back, she smiled brightly as she took in the bustling activity.

More often than not, someone seemed to mention the famed Dragon Knight, now known as the Dragon Sage. New rumors of the strange man were also running through the streets of Stafford. It appeared he recently returned from fighting enemy forces abroad.

Jade managed to suppress a giggle. Everyone in the kingdom practically knew his name. His unworldly deeds

Jay Lynn

grew with each passing of the tale. Thus far, Jade couldn't bring herself to believe any of it. Fighting and nearly killing a dragon single-handedly was nothing compared to his most recent feats.

The latest tales that the noble encountered told of the mysterious warrior/sorcerer traveling to Zerrok on a secret mission for King Titus. Some were saying he was assassinating key members of the military. Others, claimed he was causing an uprising with the slaves and peasants. Another spoke of dark arts and forbidden magic. No matter the reason, one factor appeared the same in each version: the Dragon Sage returned to Malyndor on the back of a fearsome dragon!

Jade smirked. *To think people believe such a story.*

She couldn't imagine what the next rumor would entail. He probably would be growing wings and flying around.

As their carriage pulled into the castle courtyard Jade wrapped her cloak more snugly about her shoulders. Her eyes immediately began searching the area for Alec. At long last, Garth received a letter from the elusive warrior. Though the soldier didn't share much of its contents with her, he did say Alec was once more in Marcia. Somehow, Jade just had to get a glimpse of him while she was here.

Leos stood proudly at the bottom of the stairs with a large grin spread across his face, easing the gruffness of his permanent stubble. Swinging his arms out, he strode towards them as they descended the carriage.

"Greetings, my friends," Leos boomed. "I'm pleased you were able to join me for the announcement."

Edmund laughed, gripping the other noble's arm. "You did not think we would miss such an occasion did you? I am eager to meet this admirable man you have chosen. Is it your second cousin Walter?"

The earl shook his head with a chuckle. "The introduction is not till this evening. Besides, he's not present at the moment. My son snuck off with a scouting party before sunrise."

A group of horses trotted through the portcullis and came to a stop on the other side of the courtyard.

"Oh, it appears they have returned."

Leos's gaze traveled over Jade.

She was standing a few feet behind her parents. Hands lightly clasped together, her neck was craned as she peered at the soldiers milling about. Jade wasn't the only one. Beside her, Ariel, Roderick, Eric, Garth and the rest of the Stafford Guard serving as the noble's escort seemed to be doing the same.

"Good," Edmund was saying, switching Leos's focus back to the duke. "Surely you would not be opposed to introducing your heir to your closest friend first."

Eyes flickering to Jade and back, the man smiled even brighter. "Of course not. It would be a pleasure." Taking a few steps, Leos hollered towards the dismounting scouts, "Lord Kegan, my boy, come hither. Some introductions are in order."

A tall figure turned towards them, his face masked in shadow from the deep hood of his cloak. Dusted with snow, the thick material enveloped him completely, making it impossible to discover his identity.

Crossing the paving stones with long strides, the man reached up and lowered his hood at the same time as Leos announced, "Duke Stafford, ladies, may I introduce my adopted son and heir, Lord Alec Kegan."

A shocked hush lasted for a split second before the Stafford soldiers exploded into a loud roar of happiness. Racing forward, they surrounded Alec in a flash.

Leading the pack, Garth clasped his friend around the shoulders with a smile. "So this is why you insisted I come. We definitely have some catching up to do."

Jay Lynn

Alec laughed, unable to answer as he was swarmed with pats on the back and well wishes from the men. A few curt commands and Roderick managed to get them back into formation with Garth's aid. Gripping the other warrior's forearm, the knight grinned.

"It's good to see you again, Lord Alec."

Alec gave him a self-conscious half smile. "There's no need for such formalities. Alec is fine."

"Well done," Roderick told him sincerely.

Stepping aside he cleared the way for Alec to join the other nobles.

Genuflecting respectfully, Alec greeted their guests.

"My apologizes, Duke Stafford, on my delayed greeting. Duchess Stafford, it is a pleasure to see you again."

His face a neutral mask, Edmund looked at Alec carefully. He remembered what Leos told him in the spring when he was reunited with the warrior. The earl's decision in heir shouldn't have been a surprise. It seemed his wife wasn't the only one who thought highly of the man. Edmund had been thinking a lot about what Leona said. Seeing Alec again confirmed the truth behind her words. The man behaved like a lord long before being gifted with the title.

"No apology is needed, Lord Alec. Congratulations. Lord Kegan made a wise choice."

I can't believe he gave me a compliment like that. "Thank you," the warrior replied humbly, bowing once more to the duke and duchess.

As the nobles moved onward with the earl, Alec was all at once face to face with the one woman who'd rarely left his mind since the night their paths first crossed. A small grin pulled at his lips. Alec didn't get the chance to open his mouth to speak before Jade suddenly turned on her heel and fled.

Storming off, she crossed the courtyard and rounded the side of the castle near the stables, leaving everyone, including Ariel, behind.

By the time Alec recovered, Jade was already out of sight. His brows furrowing, he took off after the lady.

Glancing at each other, the nobles as well as Roderick, Garth and Ariel trailed behind.

Paying little attention to where she was heading, Jade kept walking without slowing her pace. Her whirling thoughts couldn't seem to grasp what she discovered.

Alec was Leos's heir! It was too good to be true. Jade *was* happy for him. Yet, for some reason, the moment she saw him standing there smiling shyly, it ignited a hidden anger bubbling right below the surface.

He disappeared for almost an entire year, sparing her not a single word during that time. Now, out of nowhere, he appears as a lord? Clenching her hands, Jade bit her lower lip. There were days she missed him so badly her chest physically hurt. There were moments she feared something dreadful had befallen him. Late at night, Jade would stare at the stars wondering where he was and if he was gazing at the same sky. How dare he arrive smiling and laughing without a care when she was left holding her breath for so long? Had he missed her at all?

"Jade? Jade?" Alec called, racing towards her the minute he entered the secluded area by the stables.

She didn't answer, nor slow her steps.

"Would you please talk to me?" he asked, easily catching up. "I don't understand why you're cross; I thought you'd be glad to see me."

The wounded tone of his voice added fuel to her warring emotions. Suddenly spinning around, Jade glared at him as he skidded to a halt directly in front of her.

"Glad to see you?" she repeated with a shrill. "What were you expecting? That I would fall all over you the moment you finally decided to make an appearance?"

"Well, no—"

"I am not some mindless doll who is going to sit around and wait for you. It has been almost a year. A year, without a single word from you. There was talk of missing sages and I knew not if you might be one of them. But I do not believe you care, swordsman. If you did, you might have saw fit to send some form of correspondence."

Body stiff, Jade curled her hands into fists by her sides. Lower lip quivering, her eyes welled up with unshed tears as she continued to speak without allowing Alec to reply.

"What, pray tell, have you been doing all this time? Gallivanting around Malyndor with every female sage in the order? Or is it just Isabelle who holds your particular interest?"

"Wait, it's not—"

"Do not dare lie to me. I know about Isabelle," she cried raising her hand to slap him.

Alec easily trapped her hand within both his palms. Dropping down onto one knee he lightly kissed her smooth skin.

Jade froze. Any coherent thoughts fled her mind as her heart fluttered like a hummingbird's wings. She couldn't look away. Alec rose and gazed upon her without releasing her hand.

"I swear, Isabelle is my friend and partner, nothing more."

Jade opened her mouth to speak, but the warrior shook his head with a half smirk.

"You had your say, milady. Now let me answer these grievances you've laid against me. First, Isabelle is a wonderful person. I do care for her. She's reckless and overly optimistic. Our work can be dangerous. However, she has proven to be both loyal and trustworthy. Rest assured, the moments I have spent missing you since we parted outnumber the stars."

Releasing Jade's hand Alec revealed the necklace hidden under his tunic.

Eyes growing wide, Jade pressed her fingers against her face. "My ribbon," she whispered staring at the worn silk weaved within the wide silver chain.

"Do you remember when you gave this to me?"

She could only nod.

"It has never left my side since that day and with it, neither have you."

Burying her face in her hands, Jade's shoulders shook with a sob.

"I *had* to leave, Jade," Alec stressed. "Not because I wanted to, but because I needed to. I spent my entire life believing I was nothing. I felt as if I had to prove my worth, show everyone I could be more than an abused gladiator from Zerrok. I had yet to understand it's your actions that define you, not a title. Leos finally got me to see that. Just having the honor of being called his son is enough."

"I never thought of you as nothing," Jade whispered.

Alec ran his fingers gently through Jade's hair.

"I know that now. You were the first person who saw me as something more than just a slave." A smile drifted over his lips. "I recall seeing it in your eyes when we first met. Do you remember?"

Jade exhaled with a laugh. Holding Alec's hands, she lifted her chin with a grin.

"How could I possibly forget? You saved my life that night. If you had not come to my aid…"

Enclosing her tiny frame in his embrace, Alec set his cheek on top of Jade's silky chestnut hair. "You sure were a fiery little thing," he admitted with a chuckle. "I almost felt sorry for those drunken fools. Another minute and you probably would have sliced them with that dagger."

"What incident are you two speaking of?" Roderick demanded, crossing his muscular arms.

Two heads snapped up. Turning around Alec released Jade, but still kept a hold of one of her hands. His brows lowered as he gazed at the group now glaring at Roderick. A smirk touched his lips.

"Sorry my dear, but it looks like we've been found out," Alec told her in a mock whisper.

Jade's cheeks flushed brightly.

The knight's manner didn't soften. He continued to watch them suspiciously. *I know what I heard.* Their relationship was always a strange one, though neither would admit to it. As Roderick suspected, something happened in Grimstone of which he was not aware. This time, one of them was going to fill him in.

"What happened in Grimstone?"

Alec shot Jade a sideways glance. "You never told him?"

She shrugged with a grimace. "Was it foolish to hope I would not have to?"

The warrior sighed, "We don't seem to have a choice." Shifting his weight, he met the knight's steady gaze. "The arena dungeon wasn't the first time Lady Jade and I met."

"What?" Roderick questioned, dropping his arms to his sides as he peered at Jade briefly.

"He speaks the truth," she confirmed.

"You see, a few nights before I had managed to escape. I was making my way towards the docks in order to sneak aboard a Malyndorian vessel."

"And I...was traveling back to Grimstone Castle having engaged in my own private tour of the city. That is where I met the Thornbrook children."

"Jade!" her mother scolded amidst the group of disapproving looks.

"The short version is, I heard a young woman screaming for help," Alec continued.

"I had been cornered by three drunken hoodlums," Jade added with a shudder.

"So I ran to her aid and dispatched her attackers."

"Knocked some sense into them was more like it. We spoke briefly, never making any sort of introduction—"

"More like snapped at each other."

"I did not!"

Alec's eyes twinkled, but he said nothing.

"Alright, perhaps a little," Jade recanted. "But you were the one who told me I should not have been there. Anyway, he suddenly ran off mumbling about a ship while I returned to the castle straight away."

"By the time I reached the docks, my ship had set sail. I didn't have much choice other than to return to the arena."

As Alec's words died away, everyone, other than Edmund, showed varying displays of surprise. Roderick was the first to muster any words.

"Well by George that explains a lot. I wish you would have entrusted me with that information sooner, milady. I wouldn't have been so hard on Alec, let alone suspicious of him. He certainly wouldn't tell me your secret."

Jade flashed her beloved a grateful smile which Alec returned.

"What's done is done," the warrior said simply. "It was not my place to speak of it. As it is, things seemed to have worked out for the best."

"And what things would that be?" Edmund questioned.

Alec glanced down at Jade prior to shifting his sight to the duke. Stepping forward, the warrior dipped his proud head in a bow.

Edmund watched him carefully with a set, unsmiling expression.

It's time, Alec told himself. Heart pounding, he willed his body to keep its outward calm as he stood before the duke. Hopefully, everything he accomplished over the past year would be enough.

"Duke Stafford, with your permission, I would like to speak with you in private."

Eyes locked upon each other, Edmund waited for the warrior to squirm. He didn't. *He always did have a backbone of steel,* the noble observed. Still standing behind Alec, his daughter was gripping the skirt of her dress with bright, sparkling eyes. Edmund could not deny the vast difference in her behavior.

"It has been awhile since I was last here," he began taking his wife's arm as he started to walk back towards the front of the castle. "I believe a tour is in order, Lord Alec. What say you?"

"I would be honored, Your Grace."

"So be it. Shall we say nine o'clock? We can discuss my terms then," Edmund told him with a smirk before continuing on his way.

Alec practically did a double take. *Did the duke just give me his unofficial consent?* A rare full smile lit up the warrior's face.

Coming to stand by his side, Jade interlaced her fingers with his. "I do say that went well."

"Better than I thought," Alec admitted peering at her with a hooded gaze.

Cheeks coloring, Jade lowered her eyes. The wide grin on her lips didn't lessen.

"Milady," Ariel interrupted moving closer. "We had best get you ready for the party."

"Of course," Jade replied, mentally shaking herself.

She was so elated upon hearing her father's approval that she briefly forgot others were still present. Jade's feet refused to move. For months she yearned to be in his company. Having achieved that goal, Jade didn't want to leave Alec's side. Ever.

"Until this evening, milady," whispered the warrior as he gently kissed the top of her hand. Shifting his focus to the other woman, he flashed her a half smile. "It's good to see you, Ariel. I must thank you for your dance lessons. They came in handy."

Eyes darting between the two of them, Ariel forced a grin. "It's always a pleasure to see you, Lord Alec."

He frowned. "Alright, you can all stop doing that right now," he scolded playfully, as his gaze encompassed the group. "It's just Alec."

"You're going to have to get used to that sooner or later," Garth told him, lightly slapping his friend on the back.

"Garth is right, kiddo," Leos concurred. "In private is one thing, but there are protocols with being a nobleman you are going to have to learn and follow."

Alec raised a brow. "Is it too late to change my mind?"

"Yes," Leos laughed. "Come now, the ladies are not the only ones who need to prepare. We must make you presentable."

Alec quickly looked over his military uniform and boots. "What's wrong with this, Father? I even had my hair cut."

Leos bit back a chuckle. "There is much I still have to teach you. At least I know you shall have a worthy lady to make sure you are dressed properly."

With the early setting of the winter sun Lord Kegan's celebration began. Lords and ladies from all over the kingdom arrived to offer their congratulations, and of course, see who Leos had chosen. Having Jade near, aided Alec in bearing the numerous and at times humorous, displays of surprise. Fortunately, no one was crass enough to make any sort of retort after the introductions. Alec's position as an Emerald Sage demanded a fair amount of respect which no noble could deny.

Her hand wrapped in the crook of Alec's arm, Jade beamed brightly as she curtsied for one person after another. She had long since lost track of the number of guests entering the ballroom.

"I do believe Lord Kegan has invited the entire Kingdom," Jade giggled quietly to her suitor.

"It would seem so," he whispered in reply.

Moments later Alec stiffened.

Jade frowned, following his line of sight as she sought the source of his distress. It wasn't difficult to discover. Her fingers dug into Alec's sleeve as her gaze followed the unexpected guest striding towards them.

A smug grin on his face, Lord Vincent was quickly making his way through the short receiving line.

Jade inched closer to Alec. She never informed her father about the horrid incident which transpired on his last night in Stafford. A chill snaked down her spine at the unwanted reminder. In truth, she believed Vincent wouldn't dare show his face again. But this wasn't Stafford, and the vile man had no way of knowing who the new lord he was about to meet was. *I must speak to Father about this.* She would absolutely not allow him to make an appearance at her home.

"I will tell the Duke when we speak tomorrow," Alec softly breathed into her ear.

Jade offered him a small grin. There were moments she swore he could read her mind.

As Vincent stopped before Leos, Alec twisted his body, moving Jade slightly behind him. The earl didn't miss the deliberate adjustment.

"Greetings Lord Kegan and congratulations. I am eager to make your newest family member's acquaintance. I am sure we shall be great friends."

Leos kept a practiced smile in place which held no warmth. "As I recall, you have already met."

Vincent followed the earl's line of sight to gaze at the man standing only a few feet away. Mouth gaping, he didn't move for a full second. Then, a furious light consumed his narrowed eyes.

"Yes," he hissed stiffly. "I believe we have."

With little choice, Vincent took his turn to greet the earl's new son. His body like a statue, he made no effort to shake Alec's hand, nor did the warrior offer. His eyes shifted to

Jade. It was impossible for him to miss her close proximity to the peasant.

Watching the nobility farther down the line, she refused to acknowledge him.

Vincent's hands tightened into fists. *How dare this low bred slave touch my woman?* Not Trusting himself to speak, Vincent said nothing as he bowed and strode off. Fuming, he traveled towards the gardens in order to cool off.

After learning of Alec's departure from Stafford, Vincent was eager to return to the city. Unable to do so due to his punishment, he couldn't reverse the damage inflicted upon Jade by the Zerrokian. This was the first time his father gave him any sort of freedom since he'd returned to Parlen. Instead of improving, things somehow got increasingly worse. Who, in their right mind, would bestow on a slave a title equal to his own?

Over the next few hours, Alec was pleased to see their unwanted guest avoided them completely. Gradually, the stiffness faded from Jade's shoulders and she smiled more readily. *I missed that smile,* he thought warmly. She was the little ray of sunshine in his life. Nothing separated the two of them until supper.

As the guest of honor, Alec was seated in the center of the high table. To his right was Leos, Darin and a few of Lord Kegan's cousins. On the left was Edmund, Leona, Jade and a few other high ranking nobles.

Throughout the meal Jade repeatedly glanced down the table. Only two people were positioned between her and Alec, yet it felt like two hundred. She simply wanted some time alone with him. Not that they would truly be alone. Unofficially engaged or not, Ariel's chaperoning was sure to be constant.

The evening was progressing smoothly when suddenly the main doors of the ballroom flew open. A squad of knights from the Royal Guard stormed in. They strode towards the head table with purpose and dropped into a quick bow.

Both Leos and Edmund rose to their feet.

"Please forgive the interruption, but we are here for Lord Kegan by order of King Titus," Captain Oliver Furmon, head of the Royal Guard announced. Glancing, at Edmund he corrected, "Lord Alec Kegan, my lords."

At once, all eyes seemed to snap towards Alec at once. Calmly rising, he patted his father's shoulder. Then, with a nod he rounded the table.

Whispers circled the chamber as everyone waited to see what would take place. Why would the King send his personal knights? Was the new lord about to be arrested?

The instant Alec came to a halt in front of the soldiers, they pounded their chest plates in salute and bowed their heads.

"Evening, Captain Furnon," Alec greeted.

"I'm sorry for disturbing you on your leave my lord, but I have an urgent message for you from His Majesty." The captain looked back up at Edmund and Leos. "I have separate letters for you as well, my lords."

Oliver went to hand Alec a sealed scroll when someone scoffed loudly from the side of the room. Several men shifted their position as Vincent moved closer.

The knights scowled, while Alec on the other hand barely glanced at the man.

"Is something the matter, sir?" the captain questioned in a just polite voice.

"Not really," Vincent began snidely, with a flick of his wrist. "I just fail to see why so many intelligent people allow themselves to be blinded. There is no reason to behave as if this Zerrokian is some kind of hero for Malyndor."

"I tire of your ignorance towards my son," Leos declared, smacking his hand on the table.

"Your son? Ha. He was a glad-i-a-tor," Vincent stressed, annunciating every syllable.

"He…" echoed a loud voice throughout the space. "Is an Emerald Sage of His Majesty's forces." A tall blonde woman appeared in the doorway. "And not just any sorcerer, Alec is the Dragon Sage. I'm sure even you have heard of him. His position is more than equal to your own. So I would watch your tongue."

Sputtering, Vincent spun on his heel and stormed out of the chamber. There was nothing more he could do at the moment. Everyone heard of the Dragon Sage and his power. With so many on Alec's side, continuing the debate would be useless.

While the room was once again filled with gasps and excited whispers, Alec appeared none too pleased. As Isabelle approached, he pinched the bridge of his nose with a long sigh.

"Isabelle, I've told you before not to announce our titles so freely. The whole point of our code names is to use discretion."

"Awww, don't be cross, Alec. I was just putting the little weasel back in his place. He certainly sounded like he needed it."

Alec didn't answer.

To Isabelle's dismay, the sorcerer exchanged a quick glance with a beautiful woman at the high table. Flashing her a shy half grin, he lifted his shoulders in a shrug before turning away to retrieve his message.

Light green eyes growing wide, Isabelle's face lit up. The sorceress took off, making a bee line for the table before Alec could bring her to a halt. Propping her hip on the edge right in front of Jade, she smiled brightly.

"So you're Jade. Or should I say *Lady* Jade, my apologies." Isabelle quickly glanced behind her at Alec. Ignoring his scowl, she spun back. "I'm Isabelle Peterson. It's a pleasure to meet you, milady. I must thank you. When we were imprisoned in Zerrok, there was a few times I feared our circumstances were too dire to survive. Alec however, fought really hard so he could get back to you. I know he cares greatly, since he refused to talk about you. Only said your name once. You know how stubborn he can be. Like when we were locked in the arena dungeon—"

"Isabelle!" Alec's warning-like growl shot through the air cutting off Isabelle's monologue.

The sorceress winced. Flashing Jade a guilty smile she winked, then scurried off to join her partner.

"Yes?" she drawled innocently, standing by his elbow.

"You talk too much," he informed her dryly.

Batting large doe like eyes Isabelle leaned her head on his arm. "Sorry."

Alec sighed, "Try and remember our missions are classified."

Straightening, she gave him a quick salute. "Yes, sir."

"By the way, what are you doing here? I thought you were staying in Ariston."

She shrugged. "I decided to come along in case you needed back up against fools like that," Isabelle said mildly, pointing her thumb in the direction where Vincent disappeared. "Besides, I know how you are with crowds."

Brows lowered somewhat, Jade watched the exchange intently. When the doors flew open and the blonde beauty strode into the room, Jade instinctively knew who it was. Hiding her hands beneath the table, she gripped the skirts of her dress. The form fitting green uniform and gleaming armor suited Isabelle perfectly. *This* was the woman Alec spent his time with? From the sounds of it, they were even trapped in a dungeon together.

Jade wanted to hate her from her confident walk to her bubbly chatter. Eyes locked on the pair, her irritation quickly dissipated. There was a fondness she couldn't deny, yet it wasn't romantic in the least. The way the sorcerers spoke and looked at each other seemed to be nothing more than friendship. In fact, Alec treated Isabelle like a little sister, an irritating little sister by his current expression.

A smile pulled at Jade's lips. *I am pleased you are finally letting people in Alakaid.*

Focusing on the scroll from King Titus, Alec held up his right hand baring his engraved ring. "Surgeon, reveal."

A white magic circle appeared above the metal. Turning his hand palm side up, Alec gradually swept it over the blank paper. Words traced across the page which only the caster could see. As Alec's eyes scanned the message, his brows pleated with a frown. The sorcerer glanced at his partner.

"Have you seen this?"

She nodded. "Yes, I was already briefed."

"When do you want to take your leave, my lord?" Oliver asked.

"Immediately."

Holding the scroll out in his hand Alec set his orders alight. Turning towards the high table he gazed at Leos and the duke. Both men were re-reading their messages with an equally serious frown. Alec quickly approached them.

"Father, I regret I must depart at once. Thank you everyone for joining us for this celebration. The House of Kegan is honored by your presence."

Leos smiled. "Well said. Fear not Alec, I know well that duty to the King comes first. Try and keep Isabelle out of mischief."

Fighting a laugh, he watched as the sorceress crossed her arms with a huff.

"I will try."

Alec's gaze shifted to Edmund. "Your Grace, with your permission I will have to delay your tour until my return."

"Agreed, Lord Alec. I will, in fact, be departing for Stafford. His Majesty's call cannot be ignored. Safe journey."

"And to you as well."

Finally, Alec was able to direct his attention on Jade. Moving towards her he said, "Lady Jade, I must take my leave. However, I will seek you out as soon as I'm able. I promise it shall be a much shorter reprieve." Leaning in he whispered, "Wait for me, love?"

"Till the stars no longer shine."

Alec's eyes twinkled as he straightened.

"Go save the Kingdom, Dragon Sage," Jade added playfully.

Bowing, Alec spun about and left the room with Isabelle and the Royal Guard. Watching him disappear, Jade fought to keep her smile in place. No matter how much she wanted to be selfish and keep him with her, she couldn't. This was the path he had chosen, as a warrior and sorcerer. Jade would stand by him.

Rushing to his room to pack a bag, Jade's words echoed in Alec's mind. Knowing she felt no scorn towards him eased some of the tension of his swift departure. Within moments, he was riding out of Marcia's castle with his escorts. A long journey was ahead of them. They would be traveling through the night in order to reach Ariston as soon as possible. According to the urgent message, a major battle between several dragons broke out in the southwestern part of the kingdom. Since then, dragon sightings have been reported in every part of Malyndor.

CHAPTER 9

A loud jumble of voices mixed together, fighting to be heard within the King's private study. Dozens of high ranking officials and sages alike were summoned to discuss the sudden dragon problem. No one could recall the last time so many dragons were seen at one time. For them to be swarming the kingdom was most disturbing news.

"Quiet down!" Titus hollered over the commotion. When the noise continued on, he slammed his hand on the map table. "I said silence!"

An instant hush fell over the space. His gaze sweeping over the room, Titus let out a long slow breath.

"This arguing is not aiding us. We are already engaged in a growing conflict with The Pure, I do not wish to provoke another war with the dragons. Not all of us have forgotten the devastation it once caused."

"Which is precisely my point, Your Majesty," insisted General Claymore. "If we linger for too long, the dragons could wipe out the entire Kingdom before we are able to muster a counter-attack."

"I disagree. Acting rashly could worsen our situation," interjected Breanna.

"Grandmaster Eldridge?" Titus questioned, shifting his gaze to the other man. "What is your opinion on the matter?"

The sage's eyes scanned the topographical image of Malyndor stretched out in front of him. "While General Claymore is right to keep in mind a dragon's fearsome power, we cannot forget our responsibility to the people. Acting with haste in this case would not be wise. We don't know what these dragons seek."

"What they seek?" Jerric scoffed. "These are dragons we're talking about. We should strike them now while we can."

"If they were planning an attack, then our Kingdom would already be aflame. They wouldn't be alerting us to their presence first."

"I have to agree with Grandmaster Eldridge," General Rickman added. "Dragons don't typically hunt humans. There may be another reason for this behavior."

"Another reason?" Jerric repeated incredulously. "The stupid beasts don't need a reason. Give them enough time and they will reduce everything to ash."

"Just because we can't understand them verbally doesn't mean they're stupid," Alec pointed out reasonably. Pushing off the pillar he was leaning against, he strode towards the table. "In fact, anyone who has spent time studying them knows they are very intelligent. The Order of the Crimson Rose dedicated centuries to observing their kind. If a fight is what they sought, then nothing would stop them. It certainly didn't when they battled each other."

Jerric's brows narrowed to points. Face twitching, his lips curled back against his teeth with a snarl. "How dare you sneak in here, boy? This meeting is for the most elite counsel only. I'll have you thrown in the dungeon for this."

"*I* invited Alec," King Titus said crossly. "Lest you forget, he has more experience with these creatures than anyone else in the past three hundred years."

"That is correct." Layfon peered at Jerric's reddening face as he continued. "Though the rumors do not speak all true, Alec did indeed ride a dragon all the way from Zerrok. If anyone were able to decipher their possible motives it would be him." Waving Alec over, he looked down at the map once more. "What do you think?"

His expression a neutral mask, Alec studied the map as well. From what he'd learned since arriving in Ariston, it seems a group of half a dozen dragons crossed their border to the south three days ago. Shortly after their appearance, they were intercepted by some dragons from Ellfraya. A brutal battle took place ending with three casualties. The following day, even more dragons were reported crossing the border from Ellfraya. By now, there were sightings all the way to the coast.

Though he didn't voice such thoughts, King Titus had every right to be concerned. Alec couldn't be sure, but the enemy dragons must have been from the rogue Iron Scales Clan. If so, then why were the Ellfrayan dragons spread across Malyndor? *What are you seeking?* Alec paused. Could that be it? Were they looking for something? The only way to know for sure would be to find Cassidy and ask her. His lips pressed lightly together. Alec couldn't very well tell those present that he needed to have an audience with a dragon.

"I believe you're right, Grandmaster. Dragons tend not to act without reason. From what I've read, they have a hierarchy and are ruled by two main leaders. So many wouldn't act without cause outside of their own territory. I would recommend sending scouts to key locations to observe their movements. An armed force could provoke them unnecessarily."

"You speak as if these beasts only want peace, yet didn't one attack you after striking a defenseless village?" General Claymore questioned harshly.

"Not quite. The village was never harmed by the dragon, nor do I believe it would have been. It was the bandits who set the fire causing all the destruction."

"That doesn't explain the creature's behavior towards a human."

There were a few mumbles of agreement, but Titus held up his hand with a thoughtful frown. "I am curious, what do you mean by the dragon wouldn't have attacked the village?"

Alec crossed his arms and took a breath. It was difficult trying to convince the others without revealing his gift.

"As we all know, dragons are territorial, and though rarely seen, at least some have flourished within our borders for centuries. The bandit's assault most likely caused him to come forth and protect what is his home as well."

Titus nodded, running a hand over his chin. "Interesting..."

"It does make sense when you consider what we know of them," Layfon agreed.

"He still bears no answer for the General's question," Jerric reminded them snidely.

Alec shrugged. "Perhaps he thought he was being challenged. I did ride out to meet him."

"Surely you jest. A dragon threatened by a single human? What kind of fools do you take us for? Next you will be declaring it was a test."

"Why not?" Alec countered to the sage's surprise. "Humans undertake such diversions all the time. Dragons are equally as bright," his gaze settled on Jerric. "If not more so in some ways."

Sputtering, the master sage couldn't reply at first. "How dare you!"

"That is quite enough," Titus pronounced, ending the confrontation for the moment. "When all things are considered, we still lack key information about the situation at hand. Our knowledge of dragon-kind is limited and our inability to effectively communicate with them hinders such advancements. We can however, rely on their past behaviors.

General Rickman, send scouts from our key military outposts across the realm. I want eyes on every dragon, but no one is to engage them without my approval."

"At once, Your Majesty."

"Grandmaster Eldridge, assemble your wizards. We shall need their eyes and ears as well."

"I will assign sages to join the General's scouts."

"Good."

"Your Majesty," Alec began with a slight bow. "With your permission, I'd like to travel to the East Circle to speak with Malcolm. He knows of some ancient text which could prove useful."

Titus nodded. "Very well. Any further information would be most welcome. Once you have completed this task, return to Ariston."

"Yes, Your Majesty."

Alec dipped his head and quickly departed the space. With any luck, Cassidy would be awaiting him in Stafford. Then, the sorcerer could hopefully gain the insight needed to avoid a possibly grave misunderstanding.

Pushing open the door to his accommodations, Vincent looked around with a grimace. The small inn wasn't his normal type of lodging. The thought of remaining in Marcia Castle was not to be borne. Thus, he departed the city with all haste. Vincent only traveled a few hours prior to calling it a night. The brisk ride did nothing to quell his surly mood.

Plopping down in a chair, he propped his feet up with a groan. Eyes drifting closed, the sorcerer's face immediately invaded his mind. A wolf-like grin on his lips, the Zerrokian slave snaked his arm around Jade's waist and pulled her close. Throwing his head back with a laugh, he stared right at Vincent.

"She's mine now."

Gasping, the noble launched himself upright. Sucking in air, he pounded a fist on the chair's arm. "Damn him."

"Bad dream?" inquired a soft voice.

Head jerking up, Vincent's hand gripped the hilt of his sword. Unsheathing it in a smooth motion, he glared at the hooded intruder leaning casually against the window frame.

"How dare you enter my room? You chose the wrong person to try to rob. I shall make you regret this night."

Lunging forward, Vincent swept his sword horizontally.

The short man easily ducked under the blade and kept out of reach.

"If I wanted to rob you, Lord Vincent of Parlen, I wouldn't have alerted you to my presence."

"Do not take me for a fool," Vincent snapped. "How else would you know me if I was not your target?"

Vincent's next attack was blocked by a dagger that suddenly appeared in the mysterious man's hand. "If you wish to defeat the sorcerer Alec, then you might desire to at least hear my words," he said calmly.

The noble froze. Blade still locked against the other man's, he watched him carefully.

"Why would you care what becomes of him?"

"Let's just say those I work for would prefer if he disappeared…permanently."

A few moments ticked by before Vincent slowly withdrew his weapon. Keeping a tight hold of the hilt, he stood at the ready.

"I am listening."

The hooded figure nodded as he returned his blade to its sheath.

"My sources inform me that you believe something to be amiss with this fighter and you are correct. It is worse than you imagine."

Vincent frowned, his eyes narrowing. "How so?"

"They call him the Dragon Sage, but in truth, the beasts are his masters."

Body straightening, Vincent scoffed. "Impossible."

"You think so? Have you wondered why he acts so strangely? How others seem to bend to his will?"

The noble's sword arm dropped to his side.

"I see you have. It is part of his dark powers from the dragons. His feats were no accidents. They were staged to position him nearer to the crown. And who else would be a better bride than the closest friend of the future queen?" the man stressed, continuing to watch Vincent from the shadow of his hood.

"I have to save her," he declared returning his sword to its scabbard. "This time Duke Stafford will be sure to receive my warning."

"Hold fast, milord," the stranger said lifting a hand. "Words will not be enough over his power. The spell woven upon his victims runs deep. You will need proof."

Vincent paused. "How do I acquire it?"

"The mark of the dragon. He bears it on his back. A word of caution though, if you desire to break his sway, be sure the duke gazes upon it before you spill the sage's blood."

Two soldiers discreetly followed behind as Titus and Zachary walked down the castle's wide corridor. Having just returned from the Kingdom's western border, the prince was eager to hear their trusted counsel's opinion on the matter at hand.

"Visiting the main outposts along the border confirmed our initial reports. About two dozen dragons entered our lands. So far, none of them have been seen departing."

Titus dipped his head. "The messages I have been receiving indicate they are traveling the Kingdom in pairs. For what purpose, I still know not."

"Layfon could tell you nothing?"

Titus looked at his brother. "He does not believe they are hostile. General Claymore however, disagrees."

"Of course," Zachary said sarcastically. "He has never agreed with the wizards."

"He certainly has a point. Dragons can be dangerous, yet the simple matter is we do not possess enough information. For the time being, I have ordered scouts to monitor them at a distance. I do hope, for the sake of our people, we can avoid a war."

Zachary's brows lowered. "If it was war they wanted, then I am sure they would have attacked by now."

"I agree. Let us hope we are right."

Down the hallway, Alandra strode by dressed in travel clothes with a cloak about her shoulders.

"Alandra!" Titus called with a frown, quickening his steps.

Backtracking, his daughter peered up the corridor.

"Greetings, Father." A wide smile touched her lips. "Welcome home, Uncle Zachary."

Chuckling softly, Zachary glanced at her embroidered shirt and trousers. Alandra rarely wore dresses during the day.

"It is good to be home."

"Where are you off to?" her father questioned, crossing his arms. "I recall telling you to remain within the castle."

"You did...when the dragons were first sighted. Since it has been decided an attack is surely not to come, I thought I might travel hence to Stafford."

Titus's expression did not soften.

"Such a diversion would not be solely for leisure," Alandra pressed on. "I desire to aid our Kingdom as well. People are scared, and knowing the Royal Family is locked behind these walls is not offering them comfort. If I go to Stafford, then I can help ease their fears and be just as aptly protected."

Watching Alandra carefully, Titus fought a smirk pulling at his lips. It wasn't solely Jade's company that his daughter sought or she would have said so. He knew his strong-willed child well enough to sense that she wasn't voicing her true reasons. Did she believe he would disapprove? Or was it a fear of his refusal keeping the truth at bay?

"Alandra, why do you seek to go to Stafford, of all places, in the midst of this crisis?"

"Lady Jade is always pleasurable company," she replied smoothly.

"Who else?" he countered.

Blinking, the princess didn't have a ready answer.

"If I recall," Titus continued, "A certain sage departed for the East Circle a short while ago."

He knows too much. Alandra shrugged. "The motives I spoke of were not untrue. Yet, I cannot deny the benefit of Alec's company should our paths cross."

Titus's brows rose.

Alandra sighed, shaking her head. "As you wish, Father. I did not have the chance to converse with Alec while he was in Ariston, nor was I permitted to attend Marcia's celebration due to the current situation. Alec is my friend and trusted counsel. His well-being, I have yet to see for myself since his return from Zerrok. You, yourself Father, have encouraged me to align myself with valued individuals who will aid me in the future. Hence, I have sought to do so."

Listening to her impassioned speech, Titus frowned. "I do hope, this would not be an intimate alliance."

Eyes growing wide, Alandra leaned back as she stood there with her mouth gaping. Her and Alec? Alandra never considered him in such a light. He was her confidant, her friend. She did recently learn of another who did think of him as much more.

Laughing, Zachary placed a hand on Titus's shoulder. "Fear not brother, there is no such relationship here."

"How can you be so sure? I do not disapprove of him per say, but Alandra will be queen one day."

Zachary opened his mouth, then closed it. "Sometimes you are so blind," he mumbled. Lowering his voice the prince leaned in. "An announcement has yet to be made, but word from the ball is Alec is to be matched with the younger Lady Stafford."

Titus's eyes darted to his daughter.

A bright smile appeared on Alandra's face. "I believe it to be so. Lady Jade is quite taken with him."

"And I dare say we know Alec cares greatly for his special lady from all the teasing you and Alicia bestow upon him."

"Harmless fun," the princess replied. Waving his words off with a twinkle in her eye she added, "I think they shall make an excellent match."

"Indeed," Zachary agreed as his brother grinned with a light chuckle. "If I may, there is a matter I must discuss with Alec. I would not be opposed to escorting Alandra to Stafford. The duke's guard is skilled. She will be just as safe there as she would be here within the castle."

A hand traced the line of Titus's jaw. "I would prefer you remained here," Titus began. "However, if you are determined to take this journey and Zachary accompanies you, then I see no need to refuse your request."

Beaming, Alandra dipped into a little bob. "Thank you, Father. I assure you I shall use the utmost caution."

"I have no doubt you shall. Safe journey." Reaching forward he wrapped her in an embrace, then stepped back. Holding his daughter's gaze, the king added, "And should any dragons appear about the city…"

"I shall remain within the castle until it is safe to return to Ariston," Alandra promised. "Though I do not believe it shall be the case. None of the reports indicate any dragons lingering around heavily populated areas. What possible reason could they have to appear in Stafford?"

Cloud's hooves pounded down the surface of the forest road. Slowing his stride, Alec straightened in the saddle to peer about him. Scanning the woods he saw no other soul about. With a click of Alec's tongue, the grey steed walked off the path and moved through the trees. Cloud knew their location well and needed no further direction to find Cassidy's normal meeting spot. Entering the clearing, Alec dismounted and gazed around.

"Cassidy?" he called.

There was no reply.

Eyes searching the space, he frowned. *Come on my friend. Please be here.* Many a time she appeared suddenly when he was about. Cassidy seemed to know when he was seeking her out.

"Cassidy, I need to talk to you. Are you here?" Peering into the trees Alec searched for his friend. "Please, this is really important."

Still, there was nothing. Exhaling, Alec put his hands on his hips and dropped his chin. *What now?* he thought to himself. Cassidy was the only one who could give him the answers he sought.

Perhaps he should leave her another note with the stones. That way she would know he came to see her. Afterwards, the East Circle would be his next destination. Malcolm was the only other person Alec could think of who might be able to shine some light on the situation. Alec could always try again in a day or so.

A rustling in the brush had Alec's head snapping up. The one corner of his mouth pulled back. Alec took a step in the sound's direction.

"Cassidy, I'm glad you're here. I wanted to talk to you—"

The words died on his lips as the last person he expected to see stepped out into the clearing. Alec stiffened, his hand gripping the hilt of his blade.

"Vincent," he said with a low growl.

Damn it. How did he find me here? There was no point hoping he hadn't heard him calling for the green dragon. The triumphant gleam in his eyes was answer enough.

"I finally have you," the noble declared.

Alec didn't get the chance to respond. So focused upon the sudden appearance of his enemy, he didn't notice the six men sneaking up behind him until too late. They pounced on him, keeping Alec from drawing his blade. A scuffle broke out as the sorcerer fought to break free. The feel of cool metal encasing his one wrist registered in the back of his mind. Where had Vincent procured an anti-magic cuff?

Charging across the meadow, Cloud raced to his master's aid.

Raising his blade, one of the thugs prepared to strike.

Ramming a man in the face with his elbow, Alec managed to twist out of his grip. With the two others still holding on, the sorcerer got to his knees and launched forward, tackling the brute. Neighing loudly, Cloud was still coming towards them when a strike to the side of his head caused everything to spin before his eyes. Giving himself a shake, Alec tried to stop the sensation. The momentary lapse was enough for his enemies to regain the upper hand. Vincent stood to the side, leering at him as Alec was met with another strike to the face.

CHAPTER 10

Duke Stafford and his Battlemaster were seated in Edmund's study when a forceful knock sounded at the door. Breaking off their conversation, both men's eyes locked on the wooden entry. A frown marred his face as Edmund called for their visitor to enter.

A soldier rushed in. Breathing heavily, sweat beaded his brow as his gaze darted between the duke and Roderick.

"I'm sorry to disturb you, Your Grace, but we have a situation."

"What is it?"

"Lord Vincent has forced his way into the city. He is demanding an audience with you and nears the castle as we speak."

"Vincent?" Edmund exclaimed jumping to his feet.

Upon learning what truly transpired with the noble and his beloved daughter last year, the duke officially banished him from Stafford. As soon as the matter with the dragons was resolved, he would speak with the King about a more severe punishment. Vincent would not get away with assaulting his child. Furious that he was not told of the incident earlier, Edmund no longer possessed any lingering doubts concerning Jade's betrothal to Alec. He could not think of anyone more deserving of his daughter's hand.

"How dare he come here!" Edmund quickly rounded the desk as Roderick, too, rose to his feet with a scowl.

"How did he get inside?" the knight questioned harshly.

At the same time Edmund demanded, "Why did you allow him into the city? Remove him at once!"

The soldier paled. "We tried Your Grace, but he has a hostage with him."

"A hostage?" Roderick repeated crossly. "Who?"

"The coward. We shall see about this," Edmund said preventing the man from answering as he stormed across the room towards the door. "He wants an audience, well then he shall have it."

Roderick and the soldier swiftly followed as the duke took off down the hall. Just as they were entering the large foyer, the castle doors swung open. Vincent strode inside with half a dozen men following as they dragged a slumped over figure. A sack concealed their hostage's identity, but the blade pressed to the side of his neck was easy enough to see.

Members of the Stafford Guard flanked each side of the space as well as blocked the exit once it was sealed. All around people stopped and stared as Vincent came to a halt in the middle of the chamber.

Striding forward, the duke watched the younger lord with a face set like stone. "How dare you enter my castle after your despicable treatment of my daughter! Release this man and depart at once," Edmund ordered pointing towards the door.

Vincent's smile didn't waver. Dropping into a bow, he peered at the noble evenly. "I understand your displeasure over our little disagreement, so I brought you a gift as proof of my devotion to Lady Jade," Vincent told him retracing his steps to hover over his captive. "Behold, the Kingdom's traitor which we have so long sought," he said as he removed the covering.

Groaning, Alec flinched as the surrounding light assaulted his senses. His wrists and arms were bound with ropes. A cloth spotted with blood was tied over his mouth and his clothing was dirty and torn in several places. Blinking, the moment he saw Vincent, his eyes flashed. Two of the noble's thugs pushed down on his shoulders to keep him in place.

Eyes growing wide for a second, both Roderick and Edmund glared at Vincent with a clenched jaw.

"What is the meaning of this? Release Lord Alec this instant."

"He is no more a lord than a dog is a king. Keep your distance," Vincent snapped as a few soldiers edged closer.

A minion pressed the blade more firmly into Alec's skin, drawing blood.

"Stay where you are," Roderick commanded his men. *This is going to be tricky.* Vincent's previous behavior couldn't be forgotten. The man was like a poisonous snake, slippery and poised to strike at any moment. If they made a move right now, Alec would be dead before they could reach him. Though breathing with some difficulty, the warrior's eyes blazed proudly. He was not a man easily broken. The knight knew that well. *Hold tight a little longer, Alec.*

The duke on the other hand was not thinking as rashly as he normally would. Vincent's bright smile and twisted laugh brought forth unwanted images of Jade's vague description of the vile incident. Shaking his head, Edmund swept them away. His attention focused on the warrior glaring at Vincent's back. This was not how justice was supposed to work.

Fingers curling around the hilt of his blade, Edmund readied himself to strike. A hand gently rested on his arm, causing him to freeze for a second. The duke's gaze lowered to settle on his wife.

Her large doe-like eyes brimmed with anger and empathy, yet silently pleaded for him to calm himself.

Exhaling with a hiss, Edmund released the grip on his sword. "Very well, Lord Vincent. Since you claim to bear proof of treachery, then I shall hear you out. First, turn your prisoner over to the guard so he can be held for trial."

Vincent's men made no sign of relaxing.

"I cannot do that, Your Grace," the noble announced. "He is, without a doubt, guilty."

"That is not for you alone to decide," Roderick countered.

"The nobility cannot act above the laws of our King. It is our job to enforce those laws Lord Vincent, which include a fair trial."

The noble watched Edmund evenly. "Any means of justice cannot be done for this creature since his dark magic holds all the sway. You are all under his power, and I have come to liberate you of this twisted spell. It is time for Malyndor to see his true colors."

As Vincent was speaking, Jade and Ariel moved through the crowd. Gasping, a hand flew to her mouth as Jade gazed at the bound warrior. Her mind unwilling to process what she was seeing, Jade couldn't utter a word as she stood there staring at Alec and the crazed noble lingering close by.

Vincent continued speaking, unaware of his newest guest. "This traitorous slime you revere as a hero is, in fact, in league with the dragons swarming our beloved realm. Only a short time ago, he was in the forest outside Stafford calling for one of them by name. That's correct; he can speak with the beasts."

A strained silence filled the room. Exchanging apprehensive glances, those gathered around the space started to talk in low whispers. However, their words were not directed at the supposed traitor. They were aimed at the noble ranting to the duke.

"He is the Dragon Sage," Edmund replied with forced patience. "It is his duty to interact with dragons."

"Pray, but you understand not, Your Grace. He does not merely interact with them, he *talks* to them. I mean truly speaks with them, as if he knows what it is they say."

Edmund raised a brow.

"Do any of you rightly believe the dragon he faced outside Marcia simply left when the battle was yet to be finished? Or what about the beast he flew from Zerrok? How else would he be able to accomplish such a feat?"

"Because Alec is a gifted warrior and sorcerer," Roderick answered point-blank.

"No, you blind fool!" Vincent snapped. "This has all been a farce to get him closer to those in power."

"Tell me, Lord Vincent," Edmund began, hoping to soon find an opening for his men to move in. "Do you know why the dragons seek to take over Malyndor?"

The noble's brows lowered into a sharp point. "None of you believe me. I should have known I could not reason with you. His power is far too strong, but I will break this spell." Twisting about, Vincent addressed his men. "Turn him around."

Two more men grasped Alec's arms as they struggled to move him and then hold the spirited warrior in place.

Damn it, I have to stop this, Alec's mind shouted. Yet, with the anti-magic cuff still on his wrist, the only way to break free would be to prove Vincent right, showing everyone how strange he was. Clenching his jaw, the warrior waited for his mark to be exposed.

Pulling a dagger from his belt, Vincent's eyes flashed. "You want proof, then I shall give it to you. He is marked by the beasts. See for yourself what this traitor bears."

Grabbing hold of the back of Alec's shirt, Vincent slashed the top of it and tore the fabric down to reveal what Alec so carefully hid.

The people standing in the crowds craned their necks to get a better view.

A grin appeared once again on the noble's lips. Sure enough, there was a pale red dragon shaped birth mark between the warrior's shoulder blades. Vincent hadn't been misled by the stranger.

"See, I speak the truth. Alec is a pet of the dragons."

Roderick took a step forward. "Alec's had that mark since he was in Zerrok. Are you trying to say it was part of his plan to be imprisoned as a slave for most of his life?"

Sputtering, Vincent couldn't seem to answer.

The duke's eyes remained on the pale dragon. A frown pulled at the corners of his mouth. He couldn't place it, but something about this mark nagged at him.

"You have stated your case," Edmund said at long last. "Now release him to my men's custody."

Vincent's glee was long gone. Scowling, he shook his head. "Why will none of you believe what is before your eyes?" Spinning, the noble's narrowed gaze locked on his captive. "It would seem I have no choice. If I want to break this spell, I will have to do what *he* said." Vincent tightened his grip on the dagger and moved closer to Alec. "This creature must pay for his crimes."

"He's no creature. You are the monster here!" Jade exclaimed.

Freezing, Vincent's eyes scanned the faces of those around him until he found the woman who spoke. Green eyes shimmering like jewels, Vincent never thought she looked more beautiful. How had he missed her arrival?

"Let him go. You have gone too far as it is," she commanded.

Why is she still defending him? I cannot bear it any longer. This spell must be broken, now, Vincent thought savagely, his free hand curling into his palm.

"Enough!" the man shouted. Before anyone could react Vincent darted forward, seized Jade and pulled her into the loose ring of his men. "Here, take her," he instructed one of his underlings.

"Let go of me!" Jade shrieked.

A hand went to her belt in vain. *I forgot, I am not permitted to have a blade in the castle.* Not that it would do her much good as the man watching over her firmly gripped both her arms.

Listening to Jade struggle somewhere behind him, Alec's pulse quickened. Vincent was hurting her again. The sorcerer's entire body stiffened. Her cries of distress echoed in his mind. No other thoughts seemed to be able to grasp his attention beyond that of coming to her aid. How dare Vincent lay his filthy hands on his Jade again?

Like a flash of lightning, the atmosphere of the chamber suddenly changed. Tied to his emotions, Alec's power lashed out on its own. A faint glow emanated from his body prior to a pulse bursting forth in a shock wave which threw the thugs pinning him back.

Jade involuntarily dropped to her knees as the men flew across the room.

Irises blazing white, the sorcerer slowly rose to his feet. All eyes were glued upon Alec. The ropes binding him tore apart like paper. The metal cuff fell from his wrist and the cloth covering his mouth dissolved as he pulled it from his face.

"I warned you to never touch her again," Alec growled in a quiet, cold voice.

Face pale, Vincent could only gape. As Alec started towards him, the blade in his hand clattered onto the stone floor.

Grabbing him by the collar, Alec picked the noble clear up off the floor. A tense few seconds ticked by as he glared at his deathly white foe before throwing him onto the ground.

Vincent's body skidded across the stone, landing directly in front of members of the Stafford Guard.

Without so much as looking at him, Alec held a palm out at the thug who dared to harm his Jade. A pulse shot out sending him sailing across the chamber just as the others had.

Eyes locked on the petite woman still sitting on the floor, Alec held out his hand.

"Are you alright, Lady Jade?"

Flashing him a brave smile, Jade didn't hesitate to accept the hand he offered. Her heart wouldn't cease its pounding, but it was not fear of her rescuer causing the unusual rhythm. No matter how strange, Alec only ever used his power for good. Jade knew in her bones he wouldn't harm her.

"I am as long as you are by my side."

With Jade's fingers still resting in his palm, Alec peered around the space. Roderick's men were busy arresting Vincent and his thugs, yet the tension within the space had not dissipated. Everywhere he looked, people were staring at him and not in a good way. Alec fought the urge to cringe. Up until now, Isabelle was the only one who knew the true extent of his abilities. Talking to dragons, casting without spells, she knew it all and had kept his secret. That would no longer be possible. Isabelle he could trust, but the fearful gazes watching him held no such loyalty. Alec wasn't able to control his power when Jade was in danger and he would have to pay the price for his weakness.

The crowds' similar expressions were more or less what the sorcerer was expecting and feared. The poison of Vincent's words were taking root. Some gazed at him as though he wasn't even human.

Well, I can't deny what they just saw. I do owe the duke an explanation at least, if nothing else.

Alec couldn't begin to guess what the noble was thinking. Edmund's face was an unreadable mask. The duchess surprisingly didn't appear appalled. However, Roderick seemed to be the only one looking upon him in the same way he always did. It was as if nothing strange happened in his eyes.

Jade intertwined her fingers with Alec's.

The warmth of her small frame standing proudly beside him gave the sorcerer strength.

"Your Grace—" His words were cut off as a large shadow swept by the windows.

A deep roar filled the air, followed by frightened screams. A horn sounded from the battlements. There was a chaotic shout of commands and the ring of metal upon metal.

Alec jerked around, his eyes widening. "Oh no, Cassidy," he whispered.

She must think I'm in danger. I have to stop her. His dark brown eyes locked upon the woman by his side.

Offering him a small smile, Jade nodded her head.

Alec squeezed her fingers in thanks. Spinning around, his sight locked on Roderick as he quickly approached.

"Please, look after Jade for me."

The knight held his unwavering gaze for a moment. "Do what you must. I trust you, Alec."

"Thanks."

Kissing the top of Jade's hand, Alec raced out of the room. The door swung behind him, but didn't close all the way.

Straightening her shoulders, Jade took off in his direction.

Roderick managed to catch her arm as her father shouted, "Jade what are you doing?"

"Helping Alec. He is used to fighting alone, but he is not on his own anymore. He has me and I shall not abandon him."

Edmund's head pulled back as he gazed at the determined light shining in his daughter's eyes. "Stay with Roderick," he ordered firmly. "Let us meet this dragon of his."

Outside, Cassidy was circling back towards the courtyard as Alec flew down the steps. Arrows shot through the air. She dodged them and continued on towards her target. Seeing Alec, she released a fearsome roar.

Along the battlements the heavy crossbows were now pointing at the green dragon starting to land within the castle

147

grounds. One strike from these weapons could kill her instantly.

Acting on instinct, Alec called up a water spell and froze the crossbows in place. Joining Cassidy's side, he encased her in a shield.

"Everyone stop!" Alec shouted above the chaos. "She's not going to hurt you."

There were a few stunned moments before a few of the Stafford Guard lowered their weapons. Not all of them were willing to believe the warrior and remained at the ready.

"Lower your weapons," commanded Duke Stafford appearing at the top of the stairs.

At last, the remainder of the soldiers complied. Only then did Alec lower the barrier and turn to the green dragon.

"Cassidy, what are you doing here?"

"I felt your power surge. I feared you were in danger." Lifting a toe to touch the side of his bruised face her yellow eyes narrowed. "It seems I was right."

"I'm fine," he assured her.

A low rumble was all anyone else could understand. Another round of whispers filled the space. Soldiers tightened their grip on their weapons and servants backed away, gaping in horror. There were a few Alec noted who didn't respond with disgust or fear, but not many. Over by the barracks Garth and Nathan pushed their way to the front of the crowd.

The sorcerer's gaze focused on the duke. "I don't use dark magic, nor am I your enemy, but Vincent was right on one point. I can talk to dragons."

Cassidy nudged his shoulder and he patted the side of her face. Taking a deep breath, Alec continued, "I discovered it on my first day in Stafford when Cassidy here, came to my aid. She helped me defeat the bandits attacking Lady Jade's escort."

Slowly, some of those watching the scene intently, began to relax. The mumbling changed, shifting more to Alec's benefit.

"Dragons like Cassidy are not evil; they help protect our Kingdom—"

"See! I told you he was a traitor," interrupted Vincent's shrilled voice as he appeared on the edge of the courtyard.

How did he get free? Edmund's mind demanded. "Arrest Lord Vincent at once."

Vincent didn't cease speaking as men moved through the crowd towards him. "Your Grace would silence me for speaking the truth?"

"You are under arrest for kidnapping and attempted murder of a lord. Do not feign innocence, Vincent."

"Do none of you see? This creature's spell is strong indeed. He has you all fooled. He's in league with the dragons, and if he is not stopped, they will destroy our entire Kingdom."

Once more people's eyes shifted warily to the sorcerer standing beside the green dragon. Frightened, they didn't know who or what to believe. Whispering behind their hands, they questioned if Vincent was right or if the dragons were their friends as Alec proclaimed?

"He cannot be trusted. He's a traitor," Vincent continued to scream as he ducked behind a building with several soldiers chasing after him.

"I'm not a traitor," Alec denied in a steady voice.

Scanning the courtyard, Alec's eyes paused on Garth with a pained stare.

'Breathe,' his friend mouthed, taking a step towards him before saying something to some of the men around him.

Sucking in a shaky breath, Alec's eyes shifted to the other faces watching him intently. After everything he'd done for them, were they really so willing to think the worst of him just from a few drops of Vincent's poisonous words? Did people secretly distrust him so much? A pain radiated through Alec's chest, growing increasingly stronger. The dark glares coming from some of the staff were the sole images boring into him. Hands trembling, Alec curled them into fists as he tried to control it. The cords of his neck pressed against his skin.

"I'm no traitor," Alec repeated, his voice losing some of its strength. "From the moment I arrived I have protected you, trained you, fought beside you and even bled for you. But—but none of that matters, does it?" he questioned, his voice breaking.

They have betrayed you, the woman's voice suddenly whispered in his tortured mind.

"You've betrayed me," Alec quietly echoed. "It will never matter what I do to prove otherwise. You will only see me as an outsider…as an enemy…a monster."

Cassidy made some deep noises in her throat, but shaking his head Alec moved away.

"No," he told her firmly. "I'm marked. You wouldn't tell me what it meant, but I know now. Malcolm told me about the prophecy. I can defy the rules of magic, but look at what it has gotten me. See how they fear me. Despise me. I'm tired of people treating me like some kind of creature."

Each breath coming out in noisy gasps, Alec fought against the intense stabbing he could feel in his chest. A few drops of blood dripped from his nose. Widening his stance, Alec stretched his fingers and lifted his chin.

"If they want a monster, I'll give them one."

Eyes blazing white, Alec's power lashed out with a torrent of wind that both pushed Cassidy back and knocked everyone to the ground across the courtyard. The stones beneath his feet crumbled to dust as his hands tightened into fists once more. His aura swirling dangerously, Alec channeled his pain into a destructive force.

Still standing at the top of the castle steps, Jade watched the man she loved lose all control. Clutching her stomach, a wave of dizziness washed over her. *This is all my doing. If only I had informed Father of Vincent's evil sooner. Then he might not have brought Alec harm and caused this despair.* There had to be a way to bring him back to his senses.

"Alec, you are not evil. You have always used your powers for good because you *are* a good person," Jade called out.

Above the castle dark grey clouds threatened to block out the sun's rays. Rain poured down upon them mixed with the pinging of sleet. Close by, the crack of thunder broke through the howl of the wind. The red stain of blood began to seep from Alec's ears.

Heart pounding, Jade tried again. "Alec, I know you can stop this. You need not try to force people to despise you."

"Listen to her Alec," Garth called as he instructed people to vacate the area. "I swore my loyalty to you and no dragon will change that."

Nathan nodded his agreement. "Garth's right, little brother. The stubborn man I know wouldn't let his power control him. Fight this."

Leaking from his nose and mouth, a stream of red rolled down Alec's face like a tear. Slowly shaking his head, he just managed to answer, "It's too late. I can't stop it."

Gripping the sides of his head Alec dropped to his knees. A bolt of lightning shot down in the yard igniting a pile of hay near the stables.

"Oh no," Jade gasped as the knight pulled her back towards the castle doors.

A whirlpool twisted around the sorcerer, keeping anyone who tried to near him at bay.

"Roderick we must aid him," she pleaded. Another round of lightning struck the ground. "Alakaid. Alakaid!"

Jerking around, Edmund's eyes darted between Jade and Alec. "Alakaid," he repeated with dismay.

How could he have not seen it? The mark on his back, the prophecy he mentioned, were all linked to the name Alakaid.

He was no monster. This time, they needed to find a way to save Alec from himself.

During the chaos Alandra and Zachary arrived with their escort. Refusing to let his charge past the portcullis, Zachary watched Alec's powers run rampant. Stones throughout the courtyard were trembling and at least three fires were dancing in the rain.

Through it all, the exposed dragon mark on the sorcerer's back was glowing the same white as his eyes. Bent over, he began coughing up blood.

Stepping out into the rain, Edmund quickly joined Garth and Nathan. "Keep the area clear of nonessential personal until we can find a way to help Alec regain control before it kills him."

"If he's the one causing this storm then shouldn't we take him out?" a soldier asked with a scowl.

Frowning deeply, Edmund turned narrowed eyes upon the man. "Are you so ignorant that you have forgotten the fact that Alec has saved your life, my daughter's, mine and even King Titus himself? Such callous remarks are what caused this incident in the first place. Tell me soldier, how would you react if you believed all those you sacrificed yourself for, only sought your head?"

Mouth moving soundlessly, the man couldn't answer.

"Don't be stupid," Eric suddenly chimed in joining them from the other side. "Alec has always been one of us and we protect our own. Anyone who thinks otherwise doesn't deserve to be part of the Stafford Guard."

"Well said," Nathan agreed.

"The question is, how do we prove it to Alec?" Garth asked above the howling storm.

Gazing at the sorcerer, Edmund knew he didn't have much time left to turn the tide. It was then he saw Alec lift his blazing eyes to peer at Jade. The duke's daughter was still calling out to the warrior.

"That's it," he said to himself. Looking at the others he told them, "Alec has given up. We need to remind him there are still those who are on his side, no matter how strange his gifts."

"It just might work," Garth agreed.

"It must."

Exchanging glances, several of the other soldiers nodded. The initial shock of seeing Alec with a dragon having passed, they were left feeling guilty and foolish. Duke Stafford was correct about the warrior. They shouldn't have been so quick to judge him so poorly. When he needed them the most, they failed him.

Periodically, flashes of light lit the sky above them while stones from the courtyard were now floating in the air surrounding the sorcerer. Hunched over, the pain flowing through his body had him practically immobilized.

Cutting through the howl of the wind, Alec could make out Jade's voice calling to him. He focused upon it, sapping at the strength of her words. Unsure if he was hearing things at first, Alec swore Garth's voice joined in. Closing his eyes for a few seconds he concentrated on the sound. Growing louder, Alec could make out several other members of the guard followed by the duke himself. They were calling out to him, telling him to hold on and fight the power overwhelming him. One by one, others all across the courtyard started to add to the mix.

Come on Alec, he told himself. *Fight this. Jade still needs you.*

Exhaling with a ragged breath, Alec willed the air circling around him to dissipate. Nothing happened. Lips pressed into a thin line, he focused every ounce of energy on the task. Slowing, the winds died down and then disappeared altogether. Gaze locking on the nearest fire, Alec reached out a hand. Eyes still aglow, he silently commanded the blaze to cease. The hay morphed into a black smoldering pile as the flames went out. One after another, Alec regained control of the chaos scattered throughout the area. More blood dripped from his mouth, but he ignored it.

Soon the stones returned to their places in the ground, the rain stopped and the clouds above lightened, allowing the sun to once more shine down upon them. Lowering his arm, Alec rose unsteadily to his feet.

Cassidy rushed towards Alec as another surge rocked his body. It was nothing like the flow of energy which surrounded him previously.

Pulling itself from his body, a white light shot out of Alec's chest. Diving to the ground it twisted around his left ankle, coiled up his leg and wrapped around his waist. Moving up his spine, the energy shifted and morphed into the shape of a dragon as the spirit's head hovered above the sorcerer's shoulder.

Hearing Cassidy approaching from behind, Alec turned and held out his palm as if to stop her from growing any nearer. It was too late for her to cease her movements. In her attempt to halt her steps, the dragon ended up skidding right into Alec's hand snout first.

The moment they touched, both Alec and Cassidy seemed to freeze in place. The spirit dragon surrounding Alec snaked down his arm and flowed directly into Cassidy. Her eyes, as well as the magnificent jewel on the dragon's forehead, blazed white like the sage's. Suddenly, the translucent spirit shot back up Alec's arm and returned to his chest. Once inside him, the two were blasted apart.

Cassidy slid several feet while Alec was thrown back. Crashing to the ground, he rolled a few times before finally coming to a halt. Lying with his eyes closed, he didn't move a muscle. The mark on his back continued to glow for another second before the light faded.

Slipping from Roderick's grip, Jade raced down the steps and to his side.

Hand pressing against the stone, Alec was trying to rise onto his elbows.

Kneeling behind him, Jade helped him roll onto his back and lay his head on her lap. "You should lie still," she urged smoothing a hand over his wet hair.

"Did I hurt anyone?" he questioned quietly in a rough voice.

Jade peered around before returning her gaze to his face. "Nothing serious. Try to rest, Alec."

"I didn't mean to—" he began giving his head a slight shake. "I'm sorry. I'm so sorry Jade," his voice trailed off as he blacked out.

Biting her lip, Jade gripped Alec's shirt. *How did this happen?* Things were starting to finally work out for them. Out of nowhere, it was falling apart faster than she could even process.

"It shall be alright, Alec. Somehow. Just stay with me," Jade whispered to him as Edmund, Roderick, Garth, Alandra, Zachary, Nathan and Eric strode to her side.

Towering over Jade, Cassidy released a long steamy breath. "Why is he sorry?" her deep feminine voice wondered. "The foolish humans are the ones who betrayed you. Oh Alec, you want too badly for these people to accept you when they never will." Glancing up, she scanned the people keeping a respectful distance. "Humph, it would seem the scarred warrior, Isabelle and this girl are the only ones truly loyal. I should have taken you to Ellfraya long ago."

Mouths gaping and eyes comically wide, just about everyone was staring at Cassidy.

Her eyes narrowed. "Why are these strange creatures watching me so?" she muttered.

"Cassidy?" Jade questioned, raising her gaze to look at the dragon above her. "Cassidy, I can understand you. We can *all* understand you."

Her head pulling back, the great dragon peered around once more. "I don't believe it. You really hear my words?"

Jade nodded. "Yes. How?"

"I don't know, but..." Cassidy's eyes shifted to Alec. It must have happened when he touched her. Was this part of his abilities?

Jade's gaze followed her line of sight. "Is he going to be alright?"

There was a moment of silence. "It's difficult to say."

"I shall send for my personal physicians," Alandra declared, kneeling down by Jade's side.

"It might be better to send for Malcolm," Zachary suggested thoughtfully.

"Why would a sage be better than a doctor?"

"Because Alec is no ordinary sorcerer, as you have seen," Cassidy answered instead.

"Yes we have," Jade agreed softly. "Pray Cassidy, what is going on?"

Studying the noble for a moment, Cassidy's yellow eyes shifted to Zachary. "Why don't you ask him?"

Blinking, Alandra and Jade peered at each other with a puzzled frown before looking at the royal.

"What is she talking about Uncle Zachary? Do you know something about Alec?"

Sighing, he gradually nodded his head. "Yes, I do. Alec's full name is Alakaid Titanus Stephan Evanlor. He's your elder brother."

The following silence seemed to drag on much longer than it actually lasted.

"W-what?" Alandra stammered with disbelief. "My brother's alive?"

It couldn't be true. She had to be hearing things. For as long as she could remember, Alandra had been filling her deceased sibling's shoes, living the life which should have been his as the next ruler of Malyndor. *Is he really alive?* The moment they met, Alandra felt a strange connection to Alec which surpassed explanation. Was it possible her heart knew all along?

"How did he survive all this time?" Edmund questioned more to himself. "There was a body. We all thought…"

"I have asked myself the same questions countless time since discovering the truth. The corpse was burned beyond recognition, so his kidnappers must have made a switch. No matter how, Alec is the son of King Titus. The dragon mark proves it."

"Not that you deserve him," Cassidy hissed with venom. "Our great Emperor and Empress grant you humans a powerful gift born of our magic and you treat him like dirt. Alec should never have remained in your care. You've failed to protect him countless times and I especially blame your bloodline," she declared glaring at the prince. "Your clan was responsible for allowing him to be lost to Zerrok in the first place. We were not so easily fooled by their tricks."

"That is not fair, Cassidy. King Titus and his family have spent most of Alec's life grieving for their lost child. Nothing could be worse than that. But I do not care if he is a prince or a soldier or a goat for that matter. What do you mean by a gift from the dragons?"

Eyes searching Jade's face, Cassidy took in the way she was still clinging to the sorcerer protectively. A smile threatened to pull at her lips. Not many would stand up to a dragon.

"This is not the place to speak of it," she began conscious of the many people listening closely. "I will tell you this: unlike normal wizards, Alec has magic in his blood. That's how he was able to call up that storm without casting a spell." Cassidy bent down so only Jade could catch her words. "It's dragon's magic. Alec is essentially a dragon in human form."

CHAPTER 11

A taut silence clung in the air about a small group of riders as they raced towards Stafford. The hooves of their steeds barely touched the ground as they appeared to fly down the dusty road. Word reached them by messenger hawk briefly detailing Alec's unleashed powers and his worsening condition.

Summoning Isabelle, who arrived at the East Circle a few hours prior, Malcolm and Kalvin immediately joined her on the journey to the tiered city. Heart pounding in his chest, the quickest horse didn't feel fast enough to the Cunning Sage as they zeroed in upon their destination. A brief pause at the main gate was all that stilled the wizards' mission. Weaving their way through the city, Malcolm clenched his teeth as he dodged carts and skidded through puddles of mud. The further up they ventured, the more drenched everything became.

What happened here?

Stopping at the castle gate, his frown deepened. For the first time in years, the portcullis was sealed tight in the daylight hours. Identifying their guests, the soldiers opened

158

the passage for the sages to enter. Quickly dismounting, Malcolm didn't bother to wait for the stable boy to take the reins before he rushed towards the castle doors.

Edmund stood there waiting for the sorcerers.

"Take me to him," Malcolm said solemnly, as Kalvin and Isabelle strode up the stairs on his tail.

"Of course," Edmund agreed easily with a nod. "I am relieved you were able to get here so quickly. To be honest, I am out of my depth, especially with the dragons."

"How many are here?"

"Two. The green one arrived during Lord Vincent's disgraceful incident. The second approached shortly before you appeared. Currently, they are waiting in the back of the gardens." Glancing at Malcolm, the serious expression on the duke's face didn't lessen. "Do you expect more to come?"

"Hard to say," the sage answered honestly as they reached Alec's room. Four guards stood in the corridor at attention. "It depends on what type of a surge he experienced. When he stabilizes we'll have him ask the dragons."

Head jerking back, Edmund stilled his steps. His brows furrowed.

Malcolm, Kalvin and Isabelle continued on into the chamber.

Alec lay pale against the sheets with his eyes closed. His breathing was shallow and raspy, and his body was covered with the sheen of sweat.

Talking in hushed tones, Prince Zachary and Duchess Leona sat off to the side in the suite's living room. On one side of the bed sat Jade. Holding a cloth, she dabbed Alec's brow. Her face had a strained, pinched look to it and the hint of dark circles was forming beneath her eyes. Opposite her was Alandra. Dozing in her chair, she held Alec's limp fingers, squeezing occasionally as if she was afraid he might disappear.

As their guests entered, Jade jumped, dropping the cloth she was holding while Alandra straightened somewhat and rubbed her eyes.

"Master Malcolm, you are here. What time is it? Has morning come?"

"No, Princess, only a few hours have passed," Edmund clarified for the wizard.

Malcolm and Kalvin took the ladies' places by the bed as Jade and Alandra moved back to offer the sages some space. Isabelle shadowed Kalvin, her steps dragging as she gazed at her friend.

Coughing, specks of red dotted Alec's mouth and chin. Moaning softly, he didn't stir.

"Oh, Alec," Isabelle whispered, wiping away the blood. *I wish I'd been here to help.* "What in the world happened?"

"Vincent occurred," Jade huffed darkly, gripping the sides of her dress. Head bowed, she didn't elaborate.

Placing a gentle hand on his daughter's shoulder, Edmund told them, "Alec was ambushed by Lord Vincent outside the city, where he forth with used him as a hostage to storm into the castle, claiming Alec was a traitor to Malyndor. I have never seen such a twisted mind. Delusional and obsessed with the notion that Alec performed dark magic to trick us all. He ripped the back of Alec's tunic open where he bears a unique mark."

Edmund's gaze traveled between Malcolm and Kalvin. After a moment, his frown darkened.

Neither sage questioned the mark as they continued to study the injured wizard.

"Was it then that his powers acted on their own?" Kalvin asked.

"Briefly, when Lord Vincent took hold of my daughter. Shortly after, the first dragon landed in the courtyard."

She must have sensed he was in danger, Malcolm thought. He recalled Alec speaking of the protective creature during his visit to Marcia.

"It was not until he came to the dragon's aid that things took a dire turn. Lord Vincent declared him a traitor once more, and to my shame, there were many who appeared to lean towards the noble's side. Alec..." his words trailed off.

Glancing at the sorcerer, he sighed, "I do believe it was their reaction—the reaction of those he has loyally fought beside, which served as more then he could bear. His powers..." Edmund shook his head, lifting his shoulders. "I have never seen anything to equal them. Malcolm, he summoned a fearsome storm without even trying. Bolts of lightning struck the earth, and this strange white light pulled from his body."

Both Kalvin and Malcolm froze.

"What did it look like?" the older sage questioned a tad too quickly.

"A dragon," Zachary answered coming to stand beside the bed. "It entered the green dragon when he touched it by mistake. An energy surged between them and threw them apart once it returned to his body. The entire time his mark was aglow. Afterwards, we could understand the creature's words. We can all speak to her, Malcolm."

The two sorcerers' eyes met across the bed. Muttering in Elan, they each ran a hand over Alec. Much like when Kalvin first tested Alec's aura, the two wizards studied his magical energy. The glow surrounding their hands was different than before. Instead of white, it was a golden orange, like wisps of fire.

"It is as we feared," Malcolm said lowering his hand. "The dragon's magic has fully awakened."

Zachary slowly ran his knuckles along his jaw line. "Had it not already manifested?"

The sage turned towards the prince as he spoke. "Not completely. Parts of his magic were still dormant as his abilities grew at a steady rate."

161

"Now his powers have surfaced too quickly, overwhelming his body," Kalvin supplied. "The sudden surge is far too much for a human."

"And it's killing him," the Cunning Sage finished.

"You knew about this," Edmund accused. Eyes narrowed, his gaze shifted between Zachary and the two wizards. "How long have the three of you known Alec was the Prince?"

Beside them, Isabelle's jaw dropped.

"Come now, Edmund," the headmaster began holding up his hands. "No one here was governed by ill intent. Alec's best interests were our sole motivation."

"He is right, my friend," Zachary added reasonably. "I only realized the truth prior to Alec's first mission, but I had to agree with Malcolm's insight. Exposing Alec as a royal too soon would have been unwise and may have left him with greater scars than those with which he is already burdened."

Lips pressed into a thin line, Edmund made no retort. Prince Zachary and Kalvin recognized the truth on their own. Malcolm most likely did so from the start. No wonder he insisted on training the warrior himself. Yet, for all his foresight and supposed intelligence, Edmund wasn't able to see what was right in front of him for all those months. *How could I have been such a fool?*

Giving her head a good shake, Isabelle blinked several times. "What do you mean by 'prince'? Alec is from Zerrok. Could someone please explain what manner of amusement this is, because I don't comprehend it?"

"It is no falsehood," Alandra said, coolly lifting her chin. "Alec is in fact my elder brother, Prince Alakaid."

"How...how is that possible? I thought the Prince perished."

"Indeed. We all believed it to be so."

"We can focus on Alec's miraculous survival another time," Malcolm interjected. "Saving his life is of greater importance."

"Agreed," Kalvin said rolling his shoulders. Releasing a long breath he stared at an invisible spot on the blanket. "To do so will be difficult."

"We need to harness some of his magical energy to give him a chance to heal," Malcolm muttered tapping a finger against his cheek.

"What are you thinking?"

"An old and possibly forgotten spell."

"Hmmm, but what would we use as a vessel? Dragon's magic is different than a normal wizard's aura."

"Perhaps a dragon?" Isabelle offered while everyone else frowned as they listened to the vague conversation. "You plan on employing a mana draining spell, correct? If my understanding of the enchantment is right, then some of Alec's power will be siphoned off and placed in another living creature. None of us would be able to handle his energy, but shouldn't the dragons be able to?"

The older sages peered at each other, a silent message seeming to pass between them.

"Very resourceful, Isabelle," Kalvin praised. "You have the makings of a great master."

"Indeed. You were wasted as Jerric's student," Malcolm remarked.

Clearing his throat, the headmaster pulled the conversation back to the issue at hand. "This is a risky spell, are you sure Malcolm?"

"It's our only option."

"Then we are agreed."

"Wait a moment," interrupted Zachary. "What is it you are seeking to do? I cannot allow you to put his life in any more danger."

"His life is already in danger," the Cunning Sage replied bluntly. "If we do nothing, then Alec stands no chance of surviving this. The dragons are our only hope."

"Then what are we waiting for?" Edmund questioned, stepping closer to the bed. "Leona, pray summon the guards to aid me," he instructed, gently sitting Alec up and draping an arm about his shoulders.

Striding forward, Zachary moved to Alec's other side and placed his nephew's arm over him. "There is no need. We should hurry."

With Alec hanging limply between them, the two nobles moved as quickly as they could down the corridor. One guard rushed ahead and by the time they reached the stairs, Kayla and Garth were waiting with a stretcher. The soldiers took over, swiftly carrying Alec out of the castle and across the gardens. Nearing the back of the lush, well-manicured space, their steps slowed to a tentative crawl.

Rising to their full heights, a magnificent green and a fiery red dragon watched those approaching intently.

"Ardys!" Isabelle squeaked racing to the dragon's side. Beaming, she reached out and patted his head as he lowered it to greet her. "By my word, what are you doing here?"

"You know this dragon?" Edmund questioned with raised brows.

"But of course. Alec and I met Ardys in Zerrok. He was the one to help us escape."

"How do you know his name?" Malcolm inquired watching her closely.

"Oh, well...I mean he...I guess we kind of made it up. We couldn't very well just call him 'Dragon', now could we?"

"Wait," Jade started thoughtfully. "How would you know he is a male? I mean Cassidy is female..."

"You knew," Malcolm concluded quietly. "You knew Alec could talk to dragons and kept his secret."

Isabelle's sudden silence was confirmation enough. It was so unlike her she might have had the words guilty written across her forehead.

"Your loyalty is impressive, for a human," Cassidy suddenly said drawing everyone's attention. Eyeing Alec lying on the stretcher, she got right to the point. "He's getting worse, isn't he?"

"Yes, he is," Malcolm answered with a nod. Standing in front of the dragons the wizard gazed at one then the other. "We need your help or I fear Alec will not live through the night."

A low rumble sounded from Ardys as he exchanged a glance with Cassidy. Her eyes narrowed.

"What can we do?" she asked carefully.

"The dragon's magic is exceeding Alec's ability to control it. His body needs time to heal and adapt to the sudden increase in power. In order for him to do so, we plan on removing some of his magical energy. Just enough for him to recover," the wizard added as he heard a distinct growl.

"Why seek us out?"

"The required spell is a transference. The energy has to go into another vessel and since it is dragon's magic—"

"You need a dragon to complete your spell," Cassidy finished for him glumly.

"Correct."

There were a few seconds of uneasy silence. Still standing beside Ardys, Isabelle's gaze darted between the mighty creatures. *Are they going to say no?* She knew the dragons didn't readily trust humans. Ardys went through years of torment just as Alec did. Who knew what sorrow befell the green dragon, but this wasn't the time to be dwelling on the acts of a few evil souls. Alec needed them.

"Pray Ardys, we really need you. Alec needs you. Everyone here truly cares for him. I understand you have no reason to trust humans, but you can believe me. Alec is my best friend. I kept his secrets, stood by him in the arena and I would never betray him. I beg of you, help us."

A stream of smoke expelled from the red dragon's nostrils. Bowing his head, he gave Cassidy a sideways look.

"Are you sure?" the green dragon received a low rumbled response. "Very well." Turning to gaze at the humans she nodded. "Tell us what we need to do."

"Thank you," Isabelle whispered rubbing the side of Ardys's neck.

Malcolm motioned for the soldiers to bring Alec closer. Laying the stretcher right in front of the dragons the men quickly backed away. Malcolm and Kalvin took positions on either side prior to addressing everyone present.

"Once we begin the spell no one is to touch Alec or the dragons until the enchantment is complete. You may feel strange," Kalvin added looking up at Cassidy and Ardys. "The extra magical energy will give you heightened senses and may have other side effects until it dissipates."

"We are going to need some space and privacy," Malcolm told the small group gathered at the back of the gardens. "Isabelle can remain here in case we need another sorcerer. For the moment, I ask everyone else to move back towards the garden."

Gazing at Alec, Jade gripped her hands together. *Do not make me leave,* her heart seemed to shout at her. Opening her mouth to protest, she felt someone loop an arm around her own.

Flashing Jade a brave smile, Alandra stood beside her. "Do not fret. The sages will have him recovering shortly. Let us give them the space they require."

Biting her lip, Jade could only manage a curt nod.

Edmund, Zachary and Garth, along with the present soldiers, set about blocking off the area and ordering the staff gathering by the edge of the space to return to their work. Trying to soothe Jade's sudden shaking, the princess, Leona and Kayla walked with her down a nearby path and away from the sight of the ritual.

Looking at Isabelle with a serious glint in his eyes, Malcolm told the younger sorcerer, "Not many sages, even among the masters, know of this spell."

Eyes widening, her gaze darted to Kalvin and back.

"You must understand," the Cunning Sage continued. "Taking another sorcerer's mana is dangerous. If this spell ever fell into the wrong hands, it could be a destructive force."

"I understand Master Malcolm."

"Good."

"We should proceed," the headmaster said.

Holding their hands above the injured sorcerer, the two master sages spoke in perfect unison.

"Surgeon."

A large white magic circle formed directly over Alec's chest.

"Sumonno virtus mana-alom. Rasolee er lumina sancdamor."

As they recited the enchantment in Elan, Alec's body was encased in a golden-orange light. Like a thick swirling storm of stardust, glowing specks rose up through the magic circle, lifting into the air as they gravitated towards the dragons. Continuing to climb, the light absorbed into the jewel on both Cassidy and Ardys's foreheads.

Holding their positions, Malcolm and Kalvin stood rigid for an intense few seconds before lessening the flow of energy. Once the last few sparkles seeped into the dragons, the glow surrounding Alec's body faded and the magic symbol dispelled.

"Do you think it was enough?" Kalvin questioned, his gaze traveling between the magnificent creatures beside them and the prince.

Exhaling sharply, Malcolm lifted his shoulders. "Time will tell us. We couldn't risk syphoning anymore of his power. Not when the magic is linked to his life force."

Suddenly, Cassidy dipped her head and lightly touched Alec on the shoulder. A faint gleam passed between them so quickly that the sage was almost convinced it was a trick of the light. A soft groan reached his ears. Sinking to his knees, Malcolm leaned over the stretcher.

"Alec? Can you hear me, my boy?"

Peering through thin slits, Alec gently shifted his head to look at the sage. "Malcolm?"

"You gave us quite the fright. How are you feeling?"

He released a soft bark of laughter. "Oh, wonderful," Alec told him sarcastically.

Malcolm's shoulders sagged. *If he's making such comments then the spell must have worked.*

"Cassidy? Ardys?" the warrior murmured glancing at the dragons towering over him. "What's going on? And what are you doing here, my friend?"

"You're beginning to sound like Isabelle," Kalvin teased. "I know you have questions, but perhaps now is not the best time," he advised as Jade rushed across the grass towards them.

Alandra and Zachary trailed behind. Their dark brown heads were bent towards each other as they spoke in heated, hushed tones. Shooting her uncle one final glare, the princess quickened her pace.

Managing to sit up, Alec was nearly knocked over as Jade dropped to her knees and flung her arms around his neck.

"Do not dare frighten me like that ever again," she whispered in his ear.

The one corner of his mouth pulled back. In reply, Alec looped his arm about her and squeezed back before they put some distance between them.

"I'm so glad you're alright!" Isabelle cried pouncing on him from behind. Alandra didn't bother waiting for the sorceress to finish hugging Alec prior to wrapping her arms around him as well.

Eyes wide, Alec peered at the men standing beside the stretcher. "Did I miss something?"

"You almost died," Isabelle informed him, releasing her tight hold.

"After all the time we've spent together, how is that new?" Scowling, Isabelle swatted him with her hand.

"You did have us quite worried," Alandra admitted, her gaze lowering to the ground.

Raking his fingers through his hair, Alec sighed. "Forgive me, Princess. I...I didn't hurt anyone did I?"

Zachary shook his head. "Fortunately no. The greater concern was for your well-being."

"Quite so. Luckily, Duke Stafford sent word to us at the East Circle when he dispatched a rider to Marcia."

Alec tried not to groan at the sorceress's words. Only bits and pieces of the event were surfacing, but it must have been dire for Edmund to summon Leos.

"No doubt my father will be on his way once he hears of this. I don't wish to trouble him."

Alec's eyes narrowed as he saw the tightness around Alandra's mouth. When their gazes connected, she looked away.

"You cannot blame him for being concerned," Jade soothed placing her hand over his. "He cares greatly for you."

The corners of Alec's eyes crinkled as he shifted his sight to the noble. A reply wasn't needed. Conscious of those lingering close by, Alec slowly rose to his feet.

"Why don't you try to get some rest?" Zachary suggested. "There shall be plenty of time to discuss everything later."

"His Highness is correct. Besides, you do look a bit pale as of yet, my boy," Malcolm agreed.

"Alright, alright," Alec grumbled half-heartedly. "Only as long as everyone quits behaving as if I rose from the dead."

"You pretty much did, 'Prince Pouty'," Isabelle mumbled, earning her a quizzical frown. Flashing Alec a too bright smile, she wrapped her arm around his and led him towards the back of the castle. "Shall we go inside? I'm famished."

Shaking his head, Alec glanced down at Jade who was closely guarding his other side.

Hands tightly clenched in front of her, she lifted her shoulders with a graceful shrug.

Saying nothing more, he allowed the small group to escort him back to his chambers.

Remaining with the dragons, Malcolm and Kalvin watched the others as they disappeared into the gardens. Eyes shifting between the sage next to him and the spot where Alec was last seen, the headmaster shook his head with a sigh. Rubbing the back of his neck, he looked at Malcolm once more.

"I do believe you've grown too fond of him, my friend."

The great sage frowned, turning to peer at the other man. "Oh? Am I supposed to dislike my students? Perhaps I should treat them as Jerric does?"

Lifting his hands, Kalvin slowly twisted his head from side to side. "That's not what I mean. Alec is a good man. You've taught him well, but I worry how you shall cope once the time comes for the prophecy to be fulfilled."

Malcolm's brows lowered. "What do you speak of? I have no intention of abandoning him during the event."

There was a long pause where Kalvin opened his mouth, then closed it again. "Malcolm…you know he's going to die."

Stiffening, his eyes grew wide for a split second. The sage's gaze then narrowed to slits. "What would ever possess you to say such a thing? Alec is not only my student; he is the Crown Prince of Malyndor!"

"As I well know," Kalvin returned reasonably. "This has nothing to do with his position or my personal feelings. This is about the prophecy. I'm certain you know the meaning of those words better than even I, Cunning Sage. Your fondness of him is blinding you."

"I am not the one in need of a better grasp on his perception," Malcolm said sternly. Turning on his heel, he stormed across the grass.

"'Once to its owner, the magic returns, a new light awakens, strongly it burns.' A *new* light awakens," Kalvin called, reciting words from the prophecy. "Not an old one changed or strengthened, but a *new* light."

Malcolm's steps slowed as the other sage spoke until at last he came to a complete halt.

"We both know what those words mean," the headmaster continued. "In order for something new to be born, the old must first be extinguished. It is a law of not only magic, but life itself."

Clenching his hands, Malcolm stood with his back to Kalvin. "I refuse to believe he was only born as a vessel meant to be sacrificed for the sake of magic...for the sake of peace. Hasn't he suffered enough already?"

"If there was another way I would gladly seek it, but his power...his life force are linked together. When his magic returns to the dragons, Alec's spirit will be gone as well."

"There must be another way," Malcolm insisted spinning around. "Magic is capable of great things and not even the future is written in stone. We could be misguided by this prophecy."

Kalvin glanced at the dragons. His eyes locked on Cassidy, silently asking for her help.

A wisp of smoke escaped her nostrils as she closed her eyes and exhaled. Lowering her head, the dragon quietly said, "I was not yet hatched when Emperor Draco and Empress Shiori blessed your ancient King with a small part of their own magic. However, the story is passed down to every youngling. That is how I knew Alec was the marked one after we first met," Cassidy's eyes darted over to Ardys. "During my last journey to Ellfraya, the ritual that Alec will perform, was mentioned. All I can tell you is both Emperor Draco and Empress Shiori expect their magic to be returned to them, and when that happens..."

Bowing her head, Cassidy wasn't able to finish the words.

"So, even the dragons believe this to be his fate."

Malcolm scowled at the other sorcerer. "It changes nothing. Fate has proven time and again to be a mysterious force. There is still much we don't understand. A thousand years ago, no one would have believed a human child could be born with the power of a dragon. I'm not giving up."

His words laced with determination, the wizard strode away from his friend and allies a second time. They might deem the prince's days to be numbered, but Malcolm knew magic itself could not always be bound to the rules man judged it to have.

CHAPTER 12

Stretched out on the cool tiles of the highest rooftop, Cassidy and Ardys suddenly stiffened. Dusk was upon them. Though bright fires lit the castle and surrounding battlements, they could not lessen the inky blackness of the star dotted sky. Nor could they reveal what was hidden out above the woods. Four dark dragons were heading straight for Stafford in a diamond formation.

"It appears they came after all," Ardys observed dryly.

"So, there were members of the Iron Scales Clan hiding in Malyndor," Cassidy growled.

"We must dispose of them quickly. We can't risk any of them reporting Alec's whereabouts to the rest of the clan."

"Agreed."

Slipping away from their post, Alec's guardians swiftly moved to intercept the enemy raiders. Aiming at the dark brown dragon on point, they simultaneously released bursts of flame. The dragon dodged, diving down, as Ardys and Cassidy clashed with the next two in line. Jaws snapping and talons slashing at each other, the dragons instantly engaged in a brutal fight.

Curling her back legs beneath her, Cassidy kicked off the black dragon's stomach, launching them apart. Just as she was about to reengage, their first enemy sped up from underneath, striking her right side. Roaring in pain Cassidy whirled, briefly losing sight of both of her opponents. They came at her in a joint attack, sending the green dragon plummeting into the trees.

While the ebony creature hovered above, the bronze one set his sights on Stafford.

Charging twin navy dragons, Ardys opened his mouth as his red jewel shimmered within. He amassed a large enhanced ball of fire. The heated mass pulsed brightly as he unleashed it upon his enemies.

Bursting on impact, the blast knocked the two foes away. They tumbled through the air fighting to regain control. Recovering, the dragons shook their heads with a deep growl as they charged towards Ardys once more.

Movements bolstered with his magic, Ardys darted between the dual attacks raining down upon him. His jaw clenched around one of their throats. Spinning in a circle, he released his adversary, striking the second dragon with his twin.

Eyes flashing, his opponents shot a joint fire attack straight for the red dragon.

Ardys met the blast head-on with his own blazing flames. Smoke tainted the air as the two powerful entities collided.

Flying out of the trees, Cassidy spotted the brown dragon speeding away. Roaring, she took off in his direction, momentarily forgetting about her other foe. The black creature struck her with great force, gripping her left wing.

Diving into a barrel roll, Cassidy shook him off, twisted in the air and pounced upon her enemy. Clawing at the dragon's wings, she clamped her jaws around the bone near his shoulder. Pressing with all her might she didn't stop until she felt it break. Turning around, Cassidy made to go after their last adversary. Yelping, she was jerked back as her injured opponent grabbed her tail.

Snorting, a long line of smoke expelled from her nose. Eyeing the forest, Cassidy dove down, taking her enemy with her. Launching herself into the trees, the jewel on her forehead glowed faintly.

Snaking their way up the trunks of trees and through the canopy, thick vines lashed out, striking the black dragon.

Snarling with surprise, he accidently released Cassidy's tail.

The foliage wrapped around his body, tightly squeezing him as the green earth dragon doubled back with her talons ready to strike.

Above her, Ardys was looping around his enemies. Whipping his tail, he smashed one of the navy creatures in the face, then shot another round of enhanced fire.

The dragon crashed to the ground.

Flying straight at Ardys, his second foe locked his talons with the larger red dragon's. Boiling flames lit the back of the dark dragon's throat as he aimed to strike Ardys square in the face.

Clamping his jaw around the other creature's muzzle, Ardys cut off the attack. Without disengaging, he took hold of the dragon's wings and sent them both diving to the hard, earthen floor. Releasing his foe at the last moment, he hovered in the air as the first twin rose to fight him.

Cassidy burst from the trees nearby. Pausing, she glanced at her comrade.

"Don't worry about me. Go after him!" Ardys commanded, eyeing the bronze dragon quickly nearing the castle.

Cassidy didn't argue. Beating her wings as fast as she could, the green dragon fought to catch up. The last enemy was far ahead of her. The muscles of her wings burned, but she couldn't seem to gain enough ground.

Zipping across the open field before Stafford's outer wall, the bronze dragon was still out of range of her flames. She wasn't going to be able to stop him from attacking the city.

Speeding out of nowhere, another black dragon zeroed in on their location. Suddenly, he collided with the brown, sending them both spinning in the air.

The green dragon watched as the two twisted about, clawing violently at each other. Ramming his skull into the other creature's face, the black dragon slashed his eye. Growling, the brown managed to shake his new enemy off, but not for long.

Biting into his foe's back leg, the ebony dragon flung the other one away from the castle.

"Well, what are you waiting for?" he snapped at Cassidy.

She hadn't realized that she'd paused her flight after the arrival of the fifth dragon. Racing forward, she struck the brown one with a blast of flames as the black dragon attacked from the other side. Teamed up, they made short work of their common enemy.

Carriage speeding down the nearly vacant dirt road, Queen Kalendra gripped her hands together on her lap as her armed escorts journeyed towards Stafford. The king was away at the West Circle when the message arrived from Duke Stafford. Marked as urgent, she read the scroll at once, fearing there was ill news of the dragons. The short sentence was nothing she could have imagined.

Mind instantly going blank, Kalendra reread the words at least five times before they seemed to take hold in her thoughts.

The bearer of the dragon mark is here.

That was all Edmund's rushed script said. It was more than enough. Departing at once, the queen made all haste to the eastern city.

He was alive. Somehow, her son was alive and the only thing she could focus on was reaching his side. The carriage bounced along as they traveled the climbing layers and came to a brief stop outside the portcullis. The Stafford Guard drew themselves stiffly to attention as the royal convoy appeared in the battered courtyard. Barely registering the destruction Malcolm was beginning to repair, Kalendra glided straight up to the sorcerer.

"Take me to him," she commanded.

The sage had no need to ask to whom. There was only one person she could be referring to.

"At once," he replied bowing. *I hope Alec is ready for this.*

Malcolm could not delay the truth any longer. Turning about, he entered the castle and led the queen towards Alec's chambers. Four guards were stationed outside. Hastily stepping to the side, they cleared a path. Malcolm went into the room with Kalendra on his heels. Coming to a halt, he peered around the space with a frown.

The bed was empty and neatly made. To the left, the sitting area was unoccupied with the doors to the balcony thrown open. Striding forward, Malcolm crossed the room and looked through the doorway. There was no one outside, nor was anyone in the dressing area or wash room.

"Where is he?" Kalendra questioned, her strained voice rising in pitch.

"I don't know," Malcolm admitted.

Eyes widening, her face paled. "How can you not know? Where is my son, Malcolm? Find him!"

"I assure you, Your Majesty, he's somewhere on the castle grounds. The dragons go where he goes."

The sage didn't think the queen's face could get any paler. At the mention of the dragons, her skin became a ghostly white. Pulling the bedroom doors open with a jerk, Malcolm scanned the face of each of the guards.

"When did he leave?"

The men's eyes darted between each other.

"His Highness has not left his room all morning, Master Malcolm," one of them answered.

I didn't think he departed this way. "I see. Thank you."

Quickly disappearing down the hall, Malcolm's mind compiled a short list of places Alec would go. The click of heels shortly caught up to him. Kalendra said nothing as they neared the landing of the servants' staircase leading towards Kayla's.

Garth appeared, descending the steps.

"Garth!" Malcolm called out, increasing his pace. "Did Alec by any chance come to pay you a call?"

Bowing to the queen, the warrior shook his head with a puzzled frown. "Not at all. I haven't seen Alec since I left his room early this morning."

"Alec?" Kalendra echoed.

Her eyes narrowed on the wizard beside her. Shoulders pulling back, the royal's gaze purposely traveled between the two men.

"Your protégé, Alec? The one His Majesty named the Dragon Sage?"

"That is correct, Your Majesty."

There was a pause. "Malcolm…you and I shall have a talk later."

"Of course, my Queen," he answered smoothly, already knowing something of the sort would be forth coming.

"First, I want him located with all haste."

Garth's brows lowered into a point. "Aren't there guards outside his room?" he questioned looking at the sage.

Malcolm nodded. "No one saw him leave."

"Then I imagine he's still close by. Did you try the roof?"

"The roof?" Kalendra repeated incredulously.

The warrior flashed her a humorless smile. "I mean no disrespect, Your Majesty, but when you've survived being imprisoned in a cage for as long as we were, you tend to dislike feeling trapped. No matter how fancy the chamber may be, when there are guards outside the door, you tend to resent it. Besides, Alec is one man who doesn't need a bodyguard. Trust me, he's on the roof."

Dropping into a bow, Garth walked off down the corridor.

Mouth slightly parting, Kalendra couldn't gather her scattered thoughts. There were few who would be so bold. In some ways, it was refreshing. Kalendra didn't know of this man, Garth. However, if she had to venture a guess, then she would say he was the other Stafford gladiator Alandra mentioned. A small grin touched her lips. Part of her liked this friend of her son's.

Spinning on her heel, the queen's long brown hair sailed behind her as she retraced her steps. Two of Alec's guards were still in the corridor, while the others were frantically searching his room.

Ignoring them, Kalendra glided out onto the balcony. About ten feet long, it was deep enough to hold a small table and two chairs to the right in front of one of the suite's windows. Walking to the left, Kalendra placed a hand on the rail and looked out over the castle. One of the building's wings stood adjacent to the balcony she was standing on. The roofline of the lower structure stretched out past the balcony, with the gradual curve of the roof's pitch flowing underneath her position. Kalendra's fingers tightened on the rail as she leaned forward and looked straight down. A section of the roof was only a few feet below her, making it relatively easy to access. Sure enough, further along the tiles, was a man stretched out in the sun beside a bright red dragon.

Sprawled out in the light like a cat, the large creature raised his head to gaze at the queen. His sharp green eyes studied her for a long moment.

Kalendra froze, locked in his sights. This was her first encounter with a dragon. In the background, she could make out a green one on the edge of the gardens. These must be her son's true guardians. Heart beating wildly, Kalendra couldn't utter a word. She didn't know what powers a dragon possessed, but it felt as if the majestic creature could see into her soul.

Finally shifting his gaze, Ardys looked down on the dozing sorcerer.

Alec had his hands tucked beneath his neck and his legs stretched out in the sunlight.

Ardys blew a long gentle breath of warm air on Alec's face. Groaning, the sage swatted at the disturbance. Chuckling softly in the back of his throat, the dragon did it again.

"Alright Ardys," Alec mumbled. Shifting, he yawned without opening his eyes.

Lowering his head the red dragon nudged the warrior, rolling him onto his side.

"Hey!" Eyelids flying open, Alec pushed himself into a sitting position. "I'm awake. I'm awake. Care to tell me what's so important?"

There was a deep rumble before Alec followed Ardys's gaze to the queen. One brow lifted as he said something to the dragon Kalendra couldn't hear.

Slowly getting to his feet, the sage climbed back up the roof. Everyone stepped back as Ardys assisted Alec up over the railing.

"Thank you," Kalendra's elegant voice flowed through the air. Praying her racing heart wouldn't give way to the uncertainty within, she continued to peer up at the dragon towering above the railing. "Thank you, I am in your debt."

Dipping his head, the dragon turned away to lie back on the roof.

Her voice sounds strangely familiar, Alec thought with a frown. It had to be from his time at the castle. There had been few moments he was ever in the same room as the queen and the sorcerer couldn't recall ever hearing her speak. *Why is the Queen even here?*

Chin raised and shoulders proudly back, Alec stood before the royal with his neutral mask carefully in place. He bowed stiffly before catching sight of Malcolm standing in the doorway. A small smile touched his lips, causing Kalendra to squeeze her fingers.

"How can I be of assistance, Your Majesty?"

Eyes locked upon Alec, Kalendra opened her mouth to speak, yet no words emerged. Tears building in her eyes, she had to press her lips firmly together to keep them from quivering.

Walking up beside her, Malcolm answered instead, "In truth, we came to speak with you about something fairly important." Stepping to the side, the sage motioned for his former student to follow him inside. "You may leave," Malcolm told the guards, dismissing them from the chamber.

The door clicked shut behind them.

A deep frown briefly marred Alec's face prior to him carefully concealing it. Taking a seat near Malcolm, he said nothing as Kalendra joined them. All others having departed, the great sage rested his arms against his legs while he interlaced his fingers.

"Alec, I'm sure you can recall the conversation we had in Marcia a short while ago." He watched the younger man nod. "This is not the way I wished to finish such a discussion. Yet, time is no longer with us. And…and you deserve to know the entire truth."

Alec stiffened, observing Malcolm intently. *So, it's time for me to discover the other secret of the prophecy.* Malcolm was being unusually serious. Alec glanced at the royal quietly sitting with them. Part of him wasn't sure he wanted to know after all.

"Do you remember the words of the first two lines of the prophecy? They go like this:

"Ancient dragons, their magic combine,
the blood of one throughout his line."

Malcolm let the words sink in for a second, prior to speaking again. "You do not have the dragon's mark by mere chance. The emperor and empress dragons chose who to give a piece of their magic to all those years ago. It has been passed down through the generations in your bloodline to you, Alec. Meaning, your ancestor was there that day during the gathering."

Alec's brows furrowed. Moisture started to build on his palms and he had to resist the urge to wipe it away.

"What are you saying?"

The great sage sighed, dropping his gaze for a second. Glancing at Kalendra, he continued, "Fate has not been kind to you, my boy. I believe it is because of that, you bear an extreme dislike of all nobility, but a few. It may have also kept you from seeing the truth about yourself."

"I don't understand."

"You were never born in Zerrok, nor is your family from that kingdom."

The warrior just stared at him, his lips parting soundlessly. A coldness swept through Alec's core. After a moment, he squeezed his eyes shut. A hand rubbed the upper half of his face as he gave his head a slight shake.

"That's not possible."

"We both know anything is possible," the sage quietly returned. "Come now, my boy. The few memories you have from your childhood, and what little Theron Kinsley was able to find, must have made you question your true origins."

No. No, no, no, no, no. The sage had to be mistaken. If his parents weren't slaves, then where were they? And why was he left to suffer practically a lifetime of torment? Was it because of the mark? Had they known, as Malcolm suggested, that someone in their family would be born with it?

"What are you saying Malcolm, that I was abandoned because I'm marked?"

"No, not abandoned. You were taken by an enemy of your parents out of pure spite."

"What enemy?"

"Baron Lager Hawkins, though we could never prove it."

Alec raked his fingers through his hair with a shaky jerk. "Why would the Baron want to kidnap a child? Unless..."

"He was the son of a noble," Malcolm finished for him.

Shaking his head, Alec rose to his feet and rounded the chair. A hand gripping the back of it, he refused to meet Malcolm's eye.

"You are the first born of a noble line, and not just any line. Your—"

"Enough," Alec declared cutting off the sage's words. "I don't believe it. There's no way I'm a blue blood. And...and even if it were possible, wouldn't my family have come for me?"

"Alakaid, pray, let us explain," Kalendra suddenly implored.

His entire body tensing, Alec turned to gaze upon the queen as if moving in slow-motion. The sound of his name coming from her lips was far too familiar. Somewhere in the depths of his memories, he could hear his mother.

'Alec, are you hiding on Mommy? Alakaid?'

It can't be...

His eyes narrowed sharply and his voice sounded quietly through the room with all the warmth of a deadly winter storm.

"How do you know that name? Few have heard me say it."

Kalendra refused to look away from his piercing gaze. Mouth going dry, she licked her lips. "There is no need for you, or anyone for that matter, to say it. I know the name Alakaid well, for it was I who gave it to you. I am your mother, Alec."

Alec's expression didn't change. Unable to speak, his body appeared frozen.

The queen squeezed her hands together. "You look so much like your father did at your age. You even have the same dark hair and brown eyes as your sisters. I was foolish not to see it earlier. We believed you to be dead, Alakaid. I never dreamed after all these years that I would be fortunate enough to see you alive," Kalendra's voice cracked, as she fought off a painful sob.

"Why are you saying this?" Alec demanded, his words raw and barely above a whisper.

"Because I speak the truth. You are my son, Alakaid."

"It's true. The dragon's magic was given to King Stephan, the first ruler of Malyndor," Malcolm confirmed.

Sights lowering to the floor, Alec raked his fingers through his hair several times. "What happened?"

Kalendra twisted her fingers on her lap. Somehow, she managed to keep her gaze steady.

"One evening, some men broke into our country estate with the help of a few traitorous soldiers and took you. The Royal Guard followed suit. There was a crash. Instead of surrendering, your kidnappers set fire to the carriage, ending both their lives and at the time, what we believed to be yours. When the sages were able to diminish the blaze, there was nothing left save for a charred frame."

"So that's it?" Alec questioned.

There was something missing from her story. Clearly, he hadn't been in the carriage. Didn't they do a more thorough search? If they believed the Baron was involved, then why hadn't he been punished? Suddenly, Alec could picture the twisted smile Baron Hawkins would wear so often when he saw him. This man tormented him for years, and Alec never understood the reason for it. It made so much sense now. The Baron wasn't merely enjoying striking some worthless slave. No, he was taking his vengeance out on his enemy's child. Which would mean Alec really was the son of Queen Kalendra. Alec's grip tightened on the chair. That would also make him not just a noble, but a prince of Malyndor.

So much for family, Alec thought bitterly. All those years he was trying to find them and save his family. Here, they ruled an entire kingdom, yet hadn't bothered to protect one small boy.

Do not trust her, whispered a woman's voice within his mind.

"You left me there," Alec said, his tone devoid of emotion. Face closed off, he glanced back at Kalendra.

Face paling, she rose to her feet. "No. You are mistaken. There were scorched remains. We believed you had perished. If there had been any chance of you being alive I would not have stopped until you were found."

"I *was* alive."

A strained silence rang through the air.

"He used to beat me for no reason. Imagine learning it was all due to that monster hating your parents."

Turning away, Alec started towards the door.

"Alec, you have every right to despise me, but pray don't turn your back on your family," Malcolm said coming to stand beside the warrior.

Alec sighed heavily. "I…I don't despise you, Malcolm. I know you only seek what's best for me, but this— I can't do this right now."

Hand grasping the door handle, Alec paused as Kalendra tried to cease his flight. "Pray Alakaid, we need to talk. Your father will be arriving once word reaches him that you are here."

Malcolm closed his eyes as Alec bristled.

"Leos is my father," the younger sorcerer coldly informed her as he peered at his mother from over his shoulder. "He called me his son even when I was nothing and took me as his family. I will not betray him. *We've* never even spoke before this day, Your Majesty. I'm sorry, but you said it yourself..." Alec opened the door, his words barely above a whisper. "Your son perished."

Taking a step outside, Alec was forced to a halt. With Kalendra's voice calling his name still echoing in the sudden silence, he looked down into Isabelle's flashing eyes. Arms crossed, she blocked his path as the soldiers posted in the corridor stood still as stone.

"Where are you going?" she demanded with a frown.

How much did she hear? Alec couldn't say. At the moment, he didn't have the patience for one of the sorceress's interrogations.

"Not now, Isabelle." Alec brushed past her.

"Coward," she snapped quietly.

Spinning around, Alec towered over her with narrowed eyes and a tense jaw. "Care to enlighten me?"

"You heard me," Isabelle returned. Curling her hands into fists, she ignored her pounding heart. *He won't harm me.* Taking a deep breath she refused to avert her gaze. "I said you're a coward."

"I'm not a coward," he just about growled.

"Normally I would agree. Why are you behaving like this? I've never known you to run from anything. As for your family, they are victims just as much as you. You shouldn't blame them for thinking you were dead. You're stronger than that."

"Wait, you knew?" That's right, she called him 'Prince Pouty' only a short time ago.

"No, I didn't. Not until everyone else did after your powers exploded," she denied, holding up her hands. "Come now, Alec. This isn't like you. I know you."

Though his expression revealed nothing, Isabelle could see an internal battle within the depths of his eyes.

Turning his head away, a tendon pressed against the skin on his neck.

"You don't know what I am, Isabelle. I don't even know anymore."

Jerking away, he disappeared down the hall without so much as a backward glance. His guards jogged after him, causing Alec to quicken his pace. Must they follow him about? Alec's nails dug into the palms of his hands. The mark on his back tingled. The sorcerer couldn't risk his powers threatening to overwhelm him again. It was possible he might actually harm someone.

"I don't require an escort," Alec stiffly informed the soldiers matching his hasty steps.

"I'm sorry, Your Highness. The Duke ordered us to protect you," a man cautiously answered.

"It's Alec."

Protect him? Alec was the one to train these men. Besides *he* wasn't the one who needed a guard. Couldn't they see he was struggling to keep his magic at bay? Descending the main staircase Alec headed straight for the castle's front door.

"Cassidy! Ardys!" he hollered without breaking his stride.

Gliding towards him, Ardys landed gently in the center of the courtyard. Aiding Alec onto his back, he stretched out his wings and rose into the air without a word.

Shouting for him to come back, the soldiers stood baffled as they watched their charge soar away towards the western forest. They couldn't really force him to stay when he had his own private dragons.

Back inside the sorcerer's chambers, Kalendra dropped down into the nearest chair. "That did not fare well," she stated, her eyes focused on the floor. "He despises me. For my own son to detest me so..."

Jay Lynn

"He doesn't despise you, Kalendra," Malcolm told her, placing a hand on her shoulder. "Alec needs some time to process this. It would be a lot for anyone to discover they're a prince after being raised as a slave."

"I suppose it was too much to hope he would be pleased by the news."

"Give him time. If there is one thing I do know, it is that Alec cares greatly for his mother. He's never ceased trying to find you."

A large shadow passing by the windows caught the sage's eye. Brows lowering, he walked toward the open balcony doors. Perched on the lower rooftop, Cassidy stretched her neck to peer inside the room.

"Greetings, wizard," she purred. Catching sight of Kalendra her gaze narrowed slightly. "I see your Queen decided to pay him a visit."

"Is Alec alright?" *Why is the dragon here? Shouldn't she be with Alec?*

"He's with Ardys," she informed him as if she knew his thoughts. "Fear not, we have no intention of leaving his side."

Malcolm nodded. "Good. He needs someone to talk to at the moment."

"Agreed. You've proven yourself to be quite protective of him, which is why I'm here. We dragons may not be able to answer all the questions he is bound to have."

Behind the wizard, Kalendra walked slowly to the doorway. "I should speak with him. His situation was His Majesty's and my doing. We should never have allowed our son to be stolen."

Cassidy glared at the queen. "No, not you," she snarled prior to shifting her eyes back to Malcolm. "Come, wizard."

Lowering her one front leg, she dipped her head so Malcolm could climb onto her back.

188

His upper body pulling back for a moment, he didn't move. *I never thought I'd see the day*... Directing his gaze to the queen, he bowed. "I shall pay you a call later, Your Majesty."

There was no point in trying to argue with the dragon. If Cassidy didn't want Kalendra to join them, then she wouldn't allow it. Getting on her bad side would not be to his benefit. Besides, Malcolm was happy to get another chance to clear the air. The dragon might be able to aid him.

Bracing himself against the increasing wind, Alec didn't bother to look where Ardys was heading. It didn't matter as long as it was away from the castle. After a short flight, he was surprised to see the red dragon had landed in the meadow behind Malcolm's cottage.

"Why did you bring me here?"

"To meet someone."

"Who?"

He only just left the sage so Alec knew the dwelling was empty. Not that he minded. He wasn't sure if he wanted to see anyone else at the moment. *You certainly were keeping a hell of a secret Malcolm.* Kicking a stone into the creek, the sorcerer crossed his arms and stared blankly at the flowing water. Had he really heard them right?

"It can't be true. They are mistaken," Alec muttered unhappily.

"Oh? Who would be mistaken?" questioned a deep gravelly voice from the forest.

Alec quickly twisted around, a fireball materializing in his palm. "Who said that?"

"Ready for another match are you, marked one?"

Behind the sorcerer Ardys smiled. "He's a friend."

Stepping out of the shadows a large black dragon with blazing red eyes appeared. Though shorter than Ardys, he was still a deadly and dangerous foe. Alec didn't lower his defenses as the creature drew closer. Instinctively, he knew this was the black dragon who challenged him at the village outside Marcia. Was he here to pick another fight?

"A serious one, aren't you?" the dragon observed with the hint of a grin. He made no move to attack.

"Now isn't the best time to be toying with him, Tatsu. The human queen finally realized who he is and paid Alec a visit."

"Hmm... So, how is your mother? I didn't expect her to arrive so quickly from Ariston."

Still poised for a fight, Alec's eyes tracked Tatsu's every move. "What do you know of her?"

The large black creature snorted a waft of smoke trailing from his nose. "You sound surprised. All dragons knew the marked one would be born into the royal family."

"Then our little battle was what—an act of boredom?"

Tatsu drew in closer with a gleam in his eyes. "Perhaps, I wanted to see if you had a true dragon's spirit."

The dragon pulled back, his gaze lifting.

A frown tugged at his lips as Alec twisted to follow Tatsu's line of sight. Cassidy just arrived and as she lowered her body to the ground, the warrior knew she wasn't alone.

Brushing the hair back from his face, Malcolm slid down beaming. "I must say what a ride!" he patted Cassidy's leg. "Thank you, my friend. What a ride indeed."

Lips parting, Alec strode over to them as his gaze darted between the two. He had to fight to keep a smirk from appearing. *At least one of us is enjoying ourselves.* "I didn't expect the two of you to be so well acquainted."

Malcolm's smile grew. "I dare say its proof of the good your power is already doing for Malyndor. Communication has always been key to any lasting alliance." Catching sight of the other visitor his brows rose. "I wasn't aware you already had company."

Glancing back, Alec peered at Tatsu. "Me either. Today seems to be full of surprises."

The three dragons moved to stand beside each other prior to sitting back on their hind legs. Positioned next to his teacher, Alec gazed at them in turn. *Why do I have the feeling this meeting wasn't an accident?*

"I know not what the three of you are up to, but would you at least care to tell me your name this time?"

"I am Tatsu."

"May I ask what brings you here, Tatsu?" Alec questioned, repeating the dragon's name for Malcolm's benefit.

"Now that your powers have fully awakened, I am here to protect you as one of your guardians."

The sorcerer's eyes shifted to Ardys and then Cassidy. "Wait, so this entire time you were merely sent to watch over me? What was all that talk about being friends?"

From what the black one said, they all knew he was a prince. More and more Alec seemed to be the only one left out of the loop. This wasn't just a secret Malcolm kept hidden; his whole life was a lie! Everything he'd been searching for was all for not.

"We are friends," Cassidy insisted. "Our meeting in the woods was not planned. This forest is my home and once I knew who you were, I had to prove myself in order to be granted the honor of being named your guardian."

"That's why you were gone when I left for Marcia," he said to himself.

Cassidy nodded. "I will not fail to protect you again."

"His capture was not your fault," Ardys insisted. "I was the one to lose him the first time."

"The first time?"

Ardys exhaled grimly. "I was charged with watching over you as a child."

Taken back, Alec's mind couldn't seem to process this information. If Ardys was originally his guardian, then he must have known Alec didn't die when he was taken. The dragon would have followed his kidnappers. Meaning, the reason he was imprisoned was probably because he tracked Alec to Zerrok.

"All those years you were imprisoned were because of me," the sorcerer whispered.

"I don't regret the past, as you shouldn't. The struggles we face are what make us strong. It is what makes us warriors," Ardys told him puffing out his chest. "A pampered prince could not do what you have done, Alec. He could never do what you will have to."

Alec frowned, his gaze dropping to the ground.

Malcolm's eyes switched between Alec and the dragons as they spoke. Only able to understand Alec's words, it wasn't easy for him to track the conversation. Good thing he was the Cunning Sage.

"Don't fret about what has been," the wise sage told the younger man, placing a hand on his shoulder. "The past can't be changed. The only thing we can do is move forward and learn from our experiences."

Slowly nodding his head, Alec sighed, lifting his shoulders. "So, does anyone know how I'm supposed to unite our races?"

"Always ready for the next battle. I like it," Tatsu said approvingly.

Cassidy glared at him.

"First, it would be wise for you to learn to control your awakened powers," Malcolm answered thoughtfully. "The enchantment on your necklace may shield you from detection, however, it can't hide larger surges."

The dragons exchanged knowing glances.

"What?" Alec questioned with a frown.

"The wizard is right," Cassidy told him. "When you use greater amounts of power, it's possible for other dragons to sense it. You need to be careful with exposing your location to the enemy."

Alec grew quiet. Her words struck a chord with him. There was something else she wasn't telling him, the sorcerer could sense it. Normally, Alec didn't use much magic during battle. Glancing at Ardys he recalled his return from Zerrok. Healing the red dragon was an exception. Then there was his loss of control in the courtyard.

"They're already here, aren't they?"

"Who?" Malcolm asked.

"The Iron Scales Clan. They're rebel dragons seeking to destroy the dragon emperor and empress. King Titus said there were reports of dragons fighting each other near our southwestern border. After that, a dozen or so entered Malyndor from Ellfraya. These dragons are looking for more of the enemy, aren't they?"

Cassidy dipped her head. "That's correct, little one. Humans aren't the only ones who seek the power of the marked one. Many believe if you were to perish, then the magic within you would disappear, weakening our rulers."

"We were sent as guardians to aid Cassidy in watching over you," Ardys added.

"Humph," Tatsu grunted. "It's a good thing I arrived when I did, or it might have been all for not."

"Wait, Stafford was attacked?" Alec questioned with furrowed brows, causing Malcolm to narrow his eyes as he listened intently.

"Yes, last night. We managed to keep them from reaching the city."

"What did he say?" the sage asked.

"Stafford was attacked last night, but they took care of the enemy before they reached the city."

"I see. What are the chances of more dragons arriving?"

Cassidy spoke this time so both sages could understand what they were saying. "We should be safe for now. Even with such a massive surge, the enemy would have to be within a few hundred miles to pinpoint Alec's exact location. If there were anyone else close by, then we would have already engaged them."

"That's good, I guess."

Snorting, Tatsu gazed over at the green dragon. "I know you like him Cassidy, but you're being too soft on this human. We should take him back to Ellfraya before the Iron Scales Clan finds him again."

She shook her head and stamped a foot on the ground. "No. Emperor Draco and Empress Shiori both agreed he could remain with his kind until the time is right. He deserves to enjoy his life in the time prior to when the ceremony can be completed."

"I thought the ceremony could be done at any time."

"Not quite," Cassidy told the wizard. "From what I was told, it can only be performed when the moon is in proper alignment and sinks closer to the earth."

Fingers cupping his chin Malcolm bobbed his head. "Of course. During times when the moon is closest, the spiritual nexus holds greater power. That would enhance Alec's power as well."

"Great," Alec said throwing his hands up in the air. "Even when I am ready, I'll have to wait on the moon."

Ardys tipped his head back to gaze at the sky. After a few seconds, he sadly looked back at the warrior. "You need not worry. It shall be arriving soon."

Alec repeated what the dragon had told him to Malcolm.

Jerking back, the sage's gaze darted among the three guardians. Peering at Alec, he pressed his lips together in a thin line. If what the dragon said was true, then there wasn't much time to find a way to save the boy. Malcolm wouldn't stand there and do nothing while another student of his died.

CHAPTER 13

Standing in front of the fireplace of his study, Jerric took a gulp of brandy. The strong liquor did little to ease his nerves. The hour was late, and his manor on the outskirts of Ariston was quiet. His mantle clock chimed midnight, causing the sage to jump unexpectedly. Cursing, he wiped the moisture from his expensive tunic.

"You're unusually jumpy," observed a voice from behind his desk.

Spinning about, Jerric glared at his visitor.

Hood still in place, a man sat with his feet propped up on the gleaming surface. Twirling a knife in his hand, he made no attempt to move.

"There's no need for the dramatics, Derek. We are quite alone here," Jerric informed him snidely.

The knife paused its movement. Jerric could feel a chill creeping across his skin. Perhaps he shouldn't have said anything, but his foul mood didn't allot him much patience for the younger man's games.

With a scoff, his guest slowly lowered the hood. Actually in his mid-twenties, the hazel eyed, blond haired man's slim build and short stature gave him the appearance of a lad of fourteen or so.

Jerric knew better than to lower his guard. The man before him was the best spy he'd ever encountered.

"I see you are as pleasant as ever," Derek said returning to playing with his weapon. "Tell me, why request my presence with such haste? Clearly, it wasn't because you desire my stimulating company."

Gripping his glass, the sage took another gulp. "I see you have yet to hear the news."

"And what would that be?"

"Baron Hawkins has betrayed us. Prince Alakaid lives."

Stiffening, Derek's eyes narrowed to slits. His feet immediately dropped to the floor. Leaning forward, he pressed the top of the blade into the desk's surface.

"Impossible."

"I wish it was so. My informant at the castle says otherwise. Queen Kalendra received word that the marked one was in Stafford. King Titus will be joining them shortly." Pouring himself another drink, Jerric swirled the dark liquid around.

"How is this possible? I was told there was a body as proof of the prince's death."

Jerric nodded. "There was. I remember it well. However, upon further investigation, it would seem Lager made a switch and chose to take the boy back with him to Zerrok."

Derek's frown deepened.

The sage smiled grimly. "That's right. A powerful sorcerer, once a slave from Zerrok, returns to Malyndor only to be a continuous thorn in my side."

Watching Jerric take a long drink, Derek shook his head.

"Alec is the prince?" Rising to his feet he yanked the blade free. "This is a problem. No wonder that fool Vincent wasn't able to dispose of him. He's no match for the marked one."

A finger tapping his lips, the man stared thoughtfully at the floor. This matter could not be ignored. Now more than ever, Alec had to be disposed of. His magic was too dangerous to be left alone. Even without revealing his true identity, he upset several of The Pure's plans.

"How do you propose to deal with this pest?" Derek questioned, turning his attention back to the sage.

Jerric released a bark of laughter. "Me? You're the assassin. Alec already distrusts me. I doubt I would be able to get close. Besides, he is too well guarded in Stafford." Crossing his arms, he gazed at the dancing flames. "Facing him head on isn't an option. I've seen what that vile barbarian can do. Somehow, he must be lured to a place of our choosing where he cannot escape. A place far from the aid of others."

"I know the perfect location in Zerrok."

"Zerrok?" Jerric blinked. "Impossible. After being imprisoned twice, he will never be tempted to return there."

A smirk appeared on the man's face as an evil glint sparkled in his eye.

"Everyone has a weakness Jerric and I know just the pawn to help us exploit his."

"Oh?" the wizard inquired raising his brows. "Do tell."

Following a trail into the patch of woods behind Stafford Castle, Alec breathed a sigh of relief. Ardys blocked the way, keeping his permanent shadows from continuing to trace his every step. No one would be watching them here.

Alec drew to a stop beside his friend. "This should be far enough."

The warrior had reluctantly agreed to stay within the castle grounds until Tatsu returned from his patrol. It was time for him to begin 'dragon training' as Malcolm liked to call it. Settling himself on the ground, Alec closed his eyes as he listened to the sound of Cassidy's voice.

"Your magic is part of your life force," she told him, lowering her body to the forest floor as well. "Don't fight the power you feel rising inside you. Embrace it. Only then will you be able to fully control the spirit inside."

"I still find it strange that I will be able to summon my own spirit."

Cassidy chuckled. "Yes, I suppose it is."

Inhaling deeply, Alec let it out in a long slow breath. The world around him gradually fell away as his focus moved inward. The mark tingled lightly. Shifting, the sorcerer tried not to dwell on the strange sensation. Instead, he concentrated on a warmth in the center of his chest. The dragon mark began to glow, faintly shining through the thin material of his shirt.

Small bright orbs of light pulled from his body as if attached to a string. Soon, it grew thicker, flowing from him as it condensed into a more solid form. Something intangible told Alec to open his eyes. Hovering directly in front of him was a transparent white dragon around his size. His spirit seemed to watch him as intently as Alec was studying it. Leaning to the left, the dragon moved left also. Straightening, Alec watched it copy his movements. Bending in the other direction, the dragon shadowed the sorcerer once again.

"Wow," he whispered.

As soon as Alec even began to form the thought of pulling his spirit back to his body, the dragon returned. Exhaling with a shaky breath, the sorcerer wiped his dampening brow.

"Is that your new trick?" questioned a cheery voice standing off to the side.

Tilting his head back, Alec glanced over his shoulder at his visitor. A smirk threatened to appear at the right corner of his mouth.

"It's nothing I can teach you, I'm afraid."

The blonde sorceress shrugged. "I don't mind. I've been working on a creature summoning of my own."

Alec laughed. She never did give up. "You are a talented sage, Isabelle. What brings you here?"

"I wanted to see how you were faring. I hear His Majesty will be arriving by tomorrow."

Scowling, Alec faced forward. Quickly getting to his feet he brushed off his clothes without peering at her.

"Alec?" Brows furrowing, Isabelle watched as his invisible barriers seemed to lock in place. *Hmm...I guess he's still adjusting to that.* "I ran into your father inside the castle. We might want to avoid dangerous situations for the time being. Lord Kegan hides it well, but I could tell he is quite worried about you. Perhaps a vacation is in order?" she teased, coming to stand beside him.

"Name the place and I will gladly aid you in an escape."

Giggling, Isabelle glanced at the green dragon by Alec's side.

"How are you, Cassidy?"

"Fine." Stretching, she rose up to her full height. "You did well, Alec. Why don't you take a break? This afternoon we will engage in something more...trying," she said with a grin.

I bet I know what she has in mind. Alec wouldn't complain if he was right. He could use a more stimulating activity. Lounging about the castle was driving him mad. With Isabelle chatting away at his side, Alec left the woods and started making his way across the clearing towards the gardens at the back of the castle. There was no way to avoid the twisting paths. A straight walkway to the front courtyard didn't exist. Out of the corner of his eye, Alec could spy his assigned guards fall in line behind him. Cassidy and Ardys remained in the clearing.

Quickening his pace, Alec smoothly traveled through the ornate gardens. By now, he was fairly familiar with the overall layout. Gripping the crook of Isabelle's arm, he dashed forward, briefly leaving the soldiers' line of sight. Darting behind a shrub, the sorcerer cupped a hand over his friend's mouth to silence her startled cry as he cast a spell to shadow their forms.

Rushing down the path, the soldiers frantically gazed around, searching for their charge before splitting up to set off in different directions.

Waiting a few heart-pounding seconds, Alec loosened his grip, freeing Isabelle. Sitting on the ground she let out a bark of laughter.

"You nearly gave me a heart attack."

"Sorry. I saw an opportunity to ditch them."

"I don't blame you."

Holding out his hand, Alec helped the sorceress to her feet.

"Why anyone would think you need bodyguards is beyond my understanding," she laughed.

He shrugged as they started walking again. Turning a corner, Alec bumped into another person.

"Sorry," Alec apologized, lightly gripping Jade's upper arms to steady her as she let out a small shriek.

"Oh, forgive me," she said at the same time.

Peering down into Jade's eyes the sorcerer's fingers lingered for a moment prior to stepping back. He could recall her elation when he first woke up, but was that only because he almost perished? Some people were avoiding him. After everything which occurred, he couldn't blame her for staying away. A few steps behind her, Ariel wouldn't meet his eye.

Alec bit back a curse. For a second, he had fooled himself into believing his powers might be a good thing. They were truly an affliction.

"Excuse me, milady," Alec muttered. Bowing, he made to continue on his way. "Hi Ariel."

"Are you not going to offer to join me?" Jade questioned, a tad too quickly. *There is no need for you to sound desperate,* she mentally scolded.

Pausing, Alec's expression told her nothing. "You wouldn't mind my company?"

Beside him, Isabelle rolled her eyes and shook her head. "Ariel, is it? Pleasure to meet you, I'm Isabelle. You know I could use a tour guide. I get so lost in these gardens." Winking at Alec, she looped her arm through the other woman's. "Oh, what a beautiful fountain. Shall we take a look?"

Giving the maid no opportunity to protest, the sorceress proceeded to drag Ariel back up the path.

Giggling, Jade watched the two women slowly walk in the direction from which she came. Gliding to the warrior's side, she took Isabelle's place. A smile softly touched her lips. "Of course, Alakaid," Jade told him, her cheeks warming. "I would be much pleased to have your company."

The one side of his mouth pulled back. Strolling after Jade's chaperone and the sage, neither spoke for a moment.

"I am sorry about the bodyguards," Jade said twisting her fingers. "I saw them earlier. My father would hear nothing of their removal." She glanced behind them. "Are they waiting at the entrance?"

Alec shrugged. "Not sure. Isabelle and I gave them the slip."

"Alec!" Jade scolded, her eyes widening.

A mischievous smirk faintly appeared with a matching gleam in his eyes. "What? Ardys helped me escape from them earlier.

Her mouth gaped. "You—you do not mean…?"

"That I flew off? Of course not," he chuckled.

Fighting a smile, Jade shook her head. "It is no wonder they scarcely allow you out of their sight. They very well may have to chain someone to your side."

"Depending on whom, I might not be opposed to the idea."

A deep crimson color brightened Jade's cheeks. Peering around, Alec reached out and interlaced his fingers with hers.

A comfortable silence surrounded them as they continued their leisurely stroll.

"I heard Her Majesty came to see you yesterday morning. It must have been quite the surprise," Jade finally said.

Alec's steps came to a halt.

"Alakaid?"

He didn't answer.

"Forgive me. I should not have brought it up."

The sorcerer gently squeezed her fingers. "Don't worry about it," he flashed her an on, then off again smile.

"It must be difficult to believe. I am not certain I can believe it. To think, you are the prince. You have finally found your family."

Alec scoffed, shaking his head. How ironic. As soon as he was moving on and accepting that he would never find his mother, she suddenly appears. Alec made his own little family. He had Leos, Malcolm, Garth, Isabelle, Cassidy and his Jade. What more could he ask for? None of it seemed real. The complications of royalty made it more difficult. Part of him wanted to move forward and give them a chance, yet another part of him was still weighted down by bitter emotions.

"I don't know, Jade," he admitted quietly. "Even when I'm ready to forgive them, I don't fit in with their world. I can't behave like a prince."

"Just be true to yourself. Look how well you have adjusted to the role of a lord. Is it not but a title? No matter what course you seek, I shall always be by your side."

This time Jade squeezed his fingers.

With hooded eyes, Alec peered down at her. Nothing he could think of saying seemed right to convey what he was feeling. She kept him grounded. Jade was his light. Alec leaned down, giving Jade plenty of time to step back.

She didn't.

His lips pressed lightly against hers as his hands slid up the outside of her arms. Moving closer, Jade rested her palms on his chest. With a groan, Alec passionately increased the pressure. Everything else fell away surrounding them.

"Hey, Alec," Isabelle called. "Aren't we supposed to meet up with Garth soon?"

Pulling away, Alec tried not to laugh. *I almost let myself get carried away there.*

"Yeah, Isabelle," he replied.

A grin on his face, he looked down at Jade with shimmering eyes. The glow to her cheeks made him speechless. *She looks radiant.* Holding out his arm, Alec managed to salvage his thoughts.

"Shall we, Lady Jade?"

Her silky brown head dipped with a nod. Tucking her hand in the crook of his arm, she happily allowed Alec to escort her the remainder of the way up the path to meet Ariel and Isabelle at the fountain. Together, the four of them headed to the castle.

Exiting the gardens, Alec stiffened as he heard a voice call his name.

Relaxing on the patio with a cup of tea was none other than the queen. Kalendra smiled, rising to her feet as Alandra started walking towards them.

"Lady Jade, this is such a pleasure," she declared giving the noble woman a quick hug. "Alec, how are you fairing? I cannot believe you are my true brother! This means Jade and I shall be sisters in the near future."

"Your Highness!" Jade scolded, glaring at her friend.

Isabelle didn't think either of the couple's faces could turn any more red. Unable to say anything at first, she burst out laughing.

"Alec, if you could see your face right now."

Alandra beamed. "Isabelle, I presume. I regret not being able to make your acquaintance properly. It is a pleasure. I have heard so much about you."

"Thank you, Your Highness," the sorceress bowed. "Alec has spoken of you as well. It is an honor."

Alandra waved her words off. "There is no need for such formalities. We are all friends and family here. Pray, call me Alandra. From what I hear, you have done much for my brother. I am pleased he has such a loyal comrade."

"I agree. You have my gratitude as well."

All eyes focused in Kalendra's direction as she glided towards them.

"Good morning, Lady Jade." Pausing, the queen offered Alec a gentle smile. "Greetings Alakaid, how are you faring?"

Arm dropping to his side, Alec watched her quietly. His expression an unreadable mask, he slowly bowed. "Hello…Mother." The seconds ticked by without him adding anything further. *What am I supposed to say? All these years and my mind's gone blank.* Palms becoming slick, the warrior tapped his fingers against his leg.

A frown marring her face, Isabelle pushed against his arm. "Hey Alec, Her Majesty just asked you a question. Aren't you going to answer her?"

Wide-eyed, the three women surrounding him stared at the sorceress. Alec, on the other hand exhaled with a short chuckle. *That was just what I needed.*

"Of course," he began raking his fingers through his hair. "Forgive me. I'm doing well. How are you?"

"Quite well, thank you." Kalendra smiled.

His spunky friend was not what she expected. Kalendra didn't care for how close she was standing to Alec's side. The sorceress was practically on top of him. She appeared to have far too much influence over her son for her liking. Even more displeasing was Jade's lack of distress. How was this girl able to get so near her son when, as his mother, she could hardly get him to say a word? This friendship was most improper. She was going to have to keep a close eye on her.

"It's getting late, we best be on our way," Isabelle said glancing in the other direction.

Alec's gaze connected briefly with Jade's. Her racing heart refused to obey her as she fought the urge to reach out for him. Beaming, Jade curtsied. "Thank you for your escort, Prince Alakaid. I look forward to when we shall meet again."

A smirk touched his lips. "It was my pleasure, Lady Jade."

Chests heaving, Alec's guards appeared, blocking his escape to the courtyard. Frowns marred their faces and a soldier crossed his arms as they watched the warrior with narrowed eyes.

"With all due respect, Your Highness, you cannot keep evading us. It's our duty to protect you."

Spine stiff, Alec clenched his jaw, refusing to respond. There was no point; his orders would fall on deaf ears. These men were instructed to follow the duke's orders no matter how much he might object.

"You may stand down," Kalendra told the soldiers after studying Alec for several seconds.

Blinking, her son's gaze snapped in her direction.

"Your Majesty, our orders from Duke Stafford—" a soldier stammered.

"Your *Queen* is commanding you now," Kalendra informed him, cutting the man off. "My son is no longer in need of an escort. You may return to your regular duties."

Raising her brows, Kalendra tilted her head slightly to the side, as if daring them to defy her.

Unable to form any further protest, the guards bowed deeply and departed.

A faint smile appeared on Alec's face. "Thank you, Mother," he said dipping his head.

"Shall we see you tonight for dinner?" she questioned, brightening.

Hesitating briefly, Alec finally nodded. "Can Isabelle come?"

Lifting her hands, the sorceress shook her golden head. "Oh, that's not—"

"But of course," Kalendra smoothly insisted with no real feeling. "You must join us Miss Peterson."

"Thank you, Your Majesty," she replied cautiously. *She hates me.* Flashing the queen a strained smile, Isabelle tugged on Alec's sleeve. "We shouldn't keep Garth waiting."

"You're right. Until tonight," Alec said. Leaning to the side he gave Ariel a little wave.

She offered him a small smile in return.

"I shall look forward to seeing you...and you as well, Izzy," Jade added with a grin.

"Izzy?" the sorceress echoed scrunching up her face. Eyes sparkling, she suddenly darted forward and enclosed the noble in an embrace. "I love it! No one's ever given me a nickname before."

"May I call you Izzy as well?" Alandra questioned.

"Certainly, Princess."

Covering his face with his hand Alec's shoulders shook as he laughed.

"Come on," Alec ordered kindly, pulling Isabelle after him for a second.

Bouncing along, Isabelle followed easily. Almost immediately, she was chattering happily as they disappeared from sight.

Glancing at each other, Alandra and Jade giggled.

A frown marred Kalendra's face as she gazed at the women. "I am glad you find your competition so amusing," she quipped.

Silence fell instantly. The two nobles exchanged telling looks.

"You are mistaken, Mother. Isabelle is not Jade's competition."

"Quite so," Jade added. "She is Alec's friend and I desire for her to be mine too."

Kalendra scoffed. "Has your position taught you nothing? Royalty and nobility cannot be acquainted with commoners. They will only seek to use you for their own gain. That girl is far too close for either of you to dismiss it so easily. There is no telling what damage she might inflict. Alakaid is a prince of Malyndor. Their acquaintance must be severed."

Jade could not believe what she was hearing. Beside her, both Alandra and Ariel were gaping. Isabelle a threat? Never. Jade might have been jealous of her at first, but meeting the sage and knowing some of what Isabelle endured to help protect Alec, kept the noble from being foolishly blinded. Jade would allow no one to hurt Alec or the few people who earned his trust. The overwhelming need to shield the one she loved caused words to spill from Jade's lips. Without her even realizing, she voiced them out loud.

"You are wrong."

Kalendra's head jerked back.

I have to protect Alec. Isabelle doesn't deserve this. Jade forced herself to continue before she lost her nerve. "Being a prince does not change who Alec is, nor should it change who he has chosen as his friends. Born to nobility, I know what it is like to be burdened with so few I can trust, like Alandra and Ariel. Nothing could prevail me to sever our bond. How can you ask Alec to rid himself of such a valued friendship? Isabelle fought beside him when Alec believed he was nothing. Imagine the value of her loyalty now that he is a prince. She is *family* to him. I would hope Your Majesty would understand how important that is."

Tears threatened to roll down Jade's cheeks. Chin held high, she gripped the skirt of her dress without looking away.

The queen's mouth moved wordlessly.

Alandra glanced at Ariel, who nodded. Each lightly placing a hand on Jade's arms, they quickly urged her to go inside, leaving Kalendra still standing on the patio with all the lingering tension of a coming thunderstorm.

With news of the long anticipated arrival of King Titus, the duke's study soon became a central hive of activity. Recently joining them from his own journey, Leos waited with Edmund, Zachary, Kalendra and Alandra.

The heavy thump of his footsteps sounded in the corridor right before the door swung open. Titus appeared to fill the space as he entered the chamber. His steel grey hair was brushed back and his dark hazel eyes scanned the room beneath bushy brows which seemed to increase the scowl dominating his expression.

"What is this nonsense you dare to send me?" he questioned. Looking about the space, his expression didn't soften. "Do not tell me you have all been taken in by this imposter. Kalendra, our son perished. As much as we might wish it so, he is not returning to us."

Getting to her feet the queen moved towards his side. "Titus, I know it is difficult to believe. I did not at first, but it is true." Glancing behind him, her brows lowered. "Where is Alicia?"

"In Ariston where she belongs," he stated sternly. "I do not wish to expose her to the ill will of this imposter."

"He bares the dragon mark, Titus," Edmund told him standing beside Zachary.

"I saw it as well." Holding his brother's gaze Zachary refused to look away.

Exhaling with a hiss, Titus threw up his hands. Shaking his head, he said nothing for a moment. "It must be a hoax."

The door opened once more as Malcolm entered the study followed by Isabelle. Upon seeing the queen, the sorceress had to fight the urge not to squirm under her gaze. Relations with the royal were not improving. For the most part, Kalendra saw fit to ignore her and Isabelle knew not what was causing the icy reception. Instead, she traveled over towards Alandra.

"Hi, Alandra," she whispered.

"Greetings, Izzy," Alandra returned quietly.

All eyes were still on the king.

"Malcolm, there you are. Pray, tell everyone this foolishness is not to be borne."

Stepping further into the space, Malcolm peered at the group calmly. He'd expected Titus to be much more skeptical upon receiving the news than Kalendra. Such a discovery was difficult for all of them to take at first. The sage hoped to quell some of the royal's misgivings prior to him seeing Alec. Otherwise, Titus may well damage the fragile relationship Alec was rebuilding with his family. Or even sever it all together.

"Oh? What foolishness would that be?"

"It would appear there are those who fantasize seeing my son, alive and in Stafford no less."

"I will gladly be of service, my King. Prince Alakaid *is* alive and in Stafford."

Tossing his hands up again, Titus scoffed, "Who is this fraud, this scoundrel, who has so many under his sway? Pray, summon him so that I may—"

"For heaven's sake, Titus," Zachary snapped, "It is Alec, your precious Dragon Sage."

Jaw going slack, the king stared at him. Then, his eyes widened comically. *It cannot be true.* Though brief, he spoke to Alec several times. The sorcerer was in his study for a meeting only a few days ago. His powers were impressive, but he never thought… Glancing at Alandra, an image of Alec standing with his daughters came to mind. It had been right in front of him. Zachary once called him blind. Titus felt deceived. Alakaid—Alec was Malcolm's apprentice this entire time. By George, what was going on? Twisting around, he zeroed in on the master sage.

"Malcolm! What in blue blazes were you thinking? Are you telling me he has been right under my nose and you said not a word?"

"There was a certain amount of secrecy needed for Alec's sake. Not to mention the task of earning his trust. Had I informed him of his heritage right away, he would have rejected it immediately and possibly disappeared altogether." Shifting his attention to the other sage, he asked, "Isabelle, where is Alec?"

Swallowing hard, Isabelle tried not to focus on the nobles suddenly watching her. Keeping her eyes on Malcolm she said, "He's training with Cassidy and Ardys by your cottage, Master Malcolm."

"Who?" Titus wondered.

"They are dragons, dear," Kalendra enlightened.

"Dragons, pff." Standing beside his wife he crossed his arms. "They seem to be the source of many issues as of late."

Brushing back some stray hair with a jerky hand, Isabelle tried to ignore the churning in the pit of her stomach.

"If I may, Your Majesty, we did discover why so many of their kind have traveled to Malyndor."

"Is that so?" Lips pressed into a thin line, he let out a sharp breath through his nose. "Do tell us."

"Well…um…there are basically two separate dragon clans. The dragons from Ellfraya, who want to live in peace with humans and rebel dragons called the Iron Scales Clan, who seek to rule everything. The fight at our border was between them. They see Alec's power as a threat. According to Cassidy, the Iron Scales Clan believes if Alec perishes before his magic is passed on to the ruling dragons, it will weaken them, allowing the Iron Scales Clan to wipe out their rivals."

"Wait," Titus interrupted. "Are you saying an entire clan of dragons is hunting my son?"

"Titus, we have to stop this," Kalendra pleaded gripping his hand.

"No one is going to harm Alec. That's why the dragons are here, to protect him."

"So say you," the queen returned coldly. "I do believe we are best qualified to decide what is best for our son. Thank you for your insight, but your presence is no longer required."

Isabelle's upper body pulled back. Gaze dropping to the ground, she mumbled, "Yes, Your Majesty."

Lips parting, Alandra's eyes followed the sorceress as she quietly departed. The frown on Malcolm, Zachary and Edmund's faces didn't lessen her displeasure.

Titus raised his brows.

"I hope you are pleased with yourself, Mother."

"Not you as well, Alandra," she said stiffening.

First, Jade had employed that disgraceful display by the gardens, now her own daughter appeared ready to defend Isabelle.

"Edmund, Zachary, could you please give us a moment?" Malcolm requested, watching the strained look on Kalendra's face. "Princess?" he added as an afterthought.

Pride was an obstacle when dealing with nobility. He doubted the queen would willingly listen to anything he was about to say if there was an audience present. Thankfully, everyone left without further prompting.

Moving to stand before Kalendra, the sage sighed. "As your friend and counsel Kalendra, I must tell you that what you are doing to Isabelle is unwise."

Pushing herself to her feet, she crossed her arms and stepped closer to the windows. "She is just a commoner, Malcolm."

"We both know that has nothing to do with your treatment of her. Station has never prevented you from showing kindness in the past."

"I admit, you did seem unusually harsh, my dear," Titus said thoughtfully. "If she has done anything to offend you, I will see to it that she is properly punished."

Malcolm shook his head. "Isabelle isn't the problem."

Kalendra spun around, her arms flying apart. "How can you say such a thing? You must have noticed the way she is practically sewn to his side. My son barely utters a word without her encouragement. If that is not a problem, then do enlighten me on what is."

"Would it not serve you better to befriend her rather than push her aside?" the sage questioned, ignoring her outburst.

Tilting his head to the side, Titus narrowed his eyes. "Kalendra, are you trying to suggest *Isabelle* is a poor acquaintance of Alec's?" The royal knew of the sorceress and couldn't imagine the one he rightfully named the Just Sage as being such.

Silence.

Rubbing his chin, Malcolm exhaled. "If I may be so bold," he began, having every intent of saying what was on his mind, whether she wanted to hear it or not. "Denying Alec his friendship with Isabelle will not hasten his bond with you. Who would you remove from his company next? Garth? Lady Jade? Even Alandra perhaps?"

"There is no need to be so dramatic," Kalendra scoffed, lowering herself gracefully into a chair. Still, the tremor in her hands could not be missed.

"Malcolm has never been known for dramatics, my dear," Titus interjected reasonably. *I cannot blame her for fearing losing him again.* "My time with him has taught me that Alec is a man of few words. You must be patient. Rekindling our bond with him should not be done with haste."

"What bond?" Kalendra asked in a strained voice. "Titus, he does not even remember us."

"That doesn't mean he has no desire to, Kalendra," Malcolm informed her. "I know Alec better than most. He wants to know the family he was taken from. But pray, make no mistake, that doesn't mean he desires to part with the family he has found since coming to Malyndor."

A few seconds ticked by prior to the sorcerer continuing. "There are some things you should know about that young woman. She knew, long before the rest of us, that Alec could speak with dragons and use magic without spells, yet told no one. Alec also informed me *she* was the one who helped him during the darkest time of their imprisonment. Without Isabelle, he wouldn't have survived."

Kalendra's head jerked up at those words.

Malcolm nodded. He glanced at Titus, then back at the queen. "In my experience, Alec doesn't say much, however he does notice quite a bit. I wouldn't recommend continuing on this path. He isn't one to be controlled."

She stiffened, straightening her spine as she pulled back her shoulders. "What, pray tell, is that supposed to mean?"

"I think you are all too aware, my Queen."

Bowing, Malcolm took his leave. Right before he closed the door, his gaze connected with Kalendra's. *Don't make him choose*, he silently advised. He highly doubted she would care for the outcome should such an event come to pass.

CHAPTER 14

Breathing slow and steady, Alec lay in the grass beneath the shadow of a tree. Exhausted from the grueling training session, he dozed almost instantly after settling in the shade. At first, there was nothing but the calming darkness. As time passed, vivid images assaulted his senses. His sword slashed through the air with a flurry of motion. Fingers a frightening pale white, they clashed with the deep red staining his skin and dripping down the length of his blade. Heart pounding in his ears, Alec's chest heaved with every breath.

Lifting his gaze, the sword slipped from suddenly limp fingers. Surrounding him were the faces of every person who fell from his blade in the arena. At the front were his most recent victims. The teenage boys peered at him blankly as they stood with an eerie stillness.

Taking a step back, Alec's arm lifted of its own accord. In his hand was his sword. The warrior's lips parted, his eyes widening. *How did I...?* Weapon at the ready, Alec started forward.

Gazes filled with horror, the boys raised their arms as if to shield themselves. Their cries and pleas rang in Alec's ears, yet he couldn't control his body. Tendons pushing against the skin of his neck, he struggled to cease the descent of his arm.

"No!"

His blade cut into the first person. Alec swore his heart momentarily stopped. Without pause, his weapon slashed to the side. Closing his eyes, Alec gripped the hilt with both hands as he fought to stop the slaughter. Nothing he did worked. The more he struggled, the more the metal fused to his flesh, keeping the blade in his grasp. Then, there was silence. Swallowing repeatedly, Alec scanned the bodies at his feet.

It's not real, he told himself. *It can't be real!*

Shutting his eyes the warrior willed himself to awaken. When his lids slowly opened, his victims were once more surrounding him, staring at him, as his weapon started to vibrate in preparation of another battle.

Hands gripping the reins of her steed, Isabelle tried not to groan. How in the world did she manage to get herself into these situations? In the need to get away from the castle, the sorceress decided to take a ride out to Malcolm's and visit Alec. Saddling her horse, she was soon no longer alone. King Titus and Queen Kalendra seemed to share her idea. So here she was, at the behest of her king, riding towards the sage's cottage with the last person she wanted to see.

Pretend she's not here. Pretend she's not here.

Gaze straight ahead Kalendra spared her not a glance.

Isabelle could work with that. It was the snide, cold commands which reminded her of Jerric that she could not abide.

Nearing the dwelling, a familiar voice pierced the quiet of the forest with its distress. A chill racked her body like a frost.

Alec!

He screamed again.

215

It was an agonizing noise, the likes of which she could not recall. Racing ahead, the sorceress's eyes darted from one spot to the next as she searched for him. Cloud had paused his munching on the grass by the cottage, but she couldn't see the sage near him. Dismounting in a flash, Isabelle slid down the hill and headed towards the creek.

Alec waded up to his waist in the cool water. Head bent, he was frantically scrubbing his hands and arms.

Ardys and Cassidy were close by, speaking to him in quiet, calming tones.

Alec didn't seem to hear them. "It won't come off," he said anxiously, continuing the vigorous movements. "I can't get it off!"

Using some stones to cross the creek, Isabelle rushed to his side. She didn't even think twice about leaping into the water.

Soaking wet, Alec's hair hung in his wild eyes. Never acknowledging his friend, he continued to scrub away the invisible stains.

Gripping his arm, Isabelle gave him a good shake. "Alec, there's nothing there."

"It won't come off. Why won't it come off?"

Grabbing his hands, she moved in front of him. Blinking, the warrior gazed around. Breathing heavily, he raised his shaking fingers, examining them closely.

"Isabelle?"

His voice was raw, reminding her of that dreadful day in Terra.

"It's alright, Alec. Come on. Let's get you dried off."

Guiding him back to shore she tried to ignore the audience watching from the hillside. His expression closed off, Alec concealed the turmoil swirling within. He couldn't however, stop the tremors traveling through his limbs.

Summoning a water spell, Isabelle pulled the moisture from his clothing as Alec took a seat on the grass.

Cassidy stood hovering protectively over him.

Lowering herself to the ground beside him, Isabelle said nothing.

After a few moments, the shaking ceased. Alec was privately grateful for her silent company. Releasing a ragged sigh, he pounded the dirt with a clenched fist.

Bumping his shoulder with hers, Isabelle offered him a smile.

"Why don't I go make you a cup of coffee? It should warm you up after that swim."

Alec nodded without shifting his gaze.

"Hey," Isabelle said, tilting her head to get a better look at his face. "It wasn't your fault. You had no choice."

Alec opened his mouth then closed it. Swallowing, he tried again.

"I was still the one holding the blade."

What do I say to that? Biting her lip, the sage sighed. Hesitating, she leaned over and wrapped him in an embrace.

The warrior neither moved nor spoke.

Holding tight for a few seconds, Isabelle gradually pulled back. Forcing a smile, she told him a little too brightly, "I should fetch that coffee. I could surely use a cup myself."

Rising to her feet she brushed off her clothing.

"Thanks," came a quiet voice.

Glancing down, a real grin lightly softened her features. "Anytime."

Crossing the creek Isabelle was met on the other side by Titus.

"Isabelle," he began in a soft tone. "What, pray tell, happened to him in Zerrok?"

Gaze darting to the queen a few feet away, the sorceress shuffled her feet. "While we were in Terra our owner...forced Alec to do some terrible things. Every match he had to kill all of our opponents." She looked across the water at her friend. Still sitting with the dragons, his head was bent with his fingers buried in his dark hair. "It almost destroyed him," she finished sadly.

Following her line of sight, Titus peered at the warrior. Adjusting his belt, he stepped towards the water's edge.

"Titus, where are you going?" Kalendra questioned, eyeing the flowing creek.

"To speak with our son. Stay here, my pearl. I shall return shortly." A quick look to the guards that had joined them told the men not to follow.

Watching the dragons, Kalendra reached out towards him. "Titus—"

It was no use. His Majesty was already beginning to cross the stones.

Isabelle paused. Should she go with him? *No. I should give them a moment alone.* Perhaps hearing some advice from their king...his father, would help. The best thing she could do to aid her friend was to grant them some space. Making her way up the hill Isabelle entered the small cottage. Having been there several times, she was relatively familiar with the kitchen's contents.

Filling the kettle from the outside spigot, she didn't notice a figure now sitting at the table as she re-entered the dwelling. Lighting a small blaze, she set the kettle over the flames then turned to get some mugs.

"Eeek!" the sorceress shouted, her hand flying to her chest.

Gasping, Kalendra leaned back in the chair. "Forgive me. I did not intend to frighten you."

Holy crap. Isabelle hadn't heard the queen follow her to the cottage or enter the structure. Willing her heart to slow its pounding, she tried to recover her equilibrium.

"How may I be of service, Your Majesty?"

Needlessly fixing her hair, Kalendra rose gracefully to her feet. She started towards the sorceress and drew to a halt a short distance away. Clasping her hands, she watched Isabelle intently.

"There is something we need to discuss."

Mind elsewhere, Alec didn't hear the approach of footsteps. His gaze remained focused on the grass until a deep growl from the dragons drew his attention. Stiffening, the warrior glanced up.

Hand tucked causally by his sword, Titus surveyed him thoughtfully.

"Greetings, Alec."

No smile touched the warrior's lips. Face closed off, he made no attempt to engage in any form of small talk. "Your Majesty," he grumbled.

A strained silence fell around them. Neither made any further attempt to speak. Alec's eyes narrowed slightly.

"Is there something I can aid you with?"

His tone was just polite. A fact which caused the royal's brows to lift momentarily. "I do believe I am the one who should be asking you such a question."

Jerking away, Alec quickly got to his feet and turned his back to Titus.

"I'm fine."

"Your behavior a few moments ago says otherwise."

As Alec moved away, Titus went to follow, but stopped as Cassidy bore her teeth. Lowering her head, she glared at the man. The large red dragon acted no friendlier as Titus hovered nearby his son.

Eyeing them carefully, he didn't push onward. Briefly clenching his hands, he forced himself to remain where he was.

Alec hadn't responded to his words. Titus however, was not deterred. *Someone needs to get through to him.* He tried again.

"I know what it's like to do things you are not proud of in the midst of battle. Some sins are easier for us to forgive than others, but dwelling on those sorrows will not lessen the pain. It will only serve to slowly tear you asunder."

Head bent, Alec's jaw tightened. His shoulders pulled back stiffly as his fingers dug into his palms.

"Why do you care what becomes of me?"

"You know the reason, Alakaid," Titus told him, holding out his hands as if welcoming him.

The warrior snorted. King Titus called him by his real name, so the others must have informed him of Alec's true lineage. *The son of the king.* Alec shook his head. It was a revelation he, too, was still struggling with. Glancing towards the cottage, he noted Isabelle's self-appointed task had not been completed. *She's probably trying to give us some space.* She was a kind hearted person.

Alec swallowed hard. Thinking of his friend only served to return his mind back to the loathsome images of his nightmare. He couldn't bring himself to regret saving her, yet his selfishness cost so many others their lives. His heart knew he had no choice. Then why was his head tormenting him?

"I don't know what you expect from me, what either of you expect from me," Alec stated quietly, referring to his mother. "Malcolm insists we are of relation and I trust his judgement, but that changes nothing. You still left me to rot in a dungeon, not once...but twice. I suppose I may understand the trickery placed upon you when I was young. There is no excuse for what befell me and Isabelle in Terra. You *knew* we had been imprisoned by soldiers and left us there."

Alec finally turned to face Titus. His eyes blazed dangerously with no hint of softening.

"Did they tell you, Your *Majesty*? Do you have any idea what I did, the people I was forced to slaughter so Isabelle wouldn't pay the price?" Alec didn't give him the chance to respond. Releasing a cold bark of laughter, he pressed on. All the anger and bitterness built up inside of him seemed to spill at once, allowing him the freedom to speak his mind in a way he never had in the past.

"I'm a monster!" the warrior declared, swiping a hand to the side. "In Terra, my former master purchased us. 'Kill them all', he commanded of me during every battle. If I refused, Isabelle… So I did as he commanded. You want to know my sins? Dozens of people fell to my blade because I put her life above everything else. Lads, who had yet to become men, were slaughtered by my hand because I was selfish and weak. I…I couldn't let him hurt her. And their blood is on my hands."

Alec's eyes shifted back to his hands. His face briefly scrunched up with disgust. For a split second, he swore he could see a crimson stain on his skin. Why wouldn't it go away? Fingers curling into his palms, he looked back at Titus.

"If Ardys hadn't helped us escape I might still be there…killing. Left in a never-ending hell, all in the name of service to my King," he finished frostily.

Titus said nothing at first. Never before had someone spoken to him in such a fashion. Though not outwardly disrespectful, Alec's chilling speech was filled with venom. If it had been anyone else, Titus would have thrown him in the stocks or even the dungeon. Yet, this was his *son,* Titus acknowledged. Seeing him again, he couldn't doubt what the wizard told him. Alec's anger, as strong as it seemed, was not solely due to grievances against him. There was a lot of residual pain forged by his old master.

Telling the warrior the facts behind their search for him and his partner would do no good. Alec knew this already. It wasn't a reminder of their inability to find them that he needed to hear. In some ways, he was correct. They did fail him. He failed him.

"You are far from a monster, Alakaid. However, allowing your grief to blind you into believing so is foolish," Titus began meeting Alec's fire with fire. Speaking in a way that the warrior might see as pity would only anger him further. "Protecting the life of a friend is not dishonorable. In fact, your loyalty is quite noble. I wish it were not so, but those fated to Zerrok's arenas cannot be saved. If it had not been your blade, it would have been another's. No matter how much power one might possess, we are still but flesh. We cannot save everyone. Yet, why is it that we fight if not to protect those we care for?"

Eyes narrowed, Alec pressed his lips together in a thin line. Shifting his weight, he dropped his gaze then brushed his fingers messily through his dark hair. Behind him, Ardys nudged his shoulder.

"He's right, Alec," the great dragon told him.

Exhaling deeply, the warrior's upper body seemed to sag. In the distance, he saw Isabelle rounding Malcolm's cottage with Kalendra.

Glancing once more at the dragons, Titus dipped his head in a short bow. "Thank you for looking after my son."

Cassidy snorted. "Someone had to. None of you humans seem able to complete the task," she told him crossly. She proudly tilted her head to the side as she watched him with a frown.

The king's mouth gaped open as he jerked back. "Alakaid, did this dragon just speak to me?"

Lifting a brow, Alec turned his attention to the royal. *Hmm, no one must have told him about this part of my powers,* he mused to himself. Watching the startled expression on Titus's face caused the corners of his mouth to twitch. *Perhaps he regrets coming out here.* It would serve him right for basically calling him foolish.

"I prefer Alec, Your Majesty. This is Cassidy and Ardys, two of my guardians from Ellfraya. Somehow, I gave Cassidy the ability to communicate with humans when my powers went crazy the other day."

Alakaid did this?

It took a moment for Titus to process that piece of information. His magic was greater than the royal imagined. Titus swore he heard a faint growl, but couldn't be sure from which dragon it might have come. Neither were being particularly friendly. It seemed they blamed him for Alec's suffering as well. Titus ignored it for now. Alec was the one he needed to reach first. He was a fighter. There was no other way he would have survived this long if he didn't have a strong will. Somehow he had to rebuild the trust Alec once showed him.

"Why are you here?" Alec suddenly questioned wearily.

In a sense, he knew the answer. Alec was a prince of Malyndor, Titus's own son. While in the past the king had highly praised his skills as a warrior and sorcerer, he never showed any particular interest in him on a personal level. Alec hadn't really expected that to change. So why had Titus come all the way out here to see him? Would it not have been easier to speak with him when he returned to Stafford?

Alec didn't know. In the past few days the whole world seemed to have flipped on its axis. He was being subjected to all kinds of unwanted attention. And with the royals, it was difficult for him to know if they sought his company because they truly wanted to get to know him or if it was only because he had been revealed as a prince.

The passing silence seemed to go on forever.

"Every year on your birthday your mother and I still visit your grave," Titus began solemnly, his gaze unwavering.

Alec's brows pleated. This wasn't even close to what he was expecting to hear.

"For almost twenty years we have mourned the loss of our son, but we never forgot you, Alec. We strived to ensure both Alandra and Alicia knew of you. This is not easy for any of us. You are all grown up and I am proud of the man you have become. I was proud when I thought that you were merely

Malcolm's apprentice and I could not think of anyone else I would want to call my son."

Gazes locked together, Alec sighed. "I'm sorry for the pain your family has gone through, but I don't want to make any promises I can't keep. Being part of royalty is…difficult to accept."

"I understand completely." Titus took a step towards him. "Would it be too much for you to call me Father? Your Majesty is far too formal."

Placing a hand on Cassidy's scales Alec shook his head. "In all the years before I came to Malyndor not a single person cared for me except for Lord Kegan. He is the only father I have ever known. He took me as his son when I was nothing…no one. Calling anyone else by that name feels like a betrayal to the one man who has shown me more kindness than any other person," Alec shrugged helplessly. "I can't dishonor him like that."

Titus didn't want to, but he could understand where Alec was coming from. Leos was a good man. He resented another being able to call Alec his 'son'. There was no way to stop the warrior when he felt so strongly about it. Yet, if he must suffer this slight, then Titus could concede it to Leos…for now.

"Titus would be a welcome start. It seems strange for my own offspring to address me in the same manner as my staff when we are not in public."

Alec nodded. "If it matters that greatly, then I will try."

Fighting a frown, Titus had to resist the urge to shake him. They might not have been close, but Alec should know him well enough to accept his words at face value. The royal was not prone to making false statements in regards to his affections.

"It does matter, Alec. Though this news comes as a surprise, it is not unwelcome. I know you to be a good man and will be pleased to bestow upon you your rightful title."

Watching Isabelle and his mother making their way down the hill, Alec's brows lowered.

"Rightful title?" he repeated.

"Indeed. You are my son," Titus insisted. "As my first born, it is your right to one day assume the throne."

Alec briefly froze. *He can't be serious. Me? A king?* There was no way he could even conceive such an idea.

Titus pressed on, "I want you to return to Ariston with us and be with your family. As the future king, it is time for you to prepare for that role."

"Pardon?" For a moment Alec thought he misheard him. What of Alandra? "I can't go with you to Ariston, Titus."

Titus clenched his jaw. *Hear him out,* he mentally advised.

"I never sought to become a lord, let alone a prince. My sister..." The corners of his mouth pulled back slightly. "Alandra has trained her entire life to rule. She is a great leader and has a kind heart. I have no doubt that she will make a fine ruler." Glancing at Cassidy, he continued, "A different path has been set for me."

"Alec—"

"Finding my family is a dream come true. I could not ask for more. If you'll excuse me, Titus. I must continue with my training."

Bowing, Alec turned and walked over towards Ardys.

Brushing his fingers through his hair, Titus watched him depart with a deep sigh. *Stubborn boy.* A family trait it would seem. The conversation having ended, there was not much else Titus could do other than let him go. He would wait until another time to renew this discussion. By all means, he would not take "no" as his final answer.

Joining his wife, Titus wore a small grin for her sake.

"Shall he be returning with us?" Kalendra asked hopefully, searching her husband's profile.

"No, my pearl. I believe he requires some more time to sort this out. This news is even stranger for him than it is for us and that young man has a mind all his own." His words were mixed with a hint of both sadness and pride.

On the other side of the creek, Alec peered out at Isabelle and his parents.

Stretching out on the ground Cassidy watched him thoughtfully. "Are you sure this is what you desire?"

He slowly bobbed his head. "Yeah, Cassidy. I found them, that's what's most important." Standing beside Ardys, he leaned against the red dragon's warm scales. "A different fate awaits me other than a palace. I think I'm beginning to understand the true role I must play in this prophecy."

Neither of them responded right away.

"You would have made a great king, little one," Cassidy told him at last.

"You have wisdom beyond your years," Ardys added.

"Yeah," the warrior drawled.

So much for wisdom. He should have seen what was to come much sooner. As it was, he could not change the course that fate was about to bestow upon him. Gazing at the others, Alec tried to loosen the heavy pressure he felt resting on his chest. There was no stopping what he had to do next.

Early in the morning, Alec strolled down the long dim corridor on the way to Jade's chambers. Sunbeams starting to glow on the rugs and up the ornate walls didn't lessen the weight causing his shoulders to slump. Stretching them out, he straightened his posture and inhaled slowly, then exhaled with a sigh. Knuckles hovering by the door, he paused. Try as he might Alec couldn't muster a smile.

Rapping the solid wood, he listened and waited. There was no reply from within. Not usually prone to sleeping late, Jade always took a walk prior to breakfast. Alec was hoping to speak with her before the rest of the castle roused from its slumber.

"Lady Jade," Alec called out, knocking again. "It's Alec, can I speak with you?"

Silence.

Alec's mark tingled. Brows furrowing, his heartbeat intensified. *Please answer me.*

"Lady Jade, are you in there?"

Pressing his ear to the door, Alec tapped a finger against his leg. There was still no reply to his words. Somewhere within, he heard a faint bang of two objects colliding.

"Jade," he yelled. "I'm coming."

Stepping back, Alec pointed a hand at the door as two soldiers patrolling the area raced down the hallway. Blasting the door open, the sorcerer sped into the room.

The large empty bed was perfectly made with the thick drapes drawn back. Quickly scanning the chamber, he noted two lamps in the sitting room had puddles of cool wax beneath them. A book lay on the ground near the settee, while a cup of tea, cold to the touch, sat abandoned on the coffee table. One of the French doors leading to the balcony hung open. The glass panels were caught by the wind, causing the door to swing outward and hit the outside railing.

Alec's whole body tensed. Nails digging into his palms, he could feel his aura rising, swirling around him like an angry storm. Face hard as stone, he turned to peer at the two soldiers frantically searching the space.

"Alert Duke Stafford, Lady Jade is missing."

The flutter of movement caught the warrior's attention. Grasping the thin hilt of a dagger he sent his weapon flying through the air. By the time Alec spun around, the shadow was gone. It did however, leave him a parting gift. Pinned to the wall by his blade was a single piece of paper. Swiftly going out onto the balcony, Alec's sharp gaze searched for the wayward intruder. With no clues to the person's identity, he doubted the skilled adversary would be found.

One of the soldiers was already reading over the correspondence. His eyes locked on the prince as soon as he reentered the chamber.

"Your Highness...Alec, it's for you," he said grimly, holding the paper.

Heart thumping, Alec reached out and took the page. The words gracefully scripted across the sheet could have made his blood boil.

Lord Alec Kegan,

You are forthwith invited to an event in your honor to be held at the Imperial Tower in Zangar, Zerrok. Should you accept, your lordship and no more than four guests shall enjoy a full private tour and the hospitality of the entire Kingdom. In adherence with Zerrokian law, all magic and magical creatures are forbidden.

Sincerely,
Lord Vincent of Parlen

Alec's jaw was clenched so tightly his teeth were in danger of shattering. The edges of the paper crumpled beneath his unusually pale fingers. He gripped it so tightly his arms started to shake. Eyes aglow, Alec spun around flinging the page away from him as he stormed out of Jade's room.

The soldier quickly retrieved the note prior to chasing after the prince. His partner previously departed to raise the alarm.

Focused on nothing besides his task, Alec strode through the castle. The dragons were on a morning flight to patrol the area. He would go to the courtyard and summon them. Vincent's actions could not be ignored. Alec wouldn't let him leave this time. Not only had he dared to kidnap Jade, his 'cordial' letter to Alec was the ultimate insult.

Racing down the front steps, the sorcerer didn't even need to holler for his friends. Several roars sounded above him as three dragons soared towards the castle. Tatsu perched on the roof while Cassidy and Ardys landed upon the stone pavers.

They weren't the only ones immediately coming to Alec's aid.

Dark clouds appearing in the sky caused Garth, Roderick and Nathan to speed towards him from the barracks.

One look at the sorcerer's glowing eyes, deathly cold expression and curled fists had silent bells ringing in the warriors' minds.

"Alec, what happened?" Garth questioned, jogging to his friend's side as the royal neared the dragons.

"Lady Jade's been taken," he practically growled, "by Vincent."

Mouths momentarily gaping, they quickly recovered.

"Impossible," Roderick rejected. "This entire castle is surrounded by soldiers. He couldn't possibly break in, let alone depart here with a captive."

Nathan frowned with concern. "Are you sure her ladyship isn't taking a walk about the grounds?"

"Positive."

Tension filled Alec's entire body. He didn't want to stand here talking. It was pointless. Vincent's treachery called for action. The sorcerer knew where they were. There was no time to waste.

I have to save Jade.

"Lord Vincent left a—um note," the guard trailing him enlightened.

Everyone stilled. Their gazes briefly met with an uneasy silence.

"He's daring to ransom the daughter of a duke?" Garth questioned, his eyes narrowing.

"I wish it were that simple, sir. Lady Jade isn't mentioned by name." He stepped forward and handed Roderick the paper. "He's 'invited' Prince Alec to Zangar."

Garth's head jerked back. "You can't be serious."

While the three of them read over the short letter, Alec raked his fingers through his hair, shaking his head. He headed towards the green creature.

"I don't have time for such foolishness. Cassidy, I need you to take me to Zerrok."

Garth and Nathan moved to block his way.

"Hold fast little brother. You can't rush off into battle blindly."

"I agree with Nathan. The Imperial Tower is Zerrok's stronghold. *If* he's even there, Vincent would have to possess powerful allies in order to arrange this. He knows about your mark and your powers. This is, without a doubt, a trap."

"You think I don't know that?" Alec scoffed. "He took her. I have to do something."

Lowering his head, Ardys nudged the sorcerer. "We will help you get her back. I promise you this human will regret the day he dared to mess with dragonkind."

Standing on Alec's other side Roderick put a hand on his shoulder. He might not understand the fiery creature, yet he knew what Ardys was saying. The knight felt the same way.

"You're not alone in this, Alec. We will stand beside you in this battle or any other. Trust us to aid you."

"Yeah little brother, did you mistakenly believe we would allow you to smite an entire kingdom without us?"

Watching Nathan closely, Alec's gaze shifted between the warriors. He exhaled deeply. It appeared to be time for him to do something he never imagined: rely on another person. Crossing his arms, Alec peered at the knight.

"So what do you suggest?"

CHAPTER 15

Bobbing from side to side the ship swayed continuously as it navigated through the turbulent water. Jade moaned softly as her body rolled slightly with the movements. A hand resting against her temple, she fought a pained groan. *Why am I in such a state?* Opening her eyelids, the pounding inside her skull didn't lessen. If anything the throbbing grew.

Thick beams running adjacent to worn wooden boards, first greeted her eyes. Frowning, Jade gently twisted to peer around the space. The small cabin was sparsely decorated with a tiny porthole above the single bed on which she lay. There was no doubt in her mind that she was aboard a vessel.

"No. No, no, no," she whispered frantically as she pushed herself into a sitting position.

The horrid nightmare filling her dreams must not have been pure fiction. Meaning the moments Jade could recall were indeed true. Someone had taken her from Stafford Castle!

Chest constricting, the noblewoman was finding it difficult to breathe. *Calm thyself,* she thought soothingly. *You can figure this out.* Taking several slow breaths, she was able to gain some semblance of control over her own body.

To begin with, Jade knew it would be best to discover who her captors were. Then, perhaps she might be able to deduce what they sought. Gaze dropping to the floor, she concentrated on the last things she could remember.

Night had fallen. Ariel arrived with her tea and though she did keep Jade company for a little while, she was quieter than normal. Departing to her own room within the hour, Jade was left alone. Ignoring the urge to pace, Jade had poured herself another cup and opened a book to occupy her racing thoughts. The beverage was left untouched as a hand wrapped around her mouth, cutting off any sounds which might have risen. The sweet smell of the cloth covering Jade's face filled her lungs, sapping at her strength until darkness swarmed in. The next time she surfaced, Jade was here, trapped in this room sailing to some unknown destination.

An arm protectively encircling her stomach, Jade's other hand cupped her cheek. What little she saw told her nothing of her kidnappers. Though the skill required led her to believe that whoever came for her did not do so on a whim. Yet, to what end could someone be seeking in using her as a hostage?

Footsteps outside her door caused Jade to jump. Holding her breath without realizing it, she leaned forward as she waited to see who was behind this atrocity. Gasping, Jade almost toppled over on the bed as her visitor entered.

A smile on his face, Vincent gazed at her with bright dancing eyes.

Jade's entire body stiffened. She couldn't speak. She couldn't move. Running wasn't an option. Was there something wrong with her that this crazed demon wouldn't let her be? Jade never thought she gave him reason to believe she was anything other than indifferent to him. Why did he continue to pursue her? Nay, the man had gone so far as to kidnap her.

As he stepped further into the small space, Jade began to tremble. *I cannot escape him. Alec, pray save me.* Jade knew in her heart that her pleas would not be answered this time. She was far beyond his reach. It seemed Vincent had finally won. She was completely at his mercy.

"Good day, my dearest," he greeted with a grin.

Two men remained out in the hall as he closed the door behind him.

Some part of Jade's mind was able to pull her out of her frozen state enough to slide all the way back on the bed until she touched the wall.

Gaze traveling over her, Vincent released an elated sigh. "You cannot know how wonderful it is to have you here with me. I have dreamed of this for far too long, my dear. Now we shall be together and can finally start our lives anew."

Sitting on the edge of the bed, Vincent reached out and covered her one hand with his own.

Jade resisted the urge to pull it away. "And where...where shall that be?" she managed to ask in a fairly steady voice.

"Wherever you would like it," he declared happily.

Stafford! Jade knew it would be the wrong answer to give him. Vincent could turn dark and violent in a flash. Trying to stay on his good side seemed like the best idea she could conceive.

"That sounds splendid." Offering the noble a small brief smile, Jade didn't meet his eye. "What is our present destination?"

"Zerrok. Zangar to be exact. I am aiding an acquaintance in exchange for his services in helping me to liberate you. Do not fret," he told her patting Jade's hand before drawing back. "This shall be but a short diversion."

It took great control for her not to respond unkindly. The southern kingdom was the last place she wanted to be. Having escaped from there a second time, she was certain Alec would feel the same.

Curse you, Vincent. "Indeed," Jade replied weakly.

It was the only thing she trusted herself to say. Clasping her hands firmly on her lap, Jade remained silent for the rest of Vincent's short visit. Other than him boasting about the brilliance of his successful plan to rescue her, Jade learned little else. Who were these acquaintances of his? It must be a shady group to say the least. Jade shivered. She didn't want to think about what horrors would await once they anchored in Zerrok.

Arms crossed, Alec stood stiffly in front of the windows of Duke Stafford's study. Despite the warrior's insistence that immediate action be taken, a thorough search of the entire city was underway. The conclusion would be what he already knew: Jade was gone. Clenching his jaw, he grimly gazed at the chaos below. Staff and soldiers alike jogged about the grounds. The portcullis was sealed tight and the battlements were on high alert.

Behind him, Leos was discussing the next course of action with Titus and Malcolm while Edmund paced restlessly. Lenora had returned to her own room some time ago with the queen. Tears streaming down her face, she wasn't able to pull herself together and aid in the search. For her only child to be missing, was the duchess's worst nightmare.

"There must be more that we can do," Leos stressed, gripping the hilt of his sword. "We cannot allow Lady Jade to be held captive by that demon."

Titus sighed with a scowl. "I am in agreeance. However, we have no proof as of yet that it was he who has taken her."

"What of his note?"

"His note is quite the problem," Titus answered. "It gives no mention of Jade. On the surface it appears as nothing but a friendly invitation. Though we know that not to be the case, we must tread carefully. If I send troops to Zerrok without proper cause, it will aggravate the situation."

"Can you not send word to King David and explain the situation while we retrieve her? Pray Titus, this is my daughter." Hands curled into fists, Edmund gazed at his friend with pleading eyes.

"You know as well as we do, Edmund, that such a course would not be wise," Malcolm told him instead. "I do not believe Vincent is clever enough to pull off something like this on his own. That boy is far too impulsive. Someone is using him for a much darker purpose I fear." He glanced at Alec who was still glaring out the window. "There are few who could 'invite' someone to the Imperial Tower. Once inside, I doubt Alec would be allowed to leave. The risk is too great to blindly amble into this trap."

"I don't care if it is a trap," Alec declared spinning around. His fingers cut through the air with the effectiveness of a blade. "I will not leave Jade in the hands of someone like Vincent. He has to be stopped once and for all."

"Alec," Malcolm began placing a hand on his shoulder. "We share your frustration, but don't let your anger cloud your judgment. Who's to say that Jade is even there. Vincent could have taken her anywhere."

Turning his head to the side, Alec exhaled with a hiss. The wizard was right. The man was a liar. Alec had to be sure of his location before he charged in and unleashed his fury on whoever might be foolish enough to stand in his path.

"We do possess several spies who are in that area. I shall have messenger hawks sent to them. The moment she arrives in Zangar's port we shall know of it. Until then, no course is to be taken against Zerrok, agreed?"

It wasn't truly a question, yet Titus peered at everyone in turn as they spoke or nodded their understanding. All but Alec solemnly replied.

"Alec?"

The warrior said nothing as he clenched his jaw.

"Alakaid, are you in agreement?"

"Fine." Meeting Titus's gaze, he told him firmly, "But once she is found, I make no promises."

Not waiting for an answer, Alec strode out of the room. After he vanished, the king dropped into a chair.

"Damn it," he muttered running a hand over his face. "This will not bode well. No matter how much he may oppose, my son is not to leave Stafford."

Leos and Edmund exchanged a glance. Crossing the room, the duke came to stand beside his king. "If Vincent is indeed holding my daughter within the tower, then Alec shall be the only one capable of gaining entry. It would require an army to even have a chance at breaching their fortress. By such a time, she could already have perished."

Slowly shaking his head Titus did not waver. "Twice now he has been imprisoned within the southern kingdom. Each time has scarred him greater than the last. Alakaid shall be the next King of Malyndor. I am sorry my friend, but I cannot risk him being taken again."

"You would doom my daughter?" Edmund accused harshly. "You know what the loss of a child feels like, Titus. Jade is the only one I have. I was not blessed with others as you were."

Frowning, Titus rose to his feet. "This choice gives me no pleasure. Are you truly saying it is better to sacrifice my son over your daughter?"

Edmund didn't back down. "You know that is not what I mean. Alec's power equals a dragon. He can save her, as you well know."

"I care not what his abilities are. Alec is not invincible. Under no circumstances will I grant him permission to meet Vincent's twisted demands."

Holding up his hands, Malcolm tried to step between the two. "Pray, do not quarrel. The enemy is not in this chamber. Both of you are doting fathers and no one is requesting either of you to make a sacrifice. We must stand fast if we wish to thwart our foes."

"Malcolm is right," Leos added. "I care for both Alec and Jade as you do. If we seek it, I believe there is a way to protect them both. I know my son..." The gruff noble paused for a moment. "I know Alec well and it would appear in some ways, so does Vincent. No matter the danger, he will not deter from this challenge. We can however, prepare him our sharpest blades and our strongest armor, so that he stands all the greater chance in winning a victory."

"Victory," Titus scoffed. "Leos, five men cannot defeat the forces waiting within the Imperial Tower. Mark my words, Alakaid shall not go."

Turning on his heel, Titus stormed out of the study.

"Perhaps he is right," Edmund admitted. "It is hopeless. There is no way for so few to overtake a stronghold and survive."

"I do believe that would depend on who we send," Malcolm declared with the hint of a smirk.

Dozing here and there, Alec didn't stray far from the castle's Keep. All birds used for transporting correspondence lived on the top floor. When the hawk returned from Zerrok it would come here. Alec would then know for sure whether Vincent wrote the truth. *She better be alright,* Alec thought for perhaps the hundredth time. If he had ended the monster when he had the chance this wouldn't have happened. Alec never should have let Jade sway him otherwise.

Lying on the roof of the barracks, the warrior gazed up at the large stone structure. His fingers tapped the side of his leg without him even realizing it. Nothing worked to occupy his thoughts. How long had he been waiting here, blankly watching the azure sky for some sign? Alec couldn't say. The waning sun told him it was at the very least late in the afternoon. A small form flew by high above. Blinking rapidly, Alec rose up onto his elbows. Circling back, an elegant brown and white bird soared towards the battlements and disappeared through the highest open window of the Keep.

This is it. This has to be it.

Shifting into a crouched position on the edge of the tiles, Alec studied the Keep's sole entry to the courtyard. Like a panther awaiting its prey, he moved not a muscle. The door suddenly flew open as a soldier raced across the grounds.

Eyes tracking his path, Alec patiently held his position until the man was nearing the barracks. Leaping down, the warrior lightly landed directly in front of the soldier.

"Ah!" the man shouted jerking back. "Prince Alec, you startled me."

"Is that from Zerrok?" Alec questioned instead, gesturing to the small folded parchment clutched in the man's hand.

"I'm only to give this directly to King Titus," he replied, starting to go around the royal.

Darting forward, Alec grabbed the soldier's arm and within another heartbeat had him bent over with his arm twisted behind his back. Removing the note, Alec didn't release his grip no matter the soldier's protest. Eyes quickly scanning the small script, he said not a word.

Lady Jade arrived by ship in Zanger. She was taken to the Imperial Tower.

So the vile noble hadn't lied. Jade was there. Pressing the paper back into the man's fingers, Alec set him free. Spinning around, he set off toward the armory.

I'm coming, Jade.

Once released the soldier ran full speed to find His Majesty. His orders were to tell Alec nothing of the message. He hadn't expected the prince to be waiting to ambush him.

Seeing Titus on the front steps with Leos, the soldier dropped into a deep bow. Holding out the paper he panted, "His Highness took the note and read it. Forgive me, my King, I couldn't stop him."

Quickly glancing at the words, Titus frowned deeply. "Where is he?"

Hoofbeats pounded the ground as Cloud raced across the courtyard. Clad in short chainmail, leather armor, steel vambraces and a cloak, Alec road towards the city.

"Stop him!" Titus commanded. His gaze snapped to the currently open entry as soldiers returned to the castle. "Close the gate!"

Cloud bolted around anyone foolish enough to stand in his path. No one was going to hinder his master's flight. As the portcullis quickly began to close, Alec leapt from the saddle. Running as swift as the wind, he dove, sliding beneath the iron bars right before they sank into the ground. Rolling to a stop, he glanced back at those calling his name for but a moment. His gaze locked on Roderick. The knight didn't bother ordering for him to return. Instead, he dipped his head in a respectful bow.

Stay safe, Alec.

Alec nodded prior to disappearing from view. Raising a hand, he shot a ball of light into the air as he continued to speed down the road. Behind him, the portcullis was lifting. Soon, soldiers would be on his tail. A deep roar sounded. The one corner of Alec's mouth pulled back in a smirk. *I can always count on you, Cassidy.*

Summoning a wind spell, the sorcerer jumped high into the air. Cassidy flew by beneath him, allowing Alec to twist around in midair and land on her back.

"To Zerrok, my friend."

The green dragon answered with a grunt. Shifting her wings, she changed course. Alec frowned as shortly after their flight began, they started to descend near Malcolm's cottage.

"Why are we stopping here?" Alec questioned with a puzzled tone.

He figured Ardys and Tatsu would join them in the air. Perhaps they were resting and required waking. However, when Cassidy landed beside the modest dwelling, his other guardians were not asleep.

What is this? he wondered, trying not to voice his displeasure. They didn't have time for games.

Cassidy stretched out on the grass and folded up her wings, silently encouraging the sorcerer to dismount. Sliding to the ground, he peered around. The door to Malcolm's flew open. Adjusting cloaks and tying their weapons upon their belts, Malcolm, Isabelle, Garth and Nathan all suddenly appeared, ready for battle.

Alec's one brow rose.

"You didn't think we would allow you to breach the Imperial Tower on your own did you?" asked his former teacher with an amused voice.

"We told you we have your back, little brother," Nathan popped in.

"Zerrok could use some comeuppance," Isabelle added.

Striding over to Alec's side, Garth bumped him with his shoulder. "Have you forgotten? Vincent invited four of your comrades to join you."

Alec released a short laugh. A small smirk appeared. "I hope you know I'm flying there."

Malcolm and Isabelle smiled. Rushing over to Ardys, the sorceress patted the side of the great red dragon's face as he gave her a nudge.

"Can I go with Ardys?"

Garth and Nathan both exchanged uneasy glances.

"We thought as much," the warrior admitted. "Though I did hope you would change your mind and choose a more normal path."

Alec shook his dark hair. "Since this is a trap, we'll need all the help we can get. Vincent won't be expecting three dragons, or Malyndor's best."

Peering at the others, Alec felt his heart lift. This impossible task didn't seem so bleak with them accompanying him. There was a chance of actually coming back alive. No more waiting. Alec was going to rescue his Jade and no one, not Vincent, the armies of Zangar or even King Titus was going to stop him.

Moving to join Isabelle, another set of steps on the small porch caused Alec to pause.

His face a hard mask, Duke Stafford watched Alec without a hint of his normal friendliness. Descending the stairs, he stalked across the grass, coming to a halt several feet away from the prince.

"I am under direct orders from King Titus to ensure you do not leave Stafford." Edmund's fingers squeezed the hilt of his sword. "By any means, if necessary. As a servant to the crown, it is my duty to halt this endeavor." The duke took a few steps as he spoke. Standing still once more, his jaw clenched.

"As a father..." His hand dropped from the blade. "I implore you to do whatever *you* must to rescue my daughter. Prince Alakaid, Dragon Sage of Malyndor, pray I beg you to save Jade from that devil."

Holding Edmund's strong gaze, Alec didn't hesitate to close the distance between them. Holding out his hand, the two men gripped each other's forearms.

"I promise you, I will return with her or not at all."

A lump in his throat, Edmund could only nod. Retracing his steps, he cleared the area as the warriors climbed onto the back of the dragons and took to the air. Every part of him wanted to join this crusade. But alas, he held fast. He couldn't risk the others' lives by charging in with blind fury. As it was, the duke knew Alec would be the only one with the power to complete this mission. To think there a time he ever doubted his worth.

Forehead leaning against the cold bar of her tiny window, Jade gazed out into the city of Zangar. The thick piece of metal was unnecessary. No human could possibly fit out the thin opening. All it seemed to do was obscure Jade's view of the crowded, gloomy streets below. Not that she cared to really see them.

The moment their ship docked in the harbor, Jade's heart sank. She was quickly ushered onto the deck, down the gang plank and into an enclosed windowless carriage. Deprived of even a moment to get her bearings, she was escorted to the capital's central feature without a word from anyone.

Much like when she stood before the Grimstone Colosseum, the Imperial Tower was an imposing structure. Stretching two hundred feet tall, the central tower was flanked by first five, then three story wings which folded around it in the shape of a pentagon. At the back was Dunbrook Palace. The fortress certainly lived up to its name as the strong hold of Zerrok. Jade could imagine no way of breaking through the layers of stone and steel.

Turning away from the window with disgust, her focus shifted to her cell. If you exchanged the surrounding rock with wood, it reminded Jade of her room aboard Vincent's vessel. A single bed was pushed up against one plain wall with a small table and chair on the opposite side of the space. An equally tiny fireplace was beside the table with a bucket tucked in the corner, serving as her washroom. It was a poor comparison to even the inns Jade had previously stayed in. A proper restroom at the very least was always provided. Refusing to give that area of her chambers anymore thought, Jade peered at the solid wooden door blocking her escape. A barred opening near the top sapped at the warmth from her modest flames. Three times a day a servant tended to the pitiful blaze when they arrived with her meals. With no kindling left behind, it was difficult to fight off the unusual chill which seemed to permanently linger within the thick walls.

How did Alec survive in such harsh surroundings?

Granted, Jade knew she still had it far better than the bare, damp cells in which the warrior resided during the years he fought as a gladiator. Yet, compared to the luxury she had always known, this was an utter nightmare. The urge for some type of movement had the noble pacing the cramped space. Locked in, the endless not knowing, the vast less waiting, was driving her mad. All there was left for her to do was think. Once more, Jade's thoughts turned to Alec.

I miss you so much my love.

How would he find her here? With no way to send a message, only her captives could alert him to her whereabouts.

As if that shall happen. A cold, humorless laugh slipped past Jade's lips.

Such odds were beyond slim. Dropping down on the stiff bed, Jade sighed. There was no hope. For the first time, a darkness squeezed her chest and would not let up. It tightened, sapping at her very soul with its cold unyielding fingers. The first tear rained down on her curled hands. Another followed, and another, until her shoulders were shaking from the assault. Sucking in a ragged breath, Jade covered her face with her hands. It didn't matter if anyone heard her. Jade no longer cared about keeping up appearances. This cell would be her tomb unless, of course, Vincent chose to move her elsewhere. No matter the cost, she would never agree to be his.

Curse that man.

Alec wouldn't be able to protect her from him this time. An image of his somewhat shy half grin filled her vision. Despite the grimness of her situation, Jade felt a small smile pull at the corner of her mouth. How did he always have so much strength when he lived through these horrors? Sniffling, Jade began to wipe her face in a no-nonsense manner.

That's right. If Alec found a way out of Zerrok not once, but twice, then what would stop him from defeating the odds again? Alec always came for her. They were bonded. Jade chose him and after all they went through over the last year so they could be together, she found it difficult to believe fate would tear them asunder.

I cannot lose him again.

Rising, Jade strode back to the window. There had to be some way for her to inform Alec of her location. Jade couldn't give up. She couldn't explain it, but somehow across the distance, thinking of Alec gave her some of his strength. Taking a deep breath, Jade slowly exhaled.

"I shall find a way," she whispered to the scattered clouds outside.

As if in answer, a few rays of sunlight peeked through the grey. Nodding to herself, Jade began to twist back just as a knock sounded on the door. Without awaiting an answer, Vincent entered the small space.

Jade's body immediately stiffened in response. Seeing him now, at this pinnacle point in her turmoil of whirling emotions, hardened her resolve. It was time for him to get his comeuppance.

Keeping her expression pleasant yet neutral, Jade dropped into a graceful curtsy.

"Greetings, milord."

Holding a tray piled with food, Vincent grinned. Striding into the cramped space he told her fondly, "There is no need for such formalities sweetheart. We are alone after all and soon to be wed."

Jade's stomach churned sourly. This was not going to be a pleasant meal.

"Indeed."

Vincent might not have noted the tightness of her voice, yet he did manage to see the redness of her eyes, and the remaining sheen of tears upon her cheeks. Gaze widening, he rushed to the noblewoman's side and loosely gripped her hands.

"Jade, my dear," he began bending down to peer into her face. "Whatever is the matter? Pray, you know you can tell me anything."

Jade almost snorted. He was the cause of her distress. *I doubt he would enjoy hearing such a confession.* Though his affections were sorely misplaced, it occurred to Jade that they were indeed genuine. Vincent truly believed himself in love with her in some twisted way, and her happiness seemed to matter to the lord. This could be just the opportunity she needed.

Sighing dramatically, Jade lowered her eyelashes and sniffed.

"I do not wish to trouble you."

Pulling back slightly, Vincent rested a hand over his heart. "It would be of no trouble, my dear. Nothing is too trivial. Come," he instructed, leading her to the bed. Lowering themselves down onto the edge, he turned and peered at Jade. "Now, what is the cause of this distress?"

Jade shrugged her shoulders, trying to buy herself a moment to carefully choose her words.

"I just…I miss my mother so much. I cannot imagine how terribly frightened she must be. She knows not where I am or with whom." Jade wiped her one eye. "I wish there was some way to which I could convey my whereabouts so at the very least, my mother would know I am safe. What if she believes me to be dead?"

Sobbing, Jade covered her face with her hands. Her words were to deceive Vincent however, the heart behind them was not false. Jade really did miss her mother and the possibility of her believing Jade to be dead was quite real.

"Do not fret," Vincent soothed, patting her gently.

Many times he'd heard it said that young ladies were always close to their mothers. This situation must be difficult for her and none of it was her fault. Vincent frowned. *Damn that slave.* He was still causing his Jade pain, even after liberating her from his clutches. The noble suddenly straightened. Perhaps he could use this to his advantage to strengthen Jade's growing favor.

"I do not wish to see you unhappy, my dear," Vincent told her thoughtfully. "Would it please you if I sent for the Duchess? I know how close the two of you are."

Jade fought the impulse to jump to her feet and shriek excitedly. *This intrigue may be a success.*

"Could you?" Jade questioned squeezing his hand. "I would dearly love to see her again."

Rising to his feet, Vincent rubbed his palms together. "I see no reason why I cannot do so. Yes. Yes, I shall make the arrangements." A finger pressing against his lips, the noble's eyes lowered to the ground. "It should be done soon, prior to the first battle to come," he added quietly to himself.

"Battle?" Jade repeated incredulously.

Vincent grimaced. "I did not mean for you to hear that."

She refused to let it slide. "Who is to battle?"

"Why Zerrok and Malyndor of course. I have it on good authority that the war shall be beginning rather soon."

A chill raced through Jade's body. Skin paling, her breath temporarily caught in her throat.

"There is no cause for alarm," Vincent promised. "We shall be quite safe here in my homeland."

"Homeland?" she echoed. Jade had no idea to what he was referring. Vincent's father was the Earl of Parlen. He was, without a doubt, a true Malyndorian noble. Had Vincent completely lost his senses once more?

"I do not understand."

Tilting his head to the side, the lord puckered his lips. "I suppose you would not. Few know of my family's true origins." He nodded. "That is correct, the Brookshire bloodline are descendants of Zerrokian nobility. This kingdom is in my blood and we shall find sanctuary here."

It took a moment for Jade to form any type of response. "Then it is quite fortunate that your family has remained loyal to the land of your ancestors." Jade paused. "I thought there was an understanding between King Titus and King David which disfavored a war."

A vile, twisted smirk appeared on the man's face. "He is no longer a concern. Come," he said lifting the small table and bringing it to Jade's side. "Let us enjoy a meal together, my dear. There is no more need for us to discuss any unpleasantness."

Unable to press the issue further, Jade smiled faintly and shifted her focus to the next task at hand. Somehow, though she couldn't say how, Jade was able to eat a fair amount of the food Vincent set on her plate. After another hour of his company he departed, leaving Jade alone with nothing but the faint hope that he would deliver some sort of message to lead to her freedom.

It was dark outside when the next visitor paid Jade a call. Curled up on the bed, she was dozing peacefully when two soldiers stormed in.

"You're to come with us," the first man commanded sharply.

Flinching, Jade pushed herself into an upright position as she rapidly blinked the sleep from her eyes. Thus far, everyone had treated her politely, if not somewhat coldly. This dramatic turn was most unexpected. Jade's gaze widened slightly as she spotted the three lines marking their uniforms. These men were soldiers of The Pure. *What are they doing here?* This fortress was the stronghold of the Royal Family. Jade's heartbeat increased and her palms grew slick.

"Come with us," he barked again.

"What is our destination?" she asked cautiously.

"No questions," the second man snapped. "Just come along."

Scowling, they stepped closer to the bed. Their silent message was clear, come willingly or they would use force. Jade understood she had no choice but to obey. Pressing her lips tightly together, she withheld any further arguments. It would not be to her benefit.

This was the first time she was outside her cell since arriving at the Imperial Tower. Walking with one guard in front and the second behind her, Jade did her best to check out her surroundings. There wasn't much to see in the dimly lit corridors. Three other cells lined the end of the hall beside Jade's. As far as she could tell, the rooms were empty as she quickly passed by. At the opposite end, a few guards stood at attention beside a set of stone steps. Escorted up the steep stairway, Jade tried not to stumble. The stairs curved with the hexagonal shape of the tower and seemed to go on forever. Here and there a door appeared beside a landing, yet Jade couldn't keep track of the true number of flights she was ascending.

It was only five levels until they reached the very peak. With every step, the sinking feeling filling Jade increased. Who would be awaiting her at the top? A glow shined above them as the small group climbed the final stairwell. Reaching the open landing, Jade's brows rose. The entire length of the floor was one massive chamber. Small rivers of flames lined the outer walls with ornate metal drums lighting the more central part of the room. Mouth gaping, Jade's eyes traced the arches of the high domed ceiling. Her lips curved into a frown as she caught sight of several runes painted among the map of stars.

A hand pushed her forward from behind. The noble hadn't realized that her movement halted during her examination. Shooting the man at her flank a glare, Jade traveled further into the space. Lines painted the polished stone floor beneath her feet, forming the shape of a pentagram. Written along them was a series of magical runes similar to the ones upon the ceiling. At the very back of the chamber was a single door on the right hand side of an altar. Ominously standing before the altar were three middle-aged men of varying heights and weights. All of them were dressed in white tunics with red undershirts. On the left breast of their tunics were three blood red vertical lines like slices from a dagger.

The first man on the left was average height with broad shoulders and an equally broad girth. The one in the middle was the tallest, with a long thin beard that descended into a point like a weapon. All the way to the right was a shorter man holding a polished walking stick. His solid grey hair seemed oddly matched with his more youthful features.

The confident slyness of their grins caused Jade to withdraw a step.

"Welcome to Zangar, Lady Jade," greeted the man on the right.

His smooth voice echoed through the room, sounding much louder than it was, after the lengthy silence Jade was used to. Years of training had the noble dropping into a graceful curtsy.

"Thank you for your...hospitality. May I ask to whom I am speaking?"

"Our guest seems to be well-bred," the center man observed. "I can see why Lord Vincent holds such a strong interest in her."

"Indeed," the first man agreed. Returning his attention to Jade he told her, "We are the true and righteous leaders of mankind. We are The Pure."

"What precisely is The Pure?" Jade questioned, before she could stop herself.

Her hosts showed no signs of disapproval. In fact, the growing smiles on their faces gave the impression of being quite pleased with her inquiry.

"It represents the core of all living creatures. The pure of heart..."

"The pure of mind…" the second man added.

"The pure of spirit," the last man finished. "You may call us Lord Beltmore, Lord Sever, and Lord Desmond."

"Milords," Jade murmured, bowing once more. *Oh my stars!* Jade's mind shouted. These men weren't just any members of the extremist group. No, she was in the presence of the rulers themselves. Trying to swallow the lump forming in her throat, Jade gripped her hands together to keep them from shaking. How did Vincent find himself allied with such powerful men? And why would they waste their time on an audience with her? Jade couldn't think of any reason she would be of value to them or their twisted cause.

"You must be wondering why we have summoned you for this meeting," Sever said, causing Jade's eyes to widen.

They laughed.

"It was a natural guess to make," Desmond told her. "We merely wish to welcome you to our Kingdom and assure you that no harm shall come to you while you are staying with us."

"Indeed," Beltmore agreed. "We understand there are many people, especially the younger members of nobility, who have been unjustly influenced by the affliction of magic which is poisoning many of our neighboring kingdoms. Our mission is to purify this evil and those who willingly spread this darkness. We bear no ill will towards those uninfected and placed in a difficult situation they cannot escape from, such as yourself."

Lips parting, Jade lightly shook her head. "I do not understand. I was under the impression that I am a prisoner here. Yet, you make it sound as if I am not but a guest, milords, and Malyndor has been overtaken by some type of plague."

The men nodded gravely.

"Yes, a most contagious and horrific disease."

"Sorcery," Desmond enlightened. "The temptations of such unholy magic can taint even the purest soul with its darkness. The goodness, which used to live here before dragons brought their evil to the hands of humans, shall be restored."

"You will remain in isolation until we can determine the damage you have sustained from all your years living in a place tainted with magic."

Shoulders pulling back and chin lifting, Jade's gaze locked upon Beltmore who was the last to speak. "Sorcerers are not an enemy of mankind. You have declared them an affliction, yet they have done much to benefit the lives of countless people over the centuries. There are always those who selfishly use any form of power for evil deeds. Magic itself is not to blame. A war with Malyndor will only bring about much sorrow and death for the innocent people you claim to desire to protect. If improving their lives is what you seek, then I implore you to cease this path of destruction before it is too late."

Watching Jade's unwavering gaze, the leaders of The Pure frowned. Little did she know her spirited words would not sway them.

Lord Sever petted his long beard. "She is more corrupted than we first believed."

"I am not corrupted," Jade stressed, stamping her foot.

"Oh, I wouldn't say that," interrupted a voice.

Jade jerked back as Jerric strode into the chamber from the single door near the altar. His son, Colton, trailed behind him with a wide smirk. No words made it past Jade's lips. It was as if her mind did not desire to accept the truth standing plainly in front of her. Jerric and Colton were the traitors?

"Master Jerric," Desmond said with the hint of displeasure. "We were not expecting you to return so soon."

His eyes darted to Jade's pale face, then back at the other man.

The sorcerer shrugged. "It couldn't be helped. Our work in Malyndor has reached its end for the time being. Preparing for our guests is of greater precedence."

Unable to look away, Jade watched the two sages join the leaders. Their words didn't seem to reach her as she practically stared at them. Colton gave Jade a sideways glance. Something about his cool, arrogant expression lit a spark within her. Stiffening, Jade squeezed her hands. *Of course,* she thought to herself. No wonder their claims of all magic being a plague rang false. This was a ruse of some deeper plot. Allying themselves with wizards proved their hatred of magic was untrue, which would also mean they were tricking the soldiers under their command. Feeding off people's fears, The Pure used Zerrok's subject's ignorance to their advantage. Jade doubted that they actually sought to rid the world of all magic. She just didn't know what their real goal was. Even so, none of this shone any light onto the question of why she was here.

"Pray, tell me Master Jerric, how long have you been a part of this false war against magic?" Jade inquired softly.

Everyone stopped talking, as all eyes shifted to the noblewoman.

"What is your part of this dubious deal?" she continued. "Not a whole kingdom, surely. Vast tracks of land perhaps? The right to rule over a large fief like an earl…or a duke?"

Eyes narrowing shrewdly, Jerric said nothing for a moment. Beside him, Colton's lips pulled back with a snarl. His father cut off any forthcoming words with a quick snap of his wrist.

"You seem to be confused, Lady Jade," Beltmore soothed. "Perhaps you should rest."

I seem to have guessed correctly. Gracefully shaking her head, Jade declined. "There is no need for me to do so. I can see through the veil of your plans quite clearly. What I do not comprehend is why assist Lord Vincent in my capture? Of what value could I possibly have to your plans?"

A slow twisted smile appeared on Jerric's face. "I see you are more than just a pretty girl after all. You are a credit to your father, milady."

"Master Jerric!" chided Desmond.

The sage ignored him. "Money and power are, of course, my primary motivations. Why be a bit player where my true potential is unappreciated, when I can rise to the greatness I deserve elsewhere? As for your part in this battle—a clever lady, such as yourself, should be able to guess the role she is to play." Jerric edged closer and lowered his voice to a staged whisper. "You are his greatest weakness."

Jade paled. Eyes growing wide, her hand moved to cover her partially opened mouth.

The sorcerer nodded. A gleam shined in his grey gaze with the thought of what was to come. Soon the barbarian was going to be receiving what he had coming to him.

"We know what you mean to him," he continued. "Know that he would travel to the farthest reaches of the world or even here to this tower for you. Lady Jade, you are the key to Prince Alakaid's undoing."

"The Prince," scoffed Sever. "All these years of planning and now, at the pinnacle of our success, he shows up alive. This could have ruined everything."

"Yes," Beltmore agreed. "He should have already been taken care of."

Peering at the two men in a stunned silence, Jade's heart pounded rapidly. What did they mean they thought they took care of him? Did they have something to do with Alec's kidnapping? Something intangible drew her attention to the tall center man with a seemingly permanent scowl. The corners of his mouth twitched with amusement.

"Yes," he drawled slowly like a hiss. "We were the ones who arranged his disappearance all those years ago. The Pure has great power. It was easy for us to have the boy taken from his bed while the king and queen slept in ignorance."

"We paid Baron Hawkins a small fortune to kill the prince," Desmond enlightened.

"But he did not kill Alec," Jade said more to herself than the men before her. "He brought him back to Zerrok instead. Baron Hawkins was Alec's first master."

"And his greed surpassed our estimations. It was not until recently that we discovered the depth of his betrayal in staging the prince's death. Hawkins's foolishness cost us dearly. He should have finished him off when he was done with the boy, yet he sold him as a gladiator which transformed him into the dangerous foe Alakaid has become today."

"Even worse," Beltmore inserted, "it led the boy back to Malyndor where he was trained by their most powerful sage."

Sever's eyes sharpened like knives. "Now the Baron will pay for his grave mistake. The stain of his bloodline will be cleansed from our lands. No more will he be able to inflict any damage upon the transformation to come. Only one major obstacle stands in the way of our victory and soon he will be nothing, not even a footnote in our history."

Jerric didn't stop watching Jade's face throughout the leader's speech.

These monsters are trying to murder Alec! Vincent must be nothing more than another pawn in their deeply rooted schemes. Jade doubted they would uphold any bargain made with the exuberant noble. If they managed to succeed in their twisted plan, Alec wouldn't be the only one perishing in the Imperial Tower. Jade knew too much for them to consider setting her free.

"That's right," Jerric told her frostily. "You are the bait to trap and slay the Dragon Prince."

The fear pumping through Jade's veins up until this point released its hold. They might have her right where they wanted, and Alec would come just as they strived for, but nothing more would be as they sought. Jade knew Alec as few others did. His anger was not a crutch. It was like freshly sharpened steel just waiting for the perfect time to strike.

"You cannot hope to defeat him. Alec is more powerful than any of you," Jade returned unwavering.

Jerric smiled broadly as he pointed to the different marks painted in the space. "This room is filled with anti-magic seals that I created myself. No one can use magic here, no matter how strong they might believe themselves to be. Tell me Lady Jade, can that barbarian defeat an army without sorcery?"

Jade's gaze didn't flinch. Chin lifting, she looked at the wizard and replied in a steady voice, "Yes, he can. I do hope you are prepared to fall on his blade, traitor."

CHAPTER 16

Gripping the reins of his borrowed steed, Alec kept his dark eyes focused on the unfamiliar road. Duke Edmund had done more than merely given his blessing for the prince to defy his father's orders; he also gave Malcolm the address to one of his most trusted agents outside of Zangar.

Cool as an autumn breeze and efficient as a blade, the man quickly produced four strong steeds to personally lead them into the city with the aid of one of his sons. By the time the sun shone highest in the sky, the warriors would be at their destination.

Alec glanced up into the swirling clouds above. Vincent could employ whatever tricks he wanted. An army could stand between them and the front gate for all he cared, but it would not hinder Alec's mission. He had a few surprises of his own this time around.

Reaching the tall iron bars of the tower's outer wall the companions dismounted. Thanking their guide, Alec briefly watched him and his son lead the horses back down the bustling road. Slowly, he turned back to the gate. Eyes traveling the length of the metal, Alec inhaled deeply. No tremble raced through his body, nor did his heart beat any faster at the sight. This was what he had been waiting for. There was no going back. A controlled calm dominated his surrounding aura, much like the days of battle within the arena. Soon enough, these men would also regret crossing his sword.

"Ready?" Garth questioned standing beside him.

"Absolutely," the sage told him striding to the entrance.

Stiffening, four soldiers glared down their noses as they gripped the hilts of their blades.

"Halt right there," one of them snapped. "State your business."

Shoulders pulled back, Alec's neutral mask didn't so much as twitch. "I'm Prince Alakaid of Malyndor, here by invitation. These men are my personal guard."

Blinking, the soldiers' hands loosened their grip momentarily before tightening like a vise.

"He really came," a younger man whispered at the back of the group.

"We have been expecting you, Your Highness," announced a dapper middle-aged man who walked towards them from the guardhouse. "My name is Charles. I have been assigned the task of escorting you." He turned to look at the guards. "What are you waiting for? Open the gate."

Keys jiggled as the men rushed about to do his bidding. Eyes never leaving the visitors, the iron bars were immediately secured as soon as Alec's group cleared the passage.

"Welcome to the Imperial Tower, Prince Alakaid. As you know, magic is forbidden in Zerrok, so I trust your dragon is not with you as per the arrangement."

"Do you see it?"

The man's eyes narrowed. The threat of a frown pulled at the corners of his mouth.

"No," Charles answered coldly. He eyed Alec's hand resting lightly by his blade. "Your weapons will need to remain here."

Alec didn't bother with any form of pretense. "That's not going to happen," he stated bluntly.

"Then, I cannot allow you to continue."

Looking the man up and down, Alec lifted his chin. Behind him, his fellow warriors gripped their blades. His aura darkened, forming a visible mist which anyone could see. The Zerrokian soldiers jerked back several steps.

"Enough with this farce," Alec commanded in a firm, yet deathly quiet tone. "You know perfectly well that I'm only here for Lady Jade." His eyes shot to the next solid steel gate blocking their path. "Either take me to her or get out of my way. I have no patience for games."

Face contorting, Charles opened his mouth to speak, then clamped it closed again. Swallowing, he took a moment prior to trying again.

"Of course, Your Highness. Pray, follow me."

Striding towards the next passage, the man didn't bother awaiting a response. The doors parted with a small wave of the man's hand. Atop the battlements, the soldiers stared down at the Malyndorians as Alec led them deeper into the fortress's grounds. Just as the first gate was shut upon entering, the second one was instantly locked the moment all five visitors cleared its path. A thick sheet of tension filled the space. Crowded on each side of the courtyard was an armed battalion of soldiers. A narrow path cut through them, heading towards the main door of the Imperial Tower. Eyes tracking Alec's movements, the guards said nothing as they stood stiff as statues.

Heart racing, Isabelle fought the urge to draw her blade.

"Do you think they're going to attack?" she whispered, privately hoping her words would not spur their charge.

"Difficult to say," the great sage answered quietly. "This certainly won't make our departure without issue."

"It would be too simple for them to strike now. They must know Alec could wipe out a large force with his magic," Garth added studying the men out of the corner of his eye. "I doubt this is the trap they have set for us."

"We shall see soon enough," Alec murmured.

Massive doors held open wide to receive them, the outside daylight did little to penetrate the darkness waiting within the fortress. A tingle traced the mark on Alec's back. *Be on your guard,* he warned himself needlessly. Stepping into the gloom, a steel beam was slid across the entrance locking them inside. Glancing behind them at the sound, when Alec turned back, their escort was nowhere to be seen.

Where did he go?

"Looking for someone?" snidely questioned a condescending voice that Alec knew all too well.

"Why am I not surprised to find you here, Jerric?" Malcolm asked, his words echoing through the dark space.

He suspected the master sage for some time now, though part of him wished Kelvin was mistaken in his belief that there was a traitor within the Emerald Sages. Jerric was an egotistical man, but he was still a fellow sage. Honor and loyalty apparently meant nothing to him.

An evil laugh was the sage's only reply. Suddenly, torches came to life all around the chamber, revealing a whole slew of guards. The large space bore high stone ceilings held up by dark marble pillars spread evenly about. Long shadows cast a sinister gleam, while across the room, Jerric stood in the sole doorway to the corridor. Holding out his hands with a shrug, a smile appeared on his lips.

"I can't say I'm surprised that you figured it out, former *Grandmaster,*" Jerric mocked. "You do your sage name credit, Malcolm. Still, it must have been irksome discovering there were things you did not know. Enlighten me, just how long did it take you to uncover the truth? Or was your announcement now merely a guess?"

Malcolm's jaw tightened.

"So, it was a guess," Jerric drawled. "How frustrating for the great Cunning Sage to be unable to identify the one tearing his precious academies apart. I have looked forward to this day for a long time, old man."

"And what day would that be?

"Outwitting you, of course."

Crossing his arms, Jerric peered down at them from his beak-like nose. A smirk etched in his features, he stood proudly with all the confidence of a predator who believed he had cornered his prey.

"I assure you, boy, that day has not yet come. You are nothing, but a disgrace. Did you really believe siding with our enemies would give you the power you desire?"

The gleam in the other wizard's face was not comforting. "Yes. Because, unlike King Titus, The Pure are willing to do whatever it takes to be the strongest. You have no idea what is to come. No matter what you do, you have already lost, Malcolm." Gesturing towards the soldiers surrounding the perimeter of the chamber, Jerric continued, "You are already too late to save Zerrok. King David has perished, as will you."

The ringing silence which followed held a charged energy. Alec could not recall a time when his teacher ever looked so cross. Hands tightly curled by his side, Malcolm watched Jerric's gleeful features with sharply narrowed eyes. There was no redemption for him now. The sage was too far gone. And so, it would appear, was Zerrok. The southern kingdom had fallen.

"What of the princes?" the Cunning Sage questioned coolly. "Have you added the sin of their blood to your growing collection?"

"Not yet," Jerric sneered. "It's time someone taught you the meaning of fear. You're not as invincible as you think, Malcolm. Let us duel, just the two of us, and see once and for all who has greater power."

Pulling himself up to his full height, Malcolm stretched out his fingers. "If a duel is what you seek, then so be it." The sage quickly glanced back at his companions. "Leave this to me. Our mission must take priority. Save Lady Jade and the princes if you can. I shall join you when it is done."

Alec opened his mouth to argue, yet stopped as Isabelle's hand curved over his arm. Squeezing lightly, she let go.

Malcolm will be fine, she silently assured him.

Sighing heavily, Alec nodded. "Be careful."

The sage offered him a shadow of a smile in return. "Our situation must seem grave indeed if a youngin' like you is worrying about this old man."

Snorting, Alec shook his head as he veered to the right, edging around the wizard's battle. As he and his fellow warriors headed towards the backside of the chamber, Jerric's slimy voice demanded the older sage's attention.

"Aww, what sweet sentiments. I do hope you and your barbarian said your final goodbyes." Giving Malcolm no further reprieve, Jerric raised a palm towards the ceiling. "Airanlor, dark tempest," he hollered, summoning the first spell.

Thick grey clouds materialized overhead. The swirling mass swept over the space, extinguishing several of the flames flickering about the room. Long shadows were cast across the polished stone floor.

Watching the storm arise, Malcolm slowly drew his blade. His aura rose around him, filling his body with the rejuvenating energy.

Jutting out his chin, Jerric began to stalk towards his enemy.

"Using a sword in a magic battle," he scolded. "You never change Malcolm. After all these years you're still as unrefined as your barbarian."

Stepping forward, the great sage shrugged, causing Jerric to scowl. If he believed his mind games would work on him, then Jerric was sorely mistaken, as he was with so many other things.

Placing a hand behind his back, Jerric removed a whip from his right hip. Uncurling the material, he shot his tainted aura through it. The act was proof enough for Malcolm that there was no saving the other wizard. His spirit was so filled with malice that he could use it as a weapon.

Gradually circling each other, the two sages moved closer towards the center of the space. Meanwhile, the remaining companions strode towards the doorway on the far side of the chamber. The soldiers stationed there quickly zeroed in upon their targets. Their orders were absolute: kill the Dragon Sage.

Garth gripped the hilt of his blade as they were forced to slow their pace.

"What do you think, forty maybe fifty men?"

Alec's sharp gaze continued to scan them. "Easily. I suppose we should be honored."

Nathan scoffed, "The army outside would have been much more trouble. I do believe they are counting on the sage to pick us off."

"Then, they grossly overestimated his power," Isabelle interjected. "Jerric's ego is his greatest down fall."

Weapons firmly clutched in their hands, the three swordsmen shifted so their backs were to the center of their group where Isabelle now stood. The sorceress was stronger with support magic than she was as a warrior. This was her chance to show off some of the skills she'd honed since returning to Malyndor.

"Airanlor, gravity surge."

The air surrounding Alec, Garth and Nathan fluttered. The steel in their hands felt lighter, and when they moved, their steps swifter. Soldiers nearing them charged without hesitation. Lunging forward, Alec's blade sank into the first man. No heavier than a feather, he pulled his weapon lose and swung it in a wide circle, slashing at his opponents as

Isabelle stayed safely behind him. Hands together, her focus remained on keeping her spell active as the warriors battled around her.

Further to the left, the two master sages began their own private fight. It was more than just two men battling for survival. It was another skirmish in the age-old war of darkness versus light.

Snapping his whip, Jerric attacked repeatedly with the ferocity of a viper.

Malcolm gracefully parried each blow, inching closer as he did so. When the whip wrapped itself about his blade, the Cunning Sage released his grip, allowing Jerric to cast off his weapon. At the same time, the great sage called up both an energy ball and another surprise Jerric could not hear.

Sweeping his whip back to guard his front, Jerric realized he could not block the blast in time. Instead of summoning his own spell, the wizard leapt to the side, disappearing into the pit of one of his shadows along with his tainted weapon.

Jogging towards his sword, Malcolm's eyes continued to search the space for his missing foe. Using his foot, the mage flipped the blade into the air, taking hold of the hilt once more.

Rolling out of a shadow, Jerric attacked his adversary's exposed back with a fire ball.

In the midst of turning, the blast connected with Malcolm's left shoulder. He staggered, partially hunched over as he regained his footing.

Watching his foe, Jerric frowned. Instead of blood staining the scorched patch of clothing, electricity arched up and crackled at the spot.

Damn it, the evil sage mentally cursed.

Somehow, Malcolm had protected himself with lightning armor without Jerric being aware.

"Do you really believe such a trick is going to protect you?" Jerric sneered. "Your mind is waning, old man."

Whip in one hand, the sage started unleashing a volley of flames as he snapped his wrist with the other.

Swiftly guiding his sword through the air, Malcolm blocked each attack nipping away at him. Stepping back, his one foot suddenly sank into the floor. Edged backwards, the sage was pushed into one of Jerric's portals.

Offering his opponent no quarter, the bird-like sage struck again. While his adversary parried one of his flames, Jerric managed to land a crucial blow. The end of his whip encircled Malcolm's wrist, poisoning the other sage's aura with his malice. Both a hand and foot encumbered, Jerric knew it wouldn't be long until the master finally fell.

"How does it feel to be ensnared?"

Malcolm didn't answer. He supposed it was a good thing Jerric's ego was so unmatched. The whip loosened around his wrist, but that wasn't his main concern. It was the fire balls. At the moment, the bombardment had ceased, giving him the opportunity to change the course of this battle.

"Surgeon, lightning storm," the Cunning Sage called.

The dark clouds circling above them thundered. Streaks of color flashed through the thick grey. Then, by Malcolm's command, bolts of lightning shot down aiming for Jerric. Jumping back, he released his weapon from his opponent. Fury was etched in his twisted features.

The bright flashes, mixed with Jerric's distracted focus, allowed Malcolm to pull his leg free. Pain thumped in his left wrist as the skin changed to a blackish-purple color.

"You won't get away!" roared Jerric. Eyes blazing, he directed a hand at one of the pillars near the other wizard. "Rokon, crumble."

The stone instantly shattered. Turning to the next one, Jerric repeated his spell.

He will destroy the entire chamber at this rate, Malcolm concluded grimly, as he dodged some falling debris. Closing in upon the doorway, he spotted Alec and his friends finishing off the last of the soldiers.

They were positioned closer to the middle of the chamber. As the columns began to crash down, the warriors raced towards the doorway. With the rate at which the room was caving in, Alec knew they wouldn't make it in time. Twenty feet from their destination he spun around, lifting his hands as he summoned an air spell to suspend the rubble raining down above them.

The sorcerer directed his powers towards the two main pillars standing between the entrance to the tower and the chamber they still occupied. Jerric was nowhere to be seen as Alec glanced at his teacher racing towards them.

Throughout the chamber, stone columns burst apart, followed by a shower of stone.

Clenching his jaw, Alec kept his hands in place. A loud cracking rang out above him as his friends passed safely through the entry. Gazing up, the sorcerer saw a river of fractures quickly growing. His gazed darted between the ceiling and his teacher. *Come on. Just a little longer.*

Retracing her steps, Isabelle approached from behind.

"Let me help."

"Not this time, little lady," Garth answered for the sage. Looking at both Malcolm running towards them and Alec's strained expression, he knew there was already much weighing down upon the sage. Literally. *Now is not the time for Alec to be worrying about Isabelle, too.*

Not allowing her to argue, the swordsman picked the feisty woman up and carried her out of harm's way.

Sneaking out of a shadow by Alec's right, Jerric created a knife of ice. Face, hard like stone, he zeroed in on the prince. The others didn't matter. Alec however, he would not, could not, allow to escape from his trap alive. Body ready to spring, the evil sage gripped his weapon tighter.

"Tsumorri, freeze," Malcolm hollered pointing at the other wizard.

Ice formed over Jerric's boots and across the floor in a large circle, pinning him in place. Releasing a breath like an angry hiss, he directed flashing eyes at the master sage.

"You can't escape me!" Jerric declared with a snarl.

Snapping his whip, the evil wizard caught his adversary around the ankle. Yanked off his feet, Malcolm gazed at Alec. Their eyes met in a silent moment. Watching the grim determination gleaming in the warrior's chocolate irises, Malcolm knew his former student would not abandon him— no matter the risk to himself. Face set, he knew exactly what he must do. Raising a palm, the Cunning Sage cast one final spell.

"Airanlor, gust."

A powerful cyclone shot forward, slamming into the younger sorcerer and sending him flying backwards through the archway. Skidding across the polished stone, Alec ceased his slide. He then quickly pushed himself into a sitting position just in time to see large chunks of debris piling up where he had been standing.

"Malcolm!" the sorcerer shouted rushing to his feet. "Malcolm, can you hear me?"

There was no answer from amongst the thunder of still falling rock.

"Malcolm," Alec shouted again. "Malcolm answer me."

"Malcolm," Isabelle echoed beside him. Shoulders slumping, she all but whispered, "Oh, no. He can't be…"

Dropping to his knees, Alec couldn't seem to tear his gaze away from the rubble. *He can't be gone.* Malcolm was more than a teacher. He was a friend, a confidant and Alec knew there was still so much he had to learn from the man. No, the Cunning Sage couldn't be defeated by the likes of Jerric.

Leaping to his feet, Alec focused on the boulders. "Rokon, crumble."

Blasting the stone, his aura swirled around him, growing brighter with each strike. The sheer mass on debris was so vast that little impact had been made.

Nathan and Garth exchanged a serious glance. Nodding, Garth joined his friend's side.

"Alec," he said placing a hand on the younger man's shoulder. "We need to keep moving. Malcolm wanted you to complete this mission. Besides, Lady Jade needs you."

The blasts subsided. Slowly, the sorcerer lowered his arm. "He's still alive."

Alec's firm words left no room for discussion.

Garth didn't argue. He wanted the wizard to have survived just as much as Alec, even if the odds were against him. Now wasn't the time to discuss this. Any moment, more soldiers would be closing in upon their location.

"I'm sure he is, but we can't linger here."

With a heavy sigh, Alec finally turned away from the wreckage. "You're right. We have to rescue Lady Jade and the Zerrok princes...for Malcolm. Otherwise, he'll never let us hear the end of it."

A brief silence fell before Isabelle stepped forward. "I will go," she declared, raising her chin. "Concentrate on saving her ladyship. Let me go to the dungeon and seek out the princes."

"Are you certain?"

Isabelle dipped her head in a quick bob. "Of course. After the battles we faced in the arena, a few mere soldiers will be nothing."

Alec raised a brow. It was times like this he found it difficult to decipher if the sorceress was having a lark or not. Before he could comment, Nathan stepped forward.

"I will aid her. Splitting up is the only way to accomplish both tasks."

I don't care for weakening our numbers, but Nathan is right. If we remain together, there won't be time to rescue everyone. The sage gave them a stiff nod. "When it is done, return to the dragons. And be on your guard," Alec added. "There's bound to be more traps here."

"We will," Isabelle promised cheerfully.

"Good luck. She can be quite the handful," the gruff warrior told Nathan with a laugh as the two teams began to go their separate ways.

"I am not," she denied playfully. Spinning on her heel, Isabelle strode down the hallway in search of the dungeon.

Nathan easily matched her strides. After a few moments, he gazed around with a frown. Since departing the main chamber, they had yet to encounter another soldier. Where was everyone? A fortress of this size should be teeming with guards, yet they hadn't come across any of the enemy's forces.

"Do you know where you're going?" he questioned in a soft whisper.

Isabelle's rushed steps drew to a halt. "Actually, no, I have no idea where the dungeon is. Do you?"

The swordsman beside her shook his head. Scrunching up her nose, Isabelle's gaze dropped to the ground. No enemy soldier would volunteer such information. There must be some means for them to discover its location and quickly. The seconds seemed to loudly tick by, reverberating in the unusually quiet corridor.

"I know just the spell," exclaimed the sorceress suddenly. Holding out her hands, Isabelle's aura swirled about her like a soft breeze. "Airanlor, echo."

Sound waves vibrated from the yellow magic circles in her palms. Eyelids drifting closed, flashes of images appeared before her eyes. Focusing intently, Isabelle searched the surrounding layout for the entrance to the lower levels.

"Found it," she squealed. Turning to the warrior standing beside her, the sorceress motioned with her hand, "This way."

Moving with great haste, the two companions traveled down the corridors. All the while Nathan's eyes darted about in silent query. They paused once, allowing a small patrol to disappear from sight prior to continuing on their way.

Nothing else seemed to block their path. That changed as they came to the end of the next hall. A pair of large spiked iron gates consumed the entire breadth of the hallway. The warped metal had matching iron snakes coiled amongst the bars. Isabelle cringed at the sight of the vipers. There wasn't time to analyze the strange décor further. Four soldiers were quickly approaching.

Dashing forward, Nathan slashed his blade up at an angle. As the first man dropped, the warrior was already twisting his sword to bring it down upon the next. Their weapons slammed together with a deafening clang. Parrying another attack to his right, Nathan's blade flashed between the two men. A sword swept by at an angle. Ducking under the speeding weapon, Nathan slashed the man to his right up the side of his leg. Turning his wrist, the warrior came back with a cut to the throat.

His other opponent roared, increasing the strength and rate of his attacks. Grip tightening, Nathan raised his blade to defend against the soldier's rage-filled barrage. Pushed back, he searched for a way to turn the tide of the battle.

Nearing the metal bars of the gate, the Zerrokian soldier lifted his broad sword high into the air with both hands. Waiting until the last moment, Nathan ducked to the side. As the man's sword connected with the iron doors, the warrior jabbed him in the gut with a long dagger. He then rolled out of the way as the sword flew at him.

Blood spilling down the man's side, his movements grew more sluggish and less controlled. When their weapons connected once again, Nathan felt his spirits lift. There was a clear difference in the soldier's attacks. This was what he had been waiting for. Pushing against his opponent, the fighter increased his number of strikes. The two blades clanged back and forth as the swordsmen circled around each other. After a few counterattacks, Nathan's foe was unable to keep up. Blade planted in his chest, he dropped to the ground.

Freeing his weapon, Nathan turned to the last remaining soldier. The man faced him with a dark scowl. Holding his sword with one hand, he pulled a knife from his belt with the other.

"Out of our way," Isabelle ordered, thumping the guard on the back of the head with the hilt of her sword.

Head jerking back, Nathan raised his brows. Watching the way the sorceress swept her braid over her shoulder prior to approaching the gate had him chuckling in spite of himself.

"Hmm," she murmured studying the solid metal. "I don't suppose they'll just open it if we ask nicely?"

"Doubtful."

Isabelle shrugged. "Well, it can't be helped then. Rokon, shift."

Pointing towards the right side of the wall next to the gate, the sage slowly brought her arm down in a slicing motion. Turning to the left, she repeated the action before dispelling the magic. Nothing seemed to happen at first. A strange noise, similar to a low groan, sounded as the gate, frame and all, collapsed into the room beyond the corridor.

"Resourceful," Nathan commented with approval. "I'm glad you decided to come with us."

Isabelle didn't get the chance to answer. Her partner was engaging the next wave of enemies and he wasn't the only one upon whom they were bearing down. Drawing her blade, Isabelle met her attacker head on. The clang of metal rang out as Isabelle and her opponent battled in a dance of blades.

The man was a skilled fighter. Utilizing some of Alec's training, Isabelle suddenly dashed to the side and slashed her foe across his thigh. As he dropped to his knee, she grimly landed a final blow.

Searching for another foe, the sorceress found that none remained standing. Blood dripping from his sword, Nathan was studying the chamber's layout. A doorway, straight ahead and to the right, led down a corridor, while the two other openings on the left revealed sets of stairs.

"Which way?" he questioned, glancing down at the tall blonde by his side.

"Here," Isabelle replied, pointing at the first staircase without hesitation.

The stone steps twisted around as they descended into the dimly lit dungeon. Quickly dispatching the four guards stationed at the bottom, the companions peered about with a sigh. Their luck seemed to have come to a halt. Six doorways were spaced across the circular room. Each led to a separate corridor filled with dingy cells.

"Searching each of these is going to take time we don't have. Can you use that spell to seek the princes?"

She shook her head with a sigh. "I don't know what they look like, so it would serve no purpose."

Eyes darting between the doorways, Nathan turned back to the closest one. "It seems we have no choice but to search them all. Let us begin here."

Removing a torch from the wall, the swordsman led the way towards the first dark, musty cell block as the sorceress copied his actions. Relatively deep beneath the main structure, the dungeon contained a familiar chill that Isabelle didn't desire to recall. Water dripping down the wall beside her head, the sage paused her steps. Face paling, she couldn't seem to move her feet. The shadows cast over her surroundings took on a life of their own, intensifying as they sought to swallow her whole. Fingers lightly resting on her arm, caused Isabelle to flinch.

"Isabelle," Nathan called softly, studying her face with furrowed brows. "Are you unwell?"

Placing a hand over her pounding heart, Isabelle shook her head shakily. *I didn't expect these memories to return like this.* She never experienced something of this kind before. For such powerful sensations to completely immobilize her was unsettling. Even during her time locked in the dungeon of Terra, the sorceress couldn't recall being so frightened. *Alec was with me then*. Even with a broken spirit, his presence alone was enough to bring her comfort. The warrior was not with her in this hollow darkness. Yet, Isabelle reminded herself that she wasn't alone. Lifting her gaze, Isabelle's light green eyes met Nathan's bluish-green irises. She shook her head again. This time more steadily.

"I'm fine."

Removing his hand, the warrior twisted back in the other direction. "Stay close."

They continued on, calling the princes' names with no success. Prisoners came to the bars, reaching out towards them as they begged, threatened and cursed the two intruders to release them from their cells.

Observing the way so many of them eyed the sorceress beside him, Nathan pulled Isabelle along, ignoring the chaos of words directed their way. Whether criminals or slaves, he knew not. They didn't have the luxury of time to free any of these prisoners only for them to turn on them.

Finally reaching the end of the row, the companions stepped out into a different corridor which was linked with the other neighboring cell blocks. Turning right, Nathan began the search anew. It was taking longer than he anticipated, and now that the prisoners were all riled up, he didn't see their task improving in the near future.

"Let's keep moving," he advised.

Offering no protest, Isabelle trailed closely behind as they traveled down the next hallway. Close to the main chamber they originally started from, Isabelle's steps stilled. It took Nathan a moment to realize she wasn't with him. Frowning, he joined her side, gazing into the cell she had stopped in front of.

A youth of perhaps fourteen sat glumly by the far wall. He wasn't caked with dirt as the other prisoners were, nor was he dressed in rags. The plain tunic and dark breeches resembled that of a higher-ranking servant. Everything about him clashed when compared to the others locked within the dungeon.

"What is your name?" Isabelle asked, moving closer to the bars. Lifting the torch she tried to brighten the dark cell and get a better view of the boy inside. "I'm Isabelle," she added when he didn't respond. "Did you work in the palace?"

Her words seemed to catch his attention. Peering up at his visitor, the boy tilted his head to the side. Watching them with large eyes, he kept his arms locked around his knees as he slowly dipped his pale blond head in a bob.

Smiling, Isabelle inched closer still. *I knew it.* "We are here to rescue Prince Ashton and Prince Sebastian. Pray, do you know where they are being held?"

"Careful," Nathan warned drawing her back from the bars. "This could be one of their traps."

He found it odd that they would lock this lad here among gruff and hardened criminals unless he earned his place among them. Prisons usually had a system for housing their inmates. The area in which they began their search seemed to be for the worst of them.

"Let's go," Nathan insisted.

A rat scurried by their feet. Isabelle peered back at the youth with determination.

"How can you suggest that we just abandon him? This boy can help us."

Shuffling closer, the young prisoner stood slightly hunched over with his arms hugging himself. "You're really not with the Zerrokian Guard?"

"No. We are from Malyndor."

He took several more steps. "My name is Derek. I used to serve Prince Ashton. If you free me, I can aid you. I know where they were taken."

Brightening, Isabelle turned back toward the cell. "Agreed."

Lifting his hand, Nathan halted her actions once again. "Wait." Eyes narrowing, he gazed sternly at Derek. "How would you know of their location? A servant assigned to royalty wouldn't have knowledge of the dungeon's layout."

"The guards speak of it freely. No one has ever escaped from this prison, so they don't stay their words." He could not meet Nathan's intense gaze. Voice quivering, Derek glanced at the sorceress as he pleaded, "I don't want to die here."

"Captain Andrews," Isabelle said, giving him a probing look he didn't care for.

Despite his reservations, the warrior knew Isabelle was right. There wasn't really a choice for them. Looming over the edge of the cage, Nathan stared down at the youth with hard eyes.

"Mislead us and I *will* kill you. Understand boy?"

For the briefest moment, Nathan thought he saw a smirk cross Derek's face in the flickering light of the torch. Blinking, he dismissed it. He must have been mistaken.

The boy nodded meekly prior to being instructed to stand back.

Isabelle raised her hands and shifted her focus to the cell door. Casting a fire spell, she melted the lock. Quickly swinging the door open, the two rescuers stood to the side to let Derek pass.

Eyeing the sorceress thoughtfully, Derek didn't move right away.

Sighing impatiently, Nathan lunged forward, gripping the youth lightly by his upper arm as he tugged him out of the cell.

"You should be thanking her," the warrior grumbled. "It's time to uphold your part of the bargain. Take us to the princes."

Nodding, Derek led them back to the main central chamber of the dungeon with a murmured thanks. Gazing around for a moment, he lifted a shaky hand and directed, "This way."

Traveling all the way to the right, the small group strode down the dim corridor. The prisoners in this part were less rowdy and appeared more withdrawn, like hollow shells. Most wore clothing reduced to rags and were little more than skin and bones.

Isabelle tried not to look too closely at them as their pitiful cries echoed through the stone halls. Gripping the side of her tunic, she forced her sights to remain on the direction in which they were heading. Unlike the other corridors, halfway down there was a junction where the hall split. Turning right, then left shortly after, Derek entered another smaller side chamber. The room reminded Isabelle of the cell she shared with Alec. A chill raced over her skin.

Each room was slightly larger than the previous cells with a small single bed tucked to the side. As they entered, two men in the center cells rose and walked towards the bars. They both had sandy brown hair and hazel eyes. The one on the right was tall and medium-built with a mustache and short beard just on the bottom half of his face. His brother was equally as tall, though more on the stocky side, with hair that reached his ears in gentle waves.

"Your Highnesses," Derek greeted dropping into a deep bow. "These brave Malyndorians have come to rescue you."

The elder brother, Prince Ashton, studied their would-be rescuers. "Well done, Derek. You may rise." He lifted his solemn hazel eyes to gaze at Nathan and Isabelle.

"Do not think me ungrateful for your assistance," he began watching them closely. "Yet, how was King Titus informed of our plight so quickly? The Pure's treachery only just occurred."

Nathan knew the true meaning of the royal's inquiry. Ashton was right, even should a request for aid have been sent, it would have been much too soon for troops to be sent and offer any sort of assistance. It would seem that he wanted to know what they were really doing in his realm. Now wasn't the time to quarrel with the rightful rulers of this kingdom. More soldiers would be upon them at any moment.

"Forgive me, but time is not a luxury that we possess, Your Highness."

Glancing at Isabelle, he gave her a nod to proceed. Summoning her spell once more, the sorceress asked them to stand clear as she opened both cells. The younger prince narrowed his gaze sharply and his brows lowered to points. Even without the lock impeding him, Sebastian made no effort to depart the cell.

"Sorcery," he spat under his breath.

"Sebastian," Ashton scolded, stepping into the chamber. "Thank you for your assistance."

His face gave away nothing of what he was thinking. *Why was Malcolm insisting on us saving these men?* Her experience in Zerrok didn't offer any redeeming qualities of its monarch. Her line of sight shifted to Sebastian before moving back to Ashton. From what she could see, it was difficult to tell if these men were good or bad. Isabelle could have been peering at a block of granite for all of the emotion the older prince was revealing.

"Of course," she answered at last, realizing they had been standing in an awkward silence while she was lost in thought.

Moving towards the doorway, Nathan suddenly leapt back, raising his blade. No sooner than the second their footsteps ceased, did a pack of strange dog-like creatures suddenly race into the space.

"Oh, no!" Isabelle exclaimed.

She recognized their newest foes at once from her studies. The beasts were known as howlers. Creatures of darkness, they only allied themselves with masters of pure evil intent so they could feed off their negative energies. Short, thick black fur covered an even thicker hide. Long, razor sharp spikes trailed down their spines, matching two similar horns protruding from their skulls in an arch. Dozens of pointed teeth could be seen in their long snouts. No doubt they would be just as deadly as the steel-like extended claws on each of their four toes. Watching their intelligent crimson colored eyes, Isabelle somehow knew what their first move would be.

"Surgeon, shield," she called out, jumping in front of Nathan.

The barrier blocked a stream of flames shooting at them just in time. Without previous knowledge of howlers, someone facing these creatures wouldn't expect tongues of fire to shoot out of their mouths. How did Zerrok find these rare and allusive beasts?

"Holy shit," Nathan yelled, leaning back with wide eyes as the heat wave slammed into Isabelle's energy spell.

Ceasing their attack, the three howlers barked and snarled at each other. There was no telling what they would do next.

"Everyone stay back," Nathan ordered. They couldn't be in a worse position to battle fire-breathing demon dogs. "How do we fight them, Isabelle?"

Biting her lip, the sorceress tried to think. Only she and Nathan were armed, and her swordsmanship skills probably weren't a match for these types of foes. There was however, her more recent training. To fight a beast, there were times when you needed a creature of your own.

"I have a spell that can defeat them."

"Great, use it."

Isabelle frowned. "It's not that simple." Glancing over her shoulder, she told him, "It requires an enchantment in Elan. I'll need time to cast it, but..." She returned her gaze to their waiting foes.

It didn't need to be said. The instant she lowered the shield, the howlers would commence with another attack.

Footsteps sounded behind her as Nathan came to join the sorceress's side. Gripping the hilt of his blade, he clenched his jaw.

"Alright," the warrior said without peering at her." When I tell you, drop the shield and get behind me."

"Excuse me? Are you mad?" she whispered back. "I'm not going to hide while these things rip you to shreds."

"We don't have a choice. Let me buy you the time you require."

The exasperated sigh she emitted was answer enough. "I only need you to hold them off for a minute. Pray, don't do anything foolish."

"No promises."

Isabelle released a humorless laugh. "You sound like Alec."

Nathan couldn't help but grin briefly. "There is no need for flattery. Are you ready?"

"Quite."

Eyes locked upon the humans, the howlers growled low in the back of their throats. Rolling their shoulders, the hell hounds claws left grooves in the stone floor as they pawed the ground.

For Isabelle, everything seemed to switch to slow motion. Nathan lifted his blade and took another step forward. The howlers bared their teeth. The crimson of their eyes glowed faintly as their attention shifted to the swordsman.

"Now."

Spinning on her heel, the sorceress ducked behind the warrior. Blocking out the sounds of their battle, she quickly summoned her spell.

"Tsumorri. Sumonno orbis agel. Rasolee altor eis, Taj."

A large blue magic circle appeared on the floor. The moisture in the air crystallized, making each breath she took visible to the eye. Slowly, a pure white tiger of ice rose out of the floor.

Unaware of what was taking place behind him, Nathan slashed at the nearest howler. Snapping its jaws, the faint spark of flames danced in the rear of its throat. Throwing the creature off, he cut a long gash into the chest of a second beast bearing down on his right. Foot slipping on the suddenly frosty stones, Nathan briefly dropped his guard. A set of razor-sharp claws slashed his left arm, cutting through his vambrace and into his flesh. The three hell hounds made to pounce simultaneously. Nathan braced himself, preparing for one last stand.

Rounding the swordsman, the large ice feline charged at the hounds, throwing them backwards as he blocked their path to Nathan. As the right howler tried to get back on his feet, Taj wrapped his jaw around the back of the creature's neck. Clamping down, a deep growl sounded in his throat as the tiger snapped the hell hound's spine. The two survivors raced in for an attack. One jumped onto the ice beast's back, clawing deeply as he summoned a mouthful of fire.

His injured arm tucked against his chest, Nathan drove his blade into the howler's ribs.

"No, you don't," he muttered pulling the sword free.

Twisting around, Taj sank his teeth into the hound's shoulder, ripping open the toughened skin. The final fire beast unleashed a boiling strike on Taj's side. A puddle of water leaked onto the ground from the large melted hole in the tiger's rib cage. Baring his fangs, Taj rushed to meet the malevolent dog. They collided with a crash as the two fierce creatures became a tangled, snapping mess of teeth and claws.

Slipping out from beneath the feline's powerful grip, the howler leapt back to face his enemy once more.

Hands held out in front of her, Isabelle focused her magical energy upon her ally. The hole in Taj's side refroze as he was briefly shrouded in a glowing light. Filled with a new vigor, the ice tiger countered another fire ball with an ice blast. Steam filled the space as Taj charged forward. Swatting the temporary cloud, his massive paws hit nothing but empty air. Steam clearing, all that remained were two corpses upon the melting ice. The third howler had vanished.

"It looks like he escaped," Nathan said to no one in particular.

Taj made a noise in the back of his throat as if in agreement. Turning around, he started back towards his master. Pausing beside Nathan, the tiger lowered his head. Blue diamond-like eyes sparkled with a cunning respect. Then, to the warrior's surprise, an icy head nudged his shoulder prior to continuing on.

Smiling brightly, Isabelle greeted the tiger like an old friend. "Well done, Taj. I could not have fought this battle without you."

Purring, the tiger circled around the sage as she ran a hand over his side. Isabelle called forth another spell.

The large blue magic circle appeared in the middle of the floor. Taj went to stand within the seal. Spinning around, he faced his mistress.

"Thank you," the sorceress said once again. "Altor reditus."

In the next instant, the tiger disappeared into a swirl of snowflakes. Isabelle dropped to her knees, breathing heavily.

Nathan rushed to her side. "Are you injured?"

She shook her head. "No. Such a spell is quite draining." Isabelle eyed the blood-soaked sleeve of his arm along with Nathan's pale face. He had fought well despite his injury. She couldn't heal wounds like Alec, but at least she would be able to stop the flow of blood. Lifting a hand, the sage didn't even bother requesting the warrior's permission. He would be the one protecting them from this point onward.

"Surgeon, restore."

Gaze jerking to his arm, Nathan felt a warm tingle spread across his skin. He ripped off the tattered remnants of his sleeve. The pain from the slashes ceased, as did the bleeding, and the injured flesh was also partially healed.

"I'm afraid that is all my level of skill can do."

"You have my thanks." He knew, just as she did, that not all sages were gifted with the ability to heal. Like the color of a person's hair or eyes, magical abilities varied.

Tearing off a piece of her tunic, Isabelle gently wrapped his forearm.

Nathan watched her without a word. Once she completed her task, the swordsman rose to his feet while still examining the bandage.

"You're quite special, aren't you?" he whispered to himself.

"Did you say something?" the sage asked, gazing up at him.

Nathan shook his head, reaching down to aid her. "We should leave here without delay. I doubt those howlers will be the last enemy we encounter."

Sebastian and Derek both glanced at Ashton. His expression still unreadable, he slowly stepped forward.

"Thank you for your assistance. I believe our alliance will prove most enlightening."

CHAPTER 17

Watching Isabelle and Nathan disappear down the corridor, Alec held his position even after his friends had vanished from sight. Fingers tapping the side of his leg, he warded off a frown. Alec's gaze shifted towards the heap of rubble blocking their previous battle grounds. No matter what anyone said, he would hold on to the belief that Malcolm was still alive. Alec couldn't explain it, but it was almost as if he could sense him.

We will meet again, teacher.

Straightening his shoulders, the warrior's eyes met Garth's. The swordsman dipped his head with a firm nod. There was no going back now. All they could do was fight on. Moving in the opposite direction from their friends, the two warriors traveled up a set of twisting stone stairs. The element of surprise was not available to them. Therefore, Alec and Garth readied themselves for anything as they appeared on the next level of the Imperial Tower itself.

The rowdy noise of the semi-open chamber before them suddenly took on a moment of stunned silence. While the space was teeming with soldiers, it wasn't the armed guards Alec expected to face. The warriors had, in fact, entered the military commissary hall. Three rows of tables scattered with guards took up the center of the space. At the rear was a large pass through to the kitchen. A wide doorway to the hall was positioned near the kitchen with two other doors on either side of the chamber. To pass, they would have to defeat the entire room of soldiers.

It seemed they now knew the reason behind the lack of staff in the corridors below. In the midst of their meal, these fighters either must have believed Jerric would put a stop to their guests, or hadn't been informed that Alec and his companions arrived. None of that mattered, for the guards had quickly recovered from their frozen state and were charging at their foes.

Splitting up to meet the incoming hoard, Alec went up the center left while Garth dashed to the right. He clashed with the first fighter, their blades locking together. Overpowering the soldier Garth pressed downward, forcing his foe's sword to the side. Briefly releasing his grip with his support hand, the warrior jabbed the man in the face. As his enemy stumbled back, Garth twisted around, slashing through the next man rushing at him. Thrusting his weapon forward, he planted it in the gut of the following warrior. With a roar, Garth charged forward, using his victim as a shield to push through the massive buildup of guards. Jerking the blade free, Garth tucked his shoulder beneath the edge of the closest wooden table. Using all his might, he hurled the object into the line of soldiers now zeroing in behind him.

Charging forward like an angry storm, several enemies attacked Alec at once. The clash of his blade connecting with the opposing metal rang out like thunder. Alec whirled his sword in a flurry of movements. As he swept his left arm back, a blade of ice materialized in his grasp. Twisting the hilt, Alec simultaneously blocked attacks at both his front and back. Spinning in a circle, he sent his adversaries flying back. Another wave dashed towards him. Kicking a man in the chest to clear his path, the warrior dissolved his ice blade and rolled onto the top of the table.

Jumping up, Alec avoided the sweep of multiple weapons aimed at his legs. Eyeing the plates lying abandoned on the table, the right corner of his mouth twitched with the shadow of a smirk. Using the tip of his blade to stop a strike, Alec swiftly launched the closest plate at one of the soldiers.

The metal discus landed right on his face.

Alec's movements were a rapid blur as he used both his sword and feet to hurl whatever objects were sitting about at his enemies. Food littered the floor, causing some of the guards to slip on the newly slick surface.

Pausing his attack, Alec focused on the soldier coming straight at him. Kicking the man in the side of the head, Alec leapt into the air. Somersaulting over his foe, Alec took the man's sword out of his hand as he passed by before landing on the parallel table. Purposely gripping the dual blades, Alec firmly planted his feet on the scarred wooden surface.

"Airanlor, cyclone," the sorcerer, said summoning an enchantment.

As he once more jumped into the air to avoid being slashed, Alec spun a full seven hundred and twenty degrees, sweeping his swords along the aisle one after another. A gust of wind propelled from each blade, thundering down the length of the room as it threw anyone or anything out of its path. Seeing the mass of soldiers surrounding his friend, Alec swept his one blade up with a diagonal slash.

A blast of wind stormed across the room. Tables were destroyed and guards were tossed about like dolls as the magical attack slammed into their enemy. Unleashing an assault on Garth's other side, the remaining fighters were cleared from the exit.

"Thanks," the gruff warrior hollered, glancing over his shoulders at his friend.

Alec bobbed his head. "Let's get moving before they regroup."

Swiftly crossing the space, they headed towards the doorway with Garth in the lead. Twenty feet from their destination the swordsmen skidded to a stop as reinforcements charged into the hall. Likewise, those caught up in his wind storm were recovering their lost weapons.

Damn it, Alec mentally cursed.

Gripping his weapons, Alec shifted his attention to their flank. Simultaneously slashing his blades to the side, he cut a guard across the chest and abdomen. Turning his wrist, Alec swept his left hand back in the other direction, leaving a trail of blood down the man's front while blocking a different attack. With more soldiers quickly approaching, the warrior couldn't afford to be locked in combat with a single fighter. Kicking the man in the knee, he slid in close and rammed his elbow in the man's face. In the blink of an eye, Alec's second weapon was implanted in the guard's stomach.

"Alec, use another one of those wind blasts."

The soldiers were too close by to risk such an unpredictable attack. Once he unleashed the powerful bursts of air, Alec no longer had control over it. Garth could easily become a casualty of friendly fire. A different spell would be required.

Summoning a field of energy around his body, Alec activated a speed spell. To those around him, he was little more than a blur of motion as the sage cut through their enemies' ranks. While his two blades were engaged with other soldiers, Alec leapt up, spinning as he kicked a third foe with such force he slid across a table and fell off the other side. Wielding the duel swords with a fluid grace, Alec cleared away the men surrounding Garth. Working together the warriors defeated the rest of their attackers. With their backs towards the kitchen, Alec and Garth studied the outlying destruction.

"For a moment there I didn't think there would be an end to them," Garth huffed, trying to catch his breath.

"Yeah," Alec answered with a humorless laugh.

Appearing unexpectedly, two cooks grabbed each of the swordsmen, dragging them over the counter and into the kitchen. Grunting, Alec struggled to free himself from the iron-like fingers holding him in place. His sword was pried from his hand as another man came at him with a butcher knife. Unable to throw off his oppressors, Alec rammed the heel of his foot into the closest man's knee and pressed downward, dislocating the man's kneecap.

Crying out, the man unconsciously loosened his grip.

Alec pulled his right arm free, twisting so that his enemy was in front of him as the blade slashed downward. Removing a knife from his belt, the sage planted the blade in his other enemy's stomach. Breaking out of his hold, Alec dodged a few strikes from the armed cook prior to finishing him off.

Seeking out Garth, he watched as the gruff warrior jerked a knife out of his shoulder and used the weapon to stab his remaining adversary. Turning towards the sorcerer, he spit a wad of blood on the stone floor.

"Damn it, even their servants are a threat."

"Hold still," Alec told Garth, coming to his friend's side.

Placing a hand lightly over the wound on Garth's shoulder, he called up a spell. When the sorcerer removed his palm, the injury was completely healed.

Brows lifting, the warrior slowly shook his head. "I don't believe I'll ever get used to that. Your gift sure does come in handy though."

"Sometimes, I suppose," Alec replied with a faint smirk.

Hopping back over the counter, the two companions left the dining hall and entered a short corridor. Taking the first set of stone steps that they encountered, Alec and Garth proceeded to the next floor. Half way up the stairs everything began to shake. Bracing himself against the wall, Alec could feel a strange shift in the stone. Suddenly, the entire stairwell moved. Extending upwards, it changed direction and curved towards a different level all together.

"For a people obsessed with destroying magic, they sure have a lot of blasted mages in their keep," Garth grumbled as the spell came to an end.

"One of the soldiers must have alerted someone to the fact that we made it past Jerric."

"Care to guess what trap awaits?"

"I will pass." *You never know what demons might appear with these people,* Alec added privately. He had more than enough first-hand experience with the strange creatures that Zerrok could produce.

Gradually stalking up towards the awaiting door, Alec's body tensed. Hand tightening around the hilt of his blade, he leaned in slightly, listening for any sound which might offer some clue to the contents of the chamber beyond. Silence greeted his ears. Glancing back at Garth the two warriors nodded to each other. Disengaging the latch, Alec pushed the door open with his foot.

A figure lurking in the darkness had a dagger automatically flying from Alec's fingers. The sound of shattering glass echoed in the abyss. Brows furrowing, the warrior pushed the door open wider still. Neither swordsman cared for the images greeting their eyes. On every wall, and from what felt like every angle, were countless reflections of the two Malyndorian fighters.

This does not bode well, Garth thought sourly.

Three dark unlit passages stood before them. Garth's eyes shifted between the portals. No clue was offered as to which path through the maze of mirrors they should take. Lips pressed into a line, the warrior studied them for a moment longer.

"Brace yourself," Alec began raising a hand. "I'm going to rid ourselves of these pesky mirrors."

Garth smiled grimly. "I had the same thought."

The sorcerer's energy swirled around him as he called upon a wind spell.

"Airanlor, blast."

The forceful gust slammed into the mirrors directly in front of them. Yellow magic defense circles immediately appeared, deflecting the spell and absorbing the residual power to refuel the shield. Only a powerful master sage could have put such a backup in place.

This must be Jerric's doing.

Unless The Pure had swayed another master to their side, Jerric was the logical perpetrator. Alec glanced at the broken shards beside his dagger. Bending down to retrieve his weapon, he once more studied the surrounding glass. They were impervious to magic, yet against physical attacks remained unguarded. They could slash their way through the maze one by one, however, to do so would be not only time consuming, it could prove dangerous as well. If Jerric had the foresight to have barriers in place, then he just might have other unwanted surprises in store.

"It would seem that we're going to have to play along for now."

"Yeah," Garth agreed with a nod. "Which path should we venture down?"

Alec shrugged. The single torch on the wall behind them served as more of a distraction than a source of light. The center hallway appeared to go straight until it disappeared into the darkness. Meanwhile, the neighboring paths traveled down short corridors before twisting around a corner. No matter their choice, it would be a gamble.

"How about the middle one?"

Garth stuck out his lip while he lifted his shoulders. "Why not?"

Grasping the torch from the wall, Garth started down the maze as Alec used his power to coil a line of flames around his blade. The countless reflections made it difficult to focus. Cautiously, the two warriors strode down their chosen path.

The single corridor took them deeper into the maze before twisting around corners and bringing them to a junction one after another. Knife still in one hand, Alec marked a mirror at every intersection. Coming upon one of his inscriptions, his eyes narrowed.

"We're going in circles."

Garth exhaled with a distinct hiss. "Why does that not surprise me?"

"If their plan is simply to get us lost inside this dark tomb then they've greatly underestimated us."

Head arching back, the sorcerer shifted his attention to the ceiling. Lifting his fire higher he noticed the blaze didn't penetrate the darkness enough to reveal anything above. Returning his knife to his belt, Alec summoned a ball of light in his left palm. Without a word, he flung it up into the air where it burst and illuminated the space. The ceiling was high above them, reaching far beyond the tall rim of the mirrors. The lingering glow offered the two fighters their first true glimpse of the maze they were trapped within. It also revealed a thick yellow smoke which was beginning to swirl around their feet.

"Poison!" Garth spat as he and Alec covered their mouths.

Holding his breath, Alec's eyes darted about the space. Gazing upwards he knew what he had to do in order to free them from the poisonous cloud.

"Rokon, rise."

The stone beneath their feet quickly rose into the air until it was even with the top of the mirrors. Coughing slightly, the sage then expanded his power outward, using his spell to create a straight path across the room. *I wish I had thought of this sooner,* the sage silently mused. He might not be able to move the mirrors out of their way, but he could still manipulate everything else. If he couldn't go through them, then he would go over.

With the flames still dancing around the steel of his blade, Alec and Garth raced across their new path. Neither could see far beyond the light of their torches, yet the soft swoosh of something swiftly cutting through the air filled their ears. Suddenly stepping back, the sorcerer twisted his sword, blocking a swarm of arrows which threatened to blanket them. Manipulating the fire, he fanned it out in a circle, sending it into the darkness like a rolling wave as it burned a second volley to ash.

Behind the sage, Garth gripped his blade in one fist while holding the torch like a weapon in the other. As the next round of arrows sped towards them, soldiers appeared at the end of the stone walkway. If they didn't do something soon, it was likely the warriors would be boxed in. Glancing at Alec, their eyes met and the sorcerer gave Garth a distinct nod.

Igniting the last wisps of flame clinging to his sword, Alec directed the blaze up into an arch, creating a protective shield as he and Garth returned to the ground.

"Airanlor, blast," Alec said as their feet touched the stone floor.

With the light of his fire gone, the sorcerer had to rely on Garth's torch to dispel the smoke once more seeking to swallow them whole. The exit wasn't far ahead, yet the twisting maze was not a danger they could ignore.

"This way," Garth urged waving his friend onward. There wasn't a moment to spare.

"Wait," Alec countered. Disliking the idea of blindly running through the halls of mirrors, the sage had a different plan in mind. "Rokon, shift."

The stone beneath the mirror directly in front of them slowly began to sink into the ground. As the spell progressed, the object slipped faster into the freshly made quick sand. Directing his power in a straight line, all of the mirrors blocking their path to the other side of the space sank into the abyss below. Finishing his work, Alec returned the stone to its solid form.

"How did you…?" Garth shook his head with a laugh. Holding his flame higher, he led the way down the open corridor Alec created through the maze.

Striding past the angled mirrors, Alec's face was a mask of concentration. A flash of movement caught his attention. When nothing appeared, he almost believed that he was mistaken. Almost. No length of time would convince the sorcerer he was seeing things. Years of experience told him differently. Another flicker of motion alerted him to the soldiers' presence.

Here they come.

Rushing from the shadows, half a dozen guards zeroed in upon the warriors. The angle of the glass turned the charging men from six to six dozen.

Eyes darting across the various images in the dim light, Alec's jaw clenched tightly. An intangible instinct gave him the skill to block the most serious of blows. A cut to his upper thigh stung his flesh. Garth's reflection danced alongside the soldiers, disrupting Alec's concentration. Leaning back, a knife sliced past his left eye, just missing him. Striking the man with his foot Alec forced the guard to withdraw as another moved in to take his place.

Fingers tightly gripping the hilt of his sword, Alec mentally cursed. *Damn it! I need to get rid of these mirrors.* They were causing him more distress than he expected. There was no telling how much longer he and Garth would be able to hold out.

As the first man was thrown back, a second quickly took his place. Their blades clashing together, the sage was regaining the upper hand when more soldiers joined the reflections inside the mirrors. Pushing the guards back, he leapt into the air, somersaulting out of the way of multiple swords. The steel instead planted itself in the soldier Alec had been fighting. Even their companions were of no consequence to them. Spying a man cut Garth's arm as he struggled with his own enemies served as the last blow to Alec's careful control.

"That's quite enough," the sage growled in a low voice.

Spiritual energy rising, his aura lashed out, bringing forth Fang in a bright swirling mist. The intense power broke through the barriers protecting the mirrors and shattered the glass to dust in a twenty-yard radius. Eyes lit like an eternal flame, Alec rushed forward, reuniting with his spirit dragon as his weapon sliced the first soldier in his path.

Their battle plan having literally fallen to pieces, the Zerrokian guards couldn't seem to recover quickly enough.

Garth's thick blade cut through their ranks with brute strength and precision. Turning with a roar, he swept his sword diagonally, driving through flesh and bone as blood splattered the empty frames.

Behind him, Alec's graceful speed was no longer being hindered. Darting between the guards, the fighter alternated with his sword and knife to slash at his opponents. Nearing one of the wooden frames, he jumped up, kicking off the wall to stab a man in the back of the neck as he twisted and drove his blade into another. Landing lightly, he stood at the ready to face his next enemy. The surrounding stillness was unsettling after the previous chaos.

"It would appear this round has been won," echoed Garth's voice.

After briefly scanning the area, Alec's gaze shifted to his friend's. "I'm certain another trap awaits us."

"Without a doubt. Let us leave this chamber before the arrows begin anew."

Following Garth towards the light shining from the open doorway, Alec straightened his shoulders and lifted his chin. Their sleazy tactics would not sway him to abandon this course. He would save Jade, even if it meant bringing the entire tower crumbling down in his wake.

Sealed off from the main sections of the Imperial Tower, Alec and Garth had no other option than to ascend the next set of awaiting stairs. Traveling up several flights, Alec braced himself for another shift in the staircase. It didn't come. Instead, he and Garth eventually came to a small landing with a single metal door. Inhaling deeply, Alec nudged it open with his foot. The space before him was pitch-black.

"It better not be another blasted maze," Garth muttered as they cautiously inched further inside.

The candle light from the stairwell couldn't seem to penetrate the vast endless pit. There was nothing, no glimmer of anything awaiting them, just an eternal darkness. Suddenly, the door slammed closed. The sound of metal twisting as the steel was locked into place echoed through the walls.

"Damn it," the swordsman growled.

Alec however, wasn't peering at the portal to their rear.

"Infureono, fire ball," he said softly, watching his surroundings.

Whatever trap they had strode into was much more dangerous than the others they had faced. Alec couldn't say what told him so, but he knew they were not alone in this space. Something was there with them. Gleaming red eyes shone in the darkness. The first pair was joined by a second, third, and finally fourth pair of sharp, blazing eyes.

"Garth," Alec barked trying to quickly get the other man's attention.

"What?" There was a pause as he stood by the sorcerer's side and peered around. "Oh shit."

Clawed toes breaching the circle of light, four horned howlers appeared from the shadows with teeth bared. Stalking towards their prey, they came from each side, blocking off any chance of escape. Alec didn't know these creatures of darkness. Part of him wished Isabelle hadn't separated to search for the princes. She was sure to be aware of them.

Raise your shield, whispered an all too familiar voice.

The faintest spark in the howlers' mouths alerted Alec to their intent just as the words rang in his mind. Raising a shield like a dome, the sage blocked the fire attacks simultaneously striking from each direction. Thick blasts of flame collided with the shield and shot up into the air like a raging volcano.

Heads and necks lifted and bodies taunt, the canines snarled in a low voice as they watched the surviving humans with blazing crimson eyes. A short bark from the front howler sounded. The three others charged forward, slashing at the barrier. Unable to cause any damage, they leapt back out of range.

Alec knew they couldn't remain in this stalemate forever. They were running out of time. In order to move onward, he and Garth would have to dispose of these demon-like creatures. Rolling his shoulders, Alec cracked his neck prior to exhaling sharply.

Garth eyed him with a frown. "Pray, tell me you are not thinking of battling these things."

"If you have another option, then I'm open to suggestions."

A grunt was his sole reply.

Shifting the energy spell, Alec transformed it into a pulse which shot out, knocking the howlers across the darkened room. Strengthening their defenses he called up a fire spell, creating a blazing ring around them.

"Tsumorri, ice shield," Alec said, directing his power towards Garth.

A magical shield of ice appeared on the swordsman's left arm. Brows raised, he studied the added protection. Lightweight and cold to the touch, the frost surprisingly didn't cause any type of chill where it was secured around his arm. Beside him, instead of a shield, Alec was making a second sword.

Recovered from the surprise attack, the howlers were once again closing in upon them. In a defensive stance, Alec wasn't surprised to see the creatures walk through the encircling ring of fires he produced several feet away. Considering that they breathed flames, he more or less expected it. The fire wasn't an added guard; it was so the warriors could see. Tightening the grip on his dual hilts, Alec was ready for whatever these beasts of darkness sent his way. Or so he thought.

Pausing their advance, the howlers suddenly began to sniff the air with a new vigor. Their ears twitched. All at once, four pairs of red eyes shifted to focus upon the sage. Alec stiffened.

What the…? Damn it, why are they all targeting me?

Lacking knowledge of howlers, the sorcerer couldn't know how they fed on energy. Alec's magic was strong. The smell of his blood from the few cuts he gained in the mirror maze was too intoxicating for creatures long deprived of the presence of sorcerers. Evil souls were nothing compared to the substance this wizard could provide.

With the energy shield no longer hiding Alec's scent, Garth was completely forgotten. The gruff warrior watched as lips parting, the canines showed their moistened teeth fully and turned towards the sage. Disappearing, they suddenly seemed to have vanished from the space. A cry of pain sounding from behind him told the swordsman otherwise.

Working in unison, the howlers had commenced with a new attack upon the sorcerer, bypassing Garth completely. One had sank its teeth into Alec's injured thigh, while a second was gripping his left forearm. The remaining two pounced, aiming to slash his front and back at the same time. Alec's aura activated a barrier on its own, protecting the sage at the last second.

Driving the tip of his steel blade into the back of the one dog's neck, Alec killed the beast instantly. Instead of releasing his leg however, the corpse's jaw locked on, acting like an added weight hindering the sorcerer's movements. Flipping the blade over in his hand, Alec drove his sword in the other direction, seeking the howler latched onto his arm. At the last moment the creature released his prey and jumped back. Glancing at his forearm, Alec twisted his wrist to test the damage inflicted. The metal vambrace adorn there had protected him from much of the attack. Noting the impacted dents and hairline cracks in the armor's surface, he might well have lost his arm if he wasn't wearing it.

Racing in from the howlers' flank, Garth rammed his shield into one of the canines as he slashed it down the side. With their attention locked on Alec, the creatures had dismissed Garth from their thoughts. It was not a mistake the dog growling at him would make again. The injury to his thickened hide was minor. So as the howler lunged for a counterattack, his movements were not impeded in the least.

Wielding sword and shield as extensions of himself, Garth parried the razor-sharp talons slashing at his skin. Pressing downward on the howler's front legs with his next counterattack, the warrior then thrusted upward with his shield, smashing the canine in the snout. Drawing his blade back, he cut his enemy across the chest prior to twisting his sword to bring it once more across the dog's front to form an "x".

The creature didn't seem to be affected by the wounds or feel any of the pain from the shallow bleeding cuts.

Face hardening, Garth tucked his shield arm in to his chest as the howler pounced. Right before the hell hound about to strike, spikes of ice grew on the front of the shield to impale the beast. The shield crumbled as the corpse slid to the stone floor. Peering at his companion, Garth just caught Alec looking in his direction with his one hand extended towards him. The ice blade was nowhere to be seen, but the partially frozen dismembered head of a howler was still attached to his leg.

I knew it. He saved my neck again.

Having aided his friend, Alec's focus immediately shifted back to the two remaining howlers. The semi-frozen vice clamped to his thigh was still a handicap, though relieving the corpse of its body did help in that regard. Re-summoning a blade of ice, he spun in a tight circle. Each slash from his metal weapon was followed by the freezing slice of his magical blade. The area around the wounds crystallized, spreading an inch beyond the injured flesh.

Slipping back towards the shadows, the two howlers watched Alec thoughtfully. The fire's glow illuminated their crimson eyes as they stalked along the edge of the ring's light. A few moments passed while the demon dogs did nothing but study the sage. Then, the right one stepped closer. In response, the left canine snapped at his companion. His top lip pulling back with a snarl, the first howler turned to face the other hell hound instead. Circling each other, the two dogs began to fight amongst themselves for possession of their rare prey.

While his opponents were distracted, Alec placed the blade of his ice weapon on top of the head of the dismembered canine. The freezing spell transferred to every cell, crystallizing it until the flesh dissolved to flecks of snow. Running a hand over the wound, Alec quickly healed the bite just enough to keep it from hindering him.

Having dispatched his enemy, Garth headed straight to Alec's side. He never made it. A trap door opened up beneath his feet swallowing him into a pit of darkness.

"Garth!"

The swordsman's disappearance seemed to spur the howlers out of their fierce competition. Clawing the stone floor, they shifted their attention once again to the sage. As the two canines started to charge, Alec clenched his jaw.

"Enough of this," the sorcerer growled.

Thrusting his blades into the ground, the Dragon Sage's power reacted to his every thought without him summoning a creation spell. Spikes of ice shot upwards from the floor, impaling the twin beasts right through the chest. The moment his foes were deceased, Alec spun around, searching the darkness for the spot where his friend had vanished.

"Rokon, shift."

Sweeping his hand to the side, the opening of the trap door was revealed.

"Garth. Garth, can you hear me?" Alec hollered into the pitch-black pit.

Silence was his only answer. Taking a step forward, Alec moved to follow his companion. An image of Jade flashed before his eyes. Alec's movements ceased at once. He was not one to act impulsively. *Think Alec.*

They were close to the top of the tower. Unfortunately, there was no telling where the tunnel would lead. If this trap took him to the very bottom, then they would have to begin their journey anew, fighting countless soldiers as he and Garth made their way through the Zerrokian stronghold once again. The battles awaiting them didn't matter. Alec couldn't stand by and do nothing to help his friend. Inhaling deeply, he tucked his arms in to his sides as he prepared to jump.

Suddenly, Alec could hear Garth's voice echoing in his mind as if he was standing there beside him.

Don't even think about it.

"I can't simply abandon you," Alec said to the darkness.

Save Lady Jade. It is your duty to protect her.

Exhaling sharply, the sorcerer backed away from the hole. Hands curling into fists, he peered at the pit one last time.

"Once I rescue her, I will find you, my friend," Alec swore to the emptiness. "Don't die."

Even should he have to take this tower apart stone by stone, Alec would not break his word. The sage wasn't going to leave without the people who joined him in this battle. Zerrok had cost him far too much already. Alec wouldn't allow this cruel kingdom to take anyone else from him.

An involuntary sound of alarm escaping his lips, Garth slid down the narrow shaft to suddenly land on a cold stone floor. Head reeling, it took a moment for him to be able to study his new surroundings. A mix of straw and bone was spread upon the ground in the stifling warm space. A few torches could be seen to his left on the other side of thick iron bars. Reaching for his sword, Garth slowly rose to his feet as he bit back a curse.

A deep growl nearby caused him to stiffen. Nose poking through the bars, the sharp ivory fangs of a howler was only a foot away. Several other growls and snarls joined the creature trying to reach for him.

Blinking, Garth gazed about with a deep frown. The entire space was divided into cages. It seemed the door he fell through led to the howler's kennel.

A blast of flames shot out from the nearest creature. Dodging the heat, Garth raced to the door of the cell. Fortunately, the one he fell into didn't have an occupant. It was possible that he already slew him. Slashing the lock repeatedly, Garth was able to break free of the confined space as another blast came his way. Rushing into the narrow hall, he peered at the howlers gazing hungrily at him. The glow of fire appeared in all of their mouths. Surrounded, there was nowhere for him to flee quickly enough to avoid the attacks, nor was there anything for him to use as cover. Closing his eyes, Garth waited for the inevitable. The tip of his blade lowered to tap the stone floor. Drops of sweat slithered down the side of his face and the back of his hairline. Several seconds ticked by and still there was nothing beyond the crackling sounds of flames.

Opening one eye, then the other, Garth rapidly blinked. Brows shooting up, he heaved a sigh of relief. Magic circles on each of the cages glowed brightly, blocking the howlers' attacks from reaching the central corridor where the warrior stood. Wiping his face on a sleeve, Garth nodded to himself as he clutched his sword and started towards the exit. There wasn't any time to waste.

Edmund raised his knuckles to knock on the polished door of the king's suite. An inch from the surface, he paused. Taking a deep breath, he rapped loudly.

"Enter," called Titus's deep solemn voice from within.

Edmund quietly entered the massive suite which equaled his own quarters on the other side of the castle. The spacious sitting area was cast in a warm glow, but Titus wasn't in the ring of light. Arms linked behind his back, he stood in front of the tall windows as he gazed into the darkness beyond. A day had passed since Alec's escape from Stafford Castle. Since then, the only word they received was from their contact informing them that he had escorted Alec to the Imperial Tower's main gates. There was nothing else they could do but wait.

"Any word?" Titus questioned without turning.

The duke strode up beside him while trying to hide a worried frown. "Nothing, Your Majesty."

The royal sighed. *Damn it.* His brows lowered to a point and his lips pressed into a thin line. Why had Alec disobeyed his orders? Couldn't he see that he was just trying to protect him from a most dangerous and impossible mistake? The sinking feeling of losing his son for a second time would not subside. King David had not returned any of his messenger hawks. No matter the size of the force, unless Titus wanted to invade the southern kingdom without provocation there was nothing he could do. As a king, he could not put the whole of his realm above the life of one man. As a father, he was prepared to lead the invasion force personally to bring Alec back. If only he had been able to cease his flight in the first place.

Titus's gaze darted to the noble standing beside him. Once Alec had leapt onto the dragon's back there was little chance of safely returning him to the ground. The royal was however, aware that his son had made a brief stop at Malcolm's. It was there he must have joined his companions. For not only was the Cunning Sage missing, but Garth, Isabelle and even Captain Andrews.

Titus was aware of another who had been visiting the wizard's cottage. He returned some time after Alec's departure, placing him in the same spot as Alec during the prince's brief detour.

"Tell me," the king began clenching his jaw. "Did you even try to sway him not to go?"

Edmund didn't bother playing coy, or asking his friend of whom he was speaking. Gazing out the window, the duke's mind flashed back to the last time he saw Alec. Determination filled the man's unwavering eyes.

'I will return with Lady Jade, or not at all,' Alec had said.

Sighing Edmund closed his eyes for a moment. He believed the sage's promise, and also knew in his heart that Alec had not yet failed.

"No, I did not," Edmund answered at last. "Even should I have wanted to do so, we both know Alec could not have been stopped. His power is no match for us."

He could hear a hiss escape from Titus as the man bowed his head.

Fingers traveling to his temples, the king rubbed at the pressure pushing outward within his skull. A part of him knew what the duke's answer would be. True to himself, Edmund had not lied or tried to sugar coat his actions. It was a quality Titus valued and respected. Still, it did not help to ease the helplessness weighing him down.

"I will accept any punishment bestowed upon me, my King."

Titus turned to peer at him with a glare. "You are a noble and frustrating man, Edmund."

"I am aware."

Unable to control it, a short humorless huff escaped Titus's throat. Try as he might the initial anger he felt when it was first suggested that Alec should go to Zerrok would not rise. He was forced to admit that nothing would have kept Alec from seeking to rescue Jade.

If only I could give him aid. Titus could not understand why King David hadn't replied. Though they ruled their realms differently, both men had a peaceful co-existence. Never before had such a lengthy silence fallen between them when an official message was dispatched.

"How deep into The Pure's clutches do you believe Zerrok has fallen?"

Edmund's brow furrowed. Twisting slightly, he looked at Titus before crossing his arms.

"That is difficult to say," Edmund admitted thoughtfully. "Our sources indicate a firm holding throughout Zerrok as well as the recent presence within Rhordack. They must have some powerful allies or they would not have been able to sway sages to fight for them."

"Yes, a disturbing notion considering their stand on sorcery. Which begs the question, what is it that they really seek?"

"You believe their hatred of magic is a rouse?"

"Not entirely. It may have been a way to gain favor and control the smaller anti-magic factions, but too much of their recent deeds speak of a different motive."

"How do you mean?"

Titus exhaled deeply. "Few know of this, but it was not just the Master Sages who were targeted during the breaches at the magical academies. At the West Circle, someone tried to break into a secret vault below the school."

Edmund's brows rose to his hairline. "What? I was not aware of such a vault."

The king nodded. "Not many are. Meaning the traitor is a higher ranking sage than we feared."

"What is in the vault?"

"A library containing the entire history of magic as we know it, as well as their most powerful spells and incantations." The duke swore under his breath as Titus continued. "There are three identical libraries: one under each of the academies and a final one beneath Ariston Castle. It is said the Grandmaster protects another, yet Malcolm would never confirm such a rumor."

"The fact that our enemy knows of these vaults is dangerous enough, but does Malcolm know what they could be searching for within a den of spells?"

"He has a few ideas of what might draw their attention, but there is no way to be sure. Protecting them from the traitor is my top priority. Since the attack, I have ordered for strict magical and human defenses to be placed near each of the vaults and no one other than Malcolm, Layfon, and the Headmasters are allowed access."

Turning back to the window, Edmund was quiet for a long time. This news did not bode well. If The Pure were able to corrupt someone of such high rank in a neighboring kingdom, then what had they been able to accomplish within their own? Gazing back at Titus, he asked the question he was sure he wouldn't like the answer to.

"Are you certain King David would have replied to your message by now under normal circumstances?"

"Indeed."

Edmund took a long deep breath and slowly let it out. "Then we must consider the possibility that His Majesty never received your correspondence. Either that or…"

"Or what?" Titus questioned cautiously. He did not care for the similarities in the way he and Edmund were thinking.

"Or that the King is no longer in a position to send a reply."

Titus spun away to look out the window once again. "I have feared the same thing. It is time we closed our borders and prepared for the inevitable."

CHAPTER 18

Racing up the seemingly endless staircase, Alec finally spotted a landing. Prior to reaching it, his aura stretched out, blasting the door from the hinges. Face set, he strode into the fairly well-lit chamber. It was a surprising change compared to the dark caverns he had encountered thus far.

The space was about half the size of the other levels with plain stone walls and fires at both the front and back. No door could be seen anywhere, yet a ladder hung from the ceiling at the rear of the room. The large stone slabs on the floor abruptly ended a few feet in front of him, giving way to a uniquely decorated pattern. Eight-inch squares surrounded a larger sixteen-inch decorative piece. Each were imprinted with a different creature. Alec could make out a griffin, a drakon, a dragon and a howler. Studying the floor, he pressed his lips together thoughtfully. Fighting his way through the tower, the sorcerer knew nothing was done for no reason. Such a complex design wouldn't have been placed here without cause. There were no soldiers in sight. And no creatures lurking about that he could see.

What trickery are they hiding?

Most likely the spineless cowards would leap out when they thought he was least expecting it. Gazing around once more, Alec stepped forward, pressing some of his weight upon the plain tiles. Cursing, he moved back as the floor crumbled in the spot where his boot had been. If he hadn't been wise enough to test it first, the sage would have fallen right through. Peering at the decorative stones, Alec tilted his head to the side. Summoning a wind spell he struck the closest one etched with a griffin. A large circular blade launched from the wall and flew across the room, striking where the design was located.

Leaping back at the disturbance, Alec held his sword before him as he scanned the space for other threats. Nothing else appeared. Cautiously lowering his blade, he inched back towards the edge of the minefield. As he thought, these designs weren't mere decorations. It seemed each was a trigger for traps. Looking over the other creatures, he wondered which he should try next. Zerrokians hated dragons, so Alec doubted choosing that one would be a wise decision. This left the snake-like drakon, which he knew all too well, and the howler. Having had enough of howlers for the near future, he decided to try the snake. Targeting the tile with his power, Alec gave it a strong blast.

Firing from thin slots along the wall came a round of arrows. They passed over the tile, striking the opposite side of the chamber.

Tapping his fingers against his leg, Alec frowned. *So much for that one.* Eyes focusing on the howler, he hit the stone and waited. Gazing about the space, Alec looked for some sign of a trap being released, but nothing occurred. Glancing back at the tile, he struck it again. Still, there was nothing. Studying the pattern, Alec could see a clear path of howlers traveling out into the depths of the room. If he wanted to move forward, then he would have to follow the demon hounds.

Hopping onto the first tile, Alec paused. Once again he checked that the stone wasn't in fact a trigger of some kind.

When only silence followed, he moved forward to the next howler nearby. Jumping from one tile to the next, Alec made his way across the floor. Nearing the back wall his progress came to a stop. The ladder hung some twenty feet off; however, there were no other safe tiles that he could see. Peering around the space he searched for a howler, but couldn't seem to find any.

Exhaling through his nose, Alec gazed back at the opening. Eyeing the distance, he used an enchantment to propel himself up into the air and forward towards the ladder. Grasping the bottom rungs, the sorcerer looked up and found himself beneath a solid stone ceiling. The opening was a fake. Denied time to even process the deception, Alec's grip tightened as the ladder slipped a few inches and began to give way.

Quickly studying the ground, Alec jumped for the closest decorated tile just as the ladder completely dislodged from the ceiling. The object crashed onto the plain stones then fell through to the abyss beyond. Sword at the ready, Alec watched for either soaring arrows or flying blades, yet neither launched from their hiding places to attack him. A loud cracking noise followed by a rumbling reverberated through the chamber. Sucking in a breath, Alec slowly glanced down at the tile he was standing on. He exhaled with a groan. It was a dragon.

Suddenly, the two side walls began to move in upon him. Eyes darting around the space, Alec searched for some means of escape. The ground was quickly being swallowed up and he doubted there would be enough time to make it back to the stairwell. That left him only one other option. Sheathing his blade, Alec held a hand out towards the back wall. The sage's eyes glowed faintly as he called up a spell.

"Rokon, blast!"

A large hole appeared in the wall as the rock erupted into the shadows beyond. Using the neighboring stones to create a bridge, Alec raced through the opening and into the next chamber as the two stone slabs crashed together behind him.

Alec only vaguely paid attention to the disturbance. The room he had entered was a small cell. The blast from his spell had blown the door off the chamber and soldiers were gathering at the opening. Eyes gleaming coldly, Alec lifted his blade and strode towards his newest foes.

The first two to charge into the bleak space were immediately ejected from the room by the force of Alec's attack. Flying out of the opening, they landed in heaps on the hard ground. The gathering soldiers momentarily froze. They drew back unconsciously as Alec stepped out of the doorway.

"Get him!" a man growled, rushing towards the sorcerer.

Dodging the blow, Alec countered with a quick slash.

The half dozen soldiers surrounded him in hopes that the confined area would impede the intruder's ability to defend himself. It did not. Instead, it made the soldiers unable to escape the range of Alec's expert blade.

Making short work of the assailants, Alec gazed around prior to striding down the corridor. Peering at the handful of empty cells and bright torches lining the space, he surmised that this area was a part of the true main tower. Finally, he had broken out of its trap-infested prison.

Traveling up yet another staircase, Alec could see the soft glow of light above him as he reached the top level of the Imperial Tower. Stretching the fingers of his free hand, the warrior listened closely to every sound and watched every shadow as he stepped into the main floor. A few torches lined the outer walls, offering some light, but it wasn't enough to penetrate the depths of the center of the wide open chamber. Alec could see the general shape of the space as well as a single door on the other side of the room, yet not much else.

"Infureono, fire ball," the sorcerer said, holding out a hand.

The vastness of the high ceilings was soon apparent as the glow from his magical flames only served to illuminate the area directly around him. As Alec reached the center of the chamber, a silhouette appeared in the doorway. Cast in shadow he couldn't make out his visitor so he stayed his hand. *I can't risk harming Jade.*

Palms rising, the figure's fingers began to glow.

Flames wrapping defensively around Alec's arm, he realized too late that his opponent was another sage.

Finishing his enchantment in Elan, symbols on the ceiling and floor began to shine like the mysterious sage's hands.

Pain surged through the warrior's body. The magical seals were designed to drain mana and suppress one's aura. Though Alec's power came from his blood, he still had a powerful energy, and the effects of the spell were taking their toll.

The blaze surrounding the Dragon Sage's arm vanished as he dropped to his knees. Grimacing, his sword slipped from his trembling fingers. Bending over, his hands pressed against the floor as the room seemed to spin before his eyes. The marks glowed brighter, forcing Alec flat on his stomach.

Head to the side, the sage was only able to watch as a soldier appeared holding a torch. Moving to the right, he pressed it lightly to a trough of oil by the wall. Fire burst to life and raced along the outskirts of the chamber. Shifting to the other side of the doorway, he repeated the action, lighting the second half of the space. The chamber was suddenly cast in a bright glow, revealing the seals for Alec to clearly see. And that wasn't all he was able to observe.

A grin on his bird-like face, Colton sauntered inside. Once the sage cleared the entry, a procession seemed to follow. Six soldiers appeared leading three men in white with red tunics. Vincent trailed behind, sporting a twisted smile, after which another four soldiers entered surrounding a beautiful woman with long chestnut hair.

"Alec," Jade shouted frantically as she spotted him lying on the ground among the faintly gleaming seals. "Unhand me!" Her efforts to struggle against the iron-like fingers encircling her upper arms were in vain.

Jade's feisty voice almost made the sage smile, but seeing Vincent again robbed him of that pleasure. Eyes narrowing, everything else faded into the background as the warrior tracked his prey.

The group came to a stop by the altar where the leaders of The Pure sat upon three throne-like chairs. A self-satisfied smile spread across the noble's face as Vincent addressed the men.

"My supreme lords," he began, holding his hands out to the side. "As promised, I give you Alec, the Dragon Sage of Malyndor, sealed and delivered."

"Well done," Lord Desmond told him.

"An impressive feat," Lord Belmore agreed.

Lord Sever didn't show even the hint of a smile. "Our agreement isn't complete yet."

"Of course," Vincent soothed pleasantly with a little bow prior to turning to face his foe.

"If you harm so much as one hair upon his head I shall never forgive you, Vincent," Jade cried, pulling against her guards.

"Do not fret, sweetheart," he told her while keeping his focus upon the sage. "You shall be free of his control shortly."

Attempting to push himself off the ground, Alec clenched his jaw. "This is between you and me, Vincent. Let her be."

The grin on the noble's face grew darkly, matching a strangely evil glint in his eye. Drawing his blade, he gradually stalked towards the pinned sorcerer.

"And why would I do that?" Vincent questioned with a sneer. "Have you not heard? Jade is to be my wife. Once I dispatch you, we shall begin our life anew here in Zerrok, with my own fief as a reward for your head." Vincent continued to grow closer. "So you see slave, I have no intention of ever letting her go. Jade is mine."

"Never!" Alec roared, raising his body enough to slash at Vincent.

Eyes widening briefly, the noble leapt back just in time for the blade to sweep by. Glancing down he spotted a thin slit on the outer layer of his clothing. Gripping his sword, Vincent's eyes flashed dangerously.

"How dare you?" the noble demanded.

He continued to glare at the warrior as, despite the seals, Alec started to rise.

Managing to get to his knees, Alec sat back on his heels and peered up at Vincent with a face of stone. Though his chest was heaving from the effort, and beads of sweat gathered on his brow, the warrior was deathly calm. The mark on his back tingled with a strange, almost searing pain.

Get up, Alakaid, the voice in his mind rang out. *His spell cannot hope to hold you hence.*

Hands resting on his thighs, the tendons of his neck pressed against his skin as Alec rose to his full height.

Brows lowered to points, Colton grit his teeth as he tried to feed more energy into his incantation. The number of magical seals, paired with the sheer volume of energy connected to Colton's ancient enchantment, should be hindering the barbarian's ability to move, let alone stand. How did this strange sorcerer continue to defy the laws of magic?

"This isn't possible. What are you?"

Alec didn't answer. Gaze set, he saw nothing and no one, but the noble from Parlen. *It's time to end this.* Vincent wasn't going to slither away this time. Energy beginning to swirl about him in a fine light mist, Alec gripped his blade with both hands. His limbs felt heavy from the effects of the spell, but the warrior would not be swayed to take another course.

The two men collided with an angry, piercing clash. Each attack was parried as the foes fought without gaining any ground. The invisible chains weighing upon the sage seemed to even the divide between the two warriors' skills.

Just when their blades connected once again, Alec twisted his grip, purposely allowing Vincent to press his sword towards the ground. Stepping in close, the sorcerer pivoted so he was by the noble's side as he drove his elbow between Vincent's ribs.

Breath exhaling with a hiss, Vincent doubled over.

Alec's next blow never connected. Pain radiating through his body, the sorcerer fought to keep his grip upon his blade. Staggering back, he moved out of range of Vincent's swing as Colton's spell returned to its normal intensity.

Having escaped his near demise, Vincent smiled broadly. "What's the matter, slave? Running out of tricks already?"

His opponent made no reply as his eyes tracked every move he made. When their swords met again with an intense clang, Vincent slid to the side and stepped forward with a thrust aimed at Alec's heart.

Blocking the attack with the edge of his blade, Alec twirled in a circle, bringing his weapon down diagonally. Vincent parried at the last moment, struggling to meet the barrage of attacks suddenly raining down upon him. The sage didn't let up the assault. Twisting the hilt of his sword, he slashed first in one direction then the next.

Vincent's blade flew up into the air, exposing his abdomen.

Alec tightened his hold and lunged forward. Taking a step, his body froze as if it was chained fast on each limb. Lips pressed into a thin line, his steely gaze shifted to the other sorcerer.

Fingers spread, Colton stood with his hands in front of him as he put every ounce of his energy into the enchantment.

"Kill him," he urged Vincent through clenched teeth.

312

Alec's eyes narrowed. "Your magic can't bind me."

The glow behind the sage's dark brown eyes gleamed brightly as he tapped into the vast well of magic flowing in his blood. The mist surrounding him shined like his eyes. Lashing out, it swept across the chamber like a wind storm. Deep grooves cut into the stone, breaking the connection of several seals. Body pulsing, Alec drew his arms in close while turning his sword so that the tip of the blade was pointed downward. Lifting the weapon, he rammed it into the ground, sending a wave of power rolling over the space. A web of cracks spread through the polished surface, causing the remaining marks upon both the stone floor and ceiling to flicker and darken, losing all effect.

"No!" Colton shouted, dropping to his knees.

Lifting his chin, Alec took a deep breath and called back the strong aura shrouded about him. Pulling his blade free, his gaze returned to the sole enemy who truly earned his wrath.

Nostrils flaring and eyes unusually wide, Vincent hollered loudly as he charged straight at the sorcerer.

Alec raced to meet him. Flicking away his enemy's blade, he invaded Vincent's space to strike him in the chest with his open palm. The blow forced his opponent back momentarily, allowing the warrior to side step Vincent's next attack as he twisted the hilt of his sword and thrust it behind him into the noble's back.

The tip of the blade shone through Vincent's chest as his weapon slipped from his fingers. The color red spotted his lips. Alec pulled the blade free and peered at him with no change in his expression. With hard eyes, the sorcerer watched Vincent's corpse collapse. No smile touched his mouth from the death. Despite all he had done, killing the noble had been a last resort. There was already enough blood covering Alec's hands.

Gradually, his gaze shifted to the three leaders seated behind a row of soldiers. Nearby, Colton tried to rise as he inhaled raggedly. Finally upright, he swayed.

"Infureono, blast."

No flame came to life in the bird-like sage's hand. Completely drained of mana, his spell was useless. With no blade and no magic, the sorcerer was defenseless. His bottom lip quivered as Alec's gaze connected with his.

"Not now," Alec quipped, pointing a hand at the other sage. "Surgeon, stun."

Unable to block the enchantment, Colton was paralyzed where he stood. Inwardly cursing, he waited for Alec to deliver the finishing blow. However, the powerful sage was no longer paying him any mind.

"There is no need to be so hasty, Your Highness," Beltmore began, holding up his hands as if in surrender. "This is not what you think."

Remaining seated, Desmond added, "It is true that we recruited Lord Vincent to bring you here. Our measures, though a tad extreme, were meant to test you and not to bring you harm. A man easily defeated by one such as him could not possibly be the true savior of the realms."

Alec exhaled with a huff. "You can't possibly expect me to believe that. Only a few moments ago you were practically ordering him to slay me."

"Lord Vincent had no knowledge of the true nature of our mission. He was but a tool for a greater cause. Prince Alakaid, we need your aid to battle the dragons plaguing our beloved Kingdom."

His words caused Alec's brows to lower slightly. Could he be speaking of the rogue Iron Scales Clan? As far as he knew, they didn't venture too far from the Sea of Ash unless it was to hunt. To openly attack a kingdom would draw the attention of Ellfraya. From what Cassidy told him, the banished dragons wouldn't stand a chance in an all-out war.

Do not listen to them! Jade thought urgently, unaware that it was more his inner thoughts holding his focus. These men had no valor and their words were nothing but poison. Her earlier conversation with The Pure leaders showed Jade that they could not be trusted. These men only sought power and taking Alec's life was part of that lofty goal. A hand clamped over the noblewoman's mouth was keeping her from exposing them. With Alec's head tilted to the side and his blade aimed at the floor, she couldn't be sure that he wasn't being swayed. *I must do something.* Gathering her courage, Jade managed to wiggle her arm free enough to slam her elbow into her guard's side.

Inhaling sharply, the man's one hand loosened on her.

Biting down hard, Jade pulled her face away from his grip and shouted towards the sage, "Do not let them deceive you, these men were responsible for your kidnapping as a child."

The guard was able to regain control over the noblewoman, yet the damage was already done.

Stiffening, Alec was about to strike when Sever made his move. Removing two vials from his tunic, the man tossed the containers onto the ground at Alec's feet. Thick wafts of smoke twisted up from the broken shards, surrounding the sorcerer in a grey cloud. Holding his breath, Alec flinched as the toxin started to dissolve his clothing and burn his flesh. The soldiers inched back, leaning away from the smoke as they intently searched the cloud for their enemy.

As the elixir dissipated, all which remained were tattered pieces of the sage's cloak. The Pure lords emitted a booming chuckle as they rose to their feet with a grin. A smirk shone on even Sever's face. It had been a challenging task, but finally, the marked one was no more.

"Well done, my friend," Beltmore praised his fellow ruler. "I'm glad you always carry some of your creations with you."

His lips pulled back with a sneer. "Yes. I even created this particular mix just for him."

Their victory celebration was short lived as a soldier all the way to the right fell to the ground in a growing pool of his own blood. Everyone's attention turned in that direction, but no adversary appeared from the shadows.

Quietly sneaking up behind Jade's captor, Alec drove a knife into the man's side. Pulling the guard back, the warrior freed his beloved prior to running the steel over the soldier's throat.

Unable to control herself, Jade launched herself into Alec's embrace. Gripping the back of his tunic, she inhaled deeply. *He is here. Alakaid is really here.*

"I knew you would come," she whispered with the hint of tears.

Gaze still focused on their enemies, he rested his cheek on the top of her silky brown hair as he held her tightly to him.

"Of course love, no army could keep me from reaching you."

Smiling brightly, Jade released him and took a step back. The danger had not passed. There would be plenty of time later to enjoy their reunion. Right now, they needed to focus on finding their friends and escaping from Zerrok.

Directing Jade behind him, Alec's set gaze pierced the three startled leaders. When the prince spoke, his words were filled with all the warmth of an iceberg.

"You made a grave mistake in taking her. Jade is not my weakness, she is my greatest strength. And for harming her you will pay."

Alec allowed them no time in which to muster themselves after his chilling declaration. Dashing forward, he cut across the first two men, cleaving their swords in half as he left a groove across their chests. The soldiers fell back, pressing a hand to their wounds as the next challengers moved forward to meet Alec's blade.

At the back of the group, the three leaders made their way towards the lone doorway.

"You will not escape me." Momentarily pushing the men he was fighting off, the sage called up a spell. "Infureono, fire wall."

A tall blaze appeared, blocking off the right side of the room. Countering a few strikes, Alec cart-wheeled over a passing blade then cut low to sever the tendons in his opponent's leg. Sweeping his hand to the side, the flames followed, spreading to the other half of the space as he blocked off access to the stairs. So long as his fires burned, there was nowhere to go. Three soldiers were left standing between Alec and his targets.

Standing off to the side, Jade eyed a sword lying by her former guard's side. Retrieving the steel, she swallowed the lump trying to set in her throat. This was what she had trained for: to be able to defend herself, to protect herself. If she could be of any aid to Alec, then it would be well worth the hard work invested. Tightening her grip, Jade pulled back her shoulders and stood before the three leaders with all the determination she could muster.

The last soldier protecting them stared at the lady with raised brows. Realizing her intent, a vile smirk shadowed his features. In challenge, he held his blade at the ready while blowing Jade a kiss.

Mouth parting slightly, Jade rallied her senses and scrunched up her face with disgust. *I shall show him that I am so much more than just a pretty face.* Dashing forward, Jade struck with a slash to the man's side. The moment their blades touched, Jade's sword changed direction, attacking once more.

The smile was quickly erased from her opponent's face. Having trained with the heavy burden of armor, the lady's movements were much faster than she realized since she was now free of the excess weight. Parrying and counter-parrying, the two fighters danced in front of the bottom of the platform with no clear winner.

To the left, the last of the soldiers charged at Alec with a roar. Swiftly, the sage locked his weapon with the first man's as he connected with a kick to the second's chest. Drawing back, Alec ducked under a passing blade as he used a knife to slice his opponent's leg.

Gimping, the man held his sword steady as he waited for the next strike.

Alec didn't disappoint him. Releasing a dagger, he charged forward. As the guard deflected the flying blade, the sage moved in to slash him across the abdomen. Alec's foe dropped to the ground with blood oozing from between his fingers. Just as quickly, his remaining enemies were upon him. Relieving the deceased soldier of his weapon, Alec twisted around, blocking dual strikes. The fighters expertly moved about the chamber in the fire's dancing light. The glow shadowed Alec's features, making them appear darker and even more menacing, as he silently pushed his foes back to where the battle first began. Darting past a blade, Alec kicked the left man in the outer thigh causing him to drop to a knee. Spinning around, the warrior used the injured guard's back as a stepping stone to leap into the air and somersault over the second man. Landing lightly behind him, Alec stabbed the man with both blades.

On his feet once more, the first soldier charged at the sage with the grace of a maddened bull. Blocking the wild attack with one sword, Alec lowered his other arm, running his enemy through with the second blade.

Jerking his weapon free, the warrior scanned the area searching for Jade. He felt a mixture of dread and pride as he spotted her locked in combat with their last obstacle to The Pure leaders. The soldier had the advantage of strength and size, but Jade learned her lessons well and was using the man's power for her own gain. Light as a feather, she countered the guard's blows with a graceful swiftness few could achieve.

Striding towards them, Alec frowned. He recognized the stance she was taking. It was one of the moves he'd taught her. If all went well, Alec knew exactly how it would end. Should she fail to perform it correctly however, the blood would not be on her blade. Running full speed, Alec silently called up a wind spell to aid him.

Blade connecting with her opponent's once again, Jade pushed away the urge to cuss. This battle was more difficult than she anticipated. Luckily, she seemed to be holding her own. Yet, being locked in a stalemate was not getting her any closer to the three men whom she wanted to face. *Just a little longer.* Alec was bound to finish defeating the others soon and would join her side. Instead, she tried to think of a way to turn the tables. There was a move she recalled practicing with Alec prior to his departure. It was risky, but it could be just what she needed to defeat this foe. Mind set, Jade's next strike was to the side. As the soldier's sword went to parry the attack Jade disengaged.

It was too late for the man to pull back from the feint.

Spinning in a tight circle, Jade twisted around to the man's exposed side and struck. As her blade cut through the air, it suddenly occurred to her what was about to take place. *Oh no, he is going to fall by my blade.* Perhaps the noble wasn't as ready as she thought. It was too late to stay her sword. Closing her eyes, Jade turned her face away from the scene playing out before her. The sudden ring of metal striking metal echoed in her ears and vibrated up Jade's arms. Blinking rapidly, she glanced back at her opponent. The guard was no longer the only man present.

Alec stood between the two fighters. His sword was blocking Jade's while he grasped the hilt of a knife in the other. The tip of the short blade was buried up to the handguard in between the soldier's ribs. Pulling the blade free, Alec pushed the deceased assailant away from them.

Slowly, Jade and Alec each lowered their weapons to the floor.

"I know you are strong Jade. But as long as I'm beside you, you won't have to sully your hands with the blood of men. Let me be your shield."

Jade couldn't say if her pounding heart was from the battle she just faced or from having Alec so close, but the sincerity of his words warmed her. This was merely one of the reasons she loved him so. Smiling gently, Jade lightly touched his arm with her free hand.

"I would not be opposed to us shielding each other."

Her gaze caught sight of the three lords backing towards the other side of the altar. How could she have briefly forgotten about them? Now was not the time to get caught up in her whirling emotions.

"I fear this discussion shall have to await another time. There are those who still owe us answers."

Alec shifted his sights in the direction Jade was peering. Jaw tensing, he began to stalk towards the men. Lacking a continuous flow of power, the magical blazes blocking off any means of escape flickered and waned.

Still, instead of heading towards the doorway, The Pure leaders had been inching their way towards the opposite side of the altar.

What game is this? Alec thought sourly. Studying their calm expressions and proud stances, his lips pressed tightly together. *These men are not behaving as if they have been defeated.* Holding out his hands, Alec fed more energy into the flames, causing them to shoot up several more feet.

The lords jumped, quickly drawing away from the intense heat.

"Start talking," Alec advised, as tongues of fire curved up his fingers and snaked up his arm to wrap around his forearm.

Alec's fire spell wasn't the only enchantment which lost strength. Keeping his movements to a minimum so he wouldn't draw his enemy's attention, Colton slowly wiggled his fingers. A tingling sensation flowed through his extremities. However, he was pleased with his overall range of motion. It wouldn't be long now until he had enough mana recharged to break through the spell.

Watching the other sorcerer, Colton bit back a retort. What was it about this strange man that continued to disturb him? Colton didn't believe for a moment that he was the prince of Malyndor. There was no way a person like him was royalty. Hands curling into fists, Colton forced himself to take a slow, deep breath. Alec was a barbarian just like his father said and nothing more. Then why didn't Alec finish him off while he had the chance? Jerric would never have wasted the opportunity to get rid of an enemy.

'The strong must take power for themselves,' his father would often say. 'Otherwise, you will be trampled upon like the weak. Never be weak, Colton.'

Recalling his personal battle with Alec, the sage frowned. Eyeing his would-be target, he also thought of the way Alec fought against his father's enchantment. How could anyone think of the warrior as being weak? Colton shook his head against those poisonous thoughts. Alec was a trickster. He would not let this man sway him from that truth. Letting his aura surge around him, Colton shattered the remainder of the stunning spell placed upon him. Aiming his hand in Alec's direction, the wizard paused. As if by a will of its own, his fingers slowly curled into his palm and his arm started to lower. Giving himself a good mental shake, Colton's face hardened. Striking the warrior in the back wouldn't give him the satisfaction he desired. When he defeated Alec, Colton wanted it to be face-to-face.

"Next time, Alec," he muttered like a curse.

Turning away, Colton slipped from the chamber in search of his father.

Backed into a corner, the three lords glanced at each other strangely. Despite Alec's fiery insistence that they explain, not one of them seemed intent on doing so. Watching the blaze still waving about Alec's arm, the leaders glared defiantly.

"Why not just use your power to gain what answers you seek?" Desmond questioned coyly.

"Perhaps, because he knows he may not get the truth," Beltmore interjected placidly.

"Hmm, quite the predicament. Try to find the truth you seek, or kill us now and never know."

Alec's expression told them nothing as the two men toyed with him. Eyes scanning his adversaries, he inwardly frowned. *What are they hiding?* Observing them closely, Alec still couldn't seem to figure out what they were up to. With no weapons… Alec paused. The man known as Lord Sever wasn't engaging in this mocking display like the others. Peering at him, Alec noted that the man had a hand hidden beneath his tunic. Without batting an eye, the sage extinguished the flames around his arm to fling a strong gust at the tall lord.

Fighting to remain on his feet, Sever tried to brace himself as one after another of the remaining vials hidden in his clothing shattered. Shouting, the man stripped off his tunic and wet undershirt, throwing them on the floor. Red splotches were already bubbling up upon his skin where the toxins made contact.

"Damn you!"

"It's your own fault for thinking you could use the same trick twice," the sorcerer told him evenly.

Face twitching, the man glared up at him with narrowed eyes.

"Now then," Alec began darkly. "If you are finished underestimating me—"

The Dragon Sage didn't get the chance to complete his all too real threat. The entire top of the tower shook violently as something crashed into the domed roof from the outside. Looking upwards, Alec could see the web of cracks widen to rivers. As the next assault connected, loose pieces of plaster started to fall.

A roar sounded from the outside prior to another strike. Each one was coming faster than the next. The thunderous noise hammered away at the building with a continuous ferocity.

Behind him, Jade let out an involuntary shriek. Larger chunks were falling, some landing dangerously close by. Disregarding the men he was interrogating, Alec rushed to Jade's side.

"Surgeon, shield."

Peering over towards Colton, he went to spread the barrier around the defenseless sage as well, only to see that he had disappeared. A quick visual sweep of the space told him Colton was gone, as were the flames blocking the doorway. Focusing on protecting Jade, the sage drew his energy away from the fires to solely concentrate on his barrier.

More of the ceiling was crashing down in boulders. A hole appeared in the supposedly impenetrable roof. Soon, a large clawed foot reached in, prying the opening wider still. Once the gap was massive enough for her to easily pass, Cassidy slipped inside.

The rocks falling upon the chamber were lessening now that a mighty dragon wasn't attacking from the outside. Seeing Cassidy eased some of the tension in Alec's shoulders. Stretching out his palm, Alec shifted his attention directly above them to the falling debris.

"Tsumorri, freeze."

Leaving Cassidy's escape route clear, Alec used the ice to seal the entire ceiling prior to lowering his shield.

"That should hold for now," Alec said to no one in particular. A smile appeared on his face as he looked at the green dragon. "I can't believe you were able to break in. How are the others? Have you had any contact with them yet?"

What Alec truly wanted to know was if Malcolm had indeed survived. He didn't want to upset Jade at the moment with the details of their battles through the tower.

"Tatsu and Ardys were circling the tower in search of them," Cassidy informed him unhappily. "I have yet to see any of the others."

Alec was about to ask something more when a frown marred his features. The chamber was cluttered with various debris, but the one thing he didn't see was any sign of the three Pure leaders. *Where did they sneak off to?* The doorway was blocked. However, the exit was within the sorcerer's peripheral vision throughout the ordeal. He would have noticed if they tried to flee in that direction. Alec's gaze shifted to the area beside the altar where the men had gathered. There had to be some kind of clue to their mysterious disappearance.

As stones crashed around them, Beltmore jerked back, momentarily forgetting about the magical wall of flames surrounding the chamber. He cringed, jumping in the other direction while expecting for his skin to be burnt. The man felt no pain from his momentary lapse of memory. It was then he noticed that Alec's spell had dissipated.

"We should retreat while that demon is distracted," Sever advised.

His two partners nodded in agreement. Destroying the dragon prince would have to wait for another time. Tapping a secret pattern on the stone wall, the lord unlocked a hidden passage which stretched out behind the platform. The three men raced down the steps as they dodged the endless raining debris. Once all of them cleared the steps, Desmond pulled a lever to close the stairwell. Cast in shadow, the three lords were now locked in a pitch-black corridor. Blindly feeling the wall, Beltmore, Desmond and Sever all traveled down the hallway as quickly as they were able. Eventually, it would lead to another hidden door within the main tower. There, they would be safe from the vile sorcerer.

A light suddenly appeared streaming from a bend up ahead. The men stiffened. Without Sever's potions they were defenseless.

His hood lowered to reveal his features, Derek quickly strode towards them. A torch was clutched in one hand while a long knife was grasped in the other. He said nothing as he continued to approach menacingly.

"Derek, what are you doing here?" Beltmore questioned with raised brows. "If you seek the Dragon Sage, he is still in the chamber above."

The lethal man's expression didn't change. "My orders do not involve him at this time."

Desmond pulled back with a jerk. "Wait—no. You cannot be serious!"

"How dare you turn on us?" Sever demanded.

Derek shrugged. "You knew there could only be one true leader of The Pure when you joined my master. And you all have come to the end of your usefulness."

The torch clattered to the ground, deepening the shadows of the corridor. In the next instant, Derek seemed to disappear. The lords jerked around, squinting in the poor light for the assassin. Slipping behind them, an eerie smile stretched across the man's face as he moved in upon his first victim.

Studying the floor where he had left the three lord's company, Alec tilted his head to the side. No bodies were crushed behind the heavy stones, nor did they seem to be hiding anywhere among the boulders.

"Where did they flee?" Jade asked with a puzzled frown. It didn't seem possible for them to just vanish.

Eyeing the ground, Alec paused. Lips pressing together, he stepped closer towards the platform containing the altar and throne chairs. Among the dust were three sets of footprints. The impressions were abruptly cut off as if something else had been covering the floor where they stood. *Or nothing,* Alec privately corrected.

"Rokon, shift," the sage said, calling up a spell.

This tower had been nothing but tricks and traps. Why would this be any different? Alec knew they had been hiding something and a trap door seemed the most logical answer. Manipulating the stones, Alec slid them around until he found an opening. A dark narrow staircase was revealed at his feet. Gazing into the shaft, Alec unsheathed his weapon and summoned a fireball in his palm.

"You are not going down there are you?" Jade whispered as if there was someone standing at the very bottom listening.

"I will be fine. Wait here."

Alec knew they should depart. He knew more soldiers were bound to be on their way or even another sage, but he couldn't stay his course. He needed to know if it was possible for him to cut off his enemies' retreat in order to subdue these men. If The Pure crumbled, then he could stop their war from taking flight.

Twenty feet from the bottom step, the wizard came to an abrupt halt. A pool of liquid reflected his flame's light. Increasing the blaze, his eyes narrowed. Blood covered the floor surrounding three bodies. From the amount of red liquid he expected to find multiple lacerations covering them, but the only injuries he found during a quick exam were deep slashes to each of their necks. Whoever got to them first knew what they were doing.

With one last look, Alec exhaled deeply and turned away. There was nothing more he could do here. Instead, he shifted his focus to Jade and getting her to safety. After all, there was a promise he would not fail to keep.

CHAPTER 19

"This way!" a soldier shouted from somewhere in the adjacent corridor. "Don't let them escape."

Racing through the unfamiliar depths of the Imperial Tower, Isabelle and Nathan closely followed the two Zerrokian princes. At some point, while fleeing from the dungeon Derek became separated from the group. Isabelle hoped he was alright. With so many guards on their tail, they couldn't afford to search for the boy. At this rate, they would be lucky to escape themselves.

After leaving the dungeon, Prince Ashton had led them towards the west wing. Away from the main tower, the number of soldiers had lessened, but with so many stationed outside on the grounds, she couldn't devise a way to reunite with the dragons.

A roar sounded, rattling the windows within their frames. They were close.

"Prince Ashton," Isabelle called, quickening her steps to join his side. "Is there a large balcony or any access to the roof nearby?"

The man frowned thoughtfully. "This place was designed as a fortress, so there are no larger balconies. There is however, a small Keep nearby which we could use to get onto the roof. What are you planning?"

"To call for a ride," she answered with a grin.

Eyes narrowing, the royal glanced at the windows then back at the sorceress. "Surely you do not mean to summon that beast?"

"Quite so, he is one of our escorts."

"Indeed?" Ashton returned strangely with a frown.

Isabelle shared a glance with the warrior behind her that the prince did not miss. He opened his mouth to say something, but his less disciplined brother drew everyone's attention.

"I am not riding one of those things. It is bad enough that we are being rescued by her kind," Sebastian whined snidely. "But I shall not lower myself to associating with dragons."

Ashton's steps drew to a halt. "We spoke of this Sebastian. These people are here to help us. Their means do not matter. Without their aid, we would not be able to escape from our captors."

"Personally, I would rather stay here," the younger prince muttered tightly.

"You know we cannot," Ashton told him with a pointed look. Peering at Isabelle and Nathan, the prince gave them a slight bow. "You must forgive him. Our Kingdom's unjust fear of magic has tainted every class. My family is no exception." When Ashton looked at his brother, the younger man turned away without a word. "We are thankful for your assistance."

Loud voices and racing footsteps echoed down the corridor.

"We can't linger here," Nathan reminded everyone. "We are counting on you, Your Highness. Lead the way."

Once more taking charge, Ashton took off down the hall towards the Keep and their freedom. Outside an armored door, two wide-eyed guards slowly began to draw their weapons upon seeing their uninvited guests. Nathan didn't allow them the opportunity to gather their wits. Charging forward, he slashed both men before they were able to fully unsheathe their weapons. Checking the bodies, the warrior searched for a key.

"It only unlocks from the inside," Ashton supplied, glancing at Isabelle.

Nathan followed the man's line of sight. "Are you able to break through it?"

The sorceress strode forward and closed her eyes. Her energy was nowhere near fully restored after summoning her ice beast, yet she did have some mana to work with. Smirking, she pushed some lose strands away from her face.

"Men...always looking to destroy things. Why blast it open when there are easier ways?" she giggled. "Infureono, slice."

A faint light shone from Isabelle's finger tips. Running her hand down the seam of the door she cut through the locks. Releasing her spell, she reached forward and easily pushed the door open.

"Amazing as always," Nathan told her, keeping eye contact longer than needed prior to entering the threshold.

Blinking rapidly, the sorceress's cheeks began to flush. *What was that about? Get ahold of yourself. He was simply paying you a compliment,* she scolded, allowing the princes to go first. By the time she followed suit, Nathan was finishing off the few posted guards.

A spiral staircase in the center took them up another three flights to the top of the Keep. Nathan found the outside door quickly. After dispatching the two soldiers stationed on the surrounding deck, he motioned for the others to follow.

Isabelle pointed a hand to the sky and shot a ball of light into the air. She didn't have long to wait. A bright red dragon soared closer, circling around the Keep before coming to land on the rooftop. A wide grin lit the sorceress's features in the twilight.

"Ardys!"

The answering rumble caused her to laugh. Vaulting over the railing, Isabelle dropped down onto the lower roofline and rushed to the magical creature's side.

"I'm so glad to see you," she told him hugging the side of his face.

Watching the two strangers walking tentatively towards them, Ardys growled in the back of his throat. He didn't need to be told who they were to recognize nobility.

Isabelle patted the side of his neck. She sympathized with her friend. The sage didn't care much for the royals either, but a promise was a promise.

"I understand your feelings, my friend," Isabelle began, knowing there wasn't time to waste. "And I know it's a lot to ask, but we swore to Malcolm that we would rescue the princes. You and I both know what it is like to be locked in a dungeon. No one deserves that needlessly."

With a huff of smoke, Ardys folded his wings and held out a leg so the humans could climb aboard. Not much was said as everyone got situated and braced themselves for the flight. Lifting into the sky, Ardys circled around the perimeter of the grounds as he traveled higher into the atmosphere. The soldiers' weapons could no longer reach them, yet the great dragon could still make out the events unfolding beneath. After a few moments, Isabelle spotted a flash of green smash into the roof of the main tower.

Drawing back, Cassidy unleashed a powerful blast upon the steel tiles. Once the plates were heated, she slammed into the structure, bending the outer layer. The pattern continued until she formed a hole to the inside. Slipping through the opening, the dragon disappeared from view.

Several minutes passed before she reemerged with two passengers. As she rose into the air, Tatsu burst out from behind the tower with his own riders. The three dragons roared to each other, then quickly set off. Rising into the clouds, they headed northwest to journey towards the neighboring kingdom of Rhordack. Flying across the Sea of Narvee with additional passengers would not be wise. Not only had the dragons been engaged in their own battles while awaiting the humans, but they had yet to rest since leaving Malyndor.

Darkness added to their cover as the miles passed by far below. Peering around, Alec could occasionally make out one of the other dragons, but identifying who was with them was impossible. The sorcerer was fairly certain that Isabelle and Nathan's side mission must have been a success by the number of passengers among them. Had the great sage made it as well? He couldn't be sure.

Once within the middle kingdom, the companions followed the line of the Black Mountains. They turned north along the coast for an hour or so prior to beginning a descent. Leaning to the side, Alec gazed around at the scenery below. Cassidy was gliding towards a small clearing on the water side of the mountains. The rocks curled inward, creating a natural basin that could only be seen from the air. Thick trees clung to the ridges and grew up the mountainside adding to the area's camouflage. Once she landed, Cassidy lowered herself to the ground for Alec and Jade to dismount. To the left, was a large cave opening that Alec hadn't been able to see from the sky. Cassidy walked inside, clearing the landing field for the next dragon. Stepping back, Alec's fingers tapped the side of his leg. He craned his neck as Ardys drew closer to glide into the petit field.

Hopping down, the blonde sorceress raced to the warrior's side, hugging both Alec and Jade. The smile upon her face was almost contagious.

"I can't believe we did it," she squeaked. "We not only infiltrated the best guarded fortress in Zerrok, but we managed to save Lady Jade and the princes, too. I was sure we were all going to perish, but we survived!"

"I'm glad you had such faith in our abilities," Alec teased, keeping a straight face.

Isabelle planted a hand on her hip. "You know as well as I that this task was nearly impossible."

Behind her, Nathan was approaching with the royals as Ardys cleared the way for the black dragon. He and Alec gripped each other's forearms warmly.

"Glad to see you kept her from too much mischief," Alec greeted with a smirk on the right side of his mouth.

Nathan nodded with a smile. "I must admit that I enjoyed working with such a skilled sorceress." His gazed shifted briefly to Isabelle as he spoke, but the energetic woman was engaged with Jade in their own conversation. "Oh, perhaps I should make some introductions. Prince Ashton, Prince Sebastian, this is Alec."

Given the covert nature of their mission, he thought it best not to introduce Alec as a royal. At least, not right away to the rulers of the kingdom that they just raided without consent. They could seek forgiveness for the deception later. Getting everyone back home safely was their main objective.

Back rod straight and chin held high, the older prince stepped forward with all the grace and confidence of a man born to royalty. "I understand our rescue was only possible with your expert aid. Thank you."

Ashton held out his hand. Beside him, his brother offered a muttered 'thanks'.

Alec peered down at the royal's outstretched fingers, but didn't move. This man's family was responsible for Zerrok's slavery. They allowed people to be slaughtered in the arenas, and for innocent citizens to be captured and sold like animals. While Ashton might not be directly responsible for his suffering, he had made no effort to correct it either. In his mid-thirties, the tall sandy brown-haired man had a short beard and hazel eyes. The prince was clearly no child, and sure to have some sway in the running of his kingdom. With King David deceased, he was, in fact, the next ruler. As much as he wished to leave a good impression for the sake of his family, Alec couldn't seem to make his arm move.

"Alec, I need you," shouted Garth, drawing everyone's attention.

Saved from the awkward situation, Alec dashed to Tatsu's side. The gruff warrior had already aided a petit youth to the ground and currently had another man hunched over in his arms. Alec's face paled upon seeing his teacher. He had never observed Malcolm to be in such a state before. The wizard's skin was white, his lips contained a bluish hue and he was gasping as he sucked in shallow breaths. Alec reached up, helping Garth to lower the other sage to the ground.

"Should we take him inside?" Isabelle questioned, biting her lip as she peered at her mentor.

"There's no time," Alec dismissed.

Each passing second lowered the chance of Malcolm being able to recover. Checking the sage over, he searched for some sign of an injury. Malcolm's left hand and wrist was a strange blackish color. The unpleasant coloring was half-way up his arm and continuing to climb in thread-like veins. Even more disturbing was the green tinge swirling beneath the surface of his skin. Alec reached out to touch the wound. An electric charge zapped him, causing Isabelle to yelp in surprise. The sorcerer immediately jerked back, shaking his hand from the sting.

"What is causing this?" Jade inquired worriedly. She could not recall seeing such a strange injury before. "Is he going to pull through?"

Alec frowned. "My guess is that it's Jerric's tainted aura infecting his body. Unless it is cleansed, the energy will continue to spread and likely take his life."

"Are you able to heal this type of wound?" Garth wondered, studying the strange contagion. He never knew that magic could cause this type of harm. "Be careful not to get infected yourself."

Nodding solemnly, Alec held his hands, palm side down, over Malcolm's arm. Eyes beginning to glow softly, he called forth an energy spell.

"Surgeon, restore."

The outline of his hands glowed as Alec focused everything he could on saving his mentor and friend. The light increased, growing brighter, yet nothing seemed to happen. Shifting his hands downward, Alec located the source of the evil energy. A ring was imprinted around Malcolm's wrist where Jerric's weapon struck him. Placing his palms over top of it, Alec could gradually see a change in the dark hue of the sage's skin. Little by little his color returned to normal.

Once the wound appeared to be completely healed, Alec drew back. The raggedness of Malcolm's breathing had not eased. Nor, had there been any change to the paleness of his skin.

Something's not right, Alec thought grimly.

There were no other cuts on his skin or wounds that Alec could find as he renewed his search. Remembering Malcolm's battle with Jerric, Alec's attention shifted to the sage's legs. At the very end of their fight, Jerric's weapon struck the older sage's ankle to keep him from joining his companions.

"Help me with his boots."

Garth pulled off one while Alec removed the other. Pushing up his mentor's breeches, his face hardened. Malcolm's left leg had changed to a dark blackish color just like his wrist. The eerie, foul green tinge was dancing beneath

Malcolm's skin all the way to his knee. For someone's aura to cause such damage really was proof of Jerric's evil heart.

Stretching out his fingers, Alec took a deep breath and held his hands above the faint ring marking Malcolm's flesh. Summoning his spell, the sage set to work healing the magical wound. Just as it had done with Malcolm's arm, the tainted aura began to dissipate, and the true tint of the sorcerer's flesh was restored.

The work on his friend's leg complete, Alec wiped the sweat from his brow and sat back on his heels. It had been difficult, but all of the tainted aura seemed to be purified. Looking at Malcolm's face, he noted that the wizard's skin and lips were also starting to change back to a healthy hue.

"Nathan," Garth began, bending down by the great sage. "Help me take him inside, would you?"

"Of course," the swordsman answered easily.

As Jade waited for Alec to get back on his feet, Isabelle glanced at the sky. The surrounding darkness didn't illuminate much of the rocks or the heavens above. Another threat could be lingering nearby and they would not be aware.

"We should seek shelter," the Just Sage advised. "There's no telling when we might run into one of the Iron Scales Clan."

"Who?" Ashton questioned.

"Enemy dragons," she clarified hastily. "We should all go inside to keep from being spotted."

Alec nodded his agreement. The center of the clearing was far too open to remain in. Should they be attacked at this time, it would be difficult to defend themselves. While the area was an ideal hideout, it was certainly no fortress. Cassidy must have used it before to know of its existence.

Entering the cavern, Alec was surprised by the amount of space. While a dragon's horns nearly scraped the ceiling, the area easily housed all of the large creatures with plenty of space to spare. The single chamber was well enough hidden to allow a fire in the rear without the risk of giving them away.

Garth seemed to have come to the same conclusion. He had a small pile of kindling near the place where Malcolm was resting. Cassidy stood over him and blew a soft breath of flames, lighting it quickly. The warm glow had a soothing effect on the travelers after their ordeal in Zerrok.

Seeing their friends approaching, Garth and Nathan rose to their feet. Reaching out, the warrior gripped Alec's forearm with a grin. They each greeted the other fondly with a mix of handshakes and hugs from Isabelle.

"You did it, little brother," Nathan said approvingly. "I don't know how, but you did."

Alec glanced towards the princes sitting by the fire with their backs to the wall. Beside them, closer to the shadows, was their servant Derek.

"I see you have your own victory to be proud of. If The Pure's leaders had survived, I doubt this loss would sit well with them. As it is, I doubt we have heard the last of this anti-magical group."

As much as Alec would like the whole affair to be over, he doubted this uprising would burn itself out. Something about the efficient and decisive way the leaders had been coldly murdered caused him to believe that a far darker plot was afoot.

"You defeated their leaders?" Garth asked with a hint of pride, breaking into Alec's private thoughts.

Not even a shadow of a smirk appeared on the younger man's face. "Not entirely. Someone else delivered the final blow." Alec's gaze lowered to the dancing flames. "Someone close to them."

"It could have been a rival seeking power."

"Perhaps."

Alec wasn't so sure. An image of the slain men flashed in his mind's eye. Was this really simply one of their own turning on them? Why wait until that point? Surely there would have been other opportunities prior to his arrival. Pushing those thoughts from his mind, Alec peered at the cave's opening with a frown.

"I'll take the first watch. Everyone should get some rest. It has been a trying day."

"Oh no you don't," Nathan rejected. "I will take the first watch. Other than the dragons, I'd wager that you've done the most fighting, and healing, as I recall," he added gesturing to his own arm. "That's an order, little brother."

Alec couldn't help but chuckle. He made no remark to the fact that he was no longer a member of the Stafford Guard or technically the crown prince of Malyndor. Flashing a classic half smile, he held up his hands in surrender.

"I suppose I can't argue with my Commander."

Rising to his feet, Sebastian shuffled closer to the fire's light as the warrior strode off. "You cannot possibly mean for us to camp *here*? This is unacceptable."

"Sebastian," his brother called from behind him in a warning tone.

"No! I have done more than enough. I was locked in a filthy dungeon. I have tolerated sorcerers and their magical beasts, but I am a Prince of Zerrok. I will not sleep in the dirt!"

His face turning a deep crimson during his speech, Sebastian's body shook with tremors. The tone of his voice raised several octaves to the point that his last few words were a shrilled shriek.

Ashton strode up behind him and placed a hand on his younger brother's shoulder. Lowering his voice to a whisper, he spoke so that no one other than Sebastian could hear.

Chin dropping to his chest, Sebastian seemed only able to nod in return. Fingers curled into fists, he spun away to resume his place by the wall without peering at a single person there.

"Pray, you must excuse my brother," Ashton began, loosely linking his fingers together in front of him. "Finding yourself in a position that requires the aid of others is not always easy to accept. Misconceptions of old take time to correct. I assure you that we are both glad to be free of the dungeon and see Malyndor as a most trusted ally."

Ashton's calm, more serious demeanor was the complete opposite of his brother's heated outburst. Alec's expression revealed nothing of what he was thinking. This man's words seemed sincere. Yet, why did something about his exchange with the other prince unsettle the warrior so? Perhaps he was being overly suspicious. Still, Alec could not shake this nagging feeling in the pit of his stomach.

"Given your situation, it is natural for you to feel some anger. Those men were responsible for your father's death," Isabelle soothed compassionately.

"Yes," Alec agreed with much less empathy. "Do not however, unleash your wrath upon those who haven't earned it. You may fear and even hate magic, but don't forget that magic was responsible for your freedom. I will not force anyone to stay here. Just remember, their leaders might be dead, but The Pure's army is still very much a threat. I doubt they would give you quarter."

Gazes locked together, there was a long period of strained silence. The dark glare on Sebastian's face spoke volumes. Yet, whatever words his brother had previously shared with him discouraged the prince from voicing his thoughts. A nudge to Alec's shoulder broke the proud man's silent battle of wills.

Seeing the green dragon standing so close, Ashton quickly slid away.

"You should rest," Cassidy encouraged the sage.

The smile on Alec's lips faded as quickly as it appeared when he caught sight of the other prince's expression.

"It talks," Ashton whispered incredulously.

Alec had no intention of explaining the true nature of his powers to these men. Watching Isabelle open her mouth to speak, he loudly cleared his throat. The sorceress glanced his way prior to excusing herself as she moved towards the front of the cave to be with Nathan. Following Isabelle's lead, Alec left Garth with Malcolm by the flames to join the dragons.

Jade didn't hesitate to trail after him. She had no desire to be in the princes' company any more than he did. A small smile pulled at the corners of her mouth as she watched Alec stretch out against Cassidy's scales. The large dragon peered at him fondly. *Who could ever hate such magnificent creatures?* Jade wondered. Momentarily lost in thought, she didn't realize she was staring as Alec gazed up at her. Cheeks warming, Jade broke eye contact and shifted her focus towards the ground as she tucked a lock of hair behind one ear.

Leaning against Cassidy, Alec could feel a deep rumble in the dragon's side as she laughed. Patting the warm scales, Alec motioned for Jade to join him. A large grin lit his features as his love settled close to his side and placed her head against his shoulder. Cassidy's tail wrapped around the pair protectively before she too, closed her eyes and drifted off into a light slumber.

Resting for a few hours, the companions waited for daybreak prior to taking to the skies once more. The cover of darkness would have been preferable, but Malcolm had reservations about the Zerrok princes remaining in the darkened cave for such a long period of time. Alec couldn't say if the wise wizard was more worried about the royal's sanity or their own.

Concealing themselves above the clouds, Cassidy, Ardys and Tatsu flew north towards Malyndor. Once they crossed over the border, they shifted their flight to the east and headed in the direction of Stafford Castle. To human eyes the ground, when visible, sped past as an unreadable blur. The dragons however, were easily able to see the path they needed to take through the jet streams.

A small yelp escaped Jade's lips as Cassidy suddenly twisted to the right and dove. Alec, Malcolm and Jade were forced to grip her spikes and each other to remain on the dragon's back. The burning heat of a blaze zipped past above them. If she hadn't diverted her course when she did, then they would have been scorched.

Ahead of them, Alec saw another fireball rip through the sky, this time aimed at Tatsu. There was no mistaking it. They were under attack by dragons.

"Why are they attacking us?" Jade shouted above the wind whipping past their ears.

"They're after Alec," Malcolm clarified. "These dragons oppose Emperor Draco and believe killing Alec will weaken him."

"Stay sharp, there are at least three of them," warned Cassidy.

The moment she finished speaking, the mighty green creature released a loud roar. A dark brown dragon had sunk his teeth into her tail and jerked her backwards in the air. Twisting her head, Cassidy blasted him.

Her enemy released her and dodged the strike. However, his true aim was realized as another dragon shot up from beneath and slashed her wing, breaking one of the bones. Spiraling out of control, Cassidy quickly lost altitude.

With Jade's terrified screams filling his ears, Alec summoned a healing spell while Malcolm used an air spell to slow their descent. Their joint efforts kept them alive, but it didn't stop them from hitting the ground-hard.

His arms instinctively wrapping around Jade, Alec's aura activated on its own. It surrounded the three passengers as the impact sent them flying off Cassidy's back. Sailing across the long, untrimmed grass, Alec's head was pounding as he staggered to his feet. Peering around, he searched for the others. Jade lay several feet away while Malcolm was closer to the dragon. Aiding his love to her feet, he gazed at the wizard.

"Are you alright?"

"I'll survive," the sage grumbled.

"How are you Cassidy?"

The green dragon didn't answer. Alec and Jade raced to her side. Jade kneeled by their friend's head trying to rouse her, but it was no use. She was out cold.

"This does not bode well," the sage observed gazing at the clouds.

Three enemy dragons were circling overhead: a small brown, a larger black one and a pale bluish grey. No matter their size, they darted across the heavens unleashing a hail of fireballs upon the other two dragons.

Each burdened with human passengers, Ardys and Tatsu were having a difficult time fighting back. From below, it appeared they were continuously zigzagging through the sky. Each time they soared closer to the ground to safely offload their guests, they were cut off. There was no telling how long they would be able to dodge the blasts.

A bright red light shone upon Ardys's back. Lips parting, Alec watched as a magic circle appeared hovering in the air. A creature of flame rose from within. Stretching forth its wings, a blazing phoenix emerged in the heavens. The magical beast shrieked loudly as she charged into the nearest enemy. There was only one person among those dragons who was capable of such feats and Alec wasn't going to let her struggle alone. Turning to gaze at Malcolm, the warrior wasn't even able to voice his question.

"Just go, I will guard those here."

"Be careful," Jade added, knowing she could not stay his departure.

Alec flashed her a half grin. "Of course."

Facing the other way, the sorcerer closed his eyes. He focused inward on the energy flowing through his veins. He still had much to learn when it came to mastering the power of his spirit, yet Alec was already able to easily connect with Fang. Gathering like stardust, pale white orbs pulled from his body. They swirled together until they formed a small, long dragon. Fang patiently floated before Alec with knowing eyes. A man of few words, Alec valued the silent link binding them together. This would be their first true test, their first real battle fighting as one.

Stretching out his wings, the apparition waited for Alec to climb onto his back prior to rising. Soaring into the air, Fang headed straight for the center of the disturbance. At the very least, they needed to distract their foes long enough for Ardys and Tatsu to get their companions to safety.

Turning to meet their new opponent, the black creature shot a ball of flames. The blast was enormous, measuring much larger than any of the strikes thus far.

He must use fire magic like Ardys.

Prepared for such a violent attack, Alec raised a shield which encompassed the two of them. The blast wrapped around the barrier and harmlessly flew past.

Teeth bared, the black dragon snorted a stream of smoke. Dashing forward, he stretched out his claws and raced to meet his foe.

Lowering the shield Alec dove down, twisting around to come up behind his adversary and hit him with a bolt of lightning. Alec's spirit creature was much smaller than a normal dragon, but his size gave him an advantage when it came to speed.

With Isabelle's firebird engaged in combat with the blue dragon, Ardys used the diversion to head towards the ground. Swooping down, he landed just long enough for Nathan and Derek to dismount. Isabelle remained on his back so that she could better control her spirit beast. The further apart they were, the weaker the connection.

Eyes narrowing to slits, the black dragon relentlessly fired one blast after another at the human who dared to challenge him.

Darting around the strikes, Alec and Fang twisted through the air as if they had flown together all their lives. Once they were in position, Alec created another energy shield. When the next fireball flew at him, he redirected the blow, sending the explosion into the brown creature locked on Tatsu. The surprise attack sent the dragon tumbling through the air.

Wasting no time, Tatsu folded his wings and quickly descended. The proud black creature passed by a blur of bright red as Ardys shot up to rejoin the battle. He rammed the dark ebony foe in the back at full speed.

Roaring in pained surprise, the creature spun out of control for a brief moment. Once he regained his bearing, he was met with dual assaults from Ardys and Alec. Both claws and blade slashed across his body, cutting into his scales. Drops of blood rained down in a light crimson shower.

Recovering from his comrade's blast, the brown dragon switched places with the blue beast, freeing him to target Alec. Activating his jewel, the pale dragon increased his speed, closing the distance between him and the human in a flash. With his enemy occupied, the blue dragon had a clear opening. Crashing into Alec, he sank his teeth into Fang's neck.

A sharp pain pierced the sorcerer. Obeying Alec's every thought, Fang dissolved into a swirl of light. His spirit wrapped around him as the sage free fell. Above him, Alec's opponent jerked back, searching for his suddenly vanished rival. Alec was far from defeated. Holding his arms out to the side, he slowed his fall as Fang rematerialized around him. Raising once more, the warriors set out to return the favor.

Summoning a water spell, Alec began to coil it around his blade when his spirit called out to him. Glancing down, the sage paused for a moment. *What are you telling me?* Instead of concentrating on his weapon, Alec rested his palm on the side of Fang's neck. A bright, frosty light lined his mouth as he prepared to fire a blast. Striking at the blue dragon, Fang's now frozen breath hit him on his right shoulder, causing ice crystals to form over his side and down the dragon's wing.

Unable to move his appendage, the blue dragon spiraled out of control and crashed to the ground, hard.

His adversary fallen, Fang shifted his attention to their remaining enemies. Isabelle's firebird wasn't shining as bright, so he moved to aid her creature as Tatsu arrived to rejoin the fray.

The black injured dragon blasted his foes with another massive fireball. With one of his dragons already deceased, and his squad being quickly outnumbered, their odds for success were nearly undetectable. Soaring towards his companion, the ebony beast released another series of blasts. The sky lit up with a cloud of smoke as Ardys and Tatsu countered the attacks. Then, there was nothing. As the air cleared, the two enemy dragons had vanished. Gazing around for their foes, Alec finally spotted them disappearing into the distance. As he made to give chase, Ardys flew up beside him and shook his head.

"Let them go. We are not prepared to defend so many should they lead us into a trap."

Alec's jaw tensed. Peering at both the ground below and the strained look on Isabelle's face, he knew the dragon was right. The sorceress had to be running low on mana, and protecting the others needed to be their first priority.

"Come on, Fang," he muttered as his spirit dragon turned away.

There was nothing else he could do at the moment. Returning to the ground, Alec drew his soul back inside of him. Cassidy was beginning to wake as Malcolm finished healing the remainder of her wounds. Alec glanced at Jade. She had stayed by the green dragon's side during the length of the battle.

"How is she?"

"Quite well, thanks to you and Malcolm."

"I am perfectly capable of answering myself," Cassidy grumbled, trying not to groan as she slowly picked up her head.

The warrior ran a hand over her scales without a word. He understood her frustration. The enemy dragons had taken them all by surprise. Alec was just glad that everyone was alright.

"We should leave this place," Tatsu advised, glancing at the sky.

He received no arguments as the humans each climbed aboard their respective dragons. Fifteen minutes into their flight, the towering city of Stafford came into view. Alec drew back slightly at the sight. *I was not aware that we were so close.* This was the second time that the Iron Scales Clan had nearly attacked the city. The first time, Cassidy and the others had left no survivors to report his location. They weren't as fortunate during this battle. It wouldn't take them long to discover his connection to Stafford. *What have I done?*

It is almost time, whispered the voice he was strangely becoming used to.

Alec tried not to frown. He knew of what she spoke. The moon must be near its pinnacle place in the sky for him to complete his part of the prophecy.

Jade's hand squeezed his arm, sending a jolt of pain straight into his heart. Stafford Castle was now visible and Alec knew the threat to this fief wasn't lurking in the forest or waiting to march up the main road. It was him. The dragons had come for him and if he stayed, they could easily bring the entire city to ruin. No matter where he went, Alec was marked, and the dragons would find him.

The feel of Jade's warmth was equivalent to his plunge in the creek behind Malcolm's cottage. How could he have so selfishly put the one person he truly loved in harm's way?

345

This wasn't bandits or evil sorcerers coming to seek his head. Vincent's crazed ploy had put everything into perspective. Alec's fingers gently touched the enchanted chain bound with Jade's ribbon beneath his shirt. He could not risk putting her in anymore danger. Jade deserved to be happy and there was only one way he could see to ensure that outcome.

One at a time, the three dragons lowered themselves to the ground inside Stafford's courtyard. The main gate was closed, with the heavy steel portcullis firmly in place. Sliding down, Alec quickly asked Cassidy for the dragons to meet him in the clearing at the back of the gardens. He then turned his attention to Jade.

Helping the noblewoman to the ground, Alec wrapped his fingers around Jade's. He led her out of the courtyard while there was still a fair amount of commotion to disguise their escape. Dusk had fallen, casting the gardens in a warm glow. Once hidden from the view of prying eyes, Alec paused. He placed a gentle hand along the side of Jade's face and gazed down at her with a look she could not decipher.

"Did he harm you?" the prince questioned urgently.

Jade blinked. Alec was staring at her with such intensity that she could not seem to get her brain to focus. After the long trying ordeal she had just endured, all she wanted was to melt into the safe warmth of his arms. Strict manners kept her hands gripped in front of her.

"No, he did not. Thanks to you, I am quite safe." A smile spread across her lips, reaching all the way to her eyes. "You always seem to come to my rescue just in time."

Alec didn't return her grin. Face grim, he turned his head to the side.

"It was my fault that you were placed in danger. I deserve no thanks for that."

Jade's eyes widened. Lips parting, she shook her head. *Why must he be so severe to himself?* Reaching up, Jade's long fingers touched his dirty cheek.

"Vincent's madness was not your doing."

Alec stiffened, moving away a step. "Wasn't it?" he questioned harshly. "He became so obsessed with defeating me that he kidnapped you and gave you to our enemies. Jade, you were locked within Zerrok's stronghold because of me."

"It was not so strong when you were finished."

"This is not a joke," he stressed.

The warrior crossed his arms, seeming to close himself off from her.

Jade sighed. "I know it is not." She shrugged her shoulders and stepped closer to him. "These last few days have been the worst that I can remember. I am so relieved to be back home, to be by your side. I do not wish to tarnish this private moment that I get to share with you, Alakaid. Pray, let us not quarrel."

His true name, spoken from her musical lips, made his heart beat faster.

"Nor do I."

Alec could not keep himself from shifting his sights to peer at Jade's face. Gazing into her emerald irises, his hands slowly dropped back to his sides. No words were able to sound in his voice as he drank in the sight of her. Taking a breath, Alec went to speak, but stopped himself.

"What is it?" Jade whispered. *He is not telling me something.*

The prince shook his head without answering. Moving forward, he unexpectedly pressed his mouth against hers. Alec's lips were firm, yet gentle, as he caressed the soft skin of her shoulder before his fingers slid up to cup the back of her head.

All thoughts flew from Jade's mind. The shock of his sudden kiss stole her breath. Pressing her palms against the solid rock of his chest, she allowed herself to be swept away by the endless sensations.

Before he allowed himself to go too far, Alec gradually pulled back. His hands rested on the sides of her arms as he moved to whisper in her ear.

"I will always love you, Jade."

Watching the flushed color of her cheeks, and the sparkle in her eyes one last time, Alec spun away and vanished into the growing shadows.

Jade couldn't have found her voice to call him back even if she tried. With trembling fingers, she touched her swollen lips. This kiss had been different than the one they previously shared. While both were filled with a fire and passion, there was something bittersweet hidden beneath this kiss. Jade couldn't put her finger on it, but it almost felt as if he had been saying goodbye.

Groaning, Jade rubbed her temples. Mixed emotions and little sleep must be confusing her thoughts. There was no reason for her to be reading so much into what had been an impulsive kiss. They had all been through so much. Walking up the path, Jade set out towards the courtyard to seek her parents. Everything would be better tomorrow after a good night's rest. There would be plenty of time to speak with Alec then.

Moving with the shadows, Alec strode leisurely through the gardens and out into the clearing on the other side. Part of him was grateful of the growing lateness of the hour, for there was no one here to run into. At the moment, the prince had no desire to see any of his friends.

Cassidy, Ardys and Tatsu lay in the grass awaiting his arrival. Upon seeing them, Alec paused his steps. Tilting his head back, he gazed up at the moon. The large bright orb was almost full. How had the time come so quickly?

"We know why you have asked us here," Ardys began watching Alec closely. "There is no need to leave immediately. The ceremony cannot be completed for two nights hence."

The shadow of a smile appeared on the warrior's face. He gazed at each of the dragons in turn prior to speaking.

"I know, but there is no point in delaying what is to come. The longer I remain here, the greater the danger for those I care for."

"Alec, are you sure about this?" Cassidy questioned sadly.

He nodded.

Tatsu rose and drew his face closer to the sorcerer. "You know what's going to happen, don't you?"

It wasn't really a question. Still, Alec saw fit to answer all the same. He wasn't looking for pity. Nothing could stop his destiny, and too much sympathy just might cause him to wish for time that he cannot have.

"I do, Tatsu. It took me awhile to figure out what the prophecy really meant, but I will not run from this. It is time, I can feel it."

"Then we shall gladly be with you to the end," the green dragon told him fondly.

The strange look on Alec's face caused her to frown.

"What is it?"

Fingers tapping the side of his leg, Alec released a long slow breath. "I know you're not going to like this, my friend, but I need a favor."

"Name it," Cassidy replied easily.

He shifted his weight back and forth. "I would like you to remain here until it is done."

Cassidy's head jerked back. Eyes narrowing, a waft of smoke escaped from her nostrils.

"I know I'm asking for a lot," Alec pressed on. "But the Iron Scales Clan could attack at any time, and more importantly, you're the only one *she* will understand."

She. Cassidy knew exactly to whom he was referring. Jade meant more to Alec than anything else in this world. As much as she wanted to be by his side, she could not deny him this peace of mind. Finally, Cassidy dipped her head in agreement.

"I swear I will protect her for you, little one. It has been an honor to fight beside you," she conceded nudging him with her head. "Always know that you have the heart of a true dragon. I will never forget you, Alakaid, Prince of Dragons."

Alec chuckled, running his hand over her gleaming scales one last time. They had been through much together. Ever since he landed in Malyndor for the first time, there were days where he was almost convinced it was all a dream. No matter what was to come, the sage could not find it in his heart to regret it.

Three dragons took off into the night sky with Alec crouched low on Tatsu's back to hide his departure. They flew west towards the forest surrounding Malcolm's cottage. Once there, Cassidy pulled back, hovering above the trees as she watched the others disappear from view. Without Alec, there was no reason to remain at the castle. The green dragon planned to wait here, in the comfort of the trees, for Jade to seek her out. There was no doubt in her mind that the noblewoman would do so. By that time, the Dragon Sage would be no more.

CHAPTER 20

In the distance, flashes of light scorched the sky like an angry firestorm. Edmund knew this was no natural storm. On the edge of the horizon, the red blazes stretched across the heavens once again. Somewhere to the southwest, miles away, a battle was underway. Traveling towards the Keep, Edmund instructed his men to stand ready. He could not say for sure, but this blaze reminded him too much of dragon's fire.

"It looks like some of the creatures are battling," Roderick observed, coming to stand beside his lord. "Do you think another raid flew here from the south?"

Edmund frowned. *So, I am not the only one who thinks this is the work of beasts.* "Difficult to say. We know so little about them."

The knight nodded. "If he was here, Alec might be able to tell us. Any word from him?" *Or Jade,* Roderick wanted to add.

"Nothing but silence."

The explosions quickly erupted into a crescendo of thunderous blasts. When it was done, the heavens stilled, leaving an empty silence.

"Where will you go now?" the duke muttered.

At perhaps a day's ride away, this battle was far too close for comfort. The two men stayed on the battlements watching the waning light. Dark shadows in the distance drew the knight's attention. Frowning, he stepped forward, leaning on the thick stone wall as his gaze tracked the strange movement. Three shapes appeared as they headed straight for the castle. Eyes narrowing, Roderick pushed back from the wall. Turning to the guardhouse, he hollered for his men to ready themselves.

Soldiers raced to giant crossbows stationed along the wall and took aim. A strained, hushed quiet fell as everyone waited. The figures drew closer, visibly taking the forms of dragons. As they neared the castle, the creatures slowed their pace. Coming to a standstill, they hovered in the air just outside of the soldiers' weapons' reach. The large jewels on the dragons' foreheads began to glow, shining brightly for a few seconds before the light faded and ceased.

"Stand down!" Duke Stafford ordered at once.

As his instructions were passed along the battlements, the crossbows were lowered to the ground. Continuing along their path, the three dragons, one by one, came to land in the courtyard. Edmund dashed down the stairs and across the stone pavers seeking his daughter. He saw the familiar faces of Alec's companions, as well as a few strangers among the passengers. Reaching Cassidy, his gaze darted between the courtyard and the green dragon's back. Jade was nowhere to be seen. *Where is she?* Heart racing, the duke rushed over to Malcolm.

"Malcolm, where is Jade? Pray, do not tell me she..." Swallowing hard, he could not finish the words.

The great sage shook his head. "There is no need to fret, my friend. Jade is safe and unharmed."

"Thank the heavens," Edmund sighed, his shoulders sagging slightly.

"Indeed," Malcolm agreed, shifting to peer behind him. "Her ladyship and Alec are right...hmm," he paused. A small puzzled frown briefly touched his lips. "They were here but a moment ago."

Alec, Edmund thought with relief. How could he have forgotten about the prince? The warrior didn't seem to be anywhere either. Suddenly, Edmund caught sight of them. On the other side of the courtyard Alec was leading Jade by the hand towards the gardens at the back of the castle. They quickly disappeared from view without anyone else appearing to notice. Edmund took several steps in the direction of their fleeting forms, then stilled. *She is safe.* Tears moistened his eyes at the sight. The pressure weighing upon his chest since her disappearance faded away. As much as the duke desired to go after her, he refrained from doing so. Alec had kept his word despite all odds. If nothing else, he had earned a few private moments with his future bride. Edmund did not question Alec's honor.

Though only a few minutes passed, the ensuing seconds felt like an eternity. The dragons took flight rounding the castle, but Edmund paid them little mind.

Slowly retracing her footsteps, Jade appeared around the back of the castle.

Edmund quickly strode to meet her, noting the becoming blush which was accompanying a wide smile on her face. Wrapping his arms about her small frame, Edmund exhaled with a long sigh.

"I have dreamt of little else other than this moment since you were taken. For my own daughter to be taken from my castle—" Edmund's words cut off as he gave Jade another tight squeeze. Stepping back, the duke gently took his daughter's hands in his own. "If he harmed so much as one hair upon your head, my jewel, I swear to you there is nowhere within these realms that he shall be able to hide."

Tearing up, Jade's eyes glowed. Gripping her father's hands, she lightly shook her head. Jade had no doubt that he would do just as he said. "I am so lucky in my fortunes to have a father such as you. No, bearing his company was my only distress. Even so," Jade turned back, looking towards the gardens. "Vincent is unable to do further harm."

Eyes tracking Jade's line of sight, Edmund was easily able to understand her meaning. *It would seem Alec has already dealt with this particular issue.* The man never ceased to amaze him. Thoughts of Vincent's treachery were swept away as Leona hurried down the steps and embraced her only child.

Looking her daughter over, she cupped Jade's face between her hands. "Jade, my precious girl, I have counted the moments until we would be united once more. Did he harm you?"

Jade touched her mother's cheek with a smile. "I am unharmed, Mother. It brings me great pleasure to be home. Pray, let us put this unpleasantness behind us. He is not worth another moment's thought."

Above, the dragons passed by, heading towards the forest. Jade's lips pursed together. *I wonder where they might be traveling.*

Watching Jade's expression, Edmund fought a smile. Vincent's tyranny must not have been as heinous as he feared, for only one man seemed to be occupying his daughter's mind.

"I would surmise that the dragons are leaving to hunt. It has been a long journey for them as well. They need to rest as much as you, my jewel."

A thin smile spread across her face. "Of course."

"Come," Leona encouraged, holding out a hand. "Let us retire to a warm hearth. You must be weary after your long journey."

If her mother had said this when she first landed, Jade might have agreed. Now, Alec's touch seemed to be imprinted on her body. Jade's lips tingled at the thought of his kiss. Weary was not how she was feeling.

After a night of restless sleep, Jade woke to a sunny sky. Flakes of the first snow of the season drifted down outside the window of her new suite. During her absence, the duchess saw fit to relocate her daughter to another part of the castle. Jade's new chamber was being freshly redecorated with linens and drapes ordered from Ariston. Though most of her furniture was the same, the unfamiliar space did not offer as much comfort as she had hoped.

Gripping the shawl draped around her shoulders, Jade closed her eyes and slowly inhaled. A chill snaked about her ankles, crawling up her back as it caused her to shiver. *Is someone present?* Jade's eyelids flew open. Spinning away from the window, she ran her hands up and down her arms while visually searching her chamber. *There is nothing here,* Jade firmly scolded. The dying embers of her fire would do little to fight the outside chill. There was no reason for her to suspect another intrusion.

"He is no longer a threat," Jade murmured to the empty room.

Having witnessed the lord's demise for herself, Jade knew there was no possibility that he could be lurking about. Still, the silence of her chamber was far from peaceful. Striding across the space, Jade rushed to her door and out into the corridor. As the number of steps away from her room grew, the slower her pace and heartrate became. Jade glanced over her shoulder prior to pausing her flight. The space behind her was completely empty. Shoulders sagging, she sighed. *It would seem Vincent did more harm than I had hoped.*

In need of a calming presence, Jade continued her journey in search of Alec. A smile touched her lips. Merely being by his side was sure to be enough to settle her unease. The question was, where to seek him?

Jade first traveled out to the gardens. The rows of snow-dusted bushes gave her most beloved retreat a whimsical appearance. Flurries still drifted down from the sky, but Jade gave them little mind. Making her way to the back of the gardens, she picked up her pace. Stepping into the clearing beyond, the grin on her face faded. The surrounding area was nothing but a blanket of perfect freshly fallen snow. With no evidence of Alec or the dragons having been there anytime this morning, Jade turned back and retraced her steps.

The barracks was her next destination. In colder weather, the soldiers utilized a mix of the outdoor and indoor training areas. Entering the field behind the barracks, Jade saw several men sparring with swords and shields. Studying their faces, she fought a frown. Alec didn't seem to be among either the men in the field or those observing along the sides. Rounding the back, she headed towards the indoor hall. Torches lit the walls of the bright space giving Jade a clear view of those inside. The noble had barely arrived when the other man she sought strode to her side.

A pleasant smile adorned the gruff warrior's face. "Lady Jade," he said, greeting her fondly. "I sense that it's too early to resume your lessons. Tell me, what brings you to the barracks?"

Her eyes passing over the soldiers a second time, Jade fought for the small grin upon her face not to vanish. "As usual your senses are indeed correct. Though I do wish to begin our lessons anew, it was in seeking another swordsman which brought me hence."

Garth watched her for a second before his eyes widened thoughtfully. Turning to gaze back at his men, the warrior exhaled with a sigh. "Of that, I regret, I cannot be of any aid. I have yet to see Alec today."

Shoulders sagging, Jade's gaze shifted to the floor. "Nor has anyone else."

Where is he?

Garth looped his thumbs in his belt and sighed. "Seeing as the dragons haven't returned to the castle, Alec's most likely near Malcolm's cottage with them." When she made no reply, Garth peered at the top of her bent head. His expression softened. "Jade," he called quietly.

Blinking, the noblewoman looked back up at him.

"Give him time. He's bound to have a fair amount of anger in his heart. For any harm to come to the person you care for the most is a man's worst nightmare."

Jade frowned. "Vincent's madness was not Alec's doing."

"No, it was not. However, that doesn't stop a man from wishing he were able to prevent the misfortune from ever occurring."

A distinct sadness in Garth's voice caused Jade to turn towards him.

"Garth? Are you feeling unwell?"

He gave her a small smile which didn't even come close to reaching his eyes. "No, milady."

Liar. "What misfortune were you unable to prevent?"

A long silence fell in which Jade became certain that the warrior had no intention of answering her prying question.

When Garth next spoke, his words were barely above a whisper. "My family's murder."

Jade's lips parted, yet no words dared to come forth. A dull ache filled her heart for the kind man. Why would anyone desire to bring his family harm? Did this tragedy have anything to do with how he came to be a gladiator? One look at Garth's mournful expression and Jade knew she couldn't voice the sudden flow of questions.

"I am so terribly sorry, Garth," she said with true sincerity.

The warrior released a long sigh. "It…it matters not who bears fault. Alec cares greatly for you. He is bound to feel some responsibility. Pray, we must be patient enough to give him the space he requires."

"Of course," Jade replied with a nod. "I understand."

Though she might have said so, Jade didn't really comprehend. She believed Vincent's deceit should be strengthening her bond with Alec. Why did it seem to be pushing her and the sage apart instead?

Despite the assurance that Alec would return to Stafford when he was ready, Jade's mind would not allow her any reprieve. That night, she tossed and turned for hours on end. Kicking the covers aside with a groan, Jade dragged one of her blankets over towards a deep, comfortable chair beside the window. Curling up, she gazed longingly at the stars.

"Pray, watch over my Alec, and return him safely hence," she asked the ancient spirits.

Hopefully, someone would hear her words and send Alec back to her by morning. Eyelids drifting closed, Jade eventually dozed off where she lay. The hazy darkness of sleep morphed into the vivid images of a luxurious garden. Moonlight painted a soft glow on the surrounding foliage. Jade strode through the rows of flowers, running her fingers over the petals as she went. The path opened up to reveal the large fountain at the center of the garden. A man stood watching the flow of water with his back to her. Jade's breath caught in her throat.

"Alec," she whispered.

Jade would know him anywhere.

As the prince began to turn, Jade raced into his awaiting arms. Embracing her tightly, Alec twirled her around in a circle. His hands fluttered over the sleeves of her dress as they traveled upwards to weave their way into her long tresses. When his lips finally sought hers, Jade felt nothing but pure ecstasy. Body turning lighter than air, part of her was surprised that her feet were remaining on the ground.

Trailing kisses across her cheek Alec embraced Jade once again. "I will always love you," he breathed softly into her ear.

Jade smiled brightly. "I love you too, darling."

Just when she thought her heart might burst with happiness, Jade felt Alec's body tense. The next moment he stood in front of the fountain with a somber expression she had never seen him wear before. Lifting dull, pained eyes the prince slowly reached out towards her.

"Goodbye, love."

"Good-goodbye?" Jade questioned, a tremor racing through her like cold water. "Alec, whatever do you mean?"

Dashing forward, Jade reached for him. The moment her fingers connected with his, Alec burst apart into drops of water, as if his image had been nothing more than a reflection off the fountain's spray.

"No!" Jade cried bolting upright in her seat.

Chest heaving, she pressed a hand to her breast as she sucked in gulps of air. How could heaven shift to hell so quickly? The twisted dream had felt so real. Touching her trembling lips, Jade could still feel Alec's kiss as if he had been with her only a moment before.

Where are you?

Peering out the window, Jade caught sight of the first few rays of the sun. A new day had begun. Pulling the blanket off her lap, Jade strode to her wardrobe and searched for a gown that she could fashion without Ariel's aid. Spying her freshly laundered trousers for weapons practice, Jade grabbed the more flexible garment instead. No matter what anyone insisted, Jade needed to see Alec immediately. She would give him the space he required later. For now, the noblewoman desperately wanted to see him. Otherwise, she feared her nightmare just might come to light.

Heading across the courtyard, Jade strode as quickly as she dared towards the stables. If all went well, she should be able to sneak out of the castle grounds before her true directive was discovered. Being the daughter of the duke had its merits. Few would risk staying her course.

Just as she was entering the stable's threshold, someone called out to her. Without turning, she slipped inside as if she had not heard them. Sending a stable boy for her steed, she gripped the inside of her cloak. *Pray, do not look for me. Pray, do not look for me.*

Another set of steps approached her, despite her silent pleas. Bright smile covering her face, Isabelle waved. "Good morning to you, Lady Jade. How are you fairing? Sorry I was not able to visit you yesterday. I'm sure you're pleased to be back in Stafford."

Looking at the other woman, Jade sighed, a smile appearing on her lips in response.

"Good morning, Izzy. It is a pleasure to see you. Do not fret, considering your sudden departure with the others, I had an inkling you would be quite busy upon our return."

The bubbly sage nodded. "Indeed," she giggled. "In fact, I've just finished speaking with Malcolm." Her gaze shifted to the nearly empty hallway. "Are you going for a ride?"

Jade's smile slipped. Looking first in one direction, then in the other, she lowered her voice to a whisper. "Do not speak a word of it, but I am traveling to Master Malcolm's cottage to seek out Alec. My father does not wish for me to leave the castle grounds."

"Alec?" Isabelle repeated strangely.

Jade dipped her head in a nod. "Indeed. I…" she dropped her gaze to her hands briefly. "I must admit, I am quite worried about him. Were you aware that he has not returned to the castle since our arrival?"

Isabelle frowned. *But Malcolm said Alec hasn't been to his place.* If that was so, then where in the realms had he gone? Considering Alec's attachment to the noblewoman, Isabelle could not imagine him going too far from her side.

"Are you saying that you haven't seen Alec since the night of our return?"

"No, I have not."

The sage rubbed a hand along the side of her face. "I will go with you. This way, you will at least have an escort should you run into some unforeseen mischief."

"Really?" Jade grinned. Reaching out, she gripped the other woman's hands. "Thank you, Izzy. I am so pleased that I can rely on you as Alec does."

The blonde laughed. "I don't know about that. I seem to cause him more trouble if nothing else."

Jade shook her head. "We both know that is not true. Come," she encouraged summoning a servant to fetch Isabelle's horse. "We should depart before Sir Roderick tries to intervene."

During the short ride to the sage's dwelling, both women were unusually quiet. Jade found the lack of conversation even more unnerving. Isabelle was not one to stay her words, and for the sage to remain without some comment or another for the length of their journey, left a sour taste in Jade's mouth. Her fingers gripped the reins tightly. Did she know something that Jade did not?

Once the roof of the tiny cottage came into view, Jade urged her steed into a canter. She peered around for Cloud, but didn't see Alec's loyal horse in the open stable or grazing in the surrounding meadow. No smoke billowed from the chimney nor did a glow light the cottage from the inside. All was dark and serene. Too serene. Where was he?

"Do you see him?" Jade questioned urgently.

Isabelle's light green eyes were scanning the area. "No, I don't."

Dismounting, she tied the reins to the railing and set off around the back of the dwelling. Snow covered the ground in a thin, untouched blanket. Brows lowering, the sage carefully trekked down the slope to the edge of the swiftly flowing creek.

Jade followed close behind. Her gaze shifted to the ground as she searched for even a single set of prints.

"He has to be here," she murmured with the hint of distress.

I wish he were, Isabelle thought, for Jade's sake if nothing else. If would seem that somehow the prince had vanished. Peering about once again, her eyes narrowed. Isabelle stilled. At the edge of the forest there was a patch of trees bare of snow on the lower half of the branches. It was unnatural for a few pines to be disturbed in such a way while others were not. Helping Jade to cross the creek, Isabelle strode over towards them. Nearing the forest, her steps stilled.

Jade stood close to her side. "What is the matter? Did you find Alec?"

"No," Isabelle told her gazing at the large tracks leading into the trees. "But, I do believe I have found a dragon."

The noble's face brightened. "A dragon? Then Alec is sure to be here. Come, let us greet them."

Isabelle held out her arm to cease Jade's advance. If their battle two nights ago had taught her anything, it was that not all dragons were allies. There were some, just like humans, who would willingly bring them harm.

"Careful, Jade," Isabelle warned. "We know not if this creature is a friend. Alec's guardians wouldn't be hidden so deep within the trees that we could not see them. Perhaps, it would be better for you to remain inside while I investigate."

Jade crossed her arms. "If there is as much danger as you claim, then you very well may require my aid. I bear no desire to fight a dragon, yet I am still able to wield a sword."

When Jade refused to break eye contact, Isabelle sighed. "Well, it's not as if I can force you to remain behind."

Taking the lead, the sorceress followed the prints into the forest. The freshly fallen snow lit the surrounding space like a blank canvas. Every movement of the animals, every impression, was brightened for them to see. Heart rate speeding up, Isabelle gripped the hilt of her sword. Her eyes darted to each noise that echoed around them. *I really wish Alec was here right now.* Having a more battle-hardened warrior might have helped to ease her nerves. Still, they trudged on, traveling ever deeper into the woods.

At last they came upon a group of large rock outcroppings. Isabelle stilled her steps and motioned for Jade to move behind her. This was just the type of place which could hide a dragon.

"Hello?" she called out.

Neck straining, she listened closely for any form of reply.

"You arrived much quicker than I expected," said a deep feminine voice.

Jerking back, Isabelle and Jade glanced at each other with puzzled frowns.

"Cassidy?" they questioned simultaneously.

Walking out of a darkened overhang, the green dragon appeared in the glistening sunlight. She peered at the two humans prior to lowering herself to the ground. No smile pulled at her scaled lips as she sat in silence.

"Cassidy, I am so pleased to see you," Jade greeted fondly. If anyone would know to where the warrior had ventured off, then it would be her. "Have you seen Alec?"

Jade's words seemed to linger in the air for an extended amount of time. The small grin on her face melted away as the dragon took longer and longer to answer.

"I fear you are too late, Jade. Alec departed some time ago."

Mouth moving soundlessly, the noble's head pulled back. "What—whatever do you mean? Why is no one aware of this?"

"Yeah," Isabelle agreed. "If Alec was going on a journey, then why did he not tell us? Even Malcolm has no idea where he went."

Cassidy sighed, expelling a wisp of smoke.

"Alec didn't tell anyone because he knew those he cared for would try and stop him."

"Try and stop him?" Isabelle repeated dumbfounded. "Is he in some type of trouble? Alec should know that I would gladly fight alongside him—no matter who his enemy may be."

A small, sad smile pulled at the corner of Cassidy's lips. She had no doubt that the feisty sage would do just as she claimed, which was why the prince chose to depart as he had.

"Pray, Cassidy, where is he?" Jade asked stepping closer with fingers tightly intertwined.

"Alec has gone to Ellfraya, realm of the dragons, to fulfill his part of the prophecy."

"When do you expect him to return?"

Silence.

Jade moved nearer and placed a hand on the green creature's leg. "Cassidy?"

The dragon bowed her head and looked to the side. Alec's final request was more difficult than she surmised.

"He's not coming back, is he?" Isabelle concluded.

Jade whirled around with wide eyes. "I do not understand," she said, her gaze darting between the two. "Why would he not return?"

Cassidy shifted to peer back at the noblewoman. "Do you recall the white dragon form Alec can create?"

Both ladies nodded, leaning forward as the dragon began to speak.

"That creature is a manifestation of his soul. Alec's power is in his blood, like a dragon's. It is his very life force. According to the prophecy, the magic gifted to your ancient king by Emperor Draco and Empress Shiori must be returned in order to unite our races."

"Wait," Isabelle said, waving her hands. "So, Alec is going to use his power on the dragon rulers like that day he mistakenly did with you?"

Cassidy nodded. "The emperor and empress are connected to all dragons. To transform them will transform us all. However, once this power is united with its original owners, it will not flow back to its host."

"Did you not say that Alec's magic is his life?" Jade questioned.

"Oh my stars," Isabelle gasped. "He's going to sacrifice himself. That's why he didn't tell us. Alec knew that he is going to die."

"That cannot be!" Jade spun around searching Cassidy's yellow gaze. "Tell me she is mistaken. How could you let him depart knowing his intent?"

"Do you think my heart is as cold as my scales?" Cassidy returned sternly. "Alec means a great deal to me as well, hence why I carried out his will and awaited you here. This has always been the fate of the marked one. Had he not asked it of me, I would be by his side now."

Did they really believe it gave her any pleasure to sit here while the prince carried out his final task? Cassidy wished as much as any that there was another way to bridge the gap between their two kinds.

The harsh tone of the dragon's words caused tears to form in Jade's eyes. "Is there…is there not another way?"

Releasing a huff, Cassidy forced her voice to soften. It wasn't Jade's fault for the helplessness of their situation. Never knowing of the prophecy, the shock of Alec's deemed fate could not be easy for her to bear.

"Peace does not come without price, Jade. There is no other way."

A roaring filled the noble's ears. Leaning heavily against the dragon, she was sure that her heart had stopped beating from the sorrow of Alec's fate. Lifting trembling fingers, Jade touched her lips. It would seem her fears had been well justified, Alec *was* saying goodbye. Closing her eyes tightly, Jade curled a fist against her chest. She could not imagine what must be going through his mind. To know that the path fate had chosen for him would lead to his death, and yet, still have the courage to face it head-on, took a person of incredible strength of heart. That didn't mean he had to meet it alone.

Inhaling slowly, Jade opened her eyes and looked straight at Cassidy. "Come, my friend. Let us not delay another moment."

The dragon frowned. "What are you speaking of?"

"I speak of Ellfraya." Jade peered at Isabelle, then back at Cassidy. "Even if there is nothing we can do, Alec deserves to have the people he cares for by his side. It is my turn to lend him some of my strength. We cannot allow him to carry this burden alone."

Watching the unwavering determination in Jade's eyes, Cassidy could feel her resolve lessen. No matter the length of time she spent in their company, these humans still managed to catch her off guard.

"I'm coming too," Isabelle said, moving to stand on the magical creature's other side. "Jade's right. Alec has always been there for us. Let us offer our support this final time."

Snorting loudly, Cassidy stretched out her long, glossy wings. "You must promise to remain by my side at all times. While humans are welcome in Ellfraya, Azurartain is a sacred mountain where only dragons reside. As far as I am aware, Alec is the first human to ever set foot upon its stone. There are many who may not take kindly to either of you intruding."

"I am willing to take that risk," Jade told her sincerely.

"As am I," Isabelle added.

Cassidy studied the two women for a long moment. She had promised to look after Jade. However, she never said that she wouldn't bring her to him. As long as she protected the determined woman, then she would be keeping her word.

"Very well. Let us go find our Alec."

CHAPTER 21

Cloak wrapped tightly about his shoulders, Alec gazed at the passing scenery with renewed interest. Ardys had descended from the clouds shortly after crossing the border into Ellfraya. Alec had switched dragons during a brief stop while still in Malyndor. The ebony warrior was less inclined to have a rider than his fiery companion. Below, the thin layer of snow was quickly melting, giving him a clear view of the rolling valleys and high mountains. Alec wasn't sure what to expect of the dragon realm. The rumored fire and brimstone covered lands was sure to be false, yet the lush, thriving landscape hadn't come to mind either.

Well into their journey, Alec's escort was flanked by additional guards. In the distance, a large mountain jutted up through the horizon.

Ardys adjusted his wings, heading straight for the massive rock. This was their ultimate destination. Azurartain was more than the tallest mountain in the realm, it was the sacred home of the royal dragons themselves, and the place where the ceremony would be held. It was here that Alec would meet his fate.

As they grew ever closer, Alec studied the wondrous sight. Three main peaks dominated the mountain in increasing heights. On the far left, a series of caverns was carved into the lowest peak like a private mountain village. Most of the dragons living on Azurartain had caves linked to those entrances. The second peak was the dwelling of Emperor Draco and Empress Shiori. Below, a few openings could be seen scattered down the rock where the highest ranking dragons resided. A path was cut into the stone leading to the right and up the curving ridge towards the tallest point of the mountain. There, a large circular platform stood. Positioned directly beneath the stars, this spot was linked to the very magic of the world.

Landing on the lowest incline, Ardys and Tatsu folded their wings as a large, pale blue dragon came to meet them. His silvery eyes studied Alec crossly as the human dismounted to stand beside his friend.

"Who is this human that you dare to bring to our sacred home?"

"Calm yourself, Izor. Prince Alakaid is welcome here by order of our exalted emperor," Ardys replied, standing his ground.

The opposing creature scoffed. "Him? The marked one? I don't believe such a claim. Are you certain that he has not deceived you? Humans are quite good for employing such tricks."

Tatsu strode closer with narrowed eyes. "You are the last of us who should be commenting about tricks. With the moon almost in position, who are you to deny the marked one passage? Or is it your intent to stop our great leaders from strengthening their power?"

Izor jerked back with a snarl as several of the dragons watching the exchange began to whisper.

"There is no question of my loyalty," he snapped.

Alec took a few steps. "If you'll allow me, I can settle this quarrel easily."

The fierce creature shifted his gaze to the human with a glare.

The sage paid him no mind. If these dragons needed more proof than the word of Ardys and Tatsu, then he would show them instead. In the center of the mountain, off to the right, was a large pool. Two massive dragon statues decorated the rim at the edge of a sheer drop where the water overflowed into three waterfalls. It was upon the closest waterfall where Alec lay his focus. Holding out his hand, he said not a word. The mark on his back started to glow, as did his eyes. Alec's aura swirled around him like specks of starlight. The water spilling out of the pool slowed to a crawl prior to changing its direction. It looped into an arch and flowed back into the lake. Waving his hand, Alec twisted the stream back to its original form. He then released his control of the element, allowing the water to continue its normal flow.

Turning to look back at the other dragon, Alec questioned, "Are you satisfied?"

Izor grunted, spinning around to disappear through the growing crowd.

A small green dragon moved forward to take his place. Bowing, the creature greeted them excitedly. "Welcome, marked one. Their Majesties have sent me to act as your escort. Follow me."

Spreading his wings, the dragon lifted into the air and hovered as he waited for the others to join him.

Peering back at the small gathering, Alec's tense form didn't move. How many more of these dragons were like Izor? With the ceremony so close at hand, he knew that he couldn't trust anyone save for his guardians.

"Come Alec," Ardys encouraged.

Exhaling with a short hiss, Alec mentally shook himself.

"Stay close at all times," the red creature advised quietly.

Alec didn't miss the way his friends were both intently watching the others crowded about the flat peninsula they had landed upon. *They're not sure who can be trusted either,* the sage thought. Climbing onto Ardys's back, he pressed his lips together. It would seem he had ventured from the pot into the frying pan so to speak. So much for a warm welcome.

Following their new escort, Ardys took him higher up the mountain towards the second peak. Two black dragons were stationed as sentries outside the main carved entrance. They watched the companions silently. There was no change in their expression or any forthcoming remarks upon seeing Alec. When Tatsu and Ardys each went to pass, the guards bowed their heads respectfully.

Alec lifted a single brow. "Do you know them?"

"All living here know the Takai by sight," their escort informed him kindly.

"What is a Takai?"

There was a short pause before he answered, "In your language, it would resemble a general or an advisor. They are of the highest rank below our great Emperor and Empress."

Alec gazed back at his friends with a classic half-smirk. "You never mentioned that either of you had such esteemed titles."

"Mine was from a long time ago," Ardys informed him, brushing the comment aside.

Tatsu, on the other hand, flashed Alec a rare smile. "Impressed?"

The prince laughed. "Indeed."

Continuing along, Alec found that the great dragons' titles were not the only thing of which he had no knowledge. In his limited experience, a mountain cave was dark, fairly enclosed and bore plain ridged rock. Azurartain was so much more than that. Deep within the tunnel, the high ceilings were covered in small shards of glowing crystals. They gleamed in the darkness like tiny, far away stars. The corridor opened up into a massive space. Sunlight reflected off of a waterfall flowing at the very back of the chamber into a deep pool. The water was ice blue, revealing various crystals which lined the sides of the rock beneath the surface. The lake led to an underground river that linked with the outside waterfalls.

Tall tunnels were carved on both sides of the space and even above them in a clever tunnel system. Yet, Alec's eyes were locked on a large outcropping in the center of the water. Rising up in the shape of a vase, the arched rock formation had a flat shelf with a private ray of light shining upon it. Trees basked in the warm glow and a smaller waterfall seeped over the edge.

Alec didn't need the others to tell him this was the very place where the royal dragons lived. Such a splendid location, like a gleaming jewel out in the water, could not possibly belong to anyone else.

Clearing his throat, their escort directed his new charge to the left into another set of darkened tunnels. Once out of the sun's light, the ceiling came to life, illuminating itself. The size of the crystals grew until they were a mass of rolling waves upon the ceiling. Walking past the various rooms and tunnels, Alec noticed that the number of precious stones was increasing. At the end of the corridor, the small green dragon stepped to the side and bowed his head.

"Please wait inside," he told Alec without any further instructions.

The prince slowly walked through the doorway with a hand unconsciously gripping the hilt of his blade. Stepping out of the shadows, he entered a chamber as strange and unique as the one with the hidden lake. This space didn't possess any water as far as he could tell. Solid rock, the entire space was made up of clusters of large pale crystals in various shades. An open walkway hovered above the ground as it coiled around a central tower covered in stalagmites. The rock formations gleamed as if dusted with millions of diamonds.

Drawn to the pulsating energy of the thick pillar, Alec headed straight for the floating path and began to climb.

Arms swinging by his side he rushed onward. He couldn't say what possessed him to embark on this eager journey. It was almost as if something was calling out to him. At the top of the tower, Alec slowed his pace. His lips parted while his head tilted back to take in the entire splendor of the sight greeting his eyes.

A massive tree dominated the top of the dais. It was like nothing Alec had ever seen before. The tree's thick encrusted roots were draped over the edge of the rock while the frosted branches stretched up towards the seemingly endless ceiling. Yet, those features paled in comparison to the small clusters of crystals covering the branches like blossoms. Alec could no sooner count them than guess the number of stars in the heavens. Without being aware, the sage found himself at the base of the tree. He gazed at the bright, gleaming foliage as if in a trance. The energy radiating from the tree was oddly familiar. It called to him, pulling him closer still. Reaching out, Alec's fingers brushed a sparkling leaf.

Though his feet never left the ground, Alec felt like he was mentally jerked forward through a veil of white. The blank scenery sped by until he was deposited on the edge of a land scored black like soot. Dragons covered in plated armor etched with runes stood on each side of the battlefield. They were not the only warriors present. Swords and scepters clutched in their fists, humans, both with and without magic, surrounded a pair of shimmering blue and purple colored dragons. A figure appeared across the way from the shadows. Alec could not see the human's face, but its presence spurred both sides into action as they charged forward in a bloody clash.

Alec jerked back, stumbling a few steps as his mind tried to sort what was reality. *What was that?* The strange images had been too detailed, had felt far too real to be a dream. Fingers curling into his palm, Alec felt a slight tingle lingering behind.

"Welcome to Azurartain, Prince Alakaid," said a deep female voice from the air.

Alec spun around to see a dark blue dragon come to land on the edge of the platform. She was unlike any dragon he had ever seen. Her scales were a royal blue with swirls of purple and green like a peacock. The translucent jewel on her head changed colors as she moved to study the human with sharp, pale blue eyes. She was not the largest of her kind, however, she was the most majestic creature Alec had ever laid eyes upon.

"Thank you, Empress Shiori," Alec told her with a bow. "I owe my guardians much for seeing that I arrived safely."

The queen's gaze passed over the other dragons slowly. She offered each of them a slight nod prior to looking back at Alec. "I see only two are present."

Alec stiffened. Peering momentarily to the ground, he took a deep breath.

"Cassidy remained in Stafford to carry out a…final request."

Tilting her head to the side, Shiori sat down while she studied him quietly. "So, you do understand what is to come," she observed. "And yet you came willingly."

Turning to gaze back at the tree, Alec released a humorless laugh. "I suppose it does seem strange for someone to journey so far only to knowingly meet his death. Death…has not frightened me for some time. It comes to us all. I have no desire to end my life so quickly, yet…" Alec peered back at Tatsu and Ardys. A small smile touched the one side of his mouth. "Yet, if returning the magic in my blood will ensure a better future for those I care for, then I will meet that fate with my head held high."

Shiori blinked, her eyes widening slightly as she glanced at Ardys. A silent message seemed to pass between them as if she were asking, 'Does he speak the truth?'

The red dragon nodded solemnly.

A smile slowly stretched across her lips.

"I see."

Rising, the queen shifted her attention to the crystal tree glistening above them. Arching her neck, she gazed at the countless petals for a few seconds in silence.

"Magic links many things in the living world. It is, in fact, a lifeforce of its own. Take this tree, for instance," Shiori told him softly. "She is called Madroca. Each crystal upon her feeds off the magic of the earth, growing to form memories of our past. When touched, the history of our realms can be witnessed as if you were present."

Alec's brows furrowed. "So that's what I saw," he muttered.

"What did Madroca show you?"

"I'm not entirely sure." Alec ran a hand over the lower part of his face. "It was a fierce battle. The area was like nothing I've witnessed before. It was dark, tainted almost, and everything was scorched to dust. Dragons were pitted against each other, but there were humans present as well. They seemed to be battling alongside the dragons."

Shiori's eyes lost the sparkle they had held while Alec was speaking. Her mouth tightened as she looked upon the ancient tree. Her intense gaze almost appeared to study something the sage could not see.

Looking back at the other two dragons, the prince noted that his friends were suddenly no less serious than their queen. What event had he been granted privilege to?

"Are you alright, Empress?"

She sighed, returning her gaze to the human by her side. "It is not a time we care to remember. Humans though, seem to have forgotten it completely. There was a time when darkness ruled over all the known lands. It was brought forth by a powerful spirit not of our world. In the end, it was banished from our world at the cost of many lives." Shiori's eyes shifted back to the tree. "I do wonder why she chose to show you such a vision."

Alec shook his head. "I cannot say, perhaps because it was a time when humans and dragons worked together. This proves it is possible."

"That was a long time ago. Creating a new bridge between our kinds now will be no easy feat."

"No peace lasts forever," Alec told her, lifting his chin. "A way to bridge the gap between our races can only be to our benefit. Would you help me build that bridge?"

Alec held his hand out towards the great dragon with such unwavering determination shining in his eyes that Shiori could not answer right away. Dipping her nose, she touched his palm.

"I would be honored." A wide grin appeared, dominating her expression. "I must say, you are indeed a strange human. You have a good heart. It reminds me of your ancestor, King Stephan. I would not have chosen another to be gifted with our power."

The sage simply stared at her. Alec hadn't been expecting such high praise. Hopefully, he could continue to live up to their expectations.

"You should rest and save your strength," she advised twisting around to address his guardians. "I will have someone show you to your chambers."

"Yes, Empress," Ardys said, bowing his head.

"Of course," Tatsu replied as well.

In a gust of wind, the royal dragon ascended to disappear through a high tunnel. Alec watched her depart without a word. With the growing negative support for his very existence, he hadn't expected her to be so kind or friendly towards him. His conversation with Shiori did help to strengthen his resolve. Alec bore no lingering doubts that this was the right course for him to take.

The same green dragon appeared at the bottom of the crystal tower to lead Alec to his room. The twisting tunnels took them deeper inside the mountain where it was surprisingly warm. Stepping aside, his escort left them at the doorway with a bow. A curved slab of stone jutted out beyond the doorway to give the space some privacy. Clusters of low crystals were scattered about the room including a giant gleaming one at the center. Rays of yellow, orange and red painted the grey walls much like a warm summer sunset. A small smile touched the corner of his mouth. The image reminded him of Malyndor.

"Amazing," he whispered, watching the different hues dance throughout the space.

Behind him, Ardys and Tatsu stretched out across the entry to stay any unwelcome guests. Alec found himself more or less alone with his thoughts. Resting an arm on the hilt of his blade, the prince observed the stone lighting up his chamber. *I wonder...* Inching closer, Alec reached out to touch the crystal. His skin tingled from the radiating heat, but no images came forth in his mind's eye. With a self-disparaging sigh, Alec leaned his back against the stone and slid down to sit upon the ground. Closing his eyes, he fought a frown.

While the crystal in his room might not harbor memories like the frosted tree, its warmth did bring forth an array of images. Each one of them was centered on one person in particular: Jade. From the first moment they'd met, she'd brought new meaning to his bleak, small world of darkness.

I couldn't have come this far without you, he admitted privately. If she was here with him now, Alec would have gladly told her so. Yet she couldn't be. Not only would Alec not willingly bring her to such a dangerous place, he wasn't sure he would be able to see his final task through to the end if Jade was present.

'Save your strength,' Alec had been told.

A humorless laugh escaped his lips. Strange, for years he would rest between matches while struggling to survive in the arena. Now, he was saving his energy for a spell that was going to take his life.

"Hmm, I wonder what Jade is doing?" he quietly asked the surrounding silence.

Head bowed against the howling winds, Jade gripped one of Cassidy's spikes for dear life. Her limited experience felt like nothing without Alec by her side. Eyes squeezed tightly shut, she silently instructed herself not to look down. Isabelle's calm presence was the only thing helping to quell some of her fears as they flew through the unexpected stormfront.

Casting a spell, Isabelle's power surrounded them, protecting the companions with an invisible shield. The barrier was called up just as the dark cumulus unleashed a sheet of rain. Face, a mask of concentration, the sorceress was unusually quiet as she focused on keeping them safe.

Cassidy adjusted her wings and changed course.

"We're almost there," she informed her passengers.

Jade nodded, briefly forgetting that the green dragon couldn't see her in her current position.

"Alright," Isabelle answered for the two of them.

The sky around them started to clear and as they continued on in their new direction, the fierce wind and rain ceased. Isabelle lowered the barrier, leaning forward as an imposing mountain appeared on the horizon. Backlit by the setting sun, the very rock seemed to glow like a beacon. She didn't need to be told that this would be their destination. Placing a hand on Jade's shoulder, she encouraged her to open her eyes.

"Jade look, it's Azurartain."

Taking a deep breath, the noble slowly pried her eyelids apart. Her fear of their high elevation was momentarily forgotten. The evening light reflected off of flowing waterfalls, much like a rainbow, while the rolling peaks were painted a majestic purple. Azurartain was far from the gloomy, desolate place Jade had envisioned. It was too bad the fading light wouldn't offer her the chance to see more of this hidden gem. Jade stiffened. The sun was no longer visible in the sky and the large moon was already gleaming brightly.

"Cassidy," she called patting the dragon's neck. "When shall the ceremony begin?"

"Once darkness completely covers the sky."

Jade's gaze darted between the mountains and the moon. "Will we arrive in time?"

The noblewoman thought she heard a groan in the back of her escort's throat.

"I will do my best," Cassidy promised.

Swooping in from both sides, a pair of dark blue dragons appeared. They withheld any attacks, but eyed the humans on Cassidy's back suspiciously. The sound of a deep growl-like noise broke the quiet of the night. Cassidy replied back in a similar fashion as Isabelle and Jade each held their breath.

Pray, let us pass, Jade pleaded in her mind. They couldn't have come this far only to be sent away. The guards watched them for a long, agonizing moment. Then with a nod, they broke away to continue patrolling the skies.

Beating her wings as hard as she could, Cassidy raced to the top of Azurartain. The path to the highest peak was scattered with dragons. She knew there wouldn't be any way for her to land close to the top. Finding an area further down the path, she folded her wings to grip the rocky stairs. Aiding Jade first in her descent, she turned back to see Isabelle sliding to the ground.

"Stay close," their friend instructed. "This place is not safe for humans."

Isabelle's eyes suddenly widened. She rushed forward; her hand stretched out before her.

"Jade, come back! It's too dangerous!"

The other woman didn't seem to hear her. Already disappearing up the stairs, Jade had reached a landing and was quickly traveling down the path with no mind to those calling after her. *I need to see him. I simply must.* There were so many words built up inside of her that Jade wanted to share with Alec. More than anything, she desperately wanted the chance to say goodbye to the man who had come to mean the world to her.

Steps beginning to slow, Jade's gaze shifted to the rocks on each side of the path. In her rush to find Alec, she had journeyed too far from Cassidy's side. Dragons leered at her from every direction. Swallowing hard, Jade edged along. She could see a large dais up on the peak in the moonlight. Two large forms stood upon the stone as dragons guarding the bottom moved to the side. Jade's movements ceased. Ascending the last set of stairs, Alec joined the royals.

"Alakaid," Jade yelled, her feet taking flight of their own accord.

No longer paying mind to the possible enemies surrounding her, Jade darted around rocks and raced up the last of the steps to the plateau at the very peak. Her only thoughts were of Alec—until two dragons suddenly strode forward to block her path. Skidding to a halt, Jade slipped, falling flat on her rump.

Smoke streamed from the magical creatures' nostrils as they growled in the back of their throats. Teeth bared, they stomped the ground with extended razor-sharp talons. The dragons bent their heads to glare at the unexpected human.

Jade leaned back, her body trembling. *Help,* her mind cried out. The word stuck in her throat, failing her when she needed it most.

A loud rumble from behind the guards caused them to turn. A red dragon strode forward with an onyx one close behind. Continuing to approach Jade, the blazing creature stepped protectively over her, blocking the two guards' ability to strike. An understanding of their words wasn't necessary as the heated confrontation continued.

Jade didn't dare move or speak. Finally, the two guards gradually backed away as Cassidy joined the group with Isabelle.

"Jade, there you are," Isabelle whispered with distress as she slipped under Ardys.

The red dragon waited for the others to completely back away prior to moving aside.

"Get up," the sorceress encouraged urgently.

"Are you unharmed?" Cassidy questioned, looking the ghostly pale woman over.

Running a shaky hand over her hair, Jade nodded. "I am. Forgive me, I had not expected the dragons here to be so hostile."

"Azurartain is the one dragon sanctuary that we possess. Even so, it is the start of the ceremony which concerns them now." Cassidy lifted her gaze. The two guards had moved back to join Tatsu at the bottom of the short stairs, offering them a clear view of the platform. "It has begun."

Jade's heart sank at those words. Hands gripping Isabelle's, there was nothing else that she could do but watch.

Alec strode to the center of the ring where Draco and Shiori awaited him. Fires came to life upon the surrounding rock about the perimeter. It traveled all across the peak and part-way down the stone steps. The warm glow shone brightly upon the royal's gleaming scales, yet Jade's sights were locked on Alec and him alone. With the scene instantly illuminated, Jade quickly noticed that Alec was no longer fully dressed. At some point during her unpleasant confrontation, he had shed not only his boots and weapons, but both his tunic and undershirt as well.

A blush crept up her cheeks. Her gaze darted to the sage beside her as Isabelle's fingers tightened their hold. Peering back at Alec, Jade noticed the mark on his back had begun to glow. There was no time for any more words as the ancient magic was activated. Everything around them seemed to still as all eyes focused on the Dragon Sage.

A comforting warmth enveloped Alec as he sat with his back against the large crystal of his temporary chamber. All was still and quiet. Eyes closed, the prince dozed in relative safety knowing his friends would alert him to any forthcoming danger.

It is time, a musical voice whispered to him from the depths of his slumber.

Groaning, Alec opened his eyes. A form hovered above him. Its image was distorted by the bright light of the crystal. Blinking to clear his vision, Alec lightly shook his head.

"It's time," Ardys told him, causing Alec's brows to furrow.

Had he imagined the woman's voice this time? She came at the strangest moments. Part of him still doubted she was real. He possessed no proof that she was nothing other than a subconscious illusion.

I suppose it doesn't matter at this point. If his mind wanted to make up voices, then he would simply allow it. There was no reason to try and stop it now.

"I'm ready," Alec said rising to his feet.

Green eyes solemn, Ardys nudged the sage fondly. Words were no longer needed. They had already said all there was to say between them. Tatsu lowered himself to the ground as Alec reached the doorway.

"How about one last ride?"

The corner of Alec's mouth turned upwards with a grin. "I'm certainly not going to turn that down."

Once the companions exited the more constricting tunnels and entered the massive main chamber, the black dragon spread his wings to soar into the air. He circled tightly around the space and under the waterfall, giving Alec the best possible view. Rising back into the air, Tatsu zipped through one of the sky-bound tunnels to spiral out into the night air.

With Ardys close behind, Alec held his hands out to the side and tilted his head back with a grin. His eyes drifted closed for a moment as he reveled in the thrill of gliding across the winds. All too soon his guardian tucked in his wings to gently lower them to the ground.

Alec slid to the solid rock, resting his palm on Tatsu's dark scales. His skin prickled in the cooler night air, but the sudden chill didn't register in his mind. Heart beating quickly, the sage placed a hand on his chest and inhaled deeply.

I'm ready to meet my fate.

Walking beside his friends, Alec traveled the short distance to the highest part of Azurartain. Dragons of every color lined both sides of the path, or were sitting on small rock outcroppings and larger boulders in the higher elevations leading to the dais. While some watched him with stern expressions, there were many among the magical creatures who bowed their heads with respect. They could have flown directly to the stone, but his guardians requested this small tribute to their wingless comrade. To walk instead of fly for the last leg of their journey allowed those present to offer their respect for the human prince and the sacrifice he was about to make.

Even so, the journey was surprisingly short. In what felt like the blink of an eye, he was striding across the flat peak of the mountain towards the stone platform. The royal dragons were already awaiting him within the ring. Without pause, Alec ascended the final steps to join them. He didn't need to be told what was to come. Shiori had visited him earlier to discuss the details of the ceremony. Seeing the empress, he smiled faintly and bowed. Alec then turned to Emperor Draco. This was the first meeting the two of them shared since the royal had not been present in Azurartain when Alec first arrived.

"Greetings, Your Majesty," Alec said with a deep bow.

The king of dragons was a mighty creature with coloring similar to Shiori. He studied Alec proudly as the two gazed at each other in silence. Slowly, Draco lowered his head in a graceful bob.

"I am pleased you came, Prince Alakaid. There are few who possess such a strong character," Draco said, glancing at his mate. "I have heard much of you. I would have liked the chance to enjoy your company. Something tells me it would have led to some most interesting conversations."

Alec gave a short laugh. "Indeed. Befriending dragons has certainly been interesting thus far, and I wouldn't trade it for any price."

Shiori lifted her gaze to peer at the bright orb suspended high above them. "We should begin."

The moon was now in position. If any nearby enemies wished to make their move, this would be the time. They could not afford to delay. Nodding his understanding, Alec moved to the edge of the ring. There he set to removing his armor, weapons and boots. Pulling off his tunic, Alec's hands came to rest on the enchanted chain bound with Jade's ribbon. His fingers lingered on the cool metal for a few seconds before he unhooked the necklace and laid it on top of the pile.

His chest bare, the sage turned back to face the royals. Walking to the center of the ring, he could feel the power of the moon enhancing his magic with every step. Once in the center, his steps came to a halt. Hands sweeping out to the side, the sage turned his palms face down. His aura awakened as a beam of light illuminated the dais from above. It swirled around him like a brisk breeze, growing stronger while the dragon mark on his back shined.

"Surgeon," the sage called out.

A white magic circle appeared upon the stone. It twirled around, spinning faster as Alec moved his hands in a series of signs. He had never been taught this technique prior to the ceremony. It came to him suddenly, as if the magic in his blood was whispering each step required to complete the transference. Rising from the dust, runes in Elan appeared on the sorcerer's skin. They painted themselves across his back and down both arms as he finished the first part of the spell.

The magical seals then spread out to encompass not only Alec, but Draco and Shiori as well. Eyes glowing to match his mark, Alec chanted the necessary spell.

"Sumonno virtus mana-alom. Rasolee er lumina sancdamor."

A burst of energy erupted from beneath the sage's feet. It shot out, sweeping through the mountainside as it slammed into those watching the ceremony.

"Hold on," Cassidy told Jade and Isabelle as she moved closer, sheltering them from the burst of energy.

Back on the platform, Alec's body began to pulsate. The glowing orbs of his spirit pulled free of his physical form. Molding together, they took the shape of a great, translucent white dragon. Releasing a roar, Fang beat his wings proudly. Gaze locked on Alec, he hovered in front of the prince for a long moment. His spirit then wrapped himself around the sage, coming to hover over his shoulder.

Lowering themselves to the ground, Draco and Shiori dipped their heads so that the large jewels in their foreheads were within Alec's reach.

The prince inhaled slowly then exhaled. It was the moment he had been awaiting. *This is for you, Jade.* Without further delay, Alec placed a palm on each precious stone and closed his eyes. Emanating a roar, Fang twirled around, splitting into smaller twin versions of himself. The dragons then dove forward, twisting down Alec's arms as the dual spirits flew straight inside of the jewels. Those upon the stone platform seemed to freeze in place while the stones glowed brightly like the mark on Alec's back.

To Jade, everything played out before her eyes as if it were in slow motion.

Draco and Shiori's eyes blazed a bright white light. Then, radiating from the epicenter of the spell, the eyes and jewels of each dragon present on the mountain began to gleam as well. Even Cassidy, who had been touched by Alec's magic once before stiffened, as if frozen in time by the enchantment.

Jade and Isabelle looked around with wonder.

"Is this what took place last time?" the sorceress questioned.

Her friend gradually shook her head. "A little," Jade answered, her gaze wide as she studied the surrounding dragons. "I must say this looks far more intense."

"Hmm," Isabelle watched the dragons for a few moments. "If I were to venture a guess, I would say that the emperor and empress dragons are linked to all of the other ones. Since Alec's power is affecting them, it is in turn, affecting the rest of the dragons."

The two women peered back at the stone dais.

Teeth clenched together, Alec was hunched over as he continued to feed more power into the spell. The magic runes on his arms and back shone so intently, along with the dragon mark, that it appeared they were trying to imprint themselves on his skin. Blood started to drip from the sage's nose. His breathing more ragged, the crimson color appeared in his ears and the corners of his mouth. It began to streak down the sides of his jaw, yet Alec did not let up on his task.

One by one, the eyes and jewels of the dragons on the mountaintop lost their luster. As if surrounded in a haze, they blinked and shook their heads like someone roused from a long, deep slumber.

"Amazing," Isabelle squeaked, watching the magical creatures keenly. "I can't believe Alec's power affected all of them."

While the sorceress peered at the dragons, Jade's gaze was solely upon Alec. She took a step, inching closer as the number of creatures still under his spell lessened. At last, only Draco and Shiori remained. The moment the light gleaming in their eyes faded to nothing, Alec slumped to the ground. His body lay motionless in the vanishing ring of white.

Jade's eyes widened to large pools. Her voice could not speak, yet her mind cried out with distress. *No!* Knowing what would come had not eased the pain of witnessing such a horrific sight. Racing past the still sluggish guards, Jade did not slow her steps until she was by the prince's side. Dropping to her knees, she reached out to touch him, her trembling fingers hesitating.

"Alec?" she called out softly, silently praying that by some miracle he would answer.

When he refrained from uttering a single sound, Jade bit her lower lip. She sadly noted that the light had vanished from his mark as did the runes painting his skin from the spell. Gently, she rolled Alec onto his back.

"Alec?" she repeated with a notable quiver.

Any lingering hope that had lived on in her heart was extinguished at the sight before her. Alec's skin was an oddly pale white. His chest was still and his lips were already taking on a bluish tinge. It was then that Jade saw the blood on his face. Holding a shaking hand over his mouth, she felt nothing.

"He's not breathing," Jade wept weakly. She could hear the sound of steps approaching, yet did not dare turn her gaze away from the man laying in front of her. Jade reached out to give him a good shake. "Alec, pray get up. You cannot leave me. Alakaid, wake up!"

Her distraught pleas brought forth no change in the sage.

Cassidy lowered her head to gently nudge the human. "I'm sorry, Jade, but he's gone."

"Who is this girl?" questioned Draco.

Striding up the steps, it was Ardys who answered the emperor. "Jade is Prince Alakaid's betrothed. The blonde one is Isabelle. She is his loyal friend and a talented sage for their king."

Jaw going slack, Isabelle's eyes darted between the two dragons. "Ardys?" she drawled with a hint of disbelief. "Did you just speak? I mean human words. I...I know you can talk, but I can't usually understand you."

Isabelle suddenly found both of the royal dragons standing above her as Ardys joined her side.

"Did you say that you can understand us?"

The sorceress's head bobbed up and down.

Glancing at her mate, Shiori smiled. "A wiser gift he could not have chosen."

Never timid for long, Isabelle sighed. "I agree Your Majesty," her gaze shifted to Jade. "I just wish it had not been at the cost of his life."

Head lifting proudly and chest jutting out, Draco told her, "I understand your sorrow, but his death was honorable and dignified. He made us dragons proud to know such a mighty warrior."

"Alec was prepared to make this sacrifice," Ardys added. "It is our duty to carry on in his place."

"Indeed," Isabelle said quietly. Listening to Jade's soft bitter sobs, she didn't have the heart to put on a brave face. "I wish he had allowed us to at least say goodbye."

Alec lay suspended in a cloud of white. His body felt weightless, his limbs devoid of any feeling as if they were not but an illusion before his eyes. A swift breeze surrounded him. It lifted him into the air while the blank canvas was transformed into a large floating island. Alec's bare feet lightly touched down on a thick blanket of green grass. The azure sky bore not a single cloud. Alec held his hand out, testing the feel of the mild sun. It warmed him perfectly without the threat of scorching his skin. Behind him, was an oasis speckled with leafy palms, white sand and a pool of clear blue water. Turning back to gaze out at his surroundings, Alec spotted an endless horizon with nothing in the vastness.

He sighed, resting his hands on his hips. "Hmm, I guess I died after all."

"Not quite," unexpectedly replied the feminine voice Alec knew all too well.

Stiffening, the sage gradually turned to gaze upon a tall, beautiful woman. Her long raven hair was pulled back from her face with gem encrusted clips. Her soft, flowing blue dress was embroidered with gold thread which complimented flawless, ivory skin. A thick, braided belt adorned her slim waist and delicate sandals covered her feet. What struck Alec the most was her eyes. The pale silvery color encased a ring of bright blue.

Alec could not recall ever seeing someone like this mysterious woman before. She was surreal, like one of the drawings he had seen during his studies with Malcolm. For too long he had heard her whispers in his mind. Finally seeing the owner of that strange voice in this unearthly place further added to the sorcerer's belief that he had passed on from the living world.

"Who are you?" Alec questioned, turning fully towards her. "What are you?"

Fingers gracefully linked together, the woman offered him a kind smile. "I am the Celestial Maiden Selena. You may know me as a guardian spirit."

"Guardian spirit?" he repeated. Eyes narrowing ever so slightly, Alec shook his head. "I've never heard of such a thing."

Selena's brows lifted. "Oh? It would seem that your education is woefully incomplete." She paused for a moment. An elegant hand lifted to brush her cheek. "I wonder why Malcolm has not shared this with you. No matter, I am certain he had no intent to purposely do so."

Alec's expression did not soften in the least. He waited quietly for her to continue, watching the celestial being carefully.

"How best to explain? There are several worlds beyond the one of which you know. Celestial Maidens are part of the spirit world. We act as types of guides and help to maintain a balance between the light and the dark. There is not time to explain further. If you do not return to the mortal realm soon, then your spirit will pass on and you will indeed have perished."

Alec crossed his arms. "Wait, if this is not the spirit world, then where am I?"

Selena's expression shifted to a more solemn air. "This in-between world serves as my eternal confinement."

Alec's gaze quickly skimmed over the exquisite necklaces and rings decorating her like a piece of art. *Wait, does she mean to say that she is a prisoner?* he thought doubtfully. The sage knew what being in prison was like. This place had the appearance of a paradise, not a dungeon.

"If you're a goddess or a spirit or whatever it is that you claim, then who would have the power to imprison you?"

Strolling closer to the edge of the island, Selena looked out at the bright horizon. "I was sent here by a few of the other Maidens. Betrayed. All for seeking to aid your world in a time of great darkness beyond the limitations of our oppressive rules. It is that desire which allows me to reach out to you now, Prince Alakaid," Selena said passionately as she spun to face him. "You have given this shattered spirit cause once more. Allow me to aid you as the others have not."

Exhaling slowly, Alec peered at the celestial goddess with furrowed brows. He didn't know what to believe. Much like a dream, he could not grasp the indication that this space around him was a world not his own. He supposed there was yet a piece of him that hoped the unknown voice in his mind was not but his imagination and would cease on its own. It was not unheard of for those who lived through various torments to create certain delusions. An intangible force told the warrior this was not so.

"I will need time to consider this."

A small smile touched her lips. "For now, that is all I ask." Gasping, Selena took a quick step back while clutching her chest. "You must go," she stressed. "My power here is limited, but if you wish to reside once more in the mortal world, then I can help to send you back."

Go back?

Alec never dreamed that he would be given such a chance. Death had always been his fate, yet here was a way to overrule that destiny. He could change what was written in the prophecy. Jade's face appeared in his mind's eye. Shoulders straightening, Alec's determined gaze locked on Selena.

"What must I do?"

Selena's eyes sparkled. "Close your eyes."

Alec did as she asked.

"Reach out to your spirit. Feel him with every fiber of your being and call him back to you." Hands starting to glow, Selena pointed her palms at the mortal. "A great darkness is coming once more, Alakaid. The realms need you. As do I."

The maiden's final words ended with a whisper as Alec felt himself slip away from the warm meadow of Selena's prison. His surroundings returned to a sheet of the purest white. Focusing with every ounce of his power, Alec called out to Fang.

Hand covering her mouth, Isabelle came to stand by Jade's side. She slowly lowered herself to the ground while staring at the fallen sage. A few tears rolled down her face.

Beside her, Jade's sobs were lessening as they shifted to hiccups. The noble laid her cheek on Alec's shoulder and made no attempt to move from his side.

Isabelle curled her fingers around Alec's limp hand, squeezing tightly for a moment. "I will never forget you, my friend," she promised. Letting go, she moved to pat Jade's back. "Jade, it's time to depart."

"I cannot leave him," came a mumbled reply.

"You won't have to," Ardys told her stepping closer. "I shall carry him back to Stafford. It is the least I can do for our friend."

Sniffing, Jade pushed herself upright with a nod. "Alright."

Just as the two women were about to rise, a pulse emanated from Alec's body.

"Did anyone else feel that?" Draco questioned, dipping his nose closer to the sage.

Another pulse swept over them. The royal dragons stiffened. The jewels on their foreheads started to gleam, followed by their eyes once again.

"What's happening?" Cassidy asked, watching her rulers with wide eyes.

Pulling from the gems, sparkles of white light swirled about. Condensing together, they took on the form of a dragon before entering Alec's chest. The glow faded from Draco and Shiori. Shaking their heads, they asked what occurred, but all eyes were locked on the sage's corpse.

A healthy tint returned to Alec's skin. With a gasp, he inhaled sharply, his eyelids flying open.

The sudden movement caused both women to jump.

Rolling onto his side, Alec coughed as his body greedily sucked in fresh air.

"Impossible," Draco muttered with a scowl.

Launching herself forward, Jade wrapped both arms around his neck without a second thought. "You are alive!" she shouted. "I do not believe it. I thought we had lost you."

"We had," Cassidy confirmed. "How did you return to us?"

"Yes," Jade echoed, pulling back to study his face. "How did you?"

"I'm not sure," he answered honestly. *I want to speak with Malcolm before mentioning Selena.* Alec didn't quite know what to make of the spirit. He owed her for his safe return, yet possessed no knowledge of her kind to aid him in deciding if he should trust her. He had not the time to process all she shared about the existence of other worlds than his own.

"Jade?" he called softly to the woman still sitting surprisingly near.

"Yes?"

"Is it alright if I get off the ground?"

Jade opened her mouth to answer, then took a good look at how close she still was to his bare chest. Cheeks coloring, she quickly pulled back while tucking stray hairs behind her ear.

"Of course."

A few of the others chuckled. Heart lifting from the sight of her friend, Cassidy directed her attention back to the royal dragons. The grin lighting her face vanished as she peered at the emperor. Shiori's expression did not tell her much. Draco's, on the other hand, appeared far from pleased. A chill swept through the green creature. This unexpected turn of events could prove dangerous for the humans. Beside her, Ardys seemed to share her worry.

"We should go," he whispered urgently.

Having collected his discarded items, Isabelle allowed Alec just enough time to dress before she, too, embraced him tightly.

"You must promise never to do such a thing to us again."

Alec chuckled. The gleeful noise was short lived. Catching sight of the dragons, his body stiffened automatically. *Something's wrong.* Bowing to the emperor and empress, he ushered Jade and Isabelle over towards the green and red creatures. Alec did not get the chance to voice his concerns.

392

"Come quickly," Cassidy insisted, turning to descend the stairs.

The three humans followed close behind. At the bottom, Tatsu filed in on one side while Ardys took charge of the other. Striding through the crowded mountain path, there was a strange tension unlike anything Alec had felt during his initial appearance.

"Tatsu," he began in a low voice. "Didn't the spell work?" The dark dragon grunted. "It did. Your power gave dragons the ability to speak human words. Both Jade and Isabelle can understand us freely."

"Then why does it feel as if a battle might commence?"

Watching the other dragons out of the corner of his eye, Alec knew he was not mistaken. The general unease was difficult to miss. Surrounded by magical creatures, if a skirmish did arise their chances would not be favorable.

"They do not know what to make of your survival," Tatsu told him bluntly. "For five hundred years our rulers have patiently awaited this day with the belief that the power bestowed upon the humans would be restored. Even a small piece of their magic is stronger than what any human was ever meant to permanently possess."

"I see." *So, even though I lived today there is no telling if I will be allowed to survive tomorrow.*

"We will not allow anyone to act rashly," Ardys assured him.

Alec knew the great dragon meant his words, but his friends would have no control over any decision made by Draco and Shiori. Leaving at once would offer them some space to come to terms with this unexpected twist. Hopefully, his previous actions and a human's much shorter life span would be enough to work in his favor. One thing Alec was sure of, was that this ceremony would be the only time he would offer his life willingly to the dragons. If Selena's words proved correct, then a great evil was coming that the realms had not seen for centuries.

Just then, Jade gazed back at him with a brilliant smile. Alec felt his chest warm. If nothing else, he would not regret coming back. His journey wasn't finished. Prophecy or no, he would not leave this world without a fight. His battle had only just begun.

PRONUNCIATION GUIDE

If you feel yourself getting stuck on some of your favorite characters, or places, here is a basic guide to give you a hand.

Names/Places

Alakaid	Al-ah-kaid
Alandra	Ah-lan-drah
Ariston	Are-is-ton
Ardys	Are-diss
Elan	Ee-lan
Ellfraya	El-fray-ah
Layfon	Lay-fon
Leos	Lee-os
Malyndor	Mah-lan-door
Marcia	Mar-cee-ah
Parlen	Pair-len
Rhordack	Rod-er-ick
Roskos	Row-s-cos
Sea of Narvee	Narr-vee
Shiori	She-or-ee
Tatsu	Tat-sue
Titus	Tie-tus
Zerrok	Zah-rok

Spells

Airanlor	Air-an-lore
Infureono	In-fur-ee-on-o
Rokon	Roe-kon
Surgeon	Sir-gee-on
Tsumorri	Sue-more-ee

ABOUT THE AUTHOR

Author of *Mission Stone: Quest of the Five Flames* and *The Dragon Marked Chronicles*, Jay has been a lover of the written word from an early age. When she isn't penning her latest adventure, she enjoys reading, watching anime and spending time walking along the beach. She currently lives in Pennsylvania with her family.

Made in the USA
Middletown, DE
25 August 2023

37353878R00239